Donald Thomas and The Murder Room

>>> This title is part of The Murder Room, our series dedicated to making available out-of-print or hard-to-find titles by classic crime writers.

Crime fiction has always held up a mirror to society. The Victorians were fascinated by sensational murder and the emerging science of detection; now we are obsessed with the forensic detail of violent death. And no other genre has so captivated and enthralled readers.

Vast troves of classic crime writing have for a long time been unavailable to all but the most dedicated frequenters of second-hand bookshops. The advent of digital publishing means that we are now able to bring you the backlists of a huge range of titles by classic and contemporary crime writers, some of which have been out of print for decades.

From the genteel amateur private eyes of the Golden Age and the femmes fatales of pulp fiction, to the morally ambiguous hard-boiled detectives of mid twentieth-century America and their descendants who walk our twenty-first century streets, The Murder Room has it all. >>>

The Murder Room
Where Criminal Minds Meet

themurderroom.com

Donald Thomas (1926–)

Donald Thomas was born in Somerset and educated at Queen's College, Taunton, and Balliol College, Oxford. He holds a personal chair in Cardiff University. His numerous crime novels include two collections of Sherlock Holmes stories and the hugely popular historical detective series featuring Sergeant Verity of Scotland Yard, written under the pen name Francis Selwyn, as well as gritty police procedurals written under the name of Richard Dacre. He is also the author of seven biographies and a number of other non-fiction works, and won the Gregory Prize for his poems, *Points of Contact*. He lives in Bath with his wife.

Mad Hatter Summer
A Lewis Carroll Nightmare

Donald Thomas

An Orion book

Copyright © Donald Thomas 1983

The right of Donald Thomas to be identified as the author of this work has been asserted in accordance with the Copyright, Designs and Patents Act 1988.

This edition published by
The Orion Publishing Group Ltd
Orion House
5 Upper St Martin's Lane
London WC2H 9EA

An Hachette UK company
A CIP catalogue record for this book is available from the British Library

ISBN 978 1 4719 0431 8

www.orionbooks.co.uk

For Paris Leary

I should like to know *exactly* what is the minimum of dress I may take her in . . . I hope that, at any rate, we may go as far as a pair of bathing-drawers, though for *my* part I should much prefer doing without them.

> – C. L. Dodgson, 'Lewis Carroll', to Mrs A. L. Mayhew, on her daughter Janet, 27 May 1879

The foulest soul that lived stinks here no more.
The stench Hell is fouler than before!

> – Algernon Charles Swinburne, on the death of Charles Augustus Howell, 24 April 1890

I

November

November

I

IT WAS SEVERAL WEEKS since the chatter of college scandal had diminished to a whisper. The Angel of Death had crossed the serene Oxford sky in a moment of high summer, the shadow of his wing falling briefly as a cloud on meadow and river, clock turret, and garden quadrangle. Now that the moment was safely past, Inspector Alfred Swain sat as a friend in the Christ Church rooms of the Reverend Charles Lutwidge Dodgson.

There was no doubt that Mr. Dodgson himself had been changed by the events of that summer. To admiring correspondents he was now apt to reply that he was *not* Lewis Carroll, the "Story-Book Man," nor did he know him. A few letters were returned from Oxford with the words "Not known" scrawled across their envelopes. Like Prospero, he had drowned the secret instrument of his magic, though in Mr. Dodgson's case it was a camera rather than a book. There were to be no more photographs of little girls "in their favourite dress of nothing to wear." Even the sketchbook recorded only those in whom Mr. Dodgson had perfect trust.

On that November evening, Alfred Swain was not a policeman and scarcely a chaperone. Yet the events of the summer made his presence an advisable precaution. He gazed across the room at the young Widow Wilberforce, who sat with a shaft of lamplight sleek on her chestnut hair. For the past hour, the pair of them had watched in silent witness as Dodgson worked at a pencil drawing. His subject was Jane, the only child of Sarah Ashmole.

Presently, as if sensing her companion's eyes upon her, Roxana Wilberforce caught Swain's glance. Her soft glance relaxed in a smile of gentle adoration for her lover. He could see Dodgson but not the girl of thirteen who sat naked to be sketched. Dodgson had insisted that she must be hidden from unnecessary eyes by the woven Eden of a silk Gothic screen, its panels a paradise of hummingbirds and parakeets, a flame pattern of tropical leaves.

Dodgson sat in his dark suit, long jacket, and white bow-tie, the costume of the clergyman and scholar. Swain looked at the dark Italianate curls of the bowed head and deduced from this pose a frown of concentration on the long pale face. A pencil in the neat slim fingers hovered uncertainly over the sketching paper and then settled to its task once more. Like a caress, it followed the slight adolescent curve of waist and hip.

The girl sighed, her first indication of weariness.

"Ask me another riddle about the watch," she said quietly.

Dodgson replied without raising his head.

"Which is *better?*" It was his habit to emphasize any word over which he might stumble. "A watch that is *right* once a year, or a *watch* that is right twice a day?"

"That's only sense!" As she spoke, Swain could hear the light, soft movement of the girl's hair on her bare shoulder. "Twice a day is much better."

"Very *good!*" The pencil hovered and then settled to the paper in long exploratory sweeps. Dodgson spoke as if he had played the game so often that it no longer commanded his complete attention. "Then tell me, Jane. Would you prefer a watch which loses half a *minute* a day, or a watch that doesn't *go* at all?"

"The losing one," she said, her voice raised a little at the absurdity of such a question. "Where's the use of a watch that won't go?"

He looked up with a quick childlike smile, kind and triumphant at the same time.

"You contradict yourself, my love. *First*, you chose a watch that would be right twice a day rather than once a *year*. But it's the watch which doesn't go at all that will be right twice a day. The one that *loses* half a minute a *day* can only be right once a year. You see?"

"That's not fair!" It was a child's wail at the discovery of a cheat. "It's silly!"

Dodgson sketched quickly.

"The great privilege of mathematics, my dear, is that it can be as silly as it likes, for its conclusions are quite ineluctable."

Swain was about to say something as to the privileged unfairness of mathematics. He kept the remark to himself, however, seeing how engrossed the man and the girl were with one another. It would have been like intruding on a pair of lovers, he thought.

By nine o'clock on the November evening a river mist filled the water meadows and began to settle in droplets and patches on the grey Tudor stone of Christ Church. Cold vapour fogged the yellow outline of the lamp-panes in the wide courtyard, muffling the tiny echoes of fountain- and leaf-fall. Dampness clung to the very notes of Great Tom, tolling its hundred and one strokes as on every night since the bell had been hung in Christopher Wren's new tower two centuries before. In the stillness that followed the last of these iron reverberations, the leads of the roof sounded faintly with a steady finger-tapping of raindrops. The room was lit by a white glare of gas. Above the harsh breath of the jet, Swain could just hear the scuffle of dry leaves running before a breeze in the quadrangle below.

A silence had fallen between Dodgson and the girl. His pencil shaded the texture of lank brown hair, the setting for her brave and fair-skinned young features. How long before a woman's hardness and crudity made a caricature for him of her present beauty? How soon would the resilience of her body be marred by the weight of womanhood?

To call such anticipations a grief at the doom of nature, as though her maturity were a death, seemed absurd even to Dodgson himself. Yet as the pencil moved in surer lines, working faster towards the completion of the sketch, he was possessed by those mournful premonitions. Even now, he had become a witness to the physical tragedy of a girl who was no longer a child.

Other men would see beauty in her, of course, long after he had ceased to find it. Dodgson could almost imagine what Rossetti would make of her, a few years hence, a demon goddess naked against the tropic fire of the silk screen and the wild lush foliage. When that happened, Dodgson would be generous in his praise of artist and model. Yet his heart would be cold as winter.

In a light sweep he began to trace the outline of the Gothic screen itself, his imagination going back to the first model whom he had posed before it several years earlier. Nerissa Chantrey had stood before it, with all the naked self-assurance of a twelve-year-old. In her favourite dress of nothing to wear, he thought. It was at that time, in negotiating for Nerissa, that he had coined the euphemism to describe the nudity his camera study required. Since then he had used the words habitually in his approaches to the mothers—and in some cases the fathers—of those girls like Nerissa whom he knew to be willing models.

From time to time, he had drawn women from the nude, the models readily available in the studios of Gertrude Thomson and other London friends. On those occasions there had been no more sensuality in the pencil's caress than if he had been drawing a triangle to illustrate a proposition in Euclid. In the grey studio light, his mind was far away. It dwelt at that time on an image of Nerissa, a knowing barefoot imp who posed naked before his camera in the glasshouse on the college roof. The woman sitting in the studio was less real to him than that remembrance of summer afternoons in an Oxford lost for ever.

Gathering his thoughts, Dodgson glanced up briefly at the girl and then turned to Alfred Swain.

"I fear we have kept you far beyond your time, Mr. Swain. I had quite intended to have finished the sketch before nine o'clock. You must have grown tired of sitting in attendance so long."

Swain gave him a pleasant smile of reassurance.

"If the young lady can keep so still and be so patient, Mr. Dodgson, where's the hardship to me? It's a pleasure to see you work, sir. If I had half your gift for it, I'd take my discharge and try the academy."

Dodgson answered him with a smile and a dissuasive shake of the head, returning to his work.

"Where should we be, Mr. Swain, if you had a brace of portraits on the walls of the academy while innocent men fretted their lives away in prison cells?"

They made a joke of it now. Yet the minds of all four went back to the visions of that summer. Mr. Dodgson and the little girls. Innocence and extortion. The body of the murdered man in his plum-coloured suiting, sodden with river water. Corruption in high places and low. There had been no end to it until the August evening when Inspector Swain had started to read to himself:

Alice was beginning to get very tired of sitting by her sister on the bank and of having nothing to do: once or twice she had peeped into the book her sister was reading, but it had no pictures or conversations in it, "and what is the use of a book," thought Alice, "without pictures or conversations?"

In the words which followed, Swain had found the answer to murder and conspiracy. Perhaps the murder threatened only the innocence of the Reverend Mr. Dodgson. Yet the conspiracy was like an explosive mine beneath the fabric of English society, designed to bring down in its ruin both royalty and government, religion and moral example. Swain had already begun to think of those months of crisis as the "Mad Hatter Summer."

It had been out of the question to reveal the full truth of this to Mr. Dodgson. For that reason alone, each of the two men looked back upon the time from different standpoints.

Dodgson added the last touches to his sketch of Jane Ashmole. Beyond the velvet curtains lay the dark evening and the mist, a season of ghosts and memories of the dead. It was the time of November bonfires and the Feast of All Souls. He smiled at his two companions and went to kiss Jane for her patience.

Yet as he did so, there glimmered in the secret recesses of thought the mementoes of that time. Abandoned camera equipment in the cupboard close by. A girl who was to be his love in eternity. Belladonna, both the perfection of the girl's beauty and a gaudy poison in the innocent garden of her childhood. A crime inspired by modern lust and ancient pride. The drowned bulk

7

of the murdered man, floating on the green river surface in an Oxford twilight.

Because he believed that his greatest happiness was past, and yet would one day return for ever, Dodgson thought as he kissed the girl of that serene and sunlit afternoon by the river in early June, when the curtain had risen on his life's great melodrama.

II

Story-Book Man

2

THE LAST IMAGES of his dream faded, like the coloured fancy on the nursery wall as the lamp of the magic lantern sputtered into smoke behind the glass slide. Tiny sounds and distant voices of the upper world filled Dodgson's ears, exultation lifting him in his escape. Warmth touched his face. Even before he could open his eyes he saw behind their lids a bright apricot colour of sunlight. With a slight movement he touched the hard straw boating hat.

White flannels accompanied the dark jacket and bow-tie as he lay in the shadow of the haycocks, far across Port Meadow on the Godstow bank of the stream. So broad was the summer pasture separating the two rivers that, turning his head towards the Oxford spires, he could see the slight curvature of the earth between the Cherwell and the Isis. A ruined arch of the old nunnery seemed to spin in the air above him, against the deep summer blue.

Incommensurable magnitudes. The phrase recurred to him from that morning's lecture on the fifth book of Euclid, a discourse entirely wasted on the loutish indifference of the young men in his charge. At close quarters he watched the minute insect worlds moving about him. A ladybird, brightly lacquered as a clockwork toy, climbed the flat crown of the straw boater that

11

lay beside him and then tumbled harmlessly into the soft buttercup grass.

If, as the Fathers believed, men and women would be raised in heaven at the age of their physical perfection, why not the world also? Heaven would surely be that Oxford season that came between the white may and the June roses. Through the hum of drifting insects above him, he heard the voice that had called such thoughts to his mind while he slept. Jane Ashmole was still reading the poem begun before he had fallen into his mid-afternoon doze.

> "When round his head the aureole clings,
>   And he is clothed in white,
> I'll take his hand and go with him
>   To the deep wells of light,
> We will step down as to a stream
>   And bathe there in God's sight."

Under the starch-scented hems of her skirts the grass stirred as she shifted her hips a little before beginning the next stanza. Dodgson peeped and saw her lying propped on an elbow, reading "The Blessed Damozel" from a slim, olive-green book.

At thirteen years old, Jane Ashmole still wore her straight brown hair loose to her shoulders, not yet in the tortured shapes that the false elegance of womanhood demanded. Brown-eyed and pale-skinned, she had emerged from infancy with firm features and a smooth, strong beauty. For several years her general appearance had changed little. To the widowed mother, Sarah Ashmole, this was an irritation, as if Jane had deliberately contrived it. To Dodgson it was a delight.

"I have the bad taste to find more beauty in the undeveloped than in the mature form," he had once said to Sarah Ashmole in desperate frankness, "yet little girls are so thin from seven to ten. I think twelve or thirteen would be my ideal age." The woman had shrugged, indifferent to his views. But Jane was "invitable" alone as well as with others. Mrs. Ashmole had agreed to that. Hardly daring to breathe the words, Dodgson had asked the final question. Was Jane also "kissable"? Mrs. Ashmole received the inquiry with the same uncomprehending shrug of indifference.

He looked again at the girl and saw her lying with her pink skirt drawn up almost to her knees to reveal smartly polished boots and the shape of her firm calves. The awkward pose was characteristic of her, pale legs pressed together in a manner so self-conscious and unpractised. A child would have been less self-conscious, a woman more practised.

Turning a page of the book, Jane began the next stanza. Later, he decided, he would tell her of the day when he had photographed the book's author. What a story that would make, the group in the walled summer garden: Dante Gabriel Rossetti, dark and plump as a headwaiter, the two sisters and the mother, brother William the saturnine government clerk.

Listening to Jane's voice, staring up into the vault of blue, he longed to be somewhere more private with her. The sky was deep in colour and immensity as Gabriel could have painted it, an azure heaven of pure Pre-Raphaelite blue. Between him and its infinite expanse a light haze of gold in the warm air reflected the buttercup fields below.

Bending his arm back, he pillowed his head upon it and listened with half his attention to Jane's voice. Of course, the reading lesson was performed to win his praise. The fingers of his other hand played upon the cloth-covered buttons of his black coat, touching each of them in turn like a rosary.

As surely as mathematics, life was governed by rules. They applied with Euclidean rigour to his improvised photographic studio on the flat roof of his rooms, above the Tudor quadrangle of Christ Church. High above the trees and mellow stonework, Jane and he passed the total privacy of rare summer afternoons. At twelve years old, and now at thirteen, she had been naked before his camera a score of times. Permission was implied by Sarah Ashmole's indifference. Those golden hours had brought no discovery and no complaint. Nothing had obliged him to drown his camera in the Isis, as if it had been Prospero's book.

In years to come, looking at Jane and her mild little clergyman-scholar, who would believe it? Yet he, the modest and serious-minded cleric, knew her young body perhaps better than any husband would. Times without number the dispassionate and unblinking eye of the camera had drawn him to the line of taut adolescent thighs, the first shadowing of her breasts, the tiny delicate bone pattern where the spine curved in before the firm, half-developed swell of hips and buttocks. No disfigurement of hair had yet appeared on the narrow triangle of her loins.

The rules. His thoughts returned to them. First, only a man of evil mind could see lewdness in the beauty of Jane Ashmole, woman and child to him. That truth was as evident and absolute in Dodgson's mind as any Euclidean proposition. Moreover, to let her feel safety in being naked with him was a logical extension of their innocent love. It was, to him, the anticipation of heaven, where in the perfect age of child and woman she would bathe naked with him in those "deep wells of light," as Rossetti called them.

Beyond childhood, the adult body must become a living tomb of disease and despair. Such was the fruit of the tree of knowledge. Yet the thought of what men called death sometimes made his heart jump with anticipation of the joy of the new loves beyond it.

He watched the light wind above Port Meadow as it tore cumulus into white uncarded cotton drifts. His imagination followed the cloud's progress, swirling over the chestnut fans and river willows, the bare walls of the ruined nunnery, and borne towards Wytham Woods or the familiar Oxford towers. Now the torn shadow was falling on the eighteenth-century stonework of Peckwater Quadrangle, darkening the cool Virginia creeper on Merton wall. It was streaming like a tattered battle flag above the water meadows of Christ Church, the majestic elms of the Broad Walk. At the wider river reach, where college barges were moored like ancient pleasure galleons of Rome or Egypt, the fleeting shade passed across the water into another world, beyond lichened walls and bell notes from turret clocks.

The rules again. Never to touch or look at one of the girls lewdly, even in play, when she was naked. To hug and kiss her only when she was properly clothed. To assist only when necessary during dressing up or undressing to be photographed. This last allowance was inevitable since fancy dress was as common in his subjects as nudity. Never to force a girl who showed the least reluctance. Prudence as well as decency dictated that.

Jane had been the most forthright of any of his models. Once she had confided her feelings unprompted. Far from being uneasy, she found something "special" about being naked with an adult friend. As though, she said, she too had become adult with all the privileges that brought. The feeling came first when she was six or seven, her bathing superintended by a nursemaid. On such occasions of frankness and intimacy subjects were discussed that seemed too solemn or dangerous for normal conversation. It was as if the grown-up world also understood that the prohibitions of childhood were abandoned with its clothes.

"I fear no one will ever again pamper you as I do," Dodgson had said to her in one of these conversations, mocking himself by his own smile.

That, of course, was why Jane and others had consented to so much. He was the perfect lover for the "favourite age" of twelve or thirteen. Their knowledge of men—the men who would be husbands or lovers in the grown-up world—came casually from gossip and confidences among servants. Little of this had to do with the pleasures of love: much of it hinted at pain and brutishness. Their own eyes confirmed the annual misery and danger of childbirth, often amounting to agony and sometimes death. It was only in Dodgson's company that such girls as Jane knew they might be beautiful and pampered, naked and admired, loved and indulged, without being put to the sword of male pleasure. Love, in his presence, grew through safety and reassurance.

He was thinking of this when he realised that Jane had stopped reading and was speaking directly to him, solemn and reproving as a child, assured and familiar as a woman.

"Will it be like that after we die?" she repeated, nodding at the Rossetti volume. "After we are both dead, shall we always be together as we are now, whenever we choose? Shall I be able to say, 'This afternoon I will take a boat on the river with my Dodo'?"

Alone among his child-friends, Jane was privileged to use the endearment, which came from stumbling over his own name in pronunciation as "Do-Do-Dodgson." He was always the least uneasy when she turned upon him for his professional opinion as a man of God. Despite his thoughts, however, he was in no mood for homilies on heaven and immortality just then. With eyes closed he attempted to elude the question by an appearance of continued sleep. Jane was not to be denied.

"With my Dodo!"

She was leaning over him now, her shadow on the apricot brightness behind his lids. He felt the light warmth of her face close to his own. Quick and knowing, her lips touched him, making his own quiver in a smile. As she pulled away, he opened his eyes and looked up into her face.

His smile grew into one of contented admiration for the slight pertness in the tilt of her nose and chin, the brown hair trimmed prettily on her forehead in a brief slanting fringe. How all that might be spoilt by the "improvements" forced upon her in the name of womanly beauty! Dodgson reached for her hand and felt the cool fingers, then the warm, firm palm that responded quickly to his touch. The pressure of her fingers increased upon him.

"When I shall die . . ." She reverted again to the question.

"Oh, I daresay I shall be there long before," he said lightly, still smiling at her, "an antique old gentleman such as I am! I shall be waiting." He was so certain of the truth that there was no harm in teasing her a little.

Jane released his hand abruptly and began to display something of that tiresome coquetry which too often accompanied the transition from child to woman. She brushed her hair back quickly.

"Perhaps you may meet someone else before that," she said. "Perhaps you may marry a wife."

There was a time when the sudden thrust of such questions about marriage would have shocked him like a convulsive nausea. Now his defence was so well practised as to sound effortless.

"If I were married I should have to leave Oxford," he said wistfully. "And then who else would have me?"

"And must you never have a wife?"

"No," he said indifferently. "A College man may not marry. Yet he may have as many friends as he will, which is far the best thing. Young ladies will come to visit him. Perhaps, if he were married, his wife would forbid them. Perhaps he would not even want to see them."

Jane looked down at him sceptically.

"Not want to see them? Not even the one who sits on her bare bottom in front of his camera?"

Alone among the girl-children of his acquaintance, Jane's occasional defensive vulgarity was also to be tolerated. Not quite tolerated, indeed, but received in silence. Before he could draw breath to speak again, she scrambled up and began to walk through the meadow grass towards the riverbank, where the others had moored the skiff.

From where he lay, the copper-green shallows and luminous pools of the stream were close to him. Dodgson touched the green rushes at arm's length, thick and sappy with the soft elasticity of a girl's cool skin. Over the brown sheaths the rushes rose like classical columns, swelling out at their centre.

For the last time, he hoped, the question of matrimony had been answered. With few exceptions, a fellow of an Oxford college was debarred by statute from marriage. He was also required to proceed to Holy Orders. Neither of these stipulations was the least irksome to him. In both, he had fulfilled the letter and the spirit of the law.

The white pollen of early grasses thickened the air as he watched Jane walking away. Under the pink cotton her hips thrust with the abandon of childhood, not yet the controlled movement of a young woman.

What was it that he truly mourned? Not the loss of a mere child's appearance, for he had kissed girls of seventeen or eighteen and thought them several years younger. There were models to be hired in town who were married women with a child's body. Not appearance, then. By long experience he had learnt to dread hard-voiced independence and the impertinence of the "awkward age" as the worst disfigurement of all. Must it happen to Jane Ashmole? Perhaps only in the June heaven above the Oxford meadows would she be restored to him, for ever perfect in her regained innocence.

He could just see the stern of the skiff, beyond the cow-parsley and meadowsweet, where the river margin glimmered cool in the bright afternoon. Robinson Duckworth of Trinity, with his handsome, open face, was the chaperone of these summer afternoons. He sat on the bank in clerical coat and white flannels, a straw boater balanced humorously on the back of his head. Two girls knelt at either side of him, listening to his words. They were the daughters of Dr. Chantrey, Nerissa the elder at fourteen, Belinda at seven the youngest member of the boating party.

"Shall you be married in heaven?"

Dodgson, who had closed his eyes again in contemplation, opened them to see Jane once more standing over him. He was about to say something theological, to define heaven as a state beyond mere wedlock.

"Shall I be your bride?"

In this, he decided, Jane could not be denied. He reached up and took her hand as she stood against the faint and sunlit meadow haze. Smiling at her as he held her hand, he let go at last and watched her turn away to the others. No word was needed.

Heaven in the deep meadow sky. Perhaps not. Heaven, instead, as the cliffs and beaches of the Isle of Wight or the Sussex coast. Perpetual afternoon of summer light on groups of girl-children in bathing-drawers and vests. All of them polite, demure, yet responsive to his approach. For good measure, these charming pleasures would be tempered by lunch with Tennyson at Farringford, sunlit days with Rossetti in the gardens of Kelmscott or at Tudor House in Cheyne Walk.

Such images crowded his mind in the knowledge that several weeks hence his annual summer adventure would begin again. Against the Oxford meadowland he saw a glitter of afternoon tide stretching from the chines beyond Freshwater into the mirror fire of the Western Approaches. Warm shingle beaches below the creamy chalk of Sussex cliffs. Abruptly the mood of anticipation was dispelled by Duckworth's voice calling from the riverbank,

"Five o'clock! Five o'clock!"

The Chantrey girls joined the cry, shrill and reproving, as if to rouse Dodgson from his idleness. Drawing himself up, he dusted the pollen from his clothes. By the time that he reached the skiff at its mooring, the three girls were sitting amidships,

Duckworth in the bow with the sculls. Light and expert, Dodgson took the stern lines, pushing off from the gravelled shallows into the dappled sunlight of the stream.

At first all five of them were preoccupied in setting the little craft on its course downstream to Folly Bridge. With the lines in his hands, Dodgson watched the flat, warm countryside towards the Cumnor hills and Wytham Woods through the gaps of the willows and osiers on the bank. Fields of young wheat were already splashed by the crimson of trifolium. White bells of comfrey enlivened the green riverbank.

As the skiff moved easily with the current, he avoided the eyes of the others, knowing that the gaze of the three girls was upon him. He thought of Jane, gentle and patient; Nerissa, wise and a little suspicious with the advantage of her age; Belinda, eager and avaricious in her infancy. It was Belinda who broke the spell, the gentle pat and ripple of water on the shell, her voice confident in its own audacity.

"Tell us a story, Story-Book Man!"

Of all the girls, Belinda saw most clearly that she was the giver and Dodgson the beggar in the matter of friendship. Her voice confirmed it in every syllable.

Duckworth, in the bows, missed the water with his blade and let out a breathless guffaw.

"No time! No time!" he said, protesting like one of Dodgson's own creations on the author's behalf. "If this keeps up we shall be at Folly Bridge faster than light!"

Belinda pressed her short mane of fair hair to her mouth, as if kissing it, and pulled a face.

"Faster than light?"

"Why not?" Duckworth had his breath again now but was rowing more slowly than before.

"Because you can't travel faster than light!" Nerissa spoke, exercising the superiority of age, weary of childish talk.

"Why not?" Dodgson spoke at last, echoing Duckworth's question. The answer had fallen easily into his mind, as it generally did, while the others were talking.

"Because," said Nerissa, "what would happen to you if you did?"

"Don't you know?"
She shook her head, and so he told her.

> "Travel faster than light, and the consequence is,
> No matter how slowly you drive,
> You may finish your journey, and on the next day
> You shall watch yourself as you arrive. . . ."

"But what if you can't?" Nerissa remained unimpressed.
He had an answer for this, too.

> "As a matter of logic, the consequence is,
> If light travel faster than I,
> You shall see me in places I'm no longer in,
> By the gift of your sceptical eye."

"Bravo!" cried Duckworth. "Those who lose the wager shall take the rudder. He who wins it may now take the sculls."

They bumped the bank gently, Duckworth stepping out and steadying the bow while Jane and Nerissa sat side by side in the stern, each holding a line. Dodgson moved to the bow, taking up the sculls while his mind continued to run over the lines of the verses, seeking faults and improvements. On such afternoons he could rhyme effortlessly and endlessly, discarding almost every attempt by the time the party reached the boating station at Folly Bridge.

Beyond the boatbuilder's yard at Medley Weir, the arcadia of Wytham Woods and the buttercup meadows gave way to the dark brick of Oxford's industrial suburb. Among shabby houses rose the occasional bell tower of a Tractarian church, Romanesque or Florentine. It was an area known to Dodgson only from the distance of the river or the seclusion of a cab driving to the railway station.

Then the landscape of smoke and brick was gone. They passed under Folly Bridge to the boating station, where the freshly painted college barges lined the bank of Christ Church Meadow.

3

FROM HIS CONCEALMENT among the trees on the far bank of the river, Richard Baptist Tiptoe—familiarly known as Dicky Tiptoe—watched the skiff move downstream in the tranquil current. He caught a last sound of voices, Belinda's high-pitched peremptory demand:

"Tell us a story, Story-Book Man!"

He heard her snigger at her own pertness. Then Dicky Tiptoe closed the field-glasses he had employed during the afternoon and turned away towards the low ancient arch of Godstow Bridge. In its shadow, the boy who had been paid sixpence for his trouble was holding the two horses of Tiptoe's hired pilentum. Hairy of ear and nostril, bravely moustached, Dicky Tiptoe carried his forty years with the pace and ferocity of a bantam. Just now he was smiling to himself, thinking of the story he would tell Charlie Howell. There was not a doubt in his mind that the Reverend Mr. Dodgson was alone in the world, a beggar for the friendship of children. Tiptoe, who had experience in such matters, judged that he was a rather frightened man.

Driving back through the sunlit lanes north of Oxford, he sang quietly to himself. Dicky Tiptoe. No one who knew him could say whether the ridiculous name was the one he had been born with. He himself would have had to stop and consider the question. But there was much about him that was generally known to be true.

Richard Baptist Tiptoe had been, however briefly, a boy at Harrow School, under the famous Dr. Vaughan. He had been an officer in India after the mutiny, though no English soldier had ever served under his command. Lieutenant Tiptoe had commanded the second detachment of Native Infantry at Sedashegar, rarely seeing another Englishman. Like most subalterns in such posts, he had taken to the bottle and acquired a trio of Indian girls for his bungalow. By promising other favours here and there, his girls took care that his superiors should not hear tales of their benefactor bawling out his parade-ground commands with eyes glazed and tunic unbuttoned, berating the sepoys in the coarsest language of the barroom.

Rescued from Sedashegar by the promise of marrying money, Richard Baptist Tiptoe stepped ashore at Gravesend after a ten-year absence. Money, when it saw him in the flesh, called off the wedding. Yet as he boasted, he was "an adaptable sort of cove" and found himself employment by driving the Cambridge Mail between the Blue Boar and its London terminus at the Warwick Arms near St. Paul's.

The North-Eastern Railway put an end to the Cambridge Mail. Undismayed, Dicky Tiptoe found his way to Holywell Street, a shabby little thoroughfare running just north of the Strand. Secondhand clothes and dog-eared books crowded the windows of the narrow shops. Behind one bow-window of blistered paint and volumes of sermons a prison-hardened old man, William Dugdale, printed neat, plain-covered volumes of baroque obscenity.

Tiptoe had always possessed a certain florid facetiousness of style. At Dugdale's suggestion, he put it to work. *Vivien: A Tale of the Hindu Marriage-Bed* was a tribute to his favourite bungalow girl. He followed its success with *Nunnery Confessions, The Amorous Tour of Susie Loveit,* and *Venus at Fifteen.* The quaint, refined prose demanded by readers of the genre had been effortless to him. With a lingering pride he remembered some of his cadences as other men dwelt on the poetry of Byron or Scott. "Stripped to a negligee costume which heightened the charms of her person . . . brown velveteen skin, eyes limpid with the birth of venereal desire."

Dicky Tiptoe whistled as he cracked the whip above his horses' heads and threaded the busy Oxford streets. Brewers' drays with their powerful shires moved like galleons among the lighter craft of hansoms, yellow-painted phaetons, and the groups of riders returning to dinner from Sandford and Nuneham Courtenay.

Leaving his carriage at the stables of the King's Head in the Cornmarket, he set off with his bandy, duck-legged walk towards the University Museum, rising in its yellowish collegiate Gothic above the trees of the parks. Charles Augustus Howell, tall, olive-skinned, and strong-featured, hair carefully oiled, stood among the stone pillars of the great inner court, sunlight falling through the roof above. His tall hat was held securely under the arm of his cream suit, and he appeared to rest lightly on his gold-topped cane. As Dicky Tiptoe arrived, Howell was studying the stuffed body of the black gorilla in its glass case.

"It's done, then?" asked Tiptoe in a whisper. "Is it done?"

"Long ago." Howell continued to study the bared teeth of the dead gorilla. "And what did you discern of the learned Dodgson?"

"He'd be easily frightened," said Tiptoe thoughtfully. "He *must* be! That last letter to a girl's mother! Permission to photograph Miss Jane without her bathing-drawers! How many a time, d'you suppose, he's never asked permission? He must know there can be only one end. What we're doing is more of a kindness to the poor fellow. When the time comes, he'll cut up soft as new cheese."

To Tiptoe's slight annoyance, Howell continued to give his attention to the gorilla.

"See those teeth?" A long cream-suited arm indicated the dead animal's face. "You call that a smile? That? I'll be damned if it is! I've seen the creatures shot and clubbed in Africa. A monkey that looks like that is in real terror. No wonder if this poor brute was when they skinned him!"

Then he turned to his shabbier companion.

"Remember that," he said pleasantly, "when you next have our friend under observation."

They turned back to the entrance of the museum, through the great nave of pillars and ironwork. Just outside the main door, Howell stood in the sunlight, looking back at the courts and galleries, Romanesque arches, and steep roofs of fancy tiling.

"There is genius in that design," he said, as if the idea had only just come to him. "Not the skill of the architect but the soul of the man who created such forms. Do you know him?"

"No," said Tiptoe uneasily, "I don't believe I do."

"Professor Ruskin." Howell folded his hands on his cane in a gesture of veneration. "I shall always regard those years I spent as his secretary as the most rewarding experience of my life."

Tiptoe looked quickly to see if there was the hint of a smile pulling at his companion's lips. There was none. They walked through the sunlight to the Botanic Garden and to Christ Church Meadow. Tiptoe raised his hat to the porter at Tom Tower. Then the cream-suited aesthete and the duck-legged old subaltern beside him made their way to the Taylorian Institute where cabs could be hired for the railway station.

Leaving Duckworth to escort the three girls, Dodgson walked quickly up St. Aldate's to prepare for the evening meeting of Common Room. There was no pleasure in his anticipation. Such occasions rarely produced more than a sterile debate on the policies of the wine purchaser or measures to prevent older members from removing Common Room magazines and papers to their own quarters before the stipulated date. Yet he would have been the first to acknowledge the ferocity and animus which inspired such discussions among the college's senior members.

"What mighty contests rise from trivial things!" The line rose unbidden in his thoughts, and he smiled with a slight pedantic satisfaction at his own cleverness.

Several envelopes from the afternoon post were still at the porter's lodge, not yet delivered to individual rooms. Dodgson took those addressed to him and began to tear open the deep-blue envelopes as he crossed the quadrangle flagstones towards his corner staircase. In the hour before dinner there was an air of renewed activity around him after the stillness of the college afternoon.

Two of the envelopes were unfamiliar enough to take his quick attention as he closed the oak behind him and sat in the recess of the casement window. The first had an official appearance. From its torn fold he drew a printed slip of paper.

It were better for him that a millstone were hanged about his neck, and he cast into the sea, than that he should offend one of these little ones.

There was a second, identical envelope with nothing but his name scrawled across it, delivered by hand. Inside he found a scrap of torn paper written in the same careless script.

Tell us your story, Story-Book Man!

Dodgson held the two pieces of paper in his hand and looked out across the shaven grass of the quadrangle lawn, the fountain, and the geometrical design of gravel paths. His eyes rested on the grey Tudor shape of the square tower at the cathedral's eastern end. It was sham, of course, still raw in its new-cut stone. What an imposture it looked now! How right his opposition had been!

Presently he looked down again at the two pieces of paper, from which he had held his mind fastidiously in the aftermath of reading them. They came as no shock to him. He was prepared, as a man is prepared who has been warned long ago of an illness that will one day afflict him. It was probably by his own carelessness that the fortress of privacy had been breached. What he felt now was neither fear nor shame. Least of all had he reason for shame. It was more akin to a sudden realisation, remembering a door left open in a wall far behind him, a key unturned in a lock.

Even in the moment of danger, his gift of logic was unfailing. The text might have been cut from any one of a dozen different pamphlets issued by charities or tract societies. Yet the words written on the scrap of paper were those of Belinda Chantrey, spoken scarcely an hour before.

He excused the girls from suspicion. Not one of them had the opportunity to deliver such a note, even if the malicious sneer had been morally possible to her. Jane Ashmole was secure in the innocence of love. The Chantrey sisters were incapable of the adult wickedness that the note represented.

Who had watched him so closely as to be able to use the words of private conversation in slander of this kind? Dodgson could imagine an answer to the question.

Unwelcome though they were, the two notes were not unexpected. Discretion was a quality that Dodgson, almost deliberately, had abandoned during the past twelve months in his dealings with girl-children and their mothers alike. His conscience was clear in the matter. To any moralist, to any court of law, he could have answered for his conduct without fear. Yet he had been indiscreet, as much in committing his desires to paper as in pursuing them in practice.

To Mrs. Mayhew, wife of the Wadham chaplain, he had written a letter on the subject of how far he might undress her three daughters for the purposes of photographic art. "The permission to go as far as bathing-drawers is very charming," he acknowledged. Then in a series of notes he had urged upon the chaplain's wife the illogicality and philistinism of forbidding her daughters to be naked on these occasions with him.

Hesitant and apprehensive of Oxford scandal, the poor woman had taken refuge in the excuse that her daughters would be distressed by such proceedings. Dodgson spoke to them himself and discovered that they had no objection at all to posing "in their favourite dress of nothing to wear." He pleaded with Mrs. Mayhew in tones of facetious triumph. "Now, don't crush all my hopes. . . ." Driven from her first line of defence, the mother had agreed to Dodgson's requests on condition that she might be present herself as a chaperone. The indignity of being suspected stung him to an angry reply. He refused, ever again, to photograph the Mayhew girls—naked or clothed— "now that I know I am only permitted such a privilege under chaperonage."

The Mayhews were not his persecutors, of that he was utterly sure. What of those others whom he had implored and cajoled? Sarah Ashmole had objected, on Jane's behalf, that her daughter would not care to be naked before the camera lens. Yet she had capitulated with surprising ease when shown that Jane felt not the least repugnance.

It was unthinkable that the Mayhews, Sarah Ashmole, or such correspondents might be the authors of anonymous sneers and rebukes. What about those other men and women to whom his importunate letters might have been shown?

Sarah Ashmole, with her fair-skinned dignity and dark hair: he thought of her. She was a compliant, affectionate woman of thirty-three or thirty-four, giving friendship easily. Her weaknesses were the complement to her virtues—carelessness, imprudence, indulging her own pleasures as naturally as she permitted those of others.

For some months Dodgson had been aware of the distance that had grown between him and several Oxford families who had once been flattered by the friendship of "Lewis Carroll." There were stories of his oddity in circulation; he had known that for a long time.

As he sat in the window-seat of his room, looking down on the close-mown grass and the sand-coloured gravel paths, the name and face of one man came repeatedly to the surface of his thoughts. Thomas Godwin, like himself a senior member of Christ Church, and unlike Dodgson in almost every other respect.

Godwin with his tall brow, dark locks, and sardonic manner was a child of the Romantic rebellion in the guise of a modern scholar. Born in Germany of English parents, Godwin maintained the dark glories of Goethe, the idealism of Hegel, the religious scepticism of Göttingen. At twenty he had published a widely admired translation of *Wilhelm Meister*. With that, literary output ceased.

One of Godwin's Senior Common Room amusements was his mockery of Dodgson's piety and his contempt for the middle-aged bachelor's child-friendships. "A man among children and a child among men," Godwin had once called him to his face. "An inexhaustible stream of moral cant," was his other pleasantry, "shallow at the source and wide at the mouth."

Dodgson was not much moved by such bitter humour. It was usual enough in Oxford colleges. Yet Godwin had been Sarah Ashmole's lodger, occupying rooms in the house beyond Folly Bridge for several months in the previous year. Was it possible that he had heard something of Dodgson's pleading with Mrs. Ashmole on Jane's behalf?

With a final glance at the offensiveness of the new cathedral tower in the late sunlight, Dodgson dismissed the suspicion against Godwin. In the eyes of Dean Liddell and the governing body, Godwin's moral and doctrinal position was already equivocal. To compound this by such poisonous banter was both foolish and unnecessary. It was foolish because it would compromise his own position, unnecessary because Dodgson was so easy a target for public abuse at every meeting of Senior Common Room. Public mockery was a more gratifying game to Godwin's kind. In any case, if he had known of Dodgson's interest in Jane a year ago and had not cared, why should he care so greatly now?

There was but one way with such poisoned thoughts. Dodgson went across to the fireplace and drew aside the embroidered screen. He struck a match, watched the burning paper curl, and went to dress for dinner.

A mile away in the courtyard of the museum, Alfred Swain—of the long, intelligent features—was pondering on what he had just seen. He had come to the museum in a few hours of leisure to improve his stock of useful knowledge. Poetry was for pleasure, natural science was for improvement of the mind. That, at least, was Swain's experience. Yet he emerged into the tree-lined road outside with an uncharacteristic frown. It was not the stuffed carcases of the natural-history display that caused this grimace of puzzlement. Swain was thinking about Charles Augustus Howell and wondering what had brought him to Oxford. While there was no criminal conviction against him, Howell was "known to the police" in the most discreet way. That concerned Alfred Swain, who was a newly appointed inspector in the Criminal Investigation Department of Scotland Yard. A series of robberies among the wealthier homes of north Oxfordshire had brought him to the city. The sighting of Charlie Howell was pure coincidence. All the same, Swain stored the event in his long and tidy memory, to be thought about further when time permitted.

4

DODGSON ADJUSTED THE SCREW that stood out from the brass lens of the collodion camera. The two boxes of red polished wood that made up the body of the instrument moved one inside the other. Through the thick glass, the wickerwork sofa and its cushions came into focus, upside down.

It was rare for him to exchange his black jacket for white linen. Yet the little glasshouse on the leads above his room was oppressively hot in the June sunlight. Jane Ashmole stood on the flat roof outside it, the light breeze from meadow and river fluttering the yellow ribands of her dress. Leaning her hands on the battlemented stone, she looked down across the great quadrangle, over the cathedral roof beyond, to the elms of the Broad Walk and the distant gleam of the river itself.

Dodgson resumed his interrogation of her.

"Babies are illogical," he said severely. "Nobody is despised who can manage a crocodile. Illogical persons are despised." He gave her a moment to consider the three statements. "Answer, please!"

Jane turned the strong, pale features of her face to him—the profile of Sarah Ashmole reinforced by energy and authority at thirteen years old. She brushed back her short slanting fringe of dark brown hair.

"That's easy," she said. "Babies cannot manage crocodiles."

She gave him the taunting smile of one who knew that he had deliberately made the first problem simple.

"That's good." Dodgson straightened up from the camera. "Very good. We shall make a logician of you yet."

"Perhaps I shan't care very much for being a logician."

Her smile widened, revealing the perfection of firm white teeth, her face so captivating in its innocent teasing that his heart seemed almost to stop with the beauty of it. How easy to understand the myth of Cupid's arrow, he thought, the sudden impact that woke devotion and desire.

As if fearing that she might read too much in his eyes, he turned away to the bench on which lay two large portable wooden cases. One contained the enamel baths and rows of stoppered bottles. The other, when open, unfolded the black tent of an improvised dark-room.

"No ducks waltz," he said, beginning again with her. "No officers ever decline to waltz. All my poultry are ducks."

Jane leant her elbows on the stone of the parapet and looked directly down at the path below, as if measuring the height.

"That's harder," she said, and seemed to dismiss the problem on those grounds. Yet before he could interrupt, she added hopefully, "No officers are ducks."

Dodgson took the Hill-Norris collodion plates from their shallow trough and slid the first one into the back of the camera.

"No," he said gently, "my *poultry* are not officers."

Jane stood up and turned around triumphantly.

"There!" she said, moving across the roof like a dancer. "I shall never do logic, after all."

"You will if you try," he insisted.

By the time he had finished his preparations in the makeshift studio of the glasshouse, Jane was back at the parapet looking towards the river once more. He walked over and stood behind her so that the crown of her dark hair touched his chin. Gently he returned the pressure, but no more lasciviously than a father might have done with his daughter. She was so precious to him, so perfect a gift of God's, he thought. How could any person believe the hideousness at which the rumours and the poisonous notes hinted?

> *The marvel of a soul like thine, earth's flower*
> *She holds up to the softened gaze of God.*

The lines, which rose unprompted in his mind, reflected his love with such frankness that he dared not speak them aloud to her just then. Instead, he held her against him and directed her gaze towards the river.

Rooks in the Oxford sky above the meadow trees soared and hung in the currents of warm air. Magpies swooped low and clamorous between the branches of the Broad Walk, above the college men in their striped blazers, the women in silks and carrying parasols. From the tree-lined bank, by the barges and Folly Bridge, the sound of a gun and the dull, remote cheering of spectators marked the beginning of the last day of Eights Week.

"See the oars!" Standing behind her, clasping her to him, he extended his other arm, pointing to the gap in the trees and the mercurial glimmer of river. Dark blades scooped the water and the shells spurted out of view in a flurry of eddying pools. He could not bear to part with her yet and went on to indicate all manner of things as a pretext for their closeness.

"There the Christ Church barge." His finger stabbed at the white dismasted galleon at its mooring, crowded with straw-hatted men and women like beribboned kites in their silks. "The flag of the House at the masthead! There the new tower, and there the Deanery. And Dr. Liddell, the Dean of Christ Church, in his garden, revising the Liddell and Scott Greek Lexicon."

"Revising it?" Jane's voice was sceptical and disapproving, as if she might move from him.

"To be sure," said Dodgson quickly. "Listen!

> "Two men wrote a Lexicon, Liddell and Scott,
> One part was clever—and one part was not!
> Tell me, ye scholars who fathom this riddle,
> Which part was by Scott—and which part was by Liddell?"

"I don't believe it!" Jane broke away from him with a burst of laughter, her mood now verging towards the coquettishness that he found so displeasing in girls of any age. It was all too often, in his experience, the precursor of that awkward stage of development that first parodied and then destroyed forever the pure, unmalicious amusement of childhood. Could any woman pass from childhood to maturity unblemished by this? If there were such a creature, he believed as an article of faith that she would be Jane Ashmole.

Returning to the glasshouse, he prepared the nitrate bath for the glass slides as they were taken from the camera. It was a simple enough process, though he had not succeeded infallibly with it. The nitrate bath was a tall, narrow case about a foot square, wooden on the outside and lined with enamel on its inner surface. The glass plate, when exposed, would slide in, secure from the light.

The developing box opened to provide two enamel trays in its base and the rows of small square bottles in its lid. Dodgson took two of the bottles, drew their glass stoppers, and poured the contents into the nitrate tank. A sour mineral smell of acid filled the makeshift studio. It was perfectly safe to carry out the process in the glasshouse with the aid of the tent dark-room. By this means the glass-plate negatives would be produced. It was his normal practice to have the photographs printed from these by a professional firm in the city. In the case of the photographs he was about to take, it would be imprudent to allow others to share in the processing. It was possible, of course, to have such work done discreetly in London. On the whole, Dodgson preferred to deal with the work himself. It was time-consuming to make prints from the negatives but not, for him, difficult.

He went outside again and stood close to Jane as she turned and looked northward, beyond Peckwater, towards the square medieval towers of Merton and Magdalen. He and the girl were utterly alone on the leads of the flat roof between the grey stone of the Tudor battlements. For good or evil, their next two or three hours would be entirely uninterrupted. It was, to him, a Garden of Eden with no trees or flowers or shrubs. About them on every side lay the sublime blue of heaven and the divine fire of the sun. Together they would glimpse too briefly the love of men and women in the heavenly city.

"Truth is most beautiful when naked," he said. "Jane Ashmole is Truth. Therefore . . . ."

"Therefore, Jane Ashmole is most beautiful in her finest silks!"

She skipped away from him, spread out her skirts, and dropped a curtsy in derision.

Dodgson felt a pang, almost like the start of tears, at the apparent destruction of his hopes. Yet he knew that it was futile to argue or reprove her. When displeased, it was his custom to voice criticism later.

"Very well," he said gently. "What shall you be? The Queen of Sheba? The Lady of Shalott? A Chinese mandarin? There are costumes for them all in the cupboard."

Jane made a motion of displeasure with her mouth but her eyes were still bright with laughter.

"No!" she said, in a sudden wilful pirouette. "I shall be none of those!"

"Well, then?" He waited in the opening of the glasshouse, the sun striking lower and yet more fiercely still.

"I shall be Jane Ashmole!" she said with a triumphant flourish. How it was done he could not see. Yet as if by the pulling of a single ribbon, the dress fell from her shoulders, waist, and hips, descending in a flutter of pink silk to her feet. Beneath it she was entirely naked.

In the brilliance of the afternoon light, her pale nudity was dazzling as it was sudden. Dodgson felt again the shock which seemed to stop the rhythm of his heart by such intensity. Jane, indifferent to the effect upon him, turned in a slow circle. Her movements had the carelessness of a child and the self-confidence of a woman. In that moment it was she, not her admirer, who controlled absolutely their situation. Then, with a flick of the short slanting fringe, the dark, lank hair brushing her collarbone, she stood before him once more, hands clasped lightly over her loins. Even this was a gesture of completeness rather than prudery.

Beautiful as a butterfly and as fair as a queen. . . . The words of the song came to him with perfect aptness. Stillness had settled upon the deserted quadrangles again in the afternoon heat. Silence from the river where the ribboned and blazered crowds had turned to their picnic teas. Only from the direction of the new Gothic tower came a muffled thunder of music, the cathedral organist's Handelian chords and flourishes anticipating the next day's services.

"You shall be Jane Ashmole," he said, turning her display into a joke. "The Queen of Sheba and all the others in one."

Dodgson turned back into the glasshouse, seeing her from the corner of his eye as she scooped up her fallen clothes and followed him.

Where there was such naturalness, there could be no evil. How well he remembered the other occasion, so different, when one of Rossetti's friends had arranged a sitting by a girl of Jane's age in a private studio. There was no doubt that the intention and the girl who sat for his camera were equally innocent. Yet the woman, reputed to be the mother, had a last reserve of prudery in the matter. He remembered the girl as tall and graceful, the light brown hair sweeping from her high crown to her shoulders, framing the pale oval of her face like a nun's veil. Yet the absurd breast halter that she wore seemed to mock her innocence. Drawn round her hips was a pair of brief and close-fitting drawers like those of a ballet girl. They ran narrowly between her loins, emphasising the curve they purported to conceal. Their seat was cut high and tight in a manner more lewdly suggestive than nakedness could ever be.

Worst of all, there had been the mother, who sat in her chair just beyond the camera's field of vision. Throughout the sitting, she kept her eyes cast down and never spoke. The peculiar mixture of indifference and reproach that her silence implied was beyond bearing. "I could take no pleasure in photographing your daughters," he had told Mrs. Mayhew a few weeks later, "now that I know I am only permitted such a privilege under chaperonage." Whatever the scandalmongers might read into his words, they were the simple truth.

"You shall be Diana at the bath," he said suddenly to Jane. He had almost said Susannah, but the biblical implications of that had checked him. In the makeshift studio of the glasshouse, he draped the pink dress and skirts over the wickerwork couch and moved the table with its flowered cloth closer. Upon the table he set a bouquet of wax flowers, white and purple, and a framed oval mirror with candles in its two holders.

"Stand at the table," he said, leading her gently by the hand. "Stand a little aside from it, like this, with your back to the camera. Now, look this way into the mirror. Can you be still comfortably like that for half a minute?"

"Yes!" she said eagerly. "Oh, yes!"

It was a game now, the child's fascination with the magic of making pictures, the excitement of seeing the image grow upon the glass.

Dodgson went back and viewed her through the camera lens. Moral resolve apart, he knew that no man possessed by lewdness could make such a picture. There was too much to be done, there were too many details and processes to be remembered, for such distraction of thought. Yet even he, bringing the lens into focus by turning the brass screw, was constantly aware of Jane's natural grace. The turning of her head to the mirror gave just a suggestion of her firm profile, the lank dark hair parted over her shoulders at the nape to show the line of her neck. Her arms were held with easy unconcern, one following the contour of her body downwards in a relaxed line, the other bent at the elbow as if holding an invisible brush or comb before her. She stood so that the line of her body was not straight, the indentation of the adolescent spine, the shadowed fineness of the shoulder blades, sloped to the right a little from the gracile line of her pale shoulders. One leg was straight, taking the weight of her body, the other bent back a little at the knee, to continue a provoking lack of symmetry in her pose. The taut resilience of her buttocks and thighs had a consequent suggestion of movement even in the single photograph.

"Be patient a little longer," he said softly. Then, taking the brass cap from the lens, he held his watch in his hand and saw thirty seconds tick away. He replaced the cap.

"Now," he said, his voice quite as excited as hers by the novelty of each new picture, "see what a perfect portrait you have made!"

In the dark-room he drew the glass plate from its protective holder and slid it into the shallow trough of the first bath, where nitric and pyrogallic acids were mixed. As he worked, moving the liquid gently, drawing the plate out to inspect its density of image, he was constantly aware of the beautiful ellipse of her brown eyes, rapt as a child before a stage magician, watching him. She stood barefoot and naked beside him in total trust.

"We have it now!" he said at last, not daring to inspect his creation more closely until the process was finished. Running the glass plate through the water first, he held it carefully by one corner over the enamel bath of the developing case and poured hyposulphite gently upon it from another of the glass bottles. Once the plate was well coated, he washed it in water again and laid it on a sheet of white paper for Jane to see.

At the first glance, he knew it was superb, a picture whose accomplishment rivalled the success of his formal portraits of the Poet Laureate or Professor Ruskin.

"How easy it was!" she said excitedly, "how quick! There must be time for another! I shall be the Lady of Shalott now! See, this shall be the boat that bears me down the stream to Camelot!"

"Impossible!"

Dodgson laughed, but Jane had run to the wickerwork sofa and arranged herself upon it. Her head drooped upon the pillow, her hands lay limp and perfectly posed across her lap, one leg drawn back under the other at the knee.

" 'Under tower and balcony, by garden-wall and gallery,' " she recited, giving the words the excited shrillness of a child's playing, " 'A gleaming shape she floated by, dead-pale between the houses high.' "

Indulging her in the whim, Dodgson poured the collodion mixture carefully onto a clean glass plate, letting it run upon it until the surface was evenly coated. He tipped the excess back into the square glass bottle and returned to the camera.

The subject, Jane upon the wicker sofa, lacked all the promise of the first picture. It was, in every respect but her nudity, a conventional pose of the kind employed in child portraiture. Yet as he had done the first portrait to please himself, so he would now do this one to please her. The wickerwork sofa was in focus and he was ready to begin. At that moment, Jane's voice rose in the drama of recitation.

" 'She left the web, she left the loom, she took three paces thro' the room.' "

At first he thought, as she rose from the sofa, that she was going to advance upon him. But Jane stood, hands at her side, facing the camera with a firmness which excited and intimidated him at the same time. It would have been wise, prudent at least, to have reprimanded her and ended the afternoon's adventure at once. Yet he had turned the brass screw of the lens to keep her in focus. Now he straightened up, knowing only that such an opportunity and such a subject might never recur. Dodgson took the cap from the lens. For thirty seconds he looked steadily into the girl's frank brown eyes, thrilled by the challenge of the way her teeth touched lightly on her lower lip. As he replaced the cap, a white cloud shaded the sun for a moment and then bore its shadow onwards over the flags that flew from the towers of Merton and Magdalen in honour of the races.

That night, after Jane had been escorted home, he set to work printing the two negatives. One was a superb and evocative study of naked innocence, a child's vanity at the framed oval mirror. The second, he recognised at once, was infinitely more profound and, to him, disturbing. It was not bantering or defiant in a childish way. The image which looked back at him from the brown paper was imbued with a hint of animal ferocity, the mask fallen from a woman of thirteen.

To enforce order upon the disturbance he felt in his mind, he knelt at his bed and prayed in the manner in which he had done since his first night at Rugby School more than thirty years before. The photographs were locked in a drawer, and he knew that for some time to come they must remain there. Yet he walked to the window and drew back its curtains, looking out across the darkened sky in which the last faint light of summer dusk lingered.

"Let her be with me in eternity!"

It was not a prayer he would ever have dared to pray. Indeed, it was not a thought which he would have permitted without some sense that the demand might be presumptuous blasphemy. The need to possess her in that other state came upon him unawares, so that the words formed themselves without any thought preceding them.

For a few minutes longer he stood and looked out across the dark meadow with its golden dandelion discs. How little the world saw of the soul's drama! A man and a child walking under the trees in the early evening towards the house that lay at a little distance beyond Folly Bridge.

5

"EAT YOUR CAKE AND DON'T CRY!" said Thomas Godwin. His lips quivered a little, as if in amusement despite the severity of his tone. "Don't try to eat it and cry at the same time or you'll very probably be sick. Why is your mother not here?"

Jane, who had obediently taken a mouthful of cake, could only shake her head, hoping that the gesture would be accepted as an inarticulate disclaimer. Her pin-point tear glittered unshed.

Godwin watched her from his corner of the wooden garden seat they occupied. He had appeared unannounced through the trees after Sarah Ashmole left the teatable. They sat in the little opening at the end of the alley with its close privet hedges, among the fragrance of sweet-william and honeysuckle, heavy and stagnant in the warm midsummer day. Godwin had come through the green shade of lime and acacias. He had cut across the shrubbery slope, striding up from the road below, along which the drovers passed with their Welsh ponies for the market at Gloucester Green.

He was not her father, had no right to exercise natural authority over her, and yet he seemed to destroy all power of resistance in her.

"I daresay Mr. Dodgson makes you cry," he said, with a laugh that was almost a sniff. "I'm sure Mr. Dodgson would make me cry if I had to spend so much of my time with him."

Jane kept her gaze upon the plate in front of her. When he had taken rooms in the house, months ago, she thought of him as the Jolly Farmer with his fresh complexion. Now there was nothing jolly about him, despite his round red face. The narrow eyes, dark hair, and aquiline features were those of a cruel predator. So Jane found it easy to think of him as a hawk, whose fingers would sprout talons and whose mouth concealed a ravenous beak. He was clever, not as other Christ Church men were clever but with a hunter's calculation. She did not know that there were members of his own Common Room whom Godwin reduced to silence as easily as he paralysed Jane's own defiance.

"I wonder how I should manage to spend so much time with Mr. Dodgson," he said more gently, "with Mr. Dodgson, spinster of this parish! I wonder what I should do together with him."

"I'm sure I don't know." Because she knew what might follow and longed to prevent it, Jane attempted a reply.

"Don't you?" Godwin laughed again and his hand stroked back the lank, dark hair so that he might see her face more clearly as she bowed her head. It was a gesture to which she knew he had no right. Yet perhaps if she submitted to it, he would spare her what came next.

"Don't you?" he repeated. "Then tell me what *you* do with him, Jane! So many hours together—sometimes with the others and sometimes alone with him! Tell me what you do!"

In a few minutes, she knew, her mother would come back. The interrogation would continue but not in this manner. Then, in despair, she heard distantly from the house the notes of the piano, the familiar melodies of Mendelssohn's *Songs Without Words* as Sarah Ashmole began to play.

"We talk," she said desperately. "He tells us stories!"

"So much talk!" said Godwin in derisive admiration. He now stroked her face. "So many stories. Look me in the eye and tell me, Jane!"

So, in the summer garden among the perfume of stocks and

far from the distant bluish stars of the clematis on the wall of the house itself, the ordeal began once more.

"Look me in the eye, you bitch!" he said quietly.

The shock of the word made her lift her face and meet his gaze. Hemmed in by the teatable, she could not even slide out easily and run for the safety of the house.

"You may go, if you've a mind to," he said, when she dropped her gaze from his eyes, which seemed to hunt her own. "Nobody's hindering you."

She knew what Mr. Dodgson, "Dodo," would have replied. Yes, he would say, Nobody *is* hindering me! Nobody is sitting across the garden seat and blocking the way. Gathering all her defiance, Jane said,

"If Nobody is hindering me, you may tell him to stop!"

The effect of this was spoilt by her slight movement which knocked a small knife from the table to the ground.

"Let it stop there!" said Godwin, apparently ignoring her cleverness. "Look me in the eye and tell me what you do with Mr. Dodgson—or, if you prefer, what Mr. Dodgson does with you."

It was quite impossible, of course, even to lift her face to him. She knew, as well as Godwin did, that this encounter would never be reported to her mother. If Jane "peached," as Godwin had once called it, then Sarah Ashmole would be sure to take up the question in turn and ask what it was that Jane and her "aged, aged friend" Mr. Dodgson had done during their hours alone.

Godwin was already close to her on the seat. He put out his hand and turned her skirts back above the knee, running his palm over the stockinged expanse above the knees themselves. Jane pressed back until the wooden arm of the seat held her. She sat upright and motionless, not daring to make a sound. Whatever happened she knew she must be silent, though she had only a vague idea of what might happen.

"If you won't answer a civil question when it's put to you," Godwin said, resting his hand so that she might feel its warmth reaching her through the thin cotton, "if you *won't* answer a question when it's civilly put, then I'm sure I can't make you."

Now it was Jane who looked up, not in defiance but alarm, as if to read his intention. Godwin was looking down, watching his hand as it smoothed over the taut adolescent skin above the tops of the stockings.

"If you feel so ashamed of what you did with Mr. Dodgson that you can't repeat the details," he continued, "I'm sure I don't know what it can have been."

"It was only a story that he told!" Jane gasped from the breathlessness of fear. "That's the truth!"

"Such a long, long story!" said Godwin, still mocking her by a pretence at belief. "Then tell me this marvellous story! Now! I have time enough to spare."

"I can't!" she cried. "I don't know how!"

He sat back and folded his arms, leaving her paralysed, like the prey before the predator, the skirt hem still untidily above her knees.

"You can't, Jane," he said gently, "because you are a deceitful and impure little girl!"

"No!" The first tears, quickly checked for fear that her mother might see them and inquire, fell with this cry.

Godwin was no longer sneering or aggressive. He spoke just as if reporting something read that day in *The Times* or the *Morning Post*.

"There are places for little girls of your sort," he said casually, "places where they know how to deal with deceit and impurity. If you can't live obediently and truthfully with your mother, the justices will find a place to send you. Far, far away from here!"

It was impossible to reply. There was no reply that could be made. The brown hair fell forward as Jane lowered her face and let the tears run in silence.

Now, however, Godwin had finished with her. He stood up and walked through the trees towards the house. Jane scrambled out and ran by another way, down the length of the privet alley to the far door, escaping him at last and coming to the kitchen with its cool grey tiles and sunlit shelves.

She listened and heard the light cadences of Mendelssohn stop abruptly as Sarah Ashmole was interrupted. That meant that Thomas Godwin was in the drawing-room talking to her. Was it about Jane herself? Was it a recommendation that her misconduct should be punished by confinement in some institution? He had spoken to her in the past of reformatories where misery and brutality were the rule. Once or twice he had hinted at what she believed to be the lunatic asylum, where she might be imprisoned if her wickedness proved to be an incorrigible cast of mind.

It was easy enough to slip through the intervening room and hear the voices carrying across the hallway from the tall panelled door which stood partly open. Concealed in a doorway on her own side of the hall, Jane could even see a segment of the room. There was a stretch of tawny patterned carpet, like a lion's mane, a casement window whose leaded lights showed the sunlit roses immediately outside. On the embroidery frame, with a low chair before it, Sarah Ashmole's outline of a bright macaw was still unfinished after a year's work.

"Men like Dodgson are the worst," Godwin was saying, "your pale English curates who make a saddle of their loins! Would you have him use the girl for such purposes? A man among women—but a woman among men!"

"I'm sure you're quite wrong!" Sarah Ashmole's voice, despite her words, was interceding with him rather than contradicting his pronouncement. "It cannot be like that. If such things were true, he would have been called to account long ago. There has never been the least scandal!"

"The Liddells turned him away soon enough!" said Godwin, with his derisive laugh that sounded almost like a sniff of contempt. "Liddell may be a fool in his religion but he saw the make of Dodgson soon enough!"

"You know that's not true!"

"Is it true that Dodgson wrote letters to women last year, in Oxford, asking leave to undress their daughters for his camera? Come, my dear! You know the truth of it!"

"It may be. . . ." There was a softness in Sarah Ashmole's voice, as if Godwin had put an arm about her in a gesture of comfort. Jane listened, as she had done to several conversations about herself, and felt in awe of the man. Who was he, to speak to her mother in such a way? Had he been her father, she could have understood it. But he was not her father, merely one who had taken rooms in the house for a few months. Even the rooms had been given up some time ago. She knew he could not be her father for she was old enough to remember William Ashmole and even the candlelit tableau of his deathbed, and the day of his funeral in Christ Church cathedral.

It frightened her a little, this authority that Godwin seemed to assume so naturally with her mother. Even with Jane herself he behaved as boldly as any father could. Who was he that he should enter their lives in this way? If she was less frightened than she might have been, it was because she had been intrigued as much by the mystery as by the menace of the man. Perhaps when the mystery was revealed, she would understand. If she understood, there would be less to be afraid of, she thought.

"Quite the best thing is that she should go away for a while," Godwin was saying. "Believe me, if he cannot have her then it will not be long before he finds another sweetheart. His vanity requires it. A month or two and he will forget all about Jane in his new infatuation."

"Perhaps," said Sarah Ashmole. Her skirts brushed lightly against the carpet as she moved away from him.

"Not 'perhaps.'" Godwin pursued her with his words, if not in person. "Not 'perhaps,' but 'certainly.' The man's heart is as easy to read as an open book."

She gave way to him with a promise, its fulfilment to be delayed.

"It shall be as you suggest, but not yet. In the autumn there will be time enough. Let it be settled in the autumn."

Godwin laughed, as if teasing her obstinacy.

"So it shall be! When a man comes as a beggar, he must take whatever crumbs are offered him!"

Jane withdrew from the doorway, retracing her steps through the kitchen, along the privet alley, and back to the teatable, which the maid had not yet cleared. If they found her there, perhaps they would not suspect that she might have been in the house during the conversation.

She heard the hooves of the wild ponies and the voices of the drovers from the roadway below. Magpies chattered in the elms beyond the highway, marking the disturbance as the drovers passed. It was best after all, she decided, to rehearse a story that Mr. Dodgson might have told, in case Sarah Ashmole should ask the same questions as Godwin had done. There was one, she remembered, that had been intended for inclusion in the adventures of Alice but had never been used. It was some time since her Dodo had told it to them among the haycocks of Godstow. He had called it "The Wasp in a Wig." That would do for her present purpose.

Jane remembered the wasp who had rheumatism, asked for brown sugar, and reprimanded Alice with "Worrity, worrity! There never was such a child!" It was little enough but it would do to begin with. While she was recalling this, Sarah Ashmole appeared and sat down at the table opposite her daughter.

The mother's pale features had the same look of firm, gentle authority as her child's. Her dark eyes were softer and her hair becomingly arranged in its coiffure at the back of her head.

They sat in silence for a moment. Then Sarah Ashmole spoke, as if her words had been carefully meditated.

"You must try to understand, my dear," she said.

Jane waited, but her mother made no attempt to elaborate. Indeed, it seemed as if she abandoned the words and tried to begin again with more force.

"Mr. Dodgson is a very busy man," she said abruptly. "I wish you would not pester him so!"

"But I don't!" said Jane eagerly. "And of course I won't!"

"You do," her mother murmured, "and I fear that you will!"

"No!" Jane shook her head vigorously, suddenly relieved that all her trouble was to be ended so easily. "I never go to him unless he asks. I promise I never will. I shan't be a pest to him then, shall I?"

For all her eagerness, it was clear at once to her that the response to her mother's instruction was the wrong one. The demand made upon her was more absolute than she supposed and more sinister.

"You know what I mean!" said Sarah Ashmole sharply, though the finality betrayed hopelessness as well as impatience. She was not a woman of weak character and yet just at the moment she appeared to be one. Jane could guess at what was meant and prudently did not ask that it should be made plain in the form of a command. Yet she felt a sense of injustice and indignation after Godwin's treatment of her half an hour earlier. As he appeared at the far end of the privet alley, the girl turned her face pitilessly upon Sarah Ashmole and said loudly,

"Why does he hate me? Why does Mr. Godwin hate me?"

"What absurdity!" said Sarah Ashmole. "He doesn't hate you! He cares about you; we both do."

"He hates me!" the girl cried. "Why does he?"

As if to prevent the development of an argument that Godwin would be bound to hear, Sarah Ashmole conceded the main point.

"If he does, I'm sure I don't know why! Perhaps you have deserved his anger."

Jane was unmollified but out of concern for her mother she dropped her voice to a child's plaintiveness.

"Why does he hate me? Why should he hate me so?"

Godwin came upon them as they sat there in the silence that followed Jane's last protest. He sat down beside Sarah Ashmole, as if they were allies against her daughter's rebellion. The stillness of the adults became oppressive to the child until, once again, the tears brimmed in her eyes. Godwin behaved as if he had never left the table. He leant across and looked at the girl, examining her more closely to verify that the tears truly stood in her eyes. Then he sat back in his chair and spoke in words that were soft without being gentle.

"Eat your cake," he said quietly, "and don't cry."

Now that he was opposite her and the way from the garden seat was not blocked, Jane flung herself from it and ran towards the house.

6

THE YOUNG MAN who sat in the chair opposite Dodgson cast his eyes up to the ceiling and then down to the floor again. He looked towards the sunlit window and then stared one by one at the pictures on the walls of the tutor's room. Meanwhile, Dodgson continued to read the explanation of a problem in Euclid which the young man in cap and gown had handed to him. Far off beyond the trees, Magdalen clock chimed the hour.

As the last stroke faded, Dodgson tapped the script with his fingernail, making the paper rattle.

"*What* is a corollary?"

The young man's jaw fell slightly and his cheeks coloured a little.

"A c-c-orollary . . . that is to say, a corollary. . . ."

Dodgson was in his element now, like a duellist anticipating every thrust his opponent might make. His own habitual hesitation of speech was lost in the enthusiasm of the sport. He waited until all the young man's efforts had foundered in silence and self-consciousness.

"Do you play billiards?" he asked sharply.

"B-b-illiards?" The youth's bewilderment was most gratifying. "Billiards? Yes, sir. That is to say, I have, sometimes. . . ."

"Good. If you attempted a cannon, missed, and holed your own and the red ball, what would you call it?"

The young man judged it safe to be facetious.

"A fluke, sir? I believe I should call it a fluke."

"Exactly!" said Dodgson, rattling the paper again. "A corollary is a fluke in Euclid. Good morning!"

He stood up and held out the exercise paper at arm's length. The young man lifted his cap with the golden tassel, replaced it, and walked from the room. As the door closed, Dodgson could imagine the story of the tutorial being retold with variations, perhaps not much to his own advantage. He was not greatly concerned. It happened that he had once over-heard his own mathematical lectures being discussed and had caught the words "dull as ditchwater." That did not greatly concern him either. The subject, in this case mathematics and Euclid, mattered more than the student of it. To discover the truth of this was one of the great moral experiences of education.

More to the point, the last tutorial of the year was now over. Already the porter's lodge was almost inaccessible for the boxes and portmanteaus awaiting collection as the Trinity term came to its end and the sunlit weeks of the Long Vacation lay ahead.

Wrapping his gown about him, Dodgson went down the stairs and began to cross the quadrangle towards the Senior Common Room for the last meeting of the year. Here and there a capped and gowned undergraduate ducked his head in self-conscious acknowledgment or pulled off his cap in more formal greeting. He returned these salutes punctiliously and passed into the main entrance of Christ Church hall. Under the great staircase with the glory of its fan-vaulting, lit by reflected sun, was the inner door of the Common Room.

Most of the chairs had already been taken when Dodgson entered. The Common Room, running under the main hall of the college, was marked out by the beams across its ceiling, each of them made of iron cased in oak. The walls were hung with a succession of portraits. Above the fireplace was the white marble panel of olive leaves and berries, a relic of the ancient world brought back from Greece by one of the members half a century before. Dodgson took his chair, murmuring apologies when he noticed that both the Common Room curator and Dean Liddell himself were already in their places.

Liddell scarcely acknowledged his arrival. The dean, his head bald but for a fringe above the ears, turned fastidiously aside as he began conversation with Bayne, the curator of the Senior Common Room. Bayne was the oldest of them at the meeting, a man of almost seventy who had been curator for twenty years. He spoke with a habit of letting his head wander from side to side as if from bewilderment or nervous affliction. The meetings of the Senior Common Room consisted principally of Bayne taking offence at criticism and offering to resign, then clinging to his power as soon as the offer seemed likely to be accepted. The members of the Common Room were on the whole evenly divided in such matters, or at least indifferent. Godwin, who acted as prompter or secretary for Bayne, did so only because it gave him the opportunity to oppose Dodgson's attacks on the curator.

In terms of authority, Dean Liddell was senior to all his colleagues. Yet he contented himself with listening, head bowed, to the discussion, seldom lifting his eyes from the blotting paper on which he sketched. Dodgson glanced aside at the movement of Liddell's gold pen on the pink paper. What had seemed to be a pair of open legs was being transformed into a castle gateway. A strange isolated ellipse now became a cavalier's hat.

As soon as the meeting was under way, Dodgson launched himself into the attack on Bayne. In public affairs of this kind he returned to his habit of emphasising those words which he anticipated difficulty in uttering.

"*Why* is it, Mr. Curator, sir, that *Common* Room *will* lay in sherry?"

Bayne looked up at him, lower lip wet and trembling as it did before he spoke.

"Of course Common Room must lay in sherry," he said peevishly. "What else should Common Room do? Members of Common Room drink sherry and it must be provided."

Dodgson ignored him and spoke to the others round the table.

"It may *interest* members of *Common* Room to know that if we continue to consume *sherry* at the *present* rate, I have determined the result by a *method* of calculus. The number of bottles already laid in will *last* us for another three hundred years!"

There was a murmur of amusement round the table, some of it at the curator's discomfiture, the rest at the high figure. Dean Liddell's brows tightened in a sign of disapproval as he sketched at the face under the cavalier's hat.

"I propose," Dodgson went on, seizing the moment of triumph, "I *propose* the setting up of a Wine *Committee* to superintend the *purchase* and laying down of our *supplies* in future."

Thomas Godwin turned his sharp nose and tall brow towards Dodgson, though he spoke to the rest of the meeting. All the laughter in his eyes, all the warmth, died like a flame and was replaced by a hard gleam.

"Really, Mr. Curator, we cannot have our proceedings interrupted yet again by Mr. Dodgson's complaints. At every meeting I have attended in my time here I have listened to his carping against the college servants, his own colleagues, and the curator. A letter of Mr. Dodgson's has been sent out from the lodge unstamped. How much milk is Mr. Dodgson supposed to receive each morning and at what price? The gas supply to Mr. Dodgson's rooms is inadequate. Will his colleagues please ensure that the kitchen sends him no more smoked ham?"

Dodgson endeavoured to interrupt, stung by the unfairness with which Godwin represented his letters to the steward, but Godwin raised a hand and waved him aside.

"Mr. Dodgson requires that all ginger-beer supplied to his rooms should have glass stoppers and not corks. He objects to finding that two or three bottles in every dozen are empty." Godwin paused, as if for effect. "Little girls drink a good deal of ginger-beer on warm afternoons. I should not, myself, be surprised to find several bottles out of the dozen emptied rather easily."

"Mr. *Curator* . . ."

But Dodgson stumbled over the word and Bayne merely looked about him ineffectually. It was doubtful that he could have halted Godwin even had he chosen to.

"If I were Mr. Dodgson," said Godwin quietly, "I should make some other arrangements about the ginger-beer. Indeed, I might well conclude that a set of college rooms—at all hours of day and evening—is not the place to entertain young girls without a chaperone. To entertain some of them so frequently and for so many hours at a time!"

There was no laughter now, as Godwin sat back in his chair and awaited the response to his words. All the other members of the Common Room were looking directly or covertly at Dodgson, including old Dr. Chantrey, the grandfather of Nerissa and Belinda. Whatever dismay Dodgson may have felt at the bluntness of Godwin's attack, he gathered himself to reply. Before he could begin, Dean Liddell intervened. Godwin's attack had been well aimed but in his passion it seemed as if he had ignored both the presence of the dean and the memory of the three deanery daughters—Alice, Edith, and Lorina. Liddell put down his pen.

"You must not expect, Mr. Godwin, you must not require that your colleagues here should sit under such a shower-bath of vituperation." The voice which now addressed Godwin was gentle, but the eyes were sharp with hostility. "By demeaning one of us, you demean us all. I am no judge of what may pass for criticism in other societies of which you are a member, but you are not entitled to accuse us in such a manner here. Pray, do not do so again."

As though he expected no answer, Liddell went back to his drawing and began to add ivy to the castle gateway. Dodgson found it more difficult now to resume the reply to Godwin than he had done before Liddell's intervention. All the same he was determined to make his contribution. Godwin had put himself entirely in the wrong, drawing all the sympathy to his victim. Dodgson decided he might easily succeed in his first proposal and so carry the meeting with him.

"I *move*, Mr. Curator, that a Wine Committee be set up to superintend the purchase and laying down of wine for the future and that its constitution be presented to our next meeting in the autumn."

He waited to see if there would be a seconder or an opponent. It seemed that there was neither. Then Dean Liddell laid down his pen again and looked up.

"I oppose that," he said quietly. "The curator is well aware of any criticisms that this meeting may have had in its mind. He is the best judge of how they may best be received. There is no purpose that a Wine Committee could serve in addition to that. Indeed, if it should find itself at odds with the curator, where should we be then? No, I am bound to stand in opposition to Mr. Dodgson over this."

Bayne waited only a moment before seizing the opportunity to pass on to the next item and consign the Wine Committee to limbo.

"I am in possession of a complaint from Mr. Barclay relating to the *drains*. In the course of new building a fracture appears to have occurred near the hall. There is, in consequence, a most noxious effluvium that renders the Common Room itself quite uninhabitable from time to time. The steward's attention has been called to this but, it would appear, all in vain. . . ."

When the meeting was over, white claret was served before lunch. Godwin confronted his antagonist.

"It seems we are not to have a Wine Committee, after all, Dodgson. Does that displease you?"

"I think it unwise."

"You were a voice crying in the wilderness." Godwin paused, then continued with mocking concern. "Or perhaps such a flippant use of Holy Writ shocks you. Do I shock you, man of God? I, who care nothing for such things?"

"I fear for you," said Dodgson quietly, holding Godwin's gaze, "I fear for you as I would for a man crossing a torrent upon a wire. I am afraid to see you fall."

Godwin lifted his head back and laughed at the absurdity of it.

"And what of you?" he said at length. "What of you, Dodgson? Do you not fear for yourself more greatly still?"

He looked at his antagonist a moment longer and then walked away to speak to Bayne.

As soon as he could do so without drawing particular attention to himself, Dodgson slipped away and crossed the wide sunlit quadrangle to his own staircase in the north-west corner. All that Godwin had said in the course of the morning, the sneers and the attempts to humiliate him before the others, seemed as nothing compared to that last remark. What peril did he—and Jane—stand in by his own fault?

He took the little key and unlocked the drawer of the oak desk where he kept his private photographic prints and glass plates. The two prints of Jane Ashmole were bright and clear, not yet beginning to fade as they would do sooner or later. The sunlight through a casement window fell on the sheen of the paper as startlingly as it had fallen on the pale skin of her back. What danger did he stand in from that elegant, contrived study of Jane with her back to the camera looking naked into the dressing-mirror? No one could deny it was art, however imperfect the achievement.

It was the second print that continued to disturb him, the image of Jane facing him with a frank and implacable look in her brown eyes. Her facial expression was enough on its own. Her nakedness in this case heightened the effect of the picture but did not alter its character. The second print showed him a danger that was far beyond anything that Godwin's mean and spiteful thoughts could encompass. Godwin was a libertine, of that he had no doubt. Yet Godwin's conception of evil was limited by the conventions of libertinage and the fashionable clichés of free thought.

One day he would destroy the two pictures, wiping the image from each glass plate and then burning the paper prints. He could not do it yet. Why? There was no answer he could give that would not defy the authority of God and all his belief. He put the question from him. Godwin was crossing a torrent on a wire. In his own case, Dodgson thought, the wire crossed a measureless gulf of eternal darkness. He would destroy the plates and the prints in a day or two but not yet. Other considerations apart, he would need to make up the solution to wipe the plates clear.

With a sense that he had done all that he could for the time being, he returned the glass plates and the prints to the drawer, locked it, and dropped the key in his pocket. In the few minutes remaining before his scout would come, he knelt at the window-seat and prayed for Thomas Godwin. As he did so, he tried to put from his mind the knowledge that he was in greater fear for himself than for the enemy whose safety he sought.

7

"TELL ME WHAT AN AVERAGE is," Dodgson demanded brightly. Duckworth and the three girls who sat on the croquet lawn looked at him expectantly. Jane, who seemed to him hardly recognisable in behaviour as his companion of the other afternoon, appeared no less puzzled than the Chantrey sisters, Nerissa and Belinda.

"Well," demanded Belinda, with her infant shrillness, "what *is* an average? Tell us!"

Dodgson tilted his straw hat a little to keep the afternoon sun from his eyes as it moved clear of the trees.

"An average," he said solemnly," is a thing upon which hens lay their eggs."

"It isn't!" Belinda pressed her blonde mane to her mouth and snorted with merriment. She laughed far beyond the limit of her amusement, making a performance of it for the others.

"Ah, but it is!" said Dodgson confidentially. "Look in any book that tells you about keeping poultry. You'll find it printed there in all the best editions. 'A hen lays three eggs per day upon an average.' Therefore, an average is a thing upon which hens lay their eggs."

"I don't believe you!" cried Belinda.

Dodgson tilted his hat absurdly forward and put on an expression of extreme woe for her benefit.

"Then what a remarkably wicked little girl you are. I doubt if you could find a more wicked little girl in all history, not even if you went back to the days of Nero and Heliogabalus. Indeed, no one has ever suggested that Nero and Heliogabalus doubted that hens lay eggs upon an average."

He tilted his hat back again. Duckworth lay on the grass and looked up at the sky, his hands folded behind his head and a blade of coarse grass held in his teeth.

"It's an axiom," said Dodgson finally, as if delivering the ultimate retort to Belinda. Beyond the immaculate lawn and gravel paths, the Tudor chimneys and casements of Christ Church deanery lay golden in the yellowing sun. A light wind stirred the fruit trees of the garden and the fronds of the laburnum. From the open windows on the ground floor of the deanery, it was just possible to catch the tidal sound of voices as the Liddells' guests sat down to tea. Only Duckworth, Dodgson, and the three girls had escaped the formality of the occasion.

"What's an axiom?" Nerissa asked.

"As to that," said Dodgson facetiously, "there are no end of axioms. But the first axiom is that whatever is, is. And the second axiom is that whatever isn't, isn't. Axioms teach you to begin at the beginning."

Jane Ashmole spoke slowly, extemporising her proposition.

"Supposing you had to paint a dog green," she said.

"A dog?" Dodgson sat up suddenly and looked at her.

"Yes." She brushed her short fringe of brown hair self-consciously. "If I had to paint a dog green, I should begin at the end. With the tail. After all, it doesn't bite at the tail."

"It might do something worse to you!" giggled Belinda. Jane woke to the meaning and laughed out loud before considering whether it was proper to or not.

"Come," said Dodgson with mock severity. "Back to Croquet Castles!"

Jane ran away laughing, as if to escape the contest, and they all pursued her across the lawn. Acknowledging his precedence, the others allowed Dodgson to catch her. She put up no resistance but allowed him to lead her laughing back to the lawn.

They went across to the ten arches that had been arranged for the game. Croquet Castles was an invention of Dodgson's that he had perfected almost twenty years before. Each pair of white-painted hoops was a "castle" with a ball half way between as the "sentinel." Each player had a second ball, the "soldier," that was to be driven by the mallet to invade the other castles. A soldier who collided with a sentinel was deemed to be taken prisoner and the sentinel ball was moved into the "gate" so that the castle was fortified. The soldier who touched the flag or post in a castle was considered to have invaded it successfully. Though he had once written down the rules of the game, many of them were disregarded in the excitement of play.

Dodgson, his mouth pursed and his eyes narrowed with solemn concentration, straddled the first hoop and tapped his soldier forward. The rooks rose noisily above the meadow elms and a smoke-grey cloud darkened the river sky beyond. Duckworth counter-attacked at once. The girls joined in noisily and Belinda Chantrey cheated without compunction.

"I have you, Duckworth!" Dodgson called as two of the balls collided. "You are my prisoner now!"

Belinda stumbled and rolled laughing on the lawn in a flurry of blue cotton and petticoats.

"Wicked young person!" cried Duckworth in comic outrage. "I do believe you have driven my sentinel from his post!"

From the casement windows of the deanery the teatable conversation rose and fell. Croquet Castles was played with increasing seriousness and concentration until the shouts and banter died away, leaving only the hollow tap of the wooden mallets on the balls, the whisper of the balls themselves running on the short grass.

It was the youngest player, Belinda, who won by stealth.

"Again!" she insisted. "Another battle!"

But Jane replied, looking at Dodgson as she spoke.

"No," she said, "I think that's enough. It's only a game. A silly game for children!"

He looked at her, at the steady brown eyes and the challenge in her firm mouth and chin. Her words were merely those of the "awkward stage" that he so disliked, the months and years when the eagerness of childhood contended uneasily with a sense of feminine maturity. But there was more than that in her attitude now. As on that other afternoon, when she had stood so frankly and unashamed before the camera, challenging his timidity, they confronted each other upon the verge of a dark and unknown territory. The rooks above the elms, the croquet lawn, the other figures who stood around them, had no part in this moment. When their eyes met, even in so public a place, they were alone exclusively and, it seemed, eternally.

He did not argue with her, none of them attempted to. Nor was there any rebuke for her dismissal of the game. Jane's voice, at thirteen years old, came like that of the only adult among a group of children.

While the deanery tea was concluded and they waited for the other guests to come out into the garden, the two men and the three girls sat on the grass again in unaccustomed silence. Dodgson knew the means of ending it, rehearsing mechanically a child's puzzle he had thought of long ago.

"Once upon a time," he said, "there were three Russians. The first one was Rab and he became a lawyer. Then there was Ymra and he became a soldier. What became of Yvan?"

The others thought about this and asked him to repeat the names. Nerissa sat back on the grass, legs stretched out, supporting herself on her palms. She shook the fair hair clear of her face.

"That's easy," she said. "He became a sailor."

"Why?" asked Belinda, shrill with impatience.

"Because Rab is *bar* spelt backwards. Ymra is *army*. And Yvan is *navy*. So Yvan became a sailor."

They talked about this for a little longer. Then Jane said quietly,

"Madam, I'm Adam."

At first the others did not understand that she was continuing the game. Again it was Nerissa who caught the meaning before the rest of them.

"That's the same forwards or backwards. Anyone can see that."

"Bravo!" said Duckworth in soft admiration. "A good one that, by Jove! Very good!"

Just then the doors of the deanery opened. The Liddells' guests came out and began to form small conversational groups on the lawn. Jane went to join Sarah Ashmole, and the Chantrey sisters went across to where their parents stood.

"Poor Liddell," said Duckworth confidentially to Dodgson, nodding at the figure of the dean. "He has no small talk for occasions of this kind."

The two men separated, Duckworth carrying off the croquet mallets and Dodgson engaging Mrs. Chantrey in conversation apart from the other group. Maria Chantrey was a tall and rather awkward woman in her late thirties, her manner and movements appropriate to the wife of a scholar. The fine, light-coloured hair and fresh complexion made her seem younger than she was.

They walked together, pacing slowly towards the far hedge where the deanery garden ran down to the edge of the meadow. Dodgson came quickly and almost tactlessly to his purpose.

"I have an artist at Shrimpton's, the fine-art dealers, an excellent man at colouring photographs. If you were agreeable I should like him to colour my photographs of your girls. It would require a sitting, in order that he might get a good likeness of them, but he would not trouble you beyond that."

He was surprised that Maria Chantrey did not reply to him at first—did not, indeed, accept his offer as a matter of course.

"A single sitting would be sufficient," he added quickly. "It is only the colour of the hair and complexion that needs to be correct."

Maria Chantrey stopped and turned to him. The sincerity and goodness in her blue eyes were impregnable. He thought of the sentinels and castles in the croquet game. She laid a white-gloved hand on his arm.

"You have been so kind to our girls, Mr. Dodgson, good and generous. I do not find it easy to say what must be said now."

"That they must not have their photographs coloured?" He laughed, trying too late to make a joke of it all.

"No," she said. "That it would be better for the time being if there were no more thoughts of photography and picnics. Oh, believe me, the fault is not yours!"

"Then it can hardly be theirs!"

This seemed to increase her difficulty.

"Mr. Dodgson, there are ages at which a child may be spoilt too easily by over-indulgence, by being made to think too much of herself and her own importance. She may be too dangerously flattered by certain friendships—by association with fame."

"I cannot believe it is true of your girls," he said flatly.

"I fear it may be." There was no moving her, it seemed. "Not for the world would I allow them to lose your friendship. Yet, to be frank with you, I think it best that they should not be indulged for the time being, even in the matter of having the photographs coloured." She smiled as if at her own absurdity.

Dodgson turned over the straw boater he was carrying and looked down at it. In his mind he saw only the face of old Dr. Chantrey, the grandfather, looking expectantly at him during Godwin's outburst at the meeting of the Senior Common Room.

"I ask one thing of you, Mrs. Chantrey. Do not tell me that I must not see your daughters for this reason, if there is truly another."

"There is none," she said firmly. "I promise you."

"Then Thomas Godwin has no part in this?"

He expected her to look uncomprehending, but Maria Chantrey frowned.

"Thomas Godwin is a poisonous wretch," she said, colouring a little, "an infidel and a libertine! I hope you will not have so low an opinion of me, Mr. Dodgson, as to believe that any decision of mine could be influenced by such a man."

Again she turned and faced him with invincible sincerity.

As they walked back to the others he thought how their conversation had been like that of a mistress parting from her lover. At the moment of leaving him she tried to reassure him once more.

"It shall be just for the time being," she said.

"Ah," he said facetiously, "then I may still hope?"

For the first time, a doubt clouded her blue eyes and when she spoke he detected irritation in her voice.

"Of course you may, Mr. Dodgson."

And with that Maria Chantrey turned to her husband. The smoke-grey cloud that had hung above the meadow trees now came closer and lower. As the first isolated drops of heavy rain began to fall, the guests returned hurriedly to the shelter of the deanery.

By the time Dodgson walked back to his rooms, the rain had stopped, though the flagstones of the quadrangle were still wet and the stonework of the Tudor walls remained blotched by damp. He believed Maria Chantrey when she promised him that Godwin's malice had no part in her decision. She deceived him only by pretending that her daughters grew spoilt through their association with him. There were enough mothers in Oxford who might have spread scandal and rumour to her. That was the cause of her intervention. Thomas Godwin and his malice were superfluous.

As soon as he entered his sitting-room, Dodgson guessed what was amiss. There was a sofa cushion on the floor and the fire screen had been moved. The papers on his desk, though they were not obviously out of place, had been shifted. He tried the desk drawers and found that they were still locked. Godwin would scarcely have been such a fool—and yet his first thought was of Godwin.

He rang his bell for the porter. When the man arrived, Dodgson put the question bluntly.

"Who has been in this room this afternoon?"

"No one, sir," said the porter. "No gentlemen asked for you, nor ladies neither."

"Someone has been in here this afternoon."

"Perhaps your scout, sir?"

"My scout does not throw cushions on the floor, nor does he interfere with the papers on my desk. Someone has been in here without authority."

"Then I'm sure I don't know who, sir."

The porter had conveyed Dodgson's complaints to the steward before, about the price of milk, the quality of smoked ham, and the need to use china stoppers rather than corks for ginger-beer. He was less than sympathetic to this latest story of an imagined burglary.

"Very well," said Dodgson at length, "I require a note to be made of this occurrence in the porter's book. I shall come down to the lodge myself in half an hour and countersign it."

"That's your privilege, sir," said the porter stoically. It was the nearest he could bring himself to an expression of deference.

As soon as he was alone, Dodgson took out his keys and unlocked the desk. He had done enough now to make Godwin's position extremely dangerous—if Godwin had a hand in the matter. His first thought was for the drawer in which he kept his private photographic prints and glass-plate negatives.

With an unexpected sense of relief he saw that the two prints of Jane Ashmole lay where he had left them, on top of the others. Only when he lifted these and looked underneath did he discover that the two glass-plate negatives of the prints were gone.

8

CHARLES AUGUSTUS HOWELL had never in his life committed blackmail, not in the sense in which the world understands that term. He rather despised men like Dicky Tiptoe because they could not make the same boast. Proud in this self-knowledge, he shouldered his way patiently through the street-market crowds of St. Giles in his top boots and black cloak. The London sky, heavy with summer thunder all day, was going into a premature twilight, the colour of dark smoke.

To his victims, Charlie Howell came not as a judge but as a saviour. Not for him the soft threats of exposure to the law or the disgrace of society. He spoke gently, seeking only to prevent such catastrophes, and offered his services out of pure good nature. No court in the world could ever uphold a charge of extortion against him. It had been true in the case of a young poet, Algernon Swinburne, and in that of the reverend head-master of Harrow, Dr. Charles Vaughan. It would be doubly certain in the case of the man who masqueraded as "Lewis Carroll"—Story-Book Dodgson, as Howell preferred to call him.

Charles Howell had once been secretary to John Ruskin. He was thus well aware of the predilection shown by grown men for girl-children, the hopes and anxieties bred in them. So much was paid for so very little gratification. Yet love, when thus secretly harboured, was quite beyond price.

Algernon Swinburne had been his first success. Thinking himself secure in Howell's bawdy comradeship, the young poet had written letters to him. In these, Algy described himself by name as suffering the most obscene and ludicrous abuse in orgies of flogging perpetrated among the groves of Eton. Howell kept the letters, counting on the young man's future fame and knowing that in such an hour he might claim his reward.

Nothing would induce him to attempt the crudity of extortion. With tears in his eyes he had explained to his young friend the circumstances of his own poverty. He had pawned everything, even his own papers, believing in the confidence of the pawnbroker. How soon he was betrayed! At the first pretext the pawnbroker intended to put the letters up for public auction. They were already being read aloud to small but immensely appreciative groups of the poet's acquaintance. Howell sought nothing for himself, only to be the willing intermediary who might restore the letters to their author.

Admiral Swinburne and Lady Jane had come across even more handsomely than their son. Charlie Howell had worked long and patiently for this. His second triumph was, by contrast, a stroke of the purest fortune.

To his door had come a young woman by the name of Claire Vaughan. The second of these names—perhaps the first, too—had been assumed for the occasion. She was not a great beauty. Tall, thin, and pale, she had sharp features, slant green eyes, and red hair cropped as if a pudding basin had been put on her head and cut round.

Howell's first inclination on Claire's arrival in Southampton Row had been to kick her vigorously down the stairs. How very fortunate that he had postponed this pleasure until he read the papers she brought with her.

They were the work of the reverend gentleman, the headmaster of Harrow, Dr. Vaughan. Most were indiscreet notes written to those boys in the school who had been known as his "bitches." Discovery of these notes had led to a demand by the parents for Dr. Vaughan's resignation, even his prosecution. He was permitted to retire unmolested by the law. The archbishop of Canterbury and the prime minister, knowing of these things, had installed him comfortably as the vicar of Doncaster and master of the Temple.

So Howell had played the cards both ways. Dr. Vaughan was prepared to stand something handsome for the recovery of his papers by the honest Howell from the villains who held them. Those who had been the "bitches" were keener still. Several of the notes had been written fifteen years earlier to boys who were now men with a reputation to protect. Howell had discovered among them the commander of an infantry regiment, a coal-owner, and a champion racquets player. He was appointed without a quibble as the agent who would buy back the notes from the blackmailers of London, represented in this case solely by Dr. Vaughan's late companion, Claire.

Men who judged Charlie Howell a confidence trickster were sadly in error. Whatever he promised, he delivered. In the gaslight and the flame of the Saturday-night market the traders watched him pass. With his instinctive swagger, the dark waxed moustache, keen black eyes, and olive skin, he gave off an invincible self-confidence.

The bohemian world knew him as a man born forty years earlier in Portugal of a native mother and an English father. It knew that he had made a precarious income by diving for pearls. A rumour spread that he had lived as a sheikh in North Africa. It was then that he had managed a harem of rather faded beauties, but he did so for other men's pleasures and to his own profit. Yet he was no coward. Twenty years before, he had carried one of Orsini's bombs that exploded upon the arrival of Napoleon III at the Paris Opéra. True, the Emperor had escaped while more than a hundred men and women were killed or wounded by the lethal iron fragments and the slivers of glass. That was not Charlie Howell's fault. He sought only to aim a blow against tyranny.

In the safety of England, his loyalty and discretion to his employer, John Ruskin, had been without flaw. A mere blackmailer would at once have seized upon the sexual tragedies of the Ruskin marriage and the wistful child amours that followed.

A few years more, and he had been the truest friend to Dante Gabriel Rossetti that an artist could have hoped for. As agent to the Pre-Raphaelite Brotherhood, he had sold their paintings on commission and had kept the accounts of this punctiliously. He had been the support of his friend when Elizabeth Rossetti, with her wan beauty and lustrous russet hair, was laid in the grave at Highgate after an overdose of laudanum. Seven years later he had managed the ritual of exhumation.

At night behind the canvas screens, the gravediggers' torches fluttered and flared like banners of fire. Like the illumination in some dark Rembrandt masterpiece, the lurid glow was reflected dully from the black capes and hats of the onlookers, more brightly from the marble monuments of broken column, cross, and family tomb. When the coffin was opened, the young woman's face had scarcely suffered the first ravages of decomposition. It was still recognisable in its pale delicate beauty among the loveliness of the chestnut hair.

So Howell had taken Dante Rossetti's manuscript book of poems from the dead fingers, where the young husband had placed them in impetuous grief. They were returned to their author and promptly published to the world.

He had been a good friend, Howell thought, even to his victims. With the passage of time he saw his work as that of an agent of righteousness, punishing the wrongdoer and turning him back to the path of virtue.

Did not Dr. Vaughan merit punishment? There could be no doubt at all of that. Yet the law had not touched him. Indeed, the greatest secular and ecclesiastical powers in the land had saved him from retribution. It was left to Charles Howell to put such terror into the man that he would never err again. If that brought a handsome payment to Howell himself, it was no more than his due.

There was the matter of young Algernon Swinburne. Certainly, Howell thought, little Algy had been taught a lesson in discretion. Never again would he favour his correspondents with accounts of himself being beaten and enjoyed by whiskered old libertines. Admiral Swinburne had paid well; Howell was the first to concede it. Yet, as the traders in the street market were apt to point out, such purchases were cheap at the price.

There remained the disagreeable possibility that one day some man upon whom Howell sought to exercise moral improvement might prove ungrateful. He might even be so thoughtless as to turn for protection to the police. Howell could easily envisage the ruinous proceedings that would follow.

Yet in this, too, he exercised his innate skill. Dr. Vaughan was not well placed to appeal to the law, for he must drag down a prime minister and an archbishop as well as Howell. Young Algernon Swinburne had little better hope. Even this was not sufficient for Howell. He had devised a defence so formidable that an attempt to prosecute him would be the lighting of a fuse. The charge it would detonate had been placed so that it might bring down the entire fabric of English society.

Howell possessed certain photographs and documents. He could not use them as a blackmailer might, for one does not blackmail the royal family or a prime minister. Yet if the world ever brought him to judgment, it must bring others, too.

Among the papers were two of the notes written to another cadet on the *Britannia* by Prince Albert Victor, elder son of the Prince of Wales and third in line of succession. National honour might prefer to see these billets-doux consigned to the flames. Howell had preserved them from the flames meticulously.

At some considerable expense he had also bought the new German toy, the Stirn camera. It was made of steel, round as a tea plate but rather thicker. When worn under the waistcoat, its lens protruded through a buttonhole with the look of a button itself. Howell was one of the first to know of Mr. Gladstone's philanthropic urge to accost young prostitutes in the West End and take them home for tea and an improving talk. Howell and the Stirn camera had followed his progress.

Would they convey extreme innocence or darkest guilt, these cameos of the elderly statesman and his protégées? At the least, Howell thought, they showed the old man smiling and cooing at young women whose profession could scarcely be in doubt. The publication of such gems to the world must surely spell the ruin and disgrace of the greatest man in England.

Not that Howell wished ruin and disgrace upon a statesman whose liberal idealism he admired. The pilfered documents and the sneaked photographs were weapons too terrible to use, in his judgment, except when there was no alternative.

Story-Book Dodgson! That, of course, had been a stroke of pure fortune. Sarah Ashmole, the mother of Jane, was one of the very few women upon whom Howell had ever exercised his moral art. It was an axiom of blackmail that women paid more willingly for their indiscretions than men, as if acknowledging their guilt more readily and wishing to be punished. It had been so easy that he scarcely had the heart to continue with the poor creature.

Howell ceased to be a moral persuader and became instead a friend on the day he found Dodgson's first letter to Sarah Ashmole about Jane. "The permission to go as far as bathing-drawers is, in Jane's case, wholly delightful and will make for a truly charming portrait. It may be questionable whether a full front view could be done without them but to a back view there can be, surely, no objection. . . ."

Howell could scarcely believe his eyes, or his good fortune, when he read these words on the first of several occasions. Mr. Dodgson, clergyman and scholar of Christ Church. "The permission to proceed thus far must, I imagine, extend to Belinda. I hope it may also include Nerissa. I, at any rate, should have no objection, and the three girls may chaperone one another. . . ."

Howell had been almost overawed by the monumental presumption of the little cleric. Then he had been still more overawed by remembering Mr. Dodgson's modest style of life and the great deal of money which must have accrued to the author of *Alice's Adventures in Wonderland.*

9

CHARLES HOWELL AND DICKY TIPTOE strode across London Bridge side by side, shoulders working energetically as if they were racing one another.

"A man may have his pleasure if he chooses, Dicky," said Howell breathlessly, "but there's no reason he shouldn't pay for it!"

The bridge was crowded with working men and women going in the opposite direction, carrying outdoor work to be done at their shabby houses south of the river. There were men with bundles of umbrella frames to be covered and girls with cages of hats to which silk and binding had yet to be fastened. Among them walked grimy and barelegged coster girls going to fill their baskets, and the yellow-skinned sack-makers on their way to fetch work from the Bermondsey warehouses.

By the time Howell and Tiptoe reached the Strand, the afternoon was blazing in the ferocity of the June sun, reflected from plate-glass windows and the polished paint of carriage traffic. Howell resumed the conversation that had been broken off for want of breath a mile back.

"So it follows that if Story-Book Dodgson must have his pleasures, he mustn't expect them for nothing. Why, even an up-righter at an evangelical meat tea can't quite expect that, Dicky!"

They turned north from the Strand into the narrow streets of old soot-blackened houses that had been fashionable in the reign of George III. Most of them had been gutted to make shops on the ground floor, emporia of second-hand clothes and trinkets, with warehouses on the upper levels. The two men turned into the dingiest of all, the littered Holywell Street.

Threadbare coats and dresses drooped from long rails outside the boarded windows of the second-hand shops. Tradesmen, their clothes meaner than their own stock, leant against the doorposts in the hot afternoon sun and sucked at their white clay pipes, watching the groups of ragged children who played in the gutter. A light breeze, drawn fitfully between the tall grimy buildings, caused the garments of the dead to sway unevenly upon the rails like the bodies of criminals upon a country gallows.

It was not the "ragged trade" that had brought Howell and Tiptoe to Holywell Street. For half a century its rotting and verminous premises had been famous for something far more remarkable. Here, and in the little courts adjoining it, the flash literature of copulation and erotic cruelty had its home.

Only the "dead lead" appeared in the little windows themselves, where gaslights burnt low whatever the time or the weather. Faded by the sun, yellow photographic prints of dancing-girls lay among the dark cobwebs and dead flies behind the glass. There were books with French titles and others in English that promised much and delivered little. For all its enticement, *The Dreadful Disclosures of Maria Monk,* which sold by the hundreds to country gulls, was no more than an earnest anti-Catholic sermon issued by the Presbyterian Tract Society.

Novels such as Dicky Tiptoe's masterpiece, *Vivien: A Tale of the Hindu Marriage Bed,* were more circumspectly offered and sold in a back room, or by post to admirers of his work. Their publishers were the men who owned the little shops. From time to time, young Paul Ferdinando or old William Dugdale would be visited without warning by the police, often aided by the stalwart porters of the National Vigilance Association. Fines and a few months of imprisonment would follow before business could be resumed.

Howell pushed open the door of the first little shop, and the bell on its curved ribbon of steel gave out a cracked and brief warning. Young Ferdinando had filled the shelves immediately inside with innocent bottles of ink, rubber stamps, and packets of stationery whose condition suggested that they had remained unsold for a long time.

Ferdinando was fairer skinned than his name suggested. Like Howell he had been born in Portugal, though of a native father and an English mother. He was occupied at that moment in wrapping a package for a silk-hatted gentleman, tying the string tightly round flimsy yellow paper.

"Should you take to the photographic hobby yourself, sir," he was saying, "I can supply you with girls for ballet, or *poses plastiques,* or artists' models. I am, in a small way, a theatrical agent for the London Casino. Should you honour me with an order, I can fulfil it within the hour."

The man in the silk hat made no reply. Dicky Tiptoe smiled at Howell as the words "theatrical agent" reached him. As soon as the customer had gone, Ferdinando came forward, neatly and soberly dressed so that, with his dark hair and pale skin, one might have taken him for a conscientious curate, or perhaps an ambitious young clerk. He locked the shop door.

"Mr. Howell?"

"Theatrical agent?" said Howell, laughing at him. "Draw it mild, old fellow!"

Ferdinando shrugged.

"A figure of speech. Now, permit me a view of the two portraits, if you have them with you."

Howell went across to the counter and laid upon it a pair of prints made from the glass-plate negatives of Jane Ashmole. Ferdinando looked at the first, the rear view of the girl gazing into the dressing-mirror. He put his hand thoughtfully over his mouth, pinched his nose lightly and sniffed.

"If it was a painting, Mr. Howell, you might hang it in the Royal Academy. You might hang it there and every bishop in the land would call it beautiful."

"Damn the bishops, Ferdy!" said Tiptoe with a laugh. "Will the pictures do?"

Ferdinando looked at the second photograph in which Jane faced the camera with such questioning frankness in her eyes.

"Now that . . ." He tapped the counter lightly and repeatedly as if struggling for words. "You might ask a high price for that!"

"Have no fear," said Howell reassuringly. "I intend to ask a very high price. And I intend to get it."

"Not from me?" asked the little bookseller.

"When did I ask you for anything you could not afford, Ferdy? No, old fellow. You shall have it cheap. Dirt cheap!"

They all laughed at the innuendo, and with a certain relief.

Ferdinando went across to the door and pulled down the green canvas blind so that they would not be observed. He turned up the gas and unlocked a drawer behind the counter. From it he took the proof pages of a cheaply printed volume. Over his shoulder Dicky Tiptoe saw *The Pearl: A Journal of Facetiae and Voluptuous Reading*. Ferdinando flicked through the pages of its assorted stories. "Lady Pokingham," "The Sultan's Reverie," "Miss Coote's Confession." There were engraved illustrations in the style of brightly coloured Regency cartoons adapted to the demands of Ferdinando's customers. The young women had massive orange-coloured thighs; their lovers staggered under the weight of erections so huge as to seem like the stage property of a circus clown.

"What exactly did you have in mind?" asked Ferdinando innocently.

He knew nothing of the main plan; Howell had seen to that. Story-Book Dodgson and the business at Oxford were not for Ferdinando anyway. If he knew the plan, he would certainly demand more than he had already been promised—or, rather, half promised.

"The two photographs to be included as illustrations," said Howell simply. "A caption at the top of each, saying 'By an Oxonian.' "

Ferdinando shook his head.

"And you shall have the use of them for nothing, Ferdy!" said Tiptoe encouragingly.

Ferdinando continued to shake his head.

"It can't be done, Dicky. See here. I can have engravings

printed like letterpress. Photographs? I'd have to have each set done separately. And then how are they to be bound in? It can't be done."

"You won't do it?" asked Howell quietly.

Ferdinando tried to escape the trap.

"The man you're doing this for: does he read this sort of thing? Would he know one book from another?"

It was Tiptoe who snorted with laughter at the absurdity of it, his port-wine cheeks glowing in sheer amusement.

"Very well," said Ferdinando. "You need one copy, two perhaps, even three. I could have a few bound with the photographs inserted. Mind you, I don't say it won't be expensive if it's to be done by a good man. You must have one who can glue those pictures in so neatly that they look as if they'd been bound properly."

"That depends," said Howell. "I might do the job for myself."

"But think how much prettier it would look if I did it, Mr. Howell!"

To demonstrate his meaning, Ferdinando laid two strips of paper across the tops of the photographs. Taking his pen, he printed "By an Oxonian" to Howell's specification. Then the bookseller rummaged in a drawer and found the dismembered proofs of other volumes which provided him with captions and titles. He took two of these and placed them across the foot of each photograph.

"Now, Mr. Howell! I don't think you could ask for anything prettier than that, could you?"

The other two men looked, and Tiptoe chuckled. Howell himself smiled silently at the neatness of it all. Though the two printed captions had been cut from other illustrations, they suited the photographs of Jane Ashmole with ludicrous aptness. Under the picture of her as she faced the camera were the words, "Do you like me this way?" Under the other one there now appeared, "Or do you prefer this sort of thing, eh?"

"Name a price," said Howell quickly. "Those will do very nicely indeed."

He concealed the exultation he felt. It was always possible that Dodgson would hold out, defiant and even threatening on his own behalf. Would he refuse to save the girl as well? Howell thought not. Yet the best scheme was to twist the victim's arm a little at a time. If the bone should break, the game would be over.

"A price?" said Ferdinando thoughtfully. "I'd prefer a share, Mr. Howell. Now, don't deceive me, sir, for you couldn't if you tried. You stand to make money by this, a good deal of money. It's only just that a man who helps you should see a share of it. If it's my guess, you might even have Professor Ruskin in mind."

"Why?"

"Why, sir? Because you did ask me a second favour, you recall. A girl that can look young as the nymph in your photographs, and yet be wise in the ways of men. I have one for you, still a child at nineteen. We know the Professor's tastes, you and I."

"This has nothing to do with him," said Howell sharply. "Where is she?"

"Eating her tea in the next room." Ferdinando smiled at him confidentially. "If you want to get across a girl, never flurry her until she's got a belly full of food. Then let the grub work on her. If she's thirty, give her half an hour's digestion, if she's thirty-five let her go an hour. Talk a little bawdy to her at the same time. The one in there's young enough to be ready the minute she swallows her last mouthful."

Ferdinando laid a hand on the china knob of the door leading to the back room.

"Prudence," he said.

Howell failed to understand him.

"Why?"

"Prudence," Ferdinando repeated. "Known commonly as Prue. It's the little fool's name."

They went into the back parlour with its shabby carpet, black leaded grate, and wooden table. There was a mirror above the fireplace and a girl admiring herself in it.

Howell looked at her doubtfully. He could see why Ferdinando had chosen Prue for him, but the bookseller was less than a perfectionist in such matters. She was not too tall and was decidedly thin. At Ferdinando's insistence, she appeared now in the skin-tight, pale-blue fleshings of a ballet girl. Her legs were so slim that even her thighs appeared scarcely thicker than a man's upper arm. Her belly was flat as a child's with a backward jut of her hips, her buttocks carried high and taut. Even the curve of her breasts was as slight as that of a girl at thirteen.

"Admirable from the neck down," said Howell sceptically, "but that's not the most important thing."

"Turn round," said Ferdinando sharply to the girl. "Show your face."

When she did so, Howell's doubts were unresolved. Sooner or later, Story-Book Dodgson must be deceived by an experienced young woman who could appear as a child. Prue was slender enough in figure, petite enough in stature. Her face was another matter.

It was a peevish, mean little face with a brooding suspicion in the dark hazel eyes whose lashes had been carefully darkened. Howell's mouth tightened with disapproval as he saw the rouge on her cheeks. The nose was a little too large, the mouth a little too weak, and the jaw slack.

"Wipe your face clean," he said to the girl. She took the handkerchief that Dicky Tiptoe offered. Howell continued to look at her critically. The golden fairness of her hair had been plaited and put on top of her head in a high coiled coiffure.

"Undo your hair," he said. "Let it lie loose on your shoulders."

Prue emitted a wordless whine of protest, like the sound of an animal under coercion. But she unpinned the hair, loosened it from its plait, and then shook it free so that it swept down from her high crown to the beginning of the shoulder-blades.

"Is that the best you can do?" asked Howell, addressing the question to Ferdinando but continuing to look at the girl.

"It wasn't easy, Mr. Howell," said the little bookseller coaxingly. "A girl that must look young as thirteen and yet be old enough to know which end of a rope the knots are tied. It wasn't at all easy."

"When the time comes," said Howell, "she must know how to talk and conduct herself."

"With the hair down like that," said Ferdinando hopefully, "you'd take her for a child. Wouldn't you?"

For his answer, Howell walked across the room and raised the girl's chin gently by his finger. He smiled at her.

"How long have you been game, Prue?"

"I'm not game!" she protested, trying to turn her chin from its perch on his finger. He held her more firmly.

"What do you call game, then?"

"Why," she said, "the sort of girls that come out every night regular and get their livings by it."

"Don't you?"

"Course not!" she squealed indignantly. "Mother keeps me!"

"Not your father?"

"He's dead six months back."

Howell looked at her uncertainly. It was exactly the sort of fiction that a girl aiming at sympathy would put forward. Yet he saw that from the middle of her calves downward Prue's slender legs were cased tightly in smart black boots that she wore, incongruously, with the fleshings.

"So you wear mourning for your father?"

"Yes," she said resentfully, the mouth drawn awry in the mean little face, the hazel eyes large and full as she watched him. "Shabby, isn't it?"

He said nothing and she followed the movement of his eyes down her legs. As if to please him, she cocked one leg back, bending it at the knee.

"Nice boots, though, ain't they?" she said brightly. "A lady gived them me when father died. They're my best."

In his mind Howell was trying to imagine the effect that a young prostitute like Prue might have on Dodgson's heart. She could be got up to look like a thirteen-year-old but there was nothing to be done about her manner. Could she win her way to the man as an uneducated waif? So far as he knew, Dodgson's only interests had been in girls of good family and education.

The answer was so obvious that he could not imagine why it had not occurred to him in the first place. Illness. The dying child. Prue the consumptive. It would be quite beyond the Story-Book Man's powers to resist such an appeal. There might be a use for Ferdinando's protégée after all.

"I'm dreadful hungry again," said the girl.

Howell looked and saw that the meal provided by the bookseller for her had been no more than a slice of buttered bread and a cup of tea.

"What do you like to eat?" Howell asked.

"Pies," she said slyly, "sausage rolls. Oh, my eye, couldn't I just eat them!"

Howell looked at Dicky Tiptoe, who took the meaning at once. Tiptoe slipped out of the room, and the cracked bell on its steel ribbon clattered as he went into the street. In the dusty back room of the little shop the kettle sang on the hob once more.

"Is that what made you game, Prue?" Howell asked her.

"I'm *not* game!" she said sullenly, though her lips very nearly broke into a smile at the denial.

"Well, then," he said, "that's why you let men have you? For sausage rolls?"

She sniggered at the absurdity of the truth when it was put to her in this way.

"Yes," she said, "meat pies and pastries, too."

He went back into the shop with Ferdinando, drew the two photographs of Jane Ashmole from the drawer, and looked again at the captions as they lay there. The frank gaze held him as she faced the camera naked, the shadow of her hands not quite concealing the triangle of her loins. "Do you like me this way?" Then the print, innocent enough itself, of the girl seen naked from the back, glancing aside into her dressing-mirror. How the caption transformed it, he thought. "Or do you prefer this sort of thing, eh?"

What a fool he was ever to let Ferdinando choose the girl for him! A man must be green as a leek and soft as new cheese if an undernourished street girl of her sort could impose upon him as a child. No, thought Howell, it was the pair of photographs that would stop Dodgson like a blow to the heart. Try him with the prints alone at first. After that, if necessary, with the captions.

The more mouths there are, he thought, the more secrets may be told. That was undoubtedly true. By using the prints alone, there would be just Major Tiptoe and himself. Ferdinando would know only that he had bound three copies of his trashy magazine to include the photographs.

He was thinking of this when Tiptoe came back, bringing with him into the shop's smell of ink and paper an aroma of fresh hot pastry. Howell drew his attention to the two photographs again.

"By an Oxonian." He pointed at the upper caption of each. "What would you say to going a little further?"

Tiptoe's bluff, whiskered face looked at him in open-mouthed incomprehension.

"How's that?" he asked, his voice full of good humour and hope.

"I think," said Howell, marking the captions with a pencil, "that we'll do a proper job. Where's the harm? We'll call the pictures 'Jane, by an Oxonian.'"

Tiptoe sniggered, Howell gave a thin sardonic smile, and Ferdinando tried to look pleased on behalf of them both. They adjourned to the rear of the shop in general good humour, Tiptoe chucking Prudence under the chin and adding a pat or two of ownership.

On the far side of the little street, a row of shabby cast-off coats stirred on their rail as if under the examination of a hidden customer. A shadow fell in the bright afternoon, and Alfred Swain stood tall and thoughtful between the parted garments.

He had no business to be there. Howell was not a subject of police surveillance and, in any case, Swain was in the middle of a three-day home leave from his detail. For some of his colleagues it was a time to be the patron of drink and whores. Others paraded their wives and families with a respectable sense of pride. Swain was a mystery to them all. They looked beyond the figure of the policeman and found nothing. He seemed to come from nowhere and to go nowhere. It was identical to his technique in surveillance.

To be fair, however, Swain had begun his leave by visiting a collection of "heads" at the British Museum. He had gone to the Science Museum in South Kensington and stood admiring the new walls of the Natural History Museum, rising to completion. Then he became bored and thought of Charlie Howell. It had not been difficult to follow his trail. Howell was a scoundrel with no criminal record, the most dangerous type in Swain's view. That alone justified the sacrifice of home leave.

The mystery which he presented to his colleagues was easily solved. Beyond Inspector Swain, the policeman, there stood the figure of Alfred Swain, the policeman. Behind the mild and intellectual cast of his features, he pursued his profession with the quiet single-mindedness of an ascetic. Only the acquisition of a modest amount of formal learning was permitted to distract him. His own modesty and quietness concealed a consuming ambition. In his imagination, he saw himself at the level of supreme command, his leisure thoughts filled by a volume of verse, geology, or biblical criticism. In the honesty of solitude, Alfred Swain knew that he wanted nothing less than the place of the man who was commissioner of the Metropolitan Police. Charlie Howell, who would make a mistake sooner or later, might help him to get it.

10

In the late afternoon, the carters and showmen from Abingdon Fair blocked the length of St. Aldate's with their wagons and fancy floats. Dodgson stood in the Christ Church arch under Tom Tower and watched them turning into the street opposite, winding through the narrow ways of St. Ebbes to the fields beyond the Oxford slums.

Decked out in cheap and ragged tinsel, a procession of Tartar and Circassian horsemen in armour moved into the little streets beyond Pembroke, advertising their arrival on the way to the temporary show-ground by the river. As if to celebrate the departure of the academic season and the coming of Oxford's long summer idleness, a small brass band in the procession blasted to pieces the tranquillity of the July afternoon. The porters came out of Christ Church lodge and stood near Dodgson, watching tight-lipped.

Women riders, brown-skinned and in dirty clothes, followed the horsemen. A cart drawn by piebald horses carried a sturdy adolescent girl with a mass of fair hair over her shoulders. She held up a wand, wore a tinsel coronet, and was revealed in fleshings and the brief scrap of a skirt.

The Fairy Queen and her court swayed and jolted down the streets of the Oxford slums. A dwarf with a huge and devilish beast head covering his own brought up the rear of the group, sending the bystanders outside the little houses into delicious squeals of terror by his roaring and lunging.

Dodgson followed at a distance, entranced by the spectacle, for all its shabbiness. Even in so mean a form, the magic of make-believe was irresistible to him. Indeed, by its artless innocence it was more alluring than the London theatres which he attended at every opportunity.

It was a measure of his absorption in this world of wonder that he did not hear the sounds behind him. Yet they were only children's footsteps, after all, hurrying along in the wake of the procession. But as the street grew emptier and the circus procession passed on its way, he began to notice the pattern of the steps. They were not following him in the normal manner. They seemed to come quickly up behind him, and then scuttle away again. Yet he felt nothing and knew that no one had touched him.

"Tell us your story, Story-Book Man!"

Had the words been new to him, he would scarcely have noticed them in the distant shouts and the echoes of the street. Yet they came clearly to his consciousness in the shrill, vituperative voice of a girl who might have been Jane Ashmole's age.

Dodgson turned round slowly. In the hot dusty sunlight the street was empty. Even the doors of the narrow houses on the unlevel paving were closed. The women who had come out with children in their arms or at their apron-strings to watch the procession were now back at their stoves or wash-boilers again.

He stood still and listened. There were feet running somewhere nearby, though he could not see them. It was like hearing sounds from a parallel passage in a maze, which he could feel so close to him and yet could not find. The abuse might have come from any of the houses, any of the windows, looking on to the alley where he stood.

The shout came again, the very words from one voice and then another, in the same high-pitched vindictive tone. After the first sense of astonishment, Dodgson felt no more than irritation at the children's taunting. He walked onwards purposefully in the direction of the procession, down Tanners Lane and into the opening of Paradise Square, a small enclave of decaying houses, one of which had been turned into a tavern.

"Tell us your story, Story-Book Man!"

There was no concealment now. When he turned round, the girl was standing, hands on hips, fifty feet away at the top of the square, where it began to run downhill towards the river. He had never seen her before. She was a child of the slums, about thirteen years old with a short crop of brown hair, a full, high-boned face, and dark little eyes. Stocky and confident as a grown woman, she shouted the words after him. Dodgson turned away, ignoring her, but another child's voice shouted to the girl.

"There he goes, Sal!"

Dodgson's heart began to beat a little faster as he heard them moving after him. Yet this could not be the work of children. Who, then? He swung round once more and saw twelve or fifteen of them, mostly street boys but with several girls among them. They stood across the square with arms linked as if to prevent his escape. There was no danger, he thought, no physical danger from them. And yet he began to be afraid.

Now when he turned, they drew back. The line broke and the slum children scattered down the alleys at either side of the little square with whoops of mock terror. Slowly, as if to show any bystanders that he was unmoved by the taunting, Dodgson began to walk back the way he had come. He passed along Tanners Lane and came out into the hot street of shabby terraced cottages. Beyond the long cobbled extent of it he could see the shops of St. Aldate's, old houses whose upper floors overhung the pavement in the Elizabethan style. Tom Tower and St. Ebbes Church were just in view above the roof-tops.

"Tell us your story, Story-Book Man!"

They were behind him again. The girl with her hands still on her fat little hips remained, the leader of the others. One or two of the women from the houses were leaning in their open door-ways. The smiles on their faces suggested amusement at the discomfiture of a prig in dress clothing rather than a shared understanding of the incorrigible ways of children.

The fear returned, but not of physical assault by the children; that would have been absurd in the sunlit afternoon and against a man of his energy or build. His greater apprehension was that they would follow him to the gates of Christ Church with their shouts. He remembered the voices of nightmares long past. "Burn in hell, Mr. Dodgson, who lies with children!"

He turned, and they scattered once more. To the women in the doorways the shouts meant little. It was merely the casual ragging of a slum visitor by a gang of idling urchins. With a quicker step, he reached St. Aldate's, crossed among the traffic of cabs and wagons, and passed safely through the archway into the quiet of Tom Quad.

What disturbed him most of all, in the solitude of his rooms, was not the children themselves or even the words that the girl had shouted after him. It was the thought that the entire incident, in the lost world of the Oxford slums, had taken place no more than two or three minutes' walk from the chair in which he now sat. For the first time he felt like a man besieged.

The street children ran back to the sloping cobbled opening of Paradise Square. To one side of it was a narrow way that led past the castle mound towards the railway station. A cab had been drawn up in the opening for the past half hour. The children approached it, the girl still at their head. Through the lowered window, a man's hand appeared. In a sharp, awkward gesture he threw a handful of coins that spun and rang upon the stones. With one accord the children dived upon them, shouldering and elbowing each other in their zeal. As they did so, the iron-rimmed wheels of the cab began to turn, the hooves of the horse struck sparks from the dry cobbling, and the hansom disappeared towards the city towers.

II

"WHAT SHALL YOU DO all summer long with your Sussex aunt?" asked Dodgson facetiously.

Jane flicked her fringe impatiently, a childish habit not yet broken.

"I shall be with you," she said simply. "I shall as good as be with you, when Eastbourne is no more than twenty miles away."

Lemonade, biscuits, and ginger-beer—the dark bottles this time adorned with china stoppers—stood in the shadow of the Tudor parapet. Duckworth and the others had gone, leaving Jane alone once more with her admirer. Dodgson sat in a mahogany and cane steamer chair, the straw hat tilted a little over his eyes against strong afternoon light. Jane was leaning her elbows on the parapet, looking down at the streets and quadrangles of the old grey city, the houses clustering round the colleges as they had done since the Middle Ages, spilling down the slope towards the castle and the river.

"You shall send me a line," said Dodgson firmly. "You shall write and tell me of your holiday with your aunt."

"And you shall write to me," she said.

Dodgson laughed.

"There was a young lady I once wrote to, and not a syllable

did I get in reply. I must have written to her several times during one vacation when I was away from Oxford. I wonder if you know her. Her first name began with a 'J' and her second with an 'A.'

"They never *told* me of your letters!" Jane turned and sat on the leads beside his chair.

"And I thought you so cruel," he said quietly, stroking her dark hair. "I thought I had given my affections to a cat that only purred and rubbed itself against me as long as it thought there was cream in the cupboard!"

"But this time I shall see you," she said, moving her head against his hand. "Being so close, I shall see you."

"No, my darling," he said. "No, you must not."

"Who shall stop me?"

"Mrs. Grundy," he whispered, giving his hat brim a severe tilt.

"Who is Mrs. Grundy?"

"A very strict lady, my dear. A lady who sets it down as a matter of absolute law that a young person must not visit an old person without the permission of that young person's mama."

"But Mama lets me see you!"

"Oxford is another country, Jane. Once you are under your aunt's roof, matters will be different."

She scrambled to her feet and faced him, hands on the hips of her pink dress.

"When Mama said I might come and see you, she meant anywhere, at any time! She meant it for ever and ever, here and in Sussex, in term and vacation."

Dodgson sat up and poured the tawny ginger-beer into a glass. He let out a long sigh.

"I doubt it, my dearest. I doubt it very much indeed. I'm quite sure that your Aunt Willis would doubt it too."

Jane thought about this and appeared to sense the danger of arguing the matter further. As surely as Dodgson himself she wanted to avoid the point at which an absolute prohibition must be issued.

"Who else will you see at Eastbourne, if not me?" she asked.

Dodgson pulled a face of comic suggestiveness.

"All sorts of people, Jane. It is my second home, you know. When you are older and when I am so ancient that the world cares nothing about us, you shall see for yourself. I have had young lady-friends to visit me there once or twice, when their mamas have consented to it. But they have been awfully old, often nineteen or twenty, and sometimes more than that. Quite beyond the age at which a gentleman may take a kiss for granted without so much as a by-your-leave."

Lying back in his chair with his eyes closed against the afternoon sun, he thought that he was perhaps making too much of his scruples. Sarah Ashmole's permission for Jane to visit him had surely been a general indulgence to come to his rooms in Oxford when he chose, not merely on one occasion. Was it not logical to assume that the consent extended to the long summer weeks of the vacation in Sussex? In a quiet vision of contentment he saw himself arriving at the door of the imagined house near Lewes where Jane would be, escorting her by cab and train to the pebble beaches, the chalk cliffs, the pier, the bandstand, the glitter of sun on tide that made up his own summer idyll.

In a vision, he saw the long, firm sand where the ebbing tide had left its ripple patterns, the bright glimmer of the water's edge, and the vast extent of the sea to France. So far from the walks of the Grand Parade, the little girls played naked there. Such charming little nudities, as he called them. How to approach them? A lady might do it, a gentleman hardly could. Even to him, it would be a matter of embarrassment to *begin* an acquaintance with a naked girl! Almost forgetting Jane, he began to recite Sir Noel Paton's "Idyll" from memory.

> "For there, upon the glimmering marge,
>   Between the sea and sea-worn rocks,
>   Stood, mother-naked in the sun,
>   A little girl with golden locks."

Then he opened his eyes and smiled at Jane standing before him, her features dark from having the sun at ner back. She had tilted her chin upwards a little in a firm suggestion of defiance. Her teeth were resting on her lower lip in a manner that seemed to tease or taunt him. The expression in her dark-brown eyes was something he could not see with the light against him.

Without another word, Jane undid the dress that had proved so convenient for use in their photography. The skirts and petticoats fell together as she stepped clear and stood in naked silhouette before him.

"No," said Dodgson quietly, "that was not a part of our bargain this afternoon."

Ignoring this, Jane knelt beside his chair again and leant her head upon his knee.

"It was a bargain left over from the other afternoon," she said firmly. "It is as we were then."

"That was different, my dear." He stroked her head patiently, as if to inculcate understanding. "That was before the camera's eye!"

"And why is it respectable before the camera's eye but not before the eye of love?" she demanded softly.

There was no answer to her, so far as he knew. His eyes looked wistfully, mournfully down at the taut pallor of her body where the shapes of womanhood were apparent through the child's form, like a sculpture in its unfinished state.

"Will there be dresses in heaven?" When she put the question there was a hint of malice as well as innocent curiosity. "Will there be dresses or petticoats, frock-coats and sponge-bag trousers, silk hats and parasols? When we are together for eternity, will there be such things?"

The threatened impiety would have brought his rebuke upon her under other circumstances. Now that she had challenged him as a matter of logic, he was bound to answer her question.

"No, Jane. Nothing of that sort, I promise you!"

"Then I shall be with you now as I shall one day be with you there," she answered firmly. She began to recite certain lines, those which he remembered from the afternoon among the haycocks at Godstow with Duckworth and the Chantrey sisters. Rossetti, he thought.

"When round his head the aureole clings,
And he is clothed in white,
I'll take his hand and go with him
To the deep wells of light;
We will step down as to a stream
And bathe there in God's sight."

It was only as she finished that Dodgson remembered something else. On that first occasion Jane had read "The Blessed Damozel" from the slim olive-green book. Now she had committed the lines to memory as if they were the promise of the future that had been offered to her.

"Perhaps you shall come to the seaside," he said suddenly, "if your Aunt Willis and your mama permit it. You and I might walk upon the sand together. Could you not make friends so easily with the girl-fairies that sit among the rocks? Shall we not do photographs of one or a group? A nice little nudity that may hang in the Royal Academy next summer?"

"If you choose." Her tone suggested that she did not much relish the idea. Yet Jane had taken his hand as she recited the lines of Rossetti, and she continued to hold it now, stroking her thumb over its contours. The love of two hands, he thought, was a complete courtship and consummation in its way, a caress of infinite subtlety.

Stroking back her hair, he kissed her on the forehead and then on the cheek.

"What shall I call you?" he murmured. "Not Jane, nor dearest, nor darling. None of those names conveys what you are. So wilful at one moment and so unpredictable in everything you do. Why, I should not be surprised to come back here in October and be told that you had gone to live in Timbuctoo without your clothes, for none of the best people wear them there. Or else that you had quite thrown me over and were now the wife of the next vice-chancellor."

"What will you call me, then?" She pressed his hand to her face and kissed it.

Dodgson sat in silence, as if pretending to consider the problem for a moment.

"You shall be my Unknown Quantity," he said at length, "Jane my Unknown Quantity. She who is a woman when you expect her to be a child and a child when you think she will be a woman. She thinks Croquet Castles a silly game and acts like a baby over it, and then talks such wisdom over the most important things in heaven and on earth. She who is clothed when you want her naked and naked when you might suppose she would be fully dressed. She who is an embarrassment and a joy, a trial in her hours of happiness and a dear one in her moments of sadness. What else could one call such a creature but an Unknown Quantity? That is what you shall be to me."

He was surprised but not displeased when Jane received this declaration of love with laughter. Because a girl's reaction to his affection was always uncertain, he left himself the escape of facetiousness. Never, in all his dealings among girl-children, had he declared himself with irretrievable solemnity. Yet the avenue of retreat was not necessary with Jane, for her smooth, dark hair touched his cheek as she bent her face over his hand again and kissed it with gratitude.

"But even an Unknown Quantity must not sit all afternoon by an elderly person with none of her clothes on."

"I feel so safe," she said, as if it puzzled her. "I feel that this is home."

Once again, Dodgson sensed that the movement of their words and feelings had brought them close to dangerous ground. He stood up and raised the girl gently.

"Now you must dress and be taken back to your real home," he said, teasing her softly.

Jane did not answer, nor did she make any attempt to put on the pink dress and petticoats she had shed almost half an hour before.

"My beloved Unknown Quantity," he said gently. For the first and only time, he took her naked in his arms and kissed her.

"Now," he said, still holding her afterwards, "you need doubt me no longer. But you must dress and we must go down together. This cannot be your home, it ought not to be the place you think of as your home. Believe me, your mama loves you more than words could tell. That is where you belong and where we must go."

He turned round, as if the delight in seeing her naked did not extend to the frankness of watching her dress. Taking a tin of biscuits in one hand and a bottle of ginger-beer in the other, he led the way down from the roof to the dark tranquillity of his sitting-room.

12

Beyond the girl's window it was the time of moth-light, when only the last reflection of sun on the cloud remained as bars of crimson in the west. Wings, like torn scraps of paper blown in a wind, spun and dived across the grey lawn with its borders of shrubbery and the geranium beds now black against the fainter colours. Beyond the chestnut trees and the river meadows, quiet chimes and bells sounded among the Oxford towers.

Jane Ashmole turned in her bed from the grey light to the steady glow of flame, the golden flush of gas on the white staircase wall beyond her open door. Her own room was unlit but the light from the gilt cups of the gasolier in the hall would burn, by the custom of her infancy, until long after she was asleep. Then Hannah, in her lilac frock with white cap and apron, would close the door softly and turn down the gas for the night.

From the dining-room below, the voices of Sarah Ashmole and her guests were audible but indistinct. Lying in bed, the girl could just make out the contours of her own room in the dying twilight. The washstand with its basin and ewer stood at the foot of the bed. There were a neat dressing-table trimmed with gauze, bonnets and dresses on a chest of drawers, the black-leaded fireplace, the pictures on the walls, and the white glass globe of the lamp, seldom lit at this time of year. Jane rose in the sunlit morning and went to bed before the light had faded from the sky. Perhaps, she thought, it would be different by the next summer. Then she might be one of the dinner party in the room below. She felt no eagerness at the prospect, merely a curiosity as to what lay in store for her.

Sarah Ashmole's voice rose higher in the dining-room, as if issuing an invitation or an instruction. There was a movement of chairs, and voices gradually receded. The guests were going out onto the terrace by the laurel hedge where the men might smoke their cigars in the starlight, looking down across the Oxford skyline towards the Cumnor hills. By the time they came in again the girl would be asleep.

It was the shadow that caught her attention first, huge and distorted on the white wall of the staircase by a trick of the gaslight. Since all the guests were on the terrace, Jane never doubted that in a moment more she would see Hannah in the doorway. It was not Hannah. With puzzlement rather than alarm, she made out the shape of Thomas Godwin, who stood upon the landing and looked in at her.

Even when he came into the room, Jane Ashmole felt curiosity, indignation at his behaviour perhaps, rather than any apprehension. She was safe, surely. Her mother and the dinner guests were on the terrace, hardly twenty feet below.

Godwin sat on the edge of the bed. His fingers stroked Jane's fringe on her forehead. When she turned her face quickly away from him on the pillow, he stroked the fall of her brown hair at the back.

"What did you do with Mr. Dodgson this afternoon, Jane?"

In the semi-darkness he was more of a stranger to her than ever, a voice and shape she had never known before.

"Nothing," she said determinedly.

"Nothing?" The tall profile against the gaslit opening of the door was like that of a judge at the moment of sentence. "Nothing? How does one do nothing for three hours?"

"We sat and talked about the summer," she said defiantly, "about my Aunt Willis!"

"Believe me, Jane." The fingers stroked her hair rhythmically, as if he were trying to hypnotise her. "I am not concerned with what you may have talked about. I want to know what Mr. Dodgson did to you, perhaps what you did to him. You shall tell me."

"No!" Jane cried out, but not too loudly. More than she dreaded Godwin, she feared that the adults on the terrace below would hear her. What investigations would result from that, she thought.

"I see." Godwin's hand was moving on the back of her shoulders now, and she braced herself against him. "What a very important secret it must be." He allowed the warmth of his hand to penetrate the thin cotton of her nightgown. "Then if you will not tell me what you did with Mr. Dodgson, Jane, I will tell you instead."

She waited, knowing that by some unaccountable means he had found the truth.

"You took your clothes off for Mr. Dodgson, Jane," he said softly, "or perhaps Mr. Dodgson took them off himself."

The shock came like a bolt through her heart. Now could he know? Yet Jane knew she could not attempt a denial without betraying herself by her own voice. No one had seen them. Who could have told him? With a sick fear she wondered if it was possible that Mr. Dodgson himself might have spoken of it. The thought made her despair. Could he prize all her trust in him so little?

"You forget, Jane," said Godwin, as if he read her thoughts, "you forget how long Hannah has dressed you—since you were a very little girl. There are laces to be tied, on frocks and petticoats. No two people make quite the same bows and knots. When Hannah comes to undress you and finds that all these things have been retied in a different manner, what is she to think?"

"I can dress myself!" she gasped.

"You can, Jane, but you rarely do. I should advise you not to lie to me about it. You imagine that I have only discovered the truth of this today? On the contrary, Jane, it has happened several times before. Hannah told me because she was unwilling to go straight to your mama. What *are* we to tell your mama, Jane?"

"That I was photographed! That she gave her consent!"

"And were you photographed today, Jane? May I go to Mr. Dodgson and ask him to show me the pictures? Are we to have the charming proof that he 'borrowed' you for such nursery games this afternoon?"

She could not answer the quiet, taunting questions by which he calmly destroyed her. All her defiance of him began to dissolve in pleading. Would Mr. Godwin be placated by her promise never, never to be naked before her admirer again? She knew it would be futile to attempt such a bargain, and the knowledge of the futility made the first unshed tears sting her eyes. Godwin sat on the side of the bed, stroking the fringe of her brown hair gently, just as a father might, and prolonging the torture of his quiet interrogation.

"Are we not to have the proof of your innocent visit in so charming a camera portrait?" He paused a little, as if permitting her the chance of a reply. Then he finished the matter with casual scorn. "So you undressed for Mr. Dodgson lewdly, Jane, as a common street child might?"

"No!" Jane strove to shout with anger and to twist her face from his caresses. But Godwin's hand followed her movement and the constriction of weeping reduced the sound in her throat to a whimper.

"And you believe that tears shall wash away your sin, Jane? Yours and Mr. Dodgson's, too? Such cant you learn of such a man! Your sin, Jane, is that of a child conceived in faithlessness. Your crime is to betray and spoil the love of others!"

She understood nothing of these words. Godwin, in his cold rage, seemed rather to be talking about her to himself than speaking directly to the girl.

"You bitch!" he said at last. "You sanctimonious little slut! God and heaven on your lips! Whoredom in your heart! What a perfect little psalm-singer you will make!"

With a sudden movement, Jane turned her head on the pillow so that he could no longer see her face. Godwin's hand took her lank dark hair in a fistful and anchored her head on the pillow by it. The panic of feeling Godwin's power over her was worse than the sharp, tugging discomfort. Even when he pulled a little harder, Jane dared not cry out. To cry was to bring the others from the terrace—or Hannah from the kitchen. If they came to her, she must confess the truth of Godwin's accusations to her mother and to anyone else who was there to hear. Once that had happened, she would never again be permitted to see the one man with whom she longed to share earth and heaven.

Holding her head as firmly as ever by the hair, feeling the slight involuntary squirming of her limbs in discomfort, Godwin spoke quietly at her ear, as if to assure her there should be no respite from such taunting so long as Jane was under her mother's roof.

"Have you forgotten the warning I gave you, Jane? Forgotten it already?" His lips touched her ear as he spoke. When she flinched from this, he tightened his grip on the length of her hair and made her gasp with the pain. "There are places for little girls who debauch themselves as you have done. Places where you may be locked up safely as a child who is a sneak thief or a slut from the streets. Places of bread and water, houses of tears and beatings!"

Presently his voice stopped, and when he spoke again it was in a lighter tone, as if he had washed his hands of all that concerned the girl. He had let go of her hair and stood up.

"Perhaps it will be better if someone makes a woman of you, Jane, once you have left this house. It will quite cure you of your sickly passion for Mr. Dodgson. I feel certain that Mr. Dodgson has never made a woman of any little girl. He knows nothing of such things."

Being made a woman of: Jane had no precise idea of what he meant and yet the quiet, sneering words conjured up something dark and forbidding in her mind. They hinted at a ritual and brutal sacrifice of her childhood. With one part of her mind she fought against Godwin's suggestion. Yet more remote and secret, she felt a pulse of curiosity, a glimmer of intuition and a desire to understand.

The light had gone from the ridge of the Cumnor hills beyond the windows, the casement itself a rectangle of black. On the terrace below, the voices talked of Oxford Common Rooms and vacation plans for Switzerland or the Rhine, reading-parties in the Highlands, families and servants at Tenby or Ventnor. The voices and the sweetness of honeysuckle, the firefly points of cigars in the darkness, belonged to a world remote as antiquity from the pitiless hidden struggle of the man with the child.

"Will you go to Mr. Dodgson again, Jane?" Godwin now stood at the end of the bed looking down at her.

"No!" she cried, the word coming out with more force than she had intended, so that the sound of it carried easily to the terrace. Whether her answer was true or not, she could make no other.

Goodwin stood there looking at her for a moment more. Then he turned, going from the room and down the stairs. His vast, distended shadow was thrown again on the white staircase wall by the flames of the gasolier that shuddered briefly at his passing.

On the terrace, Sarah Ashmole reassured her guests softly as they heard Jane's last cry.

"The child has nightmares still from time to time. Who could be surprised at it when the evenings are so oppressive?"

A muffled thunder shook the atmosphere beyond the University Parks, the first scattered spots of heavy rain falling upon Merton and Magdalen.

13

"Not a penny," said Dodgson crisply, "not a halfpenny! Not one single, solitary brass farthing!" He held up a hand as if to forestall Howell's reply. "It would be quite the worst thing. I'm surprised you don't see that."

The two men took their chairs in Dodgson's rooms again, now that the Common Room's "tasting luncheon" was over and the selection of clarets had been tried.

Howell lowered his eyes, as if ashamed at what he had to say next.

"Unfortunately, my dear sir, there are places where nothing but money can protect a man's reputation. The photographic plates of Miss Ashmole . . ."

"Were stolen from this room!"

The slight figure in the black suiting and white bow-tie stood before Howell extending a teacup. He was as upright, Howell thought, as if he had swallowed the poker from the fireplace. The blackmailer interrupted the preposterous little clergyman in his turn.

"Indeed they were stolen, sir! Believe me, I have not acted as the agent for artists—Mr. Rossetti and others—without knowing what that means. You may have what you wish from dealers in pictures of this kind—provided you pay their price."

Dodgson had turned away to the tray on the table. Now he looked round at Howell again, a second teacup in his hand.

"How curious, Mr. Howell! An agent for the sale of works of art, you say?"

"Indeed," said Howell uneasily.

"Yet an hour before luncheon you announced yourself as Mr. John Ruskin's secretary. During conversation at luncheon—I apologise for the parsimonious cheese and biscuits but they serve nothing else at our tastings—you described yourself as an interior designer. How very remarkable that you should be both these things, Mr. Howell, and an agent for pictures as well!"

For the first time in their conversation a light perspiration was evident on the olive-skinned expanse of Howell's brow. In every line of the clergyman's pale face he read solemnity and concern. Why, then, did he feel that the wretched little Dodgson might be laughing at him in secret?

"You are less than fair to me, sir," he said quietly. "My words to the porter at the lodge were that I had once been Mr. Ruskin's secretary. If he informed you that I still held the post, it was not my fault. I apologise."

"Oh, Mr. Howell!" The concern deepened as Dodgson directed a flow of orange-coloured college tea into his visitor's cup. "That I could not accept! Allow a man to apologise for what was not his doing? What would you *think* of me if I insisted upon it?"

Dodgson walked away from his guest and sat on the window-seat in the deep Tudor casement.

"Then I must be frank with you, sir," Howell said sharply.

"Yes, Mr. Howell. Be frank, if you please. I should like that, of all things."

"It will be said by the world that you have abused this child and others. That after Mrs. Ashmole's refusal you compelled her daughter to undress and pose for you in such attitudes as this."

"Then the world will be wrong, Mr. Howell."

"But Mrs. Ashmole refused your request," Howell insisted.

Dodgson turned from his contemplation of the quadrangle below and looked directly at him.

"Mrs. Ashmole wrote a letter in reply to mine. She had no prudish objection to Jane's nakedness before the camera, no fear of Mrs. Grundy. Nor, of course, had the child herself. I have never photographed a subject, clothed or otherwise, unless she has been in total agreement. Mrs. Ashmole's objection was that Jane would probably be naked for some time and that there was a danger from cold or chill."

"You believed that to be her real objection?" Despite himself, Howell was fascinated by the naïvety of his victim.

"I believe what people tell me, Mr. Howell. I do them the courtesy of not regarding them as hypocrites. If Mrs. Ashmole's true objection had been otherwise, I feel sure she would have said so."

"Then you took the photographs?"

"I raised the temperature in the glasshouse, Mr. Howell, until it stood between seventy and eighty degrees. Not a difficult achievement on a hot summer afternoon. Then I took the photographs. Yes. I had, after all, met the objection which Mrs. Ashmole stated in her letter to me."

Howell felt the laughter swelling in his lungs and checked it with difficulty. The little clergyman, with the niceties of his equivocation, was almost a rogue after his own heart. All the same, he put on a solemn face and assumed a mournful voice.

"Then I am glad indeed, sir, that I came to put my good offices at your disposal. The two photographs 'By an Oxonian' now sold in those disreputable shops off the Strand have provoked some speculation. The shopman himself told me that, as he had suspected, they were by the famous Lewis Carroll."

Dodgson held up his hand.

"You may be assured, Mr. Howell, that I am not Lewis Carroll. No such person exists. When letters come to me under that title, they are returned unopened to their senders."

"Your own name will be attached to those prints soon enough," said Howell sharply, "and worse than that. Jane Ashmole will appear as she is in these two prints, illustrating books of the vilest kind, the work of men without honour or shame. You, Mr. Dodgson, in the tranquillity of your life here, can have no conception of the world to which I allude."

Dodgson turned and looked down into the sunlit quadrangle again as he replied.

"You flatter me, Mr. Howell. I have a very clear conception of the world you describe. You think that because I live here as a clergyman and a teacher, I have no idea of the wickedness of the world beyond these walls. I assure you, that world is perhaps better known to me than it is even to you."

"Then take my friendship," said Howell earnestly. "Take it for the girl's sake if not for your own. Let me find the perpetrators of this outrage. Permit me to use my own funds on your behalf to prevent the circulation of these prints. I am not a poor man, Mr. Dodgson. Indulge me in this matter. You really have no conception of the manner in which these innocent photographs will be adorned by the time they appear in print."

For a moment Dodgson said nothing. Then he turned round and stood up.

"Find the perpetrators, if you can, Mr. Howell. When you have done so, inform the police. Assure them that they shall have my cooperation."

"Then you will be brought before the world and destroyed!" said Howell incredulously.

"If I must, Mr. Howell."

"Your position at Oxford will be impossible. Your friends will become your enemies. No child will ever be trusted in your company again. The height of your fame will make your fall the greater."

"If you are right, Mr. Howell, it may be so."

Capitulation was longer delayed than in the case of most of Howell's victims. Now with the skill of the duellist he went for Dodgson's heart.

"The child, Jane Ashmole, must be destroyed with you, Mr. Dodgson. Her name could never survive such a scandal as this. For the rest of her life the story would cling to her. At the least, there would be those who believed worse of her than they did of you."

Dodgson stood without a change in his expression for a full minute.

"And what exactly, Mr. Howell, do you propose?"

So he had won after all, Howell thought! A close-run thing, though. There had been moments in the past half hour when he despaired. To have won, and to have done so with such difficulty, against the odds, made triumph sweeter still.

"Leave it to me, sir," he said simply. "Let me settle with these men as one who knows best how to touch pitch. There are but two ways of dealing with them, money or the law. But the law will destroy you as well, sir, and the girl."

Dodgson sat down in the chair opposite Howell. He studied the man's face carefully. One might take Mr. Ruskin's former secretary for a pugilist, he thought. It was the receding forehead, the high cheekbones and the aggressive jaw that suggested this so powerfully. The velvet jacket might belong equally to a true gentleman or a "sporting gent."

"Suppose I should not feel able to leave the matter to you, Mr. Howell?"

It was disconcerting to find the little clergyman, once floored, getting up to fight on. Howell took badly to the notion and dealt with it accordingly.

"Then, Mr. Dodgson, let me be plain. My concern is for you. I have an even greater concern, however, for the girl. What you stand to lose is nothing to her danger. If you will not trust me, I must go and put the facts before Mrs. Ashmole as clearly as I have put them before you. I must have authority to act—yours or hers."

"Then let us go together, Mr. Howell." There was such eagerness in Dodgson's voice that he seemed ready to set off for Folly Bridge at once. "I shall always feel proud of having been treated by Mrs. Ashmole with such exceptional confidence. If she is to be informed of what has passed between you and me this afternoon, it is surely my place to tell her."

Howell was caught off his balance for no more than a second or two. As he saw it, the fish was hooked. Yet he must play him on the line a little before he was safely landed. The poor devil was struggling now, but it would be over soon enough.

"You shall go to Mrs. Ashmole whenever you wish," he said indifferently. "Only let me see what I can do for you to begin with."

Dodgson made no reply at first. When he spoke, it was an allusion to their earlier conversation.

"I wish I could offer you money help, Mr. Howell, if that is what you need. Alas, I haven't any money."

And so the fish was landed at last. Howell could almost see the little clergyman's untruth, the casual lie, flipping and dying like the bright silver salmon in the basket. No money! Every Englishman of honour, every uprighter of Dodgson's kind regarded deceit with abhorrence. Yet each of them reserved his right to deceive and mislead others about the state of his bank balance. No money! The story-books that Dodgson wrote and little girls read had made more money for him than a gin palace and a French brothel put together. It was Howell's business to know such things. He was well aware of the recent investments Dodgson had made through Thomas Kish, the Sunderland shipbroker. In addition to his other interests, Dodgson was part owner of certain merchant steamers in a very profitable business.

No money, indeed! The best of it, as Howell knew by experience, was that a man who was less than straight over money would be easier to skittle in the end.

"Offer me your confidence, Mr. Dodgson," he said sincerely. "Let me work for you, as I have done for others."

Before his host could reply, there was a knock at the door and the scout entered.

"Steward's compliments, Mr. Dodgson, sir, and will you be requiring dinner in your rooms tonight for one or two?"

"Just one," said Dodgson quickly. "Mr. Howell is engaged to dine elsewhere tonight."

Without allowing Howell to contradict him, Dodgson escorted the sallow young man to the door and down the stone stairway in the cool darkness.

"Goodbye," he said to Howell in the archway of Tom Quad, with no suggestion in his tone that they were ever to meet again. "Goodbye, Mr. Howell. It was so very good of you to call."

Ten minutes later, sitting in a stationary cab with his confederate, Howell said,

"Don't be a fool, Dicky Tiptoe! A little patience now and he's where we want him!"

"A little patience now and we shall be eating our boots for want of cash. You were to sell him the glass plates!"

"It wouldn't have done just yet," said Howell irritably. "It wouldn't have done at all."

"You muffed it, Charlie Howell!"

Howell tapped the roof of the cab's interior and the wheels began to turn. He looked at the sun-beaten, "Indian officer" face of his companion.

"We'll get thousands later for what might only get a hundred now."

"And what about the real show?" grumbled Tiptoe. "What about Dr. Vaughan and his Harrow boys? His Royal Highness and the cadets? The Grand Old Man and his whores? When's the real show to make our fortunes?"

"When we can't be touched for it," said Howell, peering out sourly at the low windows of the Mitre Inn.

Tiptoe gave him a few moments' respite. Then he resumed the attack.

"Take the rest," he said. "Let me have the glass plates for my share. I'll settle with Story-Book Dodgson soon enough."

"No."

"Then leave him and try the Ashmole woman. There's no shortage of cash there."

"Too risky."

"Risky?" Tiptoe's bluff features were contorted with incredulity. "Ma Ashmole's been my special study, Charlie. She and her precious Thomas Godwin. The world doesn't know the half about them! Between them and Mr. Dodgson, I'll make my fortune. See if I don't."

"No," said Howell firmly, "we do just what we planned to do. We do it together."

Tiptoe turned his head away and watched the passing streets.

"You've had your try, Charlie Howell. You didn't come back with your pockets chinking with sovereigns either. I know things about these people that would make you blush to the roots of your oiled hair. So, seeing as you've had your try, it's my turn now."

Howell was genuinely puzzled by his companion's claim. He turned and looked at him, wondering what else there could be that was worth knowing about either Dodgson or Sarah Ashmole and the man he assumed to be her lover.

"What things do you know?" he asked sceptically.

"That would be telling," said Major Tiptoe firmly.

III

Major Tiptoe

14

THE FIRST DAY of the summer idyll began for Dodgson in the window of Leach's Subscription Reading-Room, which overlooked the sea. A volume of *Punch* lay open before him, in which he followed the adventures of Sir Digby de Rigby, the Hampshire baronet. Beyond the glass, on the broad paving of the Grand Parade, the women in their pink and lilac silks, the men in light summer suiting and tall hats, moved with the slow majesty of an armada under sail. The edge of the waves was hidden by the drop to the pebbles beyond the sky-blue railings. Only the alternate rush and rattle of the breakers, heard faintly at this distance, assured him that the tide was in.

After years of July and August holidays in the same resort, Dodgson knew the moods and colours of the sea as if he had never lived anywhere else. There were misty mornings, the preludes to days of heat, when the sun shone faintly on the glitter of haze, lighting the waves with the colour of ice. By noon the sea was a steel blue and the heat shimmered above the mottled white and grey of the shingle. In the afternoon the tide appeared as deep bottle-green surges before the decline of the sun and the richer, placid blue that was deepened here and there to violet by reflected gold.

To make a friend on the very first day was not unusual but always gratifying. He waited for the girl who sat beside him to finish the page of double-column print before he turned it and they both read on.

The tables of the reading room, to which he paid an annual subscription, were set out with ink, pens, and notepaper. At some of them, pairs of men played chess or draughts. At others decorous children engaged in backgammon.

Prue had come to the end of the second column. Dodgson, looking indulgently at the blonde plait worn in a pert topknot, turned the page. There was a hardness in the little face, he thought, a boldness in the line of the nose and a weakness in the chin. She was not beautiful. Indeed, he was uncertain even now why he had not dismissed her from his attention as soon as her query was answered. She had approached him, seeing his clergyman's suit under the straw boater, and asked him if he knew the times of the church services on Sunday at St. Saviour's.

Though he liked to think of himself as a High Churchman, he knew only the exterior of the new Tractarian Gothic of St. Saviour's, a miniature cathedral in brick and fancy tile. Why had he sought the girl's company? It was not merely that she spoke of her widowed father, for that was not until half an hour later. Rather, he thought, it was the pinched appearance of the hard little face, the foreboding that suggested wasting and sickness to him. Perhaps it was also the nervous solemnity with which she greeted his questions and the self-conscious propriety of her very name—Prudence.

Once again, he was the first to finish the page and his eyes returned to the scene outside. The iron spider-legs of the pier straddled the waves, and now the sun shone on the fresh white paint and the fish-silver of the roofs where stalls sold sweets and keepsakes. At a little distance along the promenade the band, each member grandly uniformed in gold braid and scarlet as any colonel of hussars, was playing "The Bird in Yonder Cage Confined."

Here and there, about the walls of the reading-room, there were advertisements for the town's amenities. The Railway Hotel offered bedrooms for two shillings and hot baths for ninepence. "Is Your Life Worth Saving?" This was an advertisement for Crisp's Life-Saving and Swimming Vests and Corsets. "Drowning is made impossible!"

Prue had finished the page once more. Dodgson closed the book and looked at her with melodramatic severity.

"Never immerse a pencil in a glass of water," he said slowly. "If you do, then you must surely be drowned."

Prue looked at him. There was no amusement in the dark hazel eyes, none of the response in her hard little face that he had grown to expect from Jane, Nerissa, and the others.

"Why?" she asked. "Why shall I be drowned?"

Dodgson took a sheet of the reading-room notepaper and dipped a pen in the inkwell. He drew a glass with a pencil standing inside it, a finger and thumb holding the pencil. His sketch extended all the way up the arm of the victim.

"Now," he said, "imagine the water level in the glass here, the pencil not dipped into it yet. Dip the pencil in a little way and what happens? The water rises, does it not?"

"Yes," she said, one hand toying with her plaited topknot.

"It rises because the volume of the pencil dipped into it will displace a similar volume of water. So the water rises an inch or so up the pencil in addition. But by doing that it immerses that next inch or so of the pencil in turn. And that displaces more water, which rises still higher up the pencil. And that once again, by the extra volume of the pencil immersed, causes a further rise."

Prue gave a self-conscious smile at the ingenuity of the trick. Dodgson continued to sketch busily over his first drawing.

"By now the water is at the man's fingers, but he cannot help himself. For the water rises up his fingers, which are much greater in volume than the pencil and displace much more water in turn. Soon it will reach his wrist and arm, rising in great surges by that time. And then, all too soon alas, the poor fellow will be found drowned, as the bills of mortality say."

As he drew the face of the drowned man in his last agony, hair on end and mouth howling open, Prue said,

"It's a trick. Like Achilles and the tortoise."

Dodgson put down the pen he had been drawing with and sat back in his leather chair. The bland clerical smile concealed the first faint warnings in his mind about the girl who stood before him, the paper in her hand.

"Now where in the world," he asked, "did you hear about Achilles and the tortoise?"

"At home," she said airily.

"Then what a very remarkable home it must be."

Perhaps it was true after all, he thought. He was so accustomed to children being coached in these matters in order to win his interest that he had been apt to overlook the possibility of clever homes outside the orbit of Christ Church and Oxford.

"If Achilles gave the tortoise a yard's start in the race," she said, "the tortoise would always be ahead. For while Achilles was running that yard, the tortoise would have moved on a little farther. And while Achilles ran that little farther, the tortoise would move an even smaller distance. The distances would get smaller and smaller but Achilles would never quite catch the tortoise."

She spoke with the bright self-assurance of the slum child. Surely someone had coached her in this. Who? And why?

"Achilles would catch the tortoise," he said, "just as you would not drown in a glass of water after all. It is a simple matter of indivisible distances."

"I know," she said, and this time Dodgson felt sure she was pretending to knowledge she did not have.

In a moment more he led her out of the subscription rooms and into the sunlight. There was a stiffer breeze blowing as the tide reached its height and swirled in green chalky breakers over the shingle. Towards Pevensey, beyond the pier, the boarding-houses with their white paint and iron balconies formed an extended curve along the sea front. To the west, the downs were rich gold with stubble after the early haymaking. Below Beachy Head the flags flew from the half-ruined Martello tower, where the lifeboat stood upon its cart.

They stood by the promenade railings where the ground began

to rise inland, the yellow broom in flower and the tamarisk stirring in the light wind.

"How long have you put your hair up like that?" he asked, nodding at the topknot of her plait.

"Not long," she said, "not always, even now."

Then, without a word, she began to unpin it, until the plait hung down its full length to her shoulder-blades. In a single gesture she unbraided it and shook the hair free about her face. For the first time she was completely a child to him, in her lavender-coloured dress, the black boots visible below the ruffles of its hem, and the kid gloves sheathing her narrow hands.

"Do you know who I am?" he asked her gently, as the laughter of a wedding party reached them from the West Rocks Hotel.

"Yes," she said, "of course. You're a clergyman. You aren't the vicar of St. Saviour's, though, or you would know the times of the services on Sunday."

It was a child's answer, he thought, too simple to have been rehearsed.

"And you," he said, "are a little girl staying with her papa at the Albion. And soon you must be there for luncheon."

As if at his words, the noon gun sounded from the grassy slope by the Martello tower.

"I can find my own way," she said quickly.

"I believe you could. However, I shall walk with you, so that you may show me how well you can find it."

So they walked together towards the Albion Hotel, whose high lantern rooms rose above the pier gates. The children bowled their hoops and the jugglers on the beach performed for pennies thrown from above. A sparkling phaeton in canary-yellow rattled past the riders and carriages on the Grand Parade, its sides announcing Lupton's Aquatic Circus, complete with underwater ballet and infant phenomenon. The splendidly uniformed bandsmen were now accompanying the comic singer who performed the lament of "Villikins and his Dinah" with a face like a sad mastiff.

"Now as Villikins vas valking the garden around—
"It was the front garden, ladies and gents, not the
   back garden—
"He spied his poor Dinah stretched dead on the
   ground.
"A cup of cold p'ison it lay by her side,
"And a billy-duct vat said that by p'ison she died . . .
"Chorus, if you please, ladies and gentlemen. . . ."

Over the stuccoed hotels of the sea front, the brightly painted
pier, and the glitter of wavelets, the notes of the song faded in
the noon haze of the channel.

It was not morning but afternoon and low tide that afforded
Dodgson his pleasantest walks. In the early days of each summer's
visit he went alone, until he had acquired enough child-friends
to last him for the remaining six or eight weeks at Eastbourne.
He had rarely made less than a dozen such friendships in July
and August, frequently far more. Indeed, if the mothers or fathers
of the girls were included, he became known to twenty or thirty
more people each year. Most of these either dropped him or
were dropped by him soon afterwards. A few had remained his
friends for many seasons.

On this occasion he returned to lunch in the rooms he always
occupied, in Lushington Road. It was a substantial homely house
midway between the promenade and the tree-lined shopping area
of Terminus Road that ran from the new railway station. When
lunch was over, the long hours until sunset stretched before him
like a vision of paradise.

He walked down across the shingle to the flat stretch of sand
uncovered by the sea. Here, with the sunlit water flooding away
almost at eye-level to the coast of France, invisible sixty miles
off, he felt the closeness and the immensity of the sea more
impressively than when viewing it from the height of the promenade. Towards Beachy Head the rocks began, and there among
the crops of stone, fishing and wading in the pools, were the
angels of delight. A few were attended by governesses who read
or knitted, upon stools in the shade of parasols. Here and there
the mother of the family watched the children. For the most part,

there were groups under the care of an older sister, herself no more than fourteen or fifteen.

On some days he would walk the sand at low tide from Beachy Head most of the way to Pevensey, mile after mile, surveying the little girls among the rocks. There was no lust in his heart; in that matter his conscience was clear. Several times in an afternoon he would approach and speak to one huddle of children or another. The friendliness and benevolence in his face were so evident that he had never been spurned in any of these encounters.

On this first afternoon he walked out along a sand-spit to a crop of dark rocks extending into the sea where the mussel women were at work with their buckets and nets in the pools. There were girls of ten or eleven among them, dressed in tight bathing-drawers and narrow-belted fisherman's jerseys that fitted them like a second skin. Most of the mussel women were older, the majority eighteen or twenty and a few twice that.

It was late by the time Dodgson reached them. The tide, which had been at its height at eleven in the morning, was now turning again. He watched them at their task, admiring the bracing of slender thighs among the younger workers, the perfect unselfconscious gymnastics of their toil. It was some while before he realised that the incoming tide had flooded the base of the sandbar on which he stood and that he was now surrounded by water.

There was no danger, of course. He could have walked easily through the six or eight inches of water that separated him from the dry sand fifty feet up the beach. It would cost him his shoes and perhaps his black clerical trousers, spoilt by the brine. He looked about him foolishly, unsure of what to do. The oldest of the mussel women came up to him.

Her hair was gathered under a black kerchief and her face was windbeaten as any man's. Yet she looked at him with the awkward smile of a child.

"My Julie shall carry you over, sir." Her head moved a little in slight formal acknowledgment.

"No," he said quickly, "I am quite able to manage, thank you."

Julie, the woman's daughter, was working at the rocks fifty yards off, wading with her nets. To Dodgson's eyes she seemed a tall, strongly made young woman in her early twenties, her brown, bare legs splashed by the water from the rock pool. With her dress tucked up, she looked at a distance as if she wore nothing but the tight fisherman's jersey that ended half-way down her thighs. Looking about him, he saw that the water had begun to swirl in a long channel already two feet deep between him and the upper beach.

"I should be too heavy for her," he said to the old woman, conceding his plight.

"Not you, sir," she said with a smile of encouragement. "Not for my Julie."

She called the girl over. Dodgson looked at the smooth dark hair, the frank open features of the young woman's sun-browned face, the water dripping and glazing her strong tanned legs. Though she was half his age, she appeared to him like some figure of the nursery, the safe comforting limbs to bear him to safety.

"You are to be my nursemaid, then?" he asked humorously.

Julie smiled at him and said nothing. There was nothing of the coquette about her, he thought, but no refinement of modesty either.

"You must go piggyback, sir," said the older woman. "That will be the easiest thing. Sit firm on her hips and clasp her shoulders with your hands."

The absurdity of his posture, as well as the necessity for finding some way to dry land, helped him to tolerate the indecency of the posture. Julie leant forward slightly and folded her hands under his knees. With his thighs against her waist on either side, his arms folded across her collarbone at the front, he saw the salt-water pond ahead of them widening rapidly, as every wavelet of the incoming tide flooded across it.

As if it were nothing to her, Julie stood forward, every movement of her body communicated to Dodgson himself. By now the water splashed almost to her knees as she carried him over it. When her foot met unevenness on the submerged sand, he felt the awkwardness of her tread as intimately as if it had been his own. Such proximity to the body of a grown woman was repugnant to him. To sit in a chair whose cushions were still imbued with a grown woman's warmth and perfume gave him a feeling of physical revulsion. The same experience with a girl of Jane's age seemed natural and clean. Dodgson endured his present predicament by compelling his mind to follow other directions.

Presently they were across and she stooped to set him down on the dry sand where the upper shingle began. She took the coin he offered. On an impulse, fearing that he might have hurt her feelings by his distant thanks, Dodgson said,

"You are a fine girl, Julie, a beautiful young woman. Be sure you guard your beauty always. It is a treasure to be watched."

There was no blushing or simpering, such as might have been expected from a woman of his own class. Julie received the mingled compliment and piety with a frank smile, looking directly at him with her fine dark eyes. A moment passed, a glimpse of her pleasure in being told she was pretty. Then she turned away and splashed back through the shallow water to gather up her nets from the distant rocks.

The open reaches of the sea were turning to marine violet under evening clouds of gunpowder grey. At the top of the shingle bank, a man who had been watching Dodgson carried over the broad pool said cheerfully,

"A tread as firm and easy as a carriage horse, sir! I salute your choice of a steed!"

Looking up at the figure above him, Dodgson was at first inclined to be irritated by the gibe. But there was no malice, no lewdness whatever in the bluff, sun-reddened face. The brave dark moustache hinted at sieges endured and lines held fast against the foe. A gold-topped stick and the military cut of the coat added to this impression.

In glancing upwards, Dodgson lost his footing on the shingle bank as the pebbles slithered down. The man above him reached down a hand. Dodgson took it and came safely up to the top of the beach.

"I believe, sir," said the stranger, "that I have the honour of addressing the Reverend Mr. Dodgson."

"I am he," said Dodgson a little breathlessly, settling the white straw boater more firmly on his head. "May I know . . ."

"Tiptoe," said the stranger, smiling under his moustaches, "Major Richard Tiptoe, late 41st Native Infantry, Sedashegar."

"We have never met, I feel sure."

Tiptoe's smile broadened, as if to embrace the opportunity of friendship more completely.

"No, sir, we have not. Yet you have done a great kindness to me. Not in person, perhaps, but to my young 'un. Prudence, sir, is mine."

"Then I understand." Dodgson took the extended hand, shaking it firmly as the quickest way to end the encounter. "You and Mrs. Tiptoe are here on holiday."

An expression of pain crossed the major's face, and his next words were subdued almost to the level of mumbling.

"Mrs. Tiptoe lies in Calcutta, sir. She was taken from me ten years ago. I have among my papers a photograph of the tablet that stands to her memory in the cathedral transept there."

"I am truly sorry to hear it," said Dodgson quietly. He did not, in truth, feel much sorrow. Yet the circumstances of the major's life appeared to explain some of the oddities of Prue's behaviour.

"I hope, sir," said the major humbly, "that you will permit me to show you that photograph one day before we go our separate ways. Mrs. Tiptoe was a lady of great refinement and accomplishments, as the tributes on the tablet record. She it was who gave our daughter the rudiments of education. Do you know, sir, Mrs. Tiptoe's maiden verse was highly spoken of by Mrs. Browning?"

"Indeed?" Dodgson contrived to sound surprised but not astonished.

The major touched a silk handkerchief to the corner of his eye, staunching the effects of the evening breeze or old grief.

"What it is, sir, for the young 'un to be brought up by a rough old soldier with none of those soft virtues."

"Yet virtue is all, Major Tiptoe," Dodgson assured him. "The softness matters little. Do you bring your daughter here for her education?"

"Would that I did!" Major Tiptoe looked bravely out towards the horizon. "No, sir, it is her constitution that requires the benefit of this air. She is better, no doubt of it. Yet a few weeks of London soot will bring back the spasms of coughing and the wasting sickness. Not serious, you understand. No spitting of blood. Indeed, here she is healthy and happy as a sandboy."

They began to walk up the steps leading to the paved promenade.

"It is my habit, Major Tiptoe, always to be frank about the occasion of my meeting such young friends as Prudence. I may tell you that it was she who spoke first. Seeing my clerical dress she thought I might know the times of the services at St. Saviour's Church."

The major looked away gallantly.

"Mrs. Tiptoe, sir! It was she who trained the girl in the way she must go. The young 'un has followed that path alone ever since. I wish I had been better able to do as much for her. If you find in your conversation with her that she lacks the courtesy of other girls of her age, I ask only that you will put it down to the tutelage of a coarse old soldier who has roughed it in the world, rather than to any natural lack of refinement in the girl herself."

On the expanse of mud still uncovered beyond the rock, a pair of fishing smacks lay stranded on their sides among the green weed of the stones, like the carcases of leviathans. Here and there on the horizon band rose the rust-coloured sails of barges, the tall stacks of colliers, clearing the Sussex coast to catch the next tide at the mouth of the Thames.

"I trust you will not have so low an opinion of me, Major Tiptoe," said Dodgson, "as to believe that my feelings can be determined by the polish of refinement rather than by deeper considerations. It is true that there is a social gulf which prevents friendships with young ladies of a certain class. Below a given line, it is unwise to let a girl have a 'gentleman friend,' even one of my age. It is for her own sake. Yet it would be absurd to suggest such a thing in the case of your own daughter."

Whatever slight Major Tiptoe might have found in these remarks he overlooked at once. He left Dodgson at the corner of Burlington Place with profuse assurances of friendship to come. With a brisk military swing of his stick, he walked quickly on past the pier gates to the grand entrance of the Albion Hotel.

Crossing the handsome vestibule with its wrought-iron gas pillars and frosted globes, the velvet ottomans and golden figures, he strode up the grand staircase.

Prudence was sitting before the mirror, her features contracted in a frown as she played experimentally with her coiffure. The major sent his tall hat skimming into one chair and laid his stick upon another. The girl rose as he came in. Tiptoe imparted a lusty amorous pat.

"To bed with you, my lass!" he said happily. "There's no more to be done today, and a doxy must do something to earn her keep!"

She made a sulky little sound. Then remembering that she had been paid for, she walked before him slowly into the other room.

15

"A MIRACLE OF THE MODERN AGE," said Major Tiptoe genially. He sat at the lunch table of the Albion Hotel where Dodgson was his guest. Sunlight through curtains of Nottingham lace shone on the white cloths and sparkled upon the glasses. Despite a breeze that blew hats across the promenade outside, there was a sense of gaiety upon the sea where the sails of yachts in the regatta rose and dipped like white butterflies above the waves. A gun sounded the beginning of another race.

Major Tiptoe beamed, paterfamilias at the head of his table. Prudence sat opposite him, her hair worn loose in its childlike manner, her body simply dressed in a dark-brown velvet with lace at the collar and cuffs.

"A hundred years ago," said Tiptoe expansively, "or let us say two, three hundred, a man would have been condemned as a sorcerer for producing those images that the camera now supplies every day for the education and betterment of mankind. You make too little of your achievements, sir. I see in the camera's magic a noble art and a learned science. Magic in the hands of such a one as your good self."

Prudence, with her eyes on her plate, cut at the mutton chop. The gown she wore was decorous enough, yet the clinging velvet suggested admirably the immature slenderness of her thighs and arms.

"It is a hobby with me," said Dodgson modestly, "no more than that. I have been fortunate in some of those, like the Laureate and Professor Ruskin, who have sat for me. Any man might make a reputation with such generosity on his behalf."

Beyond the splendid dining-room of the Albion the glass-panelled doors of polished mahogany led off to the writing-room, the billiard-room, the grand vestibule, and the smoking-room.

"Ah, no!" The major wagged his finger a little, confident in his position as host and fortified by a double share of brandy beforehand that had brought the colour more deeply to his cheeks. "Ah, no, sir! Here I may sit and gaze upon the carved monument to my dear lady-wife in Calcutta. I see it clear and true as if I stood so many thousand miles away in that cathedral transept. Yet there at my back is the sun shining on the channel and the gun sounding for the regatta."

"A painter might do it as well," said Dodgson, turning a slice of mutton on his fork, "or a copyist."

Tiptoe swallowed another mouthful of hock.

"You think me a flatterer, sir. Why should you not? Let me pledge myself. If you would return this favour, take my daughter. Make a portrait of her as nature intended her to be."

He glanced quickly to see if the innuendo had woken any response in his quest, but Dodgson continued to sit upright and unmoved in his chair.

"I will say," Tiptoe went on, "that I would rather see her mortal beauty recorded by the art of your camera than by the pencil of Gainsborough or Reynolds, or the brush of Rubens."

He glanced again to see if the last name mentioned had yet brought the little clergyman's interest to light. Dodgson set his teeth lightly upon his lip, as if about to explain something of complexity.

"I fear it is not so easy, Major. If you wished it and Prudence were agreeable of course, I daresay I could make a picture or two of her. Yet there are considerations involved whose discussion is perhaps best reserved for some other occasion."

Tiptoe had no idea whether he had caught his man or not. In his manner of speech, Dodgson gave not the least indication whether the considerations were merely those of photographic technique or whether they involved the delicate matter of how much clothing Prudence might be permitted to remove. Unless it proved to be the latter, Tiptoe thought, he had blown the price of a slap-up lunch to no purpose at all. There was, however, no need to view the matter yet in so sombre a light.

When the meal was over Dodgson went to collect two little girls of seven or eight whose acquaintance he had made in the apartments at Lushington Road. His own rooms there occupied an entire floor of the house with two bedrooms and a fine sitting-room overlooking the tree-shaded road itself. His meals were served in this room by the owner of the house, as if the property were Dodgson's and the proprietor of it merely a servant.

Presently Tiptoe saw him coming back, leading the little girls by either hand. They were decked out in silk dresses and hair ribbons, hurrying and almost skipping with excitement at the thought of what lay ahead. The major regarded them with a bitter resentment, a pair of little prigs who might threaten all his careful plans.

"The sawdust ring!" he said jovially, kissing each little girl heartily in turn. "Ah, what it is to a child's eyes!"

Beaming with insincerity, he watched Dodgson, Prue, and the little girls climb on to the seaside omnibus with its back-to-back seats down the centre, for all the world like a toast-rack on wheels. The driver in his long shabby coat cracked a whip, and the two horses lumbered off down the vista of white stuccoed houses towards the flags and drums of the circus.

On the flat grasslands edging the town, a blustering wind across the shingle made the green canvas thunder and the white ropes sing. Round the circus arena itself clustered the little booths of the hangers-on, some of the structures no more than blankets draped over a rough wooden frame. Here the gipsy girls in showy handkerchiefs told fortunes, and the sweet spicy smell of gingerbread drifted in the warmth of the enclosures. Jack-in-the-box, three shies a penny, competed with the sharps who manipulated three thimbles and a pea. Young men and girls were playing kiss-in-the-ring on the grass, the girls resisting with heads held down and cries of, "Oh, do have done then, Harry! Oh, do tickle him for me, Sue!"

In all this Dodgson saw only an invincible innocence. Even the petty cheating of the men with their three thimbles and a pea was so inept as to be forgivable. Like the colour of the theatre with its light and darkness, the charm of the circus drew him to another world, remote from reality, where dreams took a visible and tangible form. Costume and make-believe seemed the guises of truth that vanished again as they were discarded.

The summer circus on the flat grassland boasted no canvas marquee, though a semi-circle of crude boxes, embellished with royal emblems, rose above the clean white sand of the ring. Beyond the performers lay an expanse of sea, blue and mill-pond smooth at this distance.

Dodgson and the three girls took their places in the centre box for the parade of the dancing dogs and the man on stilts, the girl in clown's costume with a cockscomb and a chalked face, the girl-acrobat and the man with the brass trumpet who brought up the rear. On all sides of the arena in the bright afternoon sun were paint and gilding, looking-glasses and a smell of horses. A pair of fiddlers, who with the trumpeter, drummer, and a girl with a triangle provided the music, looked up and tuned their strings.

At last the gorgeous mysteries were revealed. For the next two hours the children laughed with delight or stared in wonder at the pony that walked on its hind legs, the comedy of the military man and the female clown, the bareback rider who jumped a score of ribbons in turn and came down safe on the horse's back after each attempt.

Dodgson's attention was caught by the three young acrobats, girls of Jane Ashmole's age, who seemed almost transformed to boys by the male dress of tights and sleeveless vests. The leader of the group, Sally, was also the trapeze-girl and returned later to perform without her companions. Dodgson could categorise her easily by the high-boned prettiness of her face, the knowing quickness of her blue eyes, the close crop of fair ringlets, and the lithe sun-browned body.

Two trapeze bars hung high up at some distance apart. A third with a rope dangling from it hung lower down between the two. Sally sprang with an urchin nimbleness at the rope and clambered up, monkey-fashion, to the first trapeze. Half frank, half fierce in her achievement, she stood in the rectangle of the trapeze itself, the sunlight on her spangled hips. Above the white sawdust she seemed to fly from one bar to the next, hanging, twisting, and turning in every attitude. The movement of each muscle showed clearly through the tight woven tricot of her costume.

Throwing herself from one high bar to the other, she landed plumb on her feet and laughed down at the spectators, as if indifferent to the drop below that might break every bone should she fall.

"A limber elf." The phrase rose in Dodgson's mind as the girl shinned down the rope again, bowed to the audience, and ran off blowing kisses back to them on her fingertips. As soon as the performance was over, he led Prudence and the two little girls to the tents of the horses to see Sally turning somersaults and practising her vaults onto the pony's back. She looked up quickly and caught his eye as he watched her, then went back to handstands and cartwheels. Dodgson kept his gaze upon her until she looked at him again, self-consciously. Then, as if responding to her invitation, he walked across.

"What a very clever young person you must be to fly like a fairy on the trapeze," he said. Sally returned his smile with a grin. "And what a brave girl, too, to perform so high above the ring."

"Go on!" she said, laughing at him. "That's nothing! That's no worse than walking tight-jeff or slack-jeff on the rope. Height makes no odds. Watch me now!"

She took a run, jumped, and with flawless skill turned a double somersault in the grassy space before landing upright and sure-footed. Dodgson laughed, clapping facetiously and calling out, "Bravo!" All the impish prettiness in Sally's face broke into life, and she went through several more of her acrobatic feats in the grass space outside the stable tents.

"Tell me," said Dodgson, as the girl stopped to regain her breath, "when you are upon the trapeze, could you stand there quite still for a length of time?"

Sally tossed her close-cropped curls as if in contempt of such doubt.

"Course I could," she said casually. "Who couldn't?"

"Long enough to have your picture taken or sketched?"

A look of doubt crossed her face. Perhaps, he thought, she was uncertain of her own skill. Or was it unease at the propriety of such a portrait? The high-boned urchin face confronted him.

"Expect so," she said. "Father might tell you."

Father, as Dodgson had discovered, was the ringmaster of the circus whose three daughters were the acrobats.

"And should you like a picture made of you while you were on the trapeze?"

"Yes!" The blue eyes broke into a smile. "Yes, if father would."

"Then you must ask him. If he consents, it shall be done."

Between her bursts of confidence, he saw that Sally had grown solemn and tense, more childish in this respect, at the thought of an ordeal before the camera's eye. Now he sought to reassure her by his questions.

"Are you a good girl, Sally? I feel sure you are! Do you teach your little sisters and obey your father always in every way?"

"Yes," she said, sounding a little frightened by his continued interrogation.

"And do you go to church and thank God for the wonderful gift of your limbs and your skill?"

"Yes," she said, with a new tone of evasiveness in her voice. "Sometimes. Whenever we can."

Listening at a distance, Prue found the entire conversation familiar. It was the sort of exchange more commonly heard, as to its tone, between an evangelist and a whore on the pavement of the Haymarket or the Ratcliffe Highway. The girls always humoured an uprighter of Dodgson's sort. Ten to one what he wanted in the end was no different than the demands of other men. If he was holy through and through, it was even more important to stay in his good books. Such was the type who could make most trouble for a girl with the law.

126

That evening Prue had cause to regret the cool disdain with which she watched Dodgson and the girl.

"You little fool!" Major Tiptoe bared his teeth under the dark moustache. "You proper little fool! You tell me you've let him slip the reins? Couldn't keep him from a circus girl? I'd rather not be you, my lass, when Ferdinando and Mr. Howell hear about this one!"

He rubbed the back of his hand for in truth he had hurt his knuckles quite noticeably in striking Prue across the face. She lay across the sofa, hugging it for protection, one cheekbone red from the impact of his fist. There would be a bruise the colour of a thunder-cloud there tomorrow. The major cursed the girl, regretting privately that he had not restrained his feelings. With such a blemish upon her, there was little immediate use for Prue in his scheme. He rubbed the back of his hand again, where the grazing had scuffed up white peelings of skin.

"Get up!" he shouted at her. Prue responded with a wordless squalling that was protest, resentment, and fear all combined. The major seized her by the braided plait of fair hair and drew her from the buttoned-leather refuge of the sofa.

"Unless you want to be knocked from here into the middle of next week," he gasped, "and then knocked back again for variation, you'll do what you're paid for! Work on him! Work on him till he must have your clothes off for his camera or bust himself. Understand?"

Again came the sulky, apprehensive mewing.

"Understand?" The major was holding her doubled over by the braid of hair, to which he gave a short jerk. She stumbled and let out a short cry.

"Understand?"

There was a squeal that might have been affirmative or not. Tiptoe gave her the benefit of the doubt. He looked at the sad and scrawny figure in her shabby underthings. Prue was powerless to do other than follow where he led her, doubled over, hands to her head, trying to ease the sharpness of the pain as he tugged her hair.

It was so easy to hold her in this manner, bending with ludicrous suggestiveness in the white bodice and pantalets, that the major could pour himself a generous measure of brandy and seltzer with his free hand. He stood at the window, looking down upon the blue evening tide, holding Prue like a dog on a leash. For all life's disappointments, Dicky Tiptoe was an optimist. At the darkest moments, it seemed as he sipped his brandy, light had shone upon him from some unexpected quarter. He thought of Sally the circus girl, and his heart began to lift again. It was in the nature of circuses to be temporary. A few days, and Dodgson would be alone once more. In the meantime, it might be possible to turn his present interest to advantage. Then, perhaps, a direct approach, offering Prudence as a model.

In his new good humour, Major Tiptoe led the stooping girl across to the open door of the water-closet. With a dexterity born of practice, he drew her forward by the hair, released her, and before she could recover her balance, propelled her through the doorway with a well-aimed kick to the rump. Without a pause, he turned the key in the lock.

Ignoring the howls from behind the door, he sat and looked down contentedly on the Wordsworthian tranquillity of the tide. But what fellow in his senses would waste time over the verses of a Wordsworth, or even the brush of a Turner, when he could have the reality set out below his window in this manner? So, at least, it seemed to Major Tiptoe as he lit his pipe, took another pull at the brandy, and gave himself to contemplation.

16

7 Lushington Road
Eastbourne
17th of July

Dear Major Tiptoe,

You will, I trust, forgive me for replying to your note in this manner, rather than discussing the matter contained therein viva voce. I find that in discussions of this kind I express myself less exactly than I would wish, so prefer to deal with them in a letter.

I should deeply regret it if there were to be any misunderstanding between us on the nature of my feelings for Prudence. I have many child-friends in whose company I take great delight, and I add to the score by dozens during my stay here every year. The majority of these friendships are pleasant but passing acquaintanceships. It would be imprudent, not to say impossible, for me to regard them in any other light.

You will, I hope, not feel offended when I tell you that I regarded your daughter's approach to me in that way. My kindness to her, as you are good enough to call it, is only what one would show to any child under such circumstances.

It was natural that I should feel for her in the two afflictions of bereavement and uncertain health. That I cannot take her under my care in the manner you seem to suggest is no slight upon her. I assure you my unwillingness to do so does not diminish the sorrow I feel for what you tell me she has suffered.

As to the matter of photography, my rules are very simple. I never take a portrait of a girl, clothed or naked, without specific permission. In the past I have always sought such permission from the mother of my subject. It would be possible that a father might consent to allow his daughter to be photographed fully dressed or in costume. Yet the studies of the nude, which you are generous enough to suggest in Prudence's case, would be out of the question. The point of a mother's consent is that she, if necessary, might act as chaperone. You will see, at once, that this could scarcely be appropriate in the case of a father.

It was kind of you to make inquiries and to discover a house in the Meads where a studio might be improvised for this purpose. However, since I shall not require such premises, it would be best to let the matter drop.

If I have misled you as to either the nature of my feelings for your little girl or what might be done by way of photographing her, I apologise. Perhaps it would save her distress if we did not meet again for the time being. I should like to think that at a later time we might resume our friendship on a less ambiguous basis.

Sincerely yours,
C. L. Dodgson

P.S. I enclose a copy of my little book *The Hunting of the Snark* for Prudence in mitigation of any disappointment.

"Bloody prig!" said Major Tiptoe, twisting his mouth as though he might spit from its corner. He crumpled the sheets of deep-blue writing paper and dropped them on the carpet. The thin volume of verse he pitched into the corner of the hotel room.

With a face darkened by a rush of blood, he scowled at the promenaders below his window.

"Bloody little prig!" he repeated. Yet his voice was calmer and more thoughtful now. He turned round, took the crumpled paper from the carpet and smoothed it out. One never knew what might not come in handy in the end.

17

As soon as lunch was over, a long stillness settled upon the houses of Lushington Road in the afternoon heat. With their tall windows, little balconies on the upper floors, the eaves overhanging each like a Florentine palace, the substantial dwellings had not yet lost the harsh yellow tone of their newly built brickwork. The broad street with flame-coloured roses in its gardens and pollarded trees along its pavements ran out of sight and sound of the sea. Only the intermittent cry of gulls or the shout of children betrayed the presence of the marine world of pier and shingle, wooden groins and yellow broom in flower upon the cliffs.

Major Tiptoe's cab stood at one end of the road, apparently unoccupied, the driver dozing upon his box with whip askew, the horses' heads drooping and tossing alternately. The blinds of the cab were down, the windows open, to allow ventilation while excluding direct sunlight on the buttoned leather of the interior. Between the edge of the window frame and the blind, Dicky Tiptoe adjusted his spyglass, surveying No. 7, Lushington Road.

A milkwoman in straw bonnet, shawl, and plain cotton frock appeared at the far end of the road. She wore the wooden yoke of the dairy across her shoulders and an ornamental silver-coloured milk pail hanging by a leather strap on either side at the level of her hips. She knocked at each house in turn, sometimes calling "Milk down below!" when there was no response.

The milkwoman passed and Major Tiptoe continued to wait patiently. If Dodgson had given lunch to the circus girl Sally, he thought, the little clergyman would leave her to "digest a while" afterwards, like any seducer with his victim.

There was not long to wait, however. Looking at the front of the house, the major could see that a camera might be used only in one area of Dodgson's apartments. It must be either within the immediate light of the tall windows or, more probably, on the little balustraded balcony outside. The stonework surrounding it would conceal both the photographer and his model at least to their waists.

That was a pity, in Dicky Tiptoe's opinion. He had come equipped with a camera of his own on this occasion, a German novelty which had done him excellent service in such situations before. It was the latest Stirn camera, which looked like a pair of saucers fastened together in a convex shape. Charlie Howell had seen its possibilities at once. Tiptoe had proved a ready pupil and already used the device to record his victims' indiscretions. Compact though it was, the little Stirn camera would hold four plates at a time, each of them three inches by one inch. With four plates, and considerable experience, Major Tiptoe had been able to bring embarrassment and even fear to a number of men and women.

No need for concealment of the Stirn on this occasion, he thought. Taking it carefully, he brought the balcony of Dodgson's sitting-room into line. It was too much to hope for a truly startling picture, but even a snapshot of two people in the street together had been known to cause consternation in one of them at least.

There was movement behind the windows of the room, he could make that out unquestionably. The tall window opened and Dodgson himself appeared on the balcony, bareheaded and only the upper half of his body visible in the black jacket. Somewhere in the shaded coolness of the room itself the girl laughed. It was the bantering call of the street urchin. "Go on! Take a proper picture of us, then!"

Sally came out onto the balcony as well, and Major Tiptoe

caught his breath with delight. She had changed from her frock and bonnet into the tights and vest of the trapeze performer. Where had she changed? In Mr. Dodgson's apartments, almost in the presence of the sanctimonious little prig himself! He must have seen her, watched her as she did so. After all, thought the major, a man who was prepared to take pictures of a girl naked need hardly scruple to see her change out of one set of things and into another. And how was she to lace and tie herself? The major chortled with a mixture of outrage and satisfaction. How busy the little prig's hands must have been, touching and fumbling!

Just within the window, the sunlight caught the polished wood of the camera with its reddish hue. Easy to see, thought Tiptoe, how the best photograph might be taken up there. Sally posed in full sunlight on the balcony, the camera set back in the shadow of the room a little to give enough distance. Despite himself, he gave Dodgson credit for professional skill.

Sally was standing close to Dodgson now, the high-boned imp-ishness of her face almost pressing his shirt front as he brushed her fair hair so carefully curled at its edges. As Dodgson smoothed the hair in place, the attitude of the two was not quite an embrace but it was close enough. Major Tiptoe aimed the lens of the Stirn camera and exposed the first plate.

Then he saw how Sally was to be posed for her portrait and he almost regretted having wasted one of his four chances. She leapt up and stood hazardously on the broad stone ledge of the balustrade, parading in her tights, legs slim and agile, hips and buttocks tautly rounded under the thin material. Dodgson, laugh-ing, drew her down and made her lie like an odalisque upon the ledge, hands folded and cushions supporting her head. He bowed his face and kissed her lightly. The major pressed the shutter of the Stirn camera with a sense of triumph.

For the next hour he waited with great forbearance, as it seemed to him, while Dodgson arranged and rearranged the pose of his victim between each exposure of the plates. Surely, Dicky Tiptoe thought, some of those portraits were going to have more than a touch of lewdness to them? His jubilation was mingled with contempt for the little man who had spurned his offer of Prudence naked. There was no mother's permission or presence as a chaperone in Sally's case. And what of Mr. Dodgson's fine distaste for avoiding the daughters of the lower orders? How had it been phrased? "I have learned my technique of composition from many years of experience in photography. My favourite subjects are children but not peasant girls formed by generations of labourers. There is a marked difference between them and the natural grace of the upper-class child."

The major gave a grim little smile at the thought that a single glance at the legs of a fourteen-year-old circus girl like Sally had been enough to melt Dodgson's principles in the course of a single afternoon. Just at that moment, Dicky Tiptoe felt his heart swell with an uneasy sense of virtue. He was a rogue and knew it. There was not much in his life that would bear close moral examination. Yet he knew he was no hypocrite. At times like this, faced by the furtive lechery of the respectable class, he believed in his own honesty. Perhaps it was the only matter in which he was morally superior to his victims. But was it not the most important to a man's character? Like Howell, he saw himself as punishing those whom the law would never trouble. He robbed men who had imposed upon society by their moral dishonesty and grown rich by it. Who could say that Dr. Vaughan of Harrow or the Grand Old Man himself did not deserve to be milked of their takings? Major Tiptoe lived by such thoughts as these. They reconciled him to the trade of genteel extortion and, to that extent, made him grow almost fond of his skill in it.

Dodgson was standing over Sally again, rearranging the position of her body as she lay on the stone balustrade. He stooped and kissed her gently once more. The shutter of the little Stirn camera moved. By four o'clock the last portrait of the afternoon had been taken on the balcony of Lushington Road, and Dodgson led his cheeky young model into the darkness of the sitting-room, laughing and chiding her gently for her vulgarity.

Other men would have turned and left at this point. Not Dicky Tiptoe. Though his work was done, there was one pleasure, a kind of moral satisfaction that he could not deny himself. He waited for almost half an hour until the carriage that had been summoned to take Sally away drew up on the opposite side of the road. The girl came down in Dodgson's company. As he handed her into the little carriage, Major Tiptoe was able to see that she carried two books presented to her by her admirer. One he recognised as *The Hunting of the Snark*. The other was visible by its black calf binding as a newly purchased copy of the Bible.

In the seclusion of the cab, Dicky Tiptoe rolled and hooted with laughter till the tears stood in his eyes. It was too priceless for words, he told himself, too utterly preposterous. He could almost have gone out and embraced Dodgson with the warmth of one rogue greeting a brother.

"Oh, you splendid, superb whited sepulchre," he cried to the back of the retreating clergyman, "you first-rate prime hypocrite!"

Dicky Tiptoe was in such a jolly mood that he even stopped at the butcher's shop in Terminus Road and bought a little raw steak for Prue to wear on her black eye.

18

"THE TIDE HAS TURNED NOW," said Dodgson, pointing with his stick to the foam that drained back down the shingle. "By this afternoon there will be miles of sand uncovered. We shall print our steps there like African explorers, and yet you shall be safe with your Aunt Willis again long before suppertime."

Jane Ashmole walked beside him on the narrow planking of the pier. By ten o'clock in the morning the band was tuning up, the first riders were cantering on the esplanade, and the children bowled their hoops or whipped their tops with impatience for the day's excitement. Dodgson glanced sidelong at the girl in her emerald-green dress and matching ribbon in her shiny dark hair. She was visibly fresher, if not visibly younger, than Prudence. Yet she carried herself with a natural grace that merely emphasised the shop-worn childishness of Major Tiptoe's protégée.

"I shan't mind if I'm safe or not with her," said Jane at length. "I can be safe here just as easily."

Dodgson laughed and they turned in the sunshine at the pier-head where the band played, facing the white stucco terraces of the Marine Parade. He sought an excuse to lay his arm round her shoulders.

"Over there," he said, his finger pointing through the morning mist and his chin resting on her silky hair as he held her to him, "stand the ruins of Pevensey Castle. Do you see? And on the other side is the round Martello tower, built to keep Napoleon from landing."

"How very curious!" she said, mocking him. "And how convenient to have such things pointed out by one who knows them so well."

Dodgson experienced a moment's chill. Too often he had been separated from a girl of Jane's age whom he had loved, only to encounter her after a few weeks as a young woman, utterly removed in spirit from the child he had so lately known. It was not the change alone that saddened him but the speed of it, as if a sudden death of the spirit had destroyed a familiar friend. The miracle of Jane Ashmole was that though she mocked him in this manner, she was to him as she had always been, turning in his arms now and smiling back at him.

They walked towards the pier gates where the little kiosks sold china keepsakes, clay pipes, and home-made candies whose boiling filled the summer air with a sweet scent of nougat.

With Jane upon his arm, Dodgson walked past the long Georgian façade of the Burlington Hotel towards the yellow-green slope of the downs and the chalk cliffs of Beachy Head.

"Instruct me," he said facetiously, tipping his straw hat to a family he had met at the Devonshire Park Theatre one night. "How does one pass a summer with one's Aunt Willis in Lewes?"

Jane thought about this for a moment, swinging her hips a little and tossing her hair as though this might aid her concentration.

"One sews a little," she said, "one reads a lot—and one has Mr. Whitely the curate to tea every Thursday."

"Perhaps," Dodgson looked at her doubtfully, "perhaps he has designs upon you, this Mr. Whitely."

They were alone now on a path that ran midway between the level of the sea and the higher ground. Pine trees stood black against the blue quiescent water of the slackening tide. Jane turned about, walking backwards and facing him as she sang:

"Oh, the man who marries me must have silver and gold,
A chariot to ride in, and be handsome and bold.
His hair must be curly as any watch spring,
And his whiskers as big as a brush for clo-thing!"

Before Dodgson could applaud her, she turned and ran, heels
flying and green hem rippling, racing ahead of him, the woman
turned to child again. He caught her up and continued his gentle
interrogation.

"And am I to take it that he is your suitor, *ce jeune monsieur
Whitely?*"

"Oh, you fool!" Jane slipped her hand in his. "He is *old* Mr.
Whitely, and he is my Aunt Willis's suitor, I'm sure. But if you
tell anyone that, I shall be most cruelly scolded."

Dodgson laughed at her, letting go of her hand, and Jane raced
ahead again, like a child released after long hours in school. No
other girl of her age, even one of whom he was fond, would have
been permitted to call him a fool, even in play. With Jane he did
not mind. The reason was one he could scarcely fathom beyond
knowing that it lay not within him but within the girl herself.

They walked down together to the shingle, swaying and start-
ing over the shifting pebbles of the long bank. Below them the
tide's withdrawal had uncovered the first dark-brown stretch of
sand between the rotten, shell-encrusted wood of two groins.
Farther out, the serrated row of rock tips appeared above the
falling water at each new trough in the waves. In one hand Dodgson carried the leather wallet with his sketching paper and pencils.
By the other hand he held Jane to prevent her from falling on
the pebbles. At last they stood together by the tiny stream that
drained down the firm sand. Coal dust from the colliers and white
or grey shell fragments from the gulls' supper gathered in the
ripple patterns left behind.

"A little more," said Dodgson breathlessly, "and then we must
turn back for lunch."

"I should rather not." Jane looked away from him across the
tranquil water. "I should rather not go back to lunch—to Lewes,
to Oxford, ever again."

It had never happened with any other girl or child that he found himself so much a mere partner in the relationship, not even an equal partner as it now seemed. It would have been so easy, as he thought afterwards, to impose his authority and take her back. Yet he did not. The reason was one he could not have given, until it was too late and the reason did not matter.

"Please," said Jane, the brown eyes under the brief slant of her fringe regarding him hopefully, "please let us go on. There is only today!"

"And what of Mrs. Dyer's lunch?" he asked, as if it were the best argument he could put forward.

"It will grow cold," said Jane in a satisfied tone, slipping her hand into his.

"She will tell the world we have been drowned."

Jane let slip his hand, ran forward several paces, jumped and turned. She called back to him,

" 'The funeral bak'd meats did coldly furnish forth the marriage tables,' didn't they?"

He felt sure that she used the line without the least awareness of its strange applicability to the love between them.

"Does your Aunt Willis encourage the reading of such very advanced literature as *Hamlet*?" he shouted after her.

"Oh, yes!" she cried. "Anything with a ghost in it, to be read after dark by the light of the fire!"

"Wait till we come to the rocks," he called, "and I will draw you such a ghost as shall haunt you by the light of noon!"

She gave a cry of feigned terror and began to run, in a scurry of green skirts. Dodgson gained upon her by easy strides, chanting as he did so.

> "I saw a monster come with speed,
>   Its face of grimmliest green,
> On human beings used to feed,
>   Most dreadful to be seen."

Jane gave another cry as he caught her gently in his arms and concluded the verses.

"Amidst my scarcely stifled groans,
Amidst my moanings deep,
I heard a voice, 'Wake, Mr. Jones,
You're screaming in your sleep!' "

The girl swung to and fro as he held her, laughing at every line of the recitation.

As they walked on, the sand and shingle gave way to uneven plateaus of dun-coloured rocks where the seaweed lay dark and crisp at low tide. The last gables of the houses were hidden by the beginning of the tall chalk cliff.

"I'll tell you who time gallops withal," he said softly, his hand holding hers on the rock ledges. "He gallops with Jane Ashmole and her aged, aged friend, for though suppertime is an eternity away, they think it comes too soon."

He steadied her as she undid her shoes and took them off, her stockings too, walking barefoot through the warm shallow pools where the fine green weed floated in their depths like drowned hair. By the time they found a recess in the taller rocks and sat down, the tide was no more than a distant whisper, the Hastings cliffs appearing like a desert mirage over an arid plain of stone.

Opening his sketching case, he found a tin of humbugs and offered it to her. Then with pad and pencil he drew a ghost, its dark mouth wide with horror, its eyes a pair of white circles with tiny central dots. With rapid strokes he gave it braided hair that stood on end and two neat upper teeth. Its body consisted of a head, long bird legs with claws, and two enormous hands. He set it in a cave, looking out onto a rocky beach of the sort where they sat. Quickly he sketched a pair of figures clinging to one another in terror.

"Ghost frightening excursionists," he said, pronouncing the words as he wrote them under the sketch. Then he tore the page from the pad and laid it aside.

"Draw me," she said simply.

"Must I? It will hardly do you justice as a camera might."

"But it will be a picture of me as I seem to you," she insisted quietly. "I should like that."

141

He laughed and chose another pencil from the case. Jane stood a moment and he knew what was about to happen. There was no reason to prevent her, except caution. Yet caution was impossible to him at that moment. She laid the green dress and white petticoats carefully on the clean, smooth surface of a pale stone, presently adding the bodice and pantalets. She quoted back at him, with variations, the lines from Sir Noel Paton's "Idyll" that he had recited to her on the roof above his Christ Church rooms.

> "For here, upon the glimmering marge,
> Between the sea and sea-worn rocks,
> Stands, mother-naked in the sun,
> Jane Ashmole with her dark brown locks."

She stood in profile as she spoke the lines, then turned her face to him with firm chin raised a little, her upper teeth just touching the lower of her parted lips in an expression of teasing challenge. Dodgson looked steadily back at her brown eyes, the short fringe of dark hair, the strong, honest lines of her young face.

"You forget, my dear," he said quietly. "I have no leave from your Aunt Willis for such a sketching expedition as this."

"You have my leave," she said, turning her body to him. "You have my leave now and forever."

The words were so old for a voice so young that he hesitated a moment before answering her.

"If I did my duty, Jane, I should take you home at once."

She looked at him with quiet surprise and took a step forward on the smooth rock.

"How strange you are," she said. "This is home, safe with you. My Aunt Willis is kind but that is not home to me. I love Mama, but my home will not always be with her. Whenever I am with you, wherever it may be, I shall always be at home. How could it be otherwise?"

He smiled and took her hand. The gesture concealed from her, though not from himself, his fear of a woman's words in the mouth of one who was almost visibly a child. Looking down, he saw the sheet of paper torn from the sketching pad, lying in bright sun. The ghost—the monster in the cave with its mouth open and hideous, its wide staring eyes. Jane was no monster to him, yet beyond her lay a dark cave of his inexperience from which her words seemed to come. With a shock, he realised that by the law of England she was a woman, legally competent to consent to her own seduction. Parliament had decided the matter by statute four years earlier when the age was raised from twelve to thirteen.

The expression in her eyes grew more gentle and her firm, pale features seemed to soften as if she guessed the secret apprehensions that he harboured, the fear of her demands upon him that barred the way like the comic monster frightening the two excursionists in the sketch. Tightening her hold on his hand, she lowered herself and sat where a skin of dry sand covered a narrow space between two shelves of rock.

"Now you shall sketch me, please!" She might have been a nurse encouraging a timid child. Letting go of his hand, Jane sat upright, her knees drawn up a little, and one foot crossed over the other.

Looking down at her, Dodgson felt more naked than she. All his logical facetiousness and extravagant, comic horrors by which he had amused and dominated Jane and her kind were lost to him. His authority was gone. The girl might have taunted or insulted him now as much as she pleased, and he would scarcely have known how to reply. As it was, Jane smiled again and said rather shyly,

"What a boast you are! I don't believe you can sketch at all! Was it all a story?"

"And what a goose you are to doubt it!" he said at once.

In the words of the nursery, the banter of children, they were safe again. The danger and the hope had passed together for the time being. Dodgson sat on one of the adjacent ledges of rock and took a pencil from his sketching case. Then he set the pad upon his knee and began to work.

His pencil traced the firm line of her back, the slope of the shoulder and arm, and the straight dark hair whose ends curled on her back just below the level of her collar. In profile, she presented a firm mouth and chin, the eyes seeming to slant a little at this angle. Beyond her he filled in the chalk cliffs and a crown of pale green turf, the glimmering emerald tide that appeared to rise slightly above the level of the beach with the curve of the earth. The stones and rocks in the foreground varied from pure white to the dark, dry, seaweed drapery against which she sat.

Usually when he worked with such intensity time passed very quickly for him, and every glance at his watch was a cause of astonishment. This time the long afternoon, which had begun even before lunchtime, passed with a slowness that was itself mysterious to him.

Back towards Eastbourne and the flat line of the coast beyond the Pevensey level, the world seemed empty but for himself and the girl. With no interruption, he completed his sketch of Jane, sitting between the ledges of rock, before the sun had passed far behind his back. The girl stretched out on the thinly sanded rock and Dodgson looked down at his drawing of her, marvelling at the unaccustomed ease and skill with which he had completed the picture. The power that had guided him was not in his fingers but in his mind.

Turning the smooth paper, he began again, tracing the outline of the fair-skinned body as she half sat and half reclined sideways on her elbow facing him. Her legs were drawn up a little, one bent back slightly under the other at the knee. His pencil followed the line of the slender waist, the half-formed swelling of her breasts that had been hidden from him in the previous pose, the softer curve of hip and thigh. As easily as before, he caught the effect of the lank brown hair on her white shoulders as she turned her head a little and looked across the expanse of rock and sand towards the distant whisper of the tide.

When he had finished, Jane got up and stood before him as unself-consciously as if she had been wearing the green dress and all her clothes. She moved with such ease and naturalness to the rock on which he had perched to make his sketches that he thought of her as a young goddess of an ancient sea, risen from the foam like Venus Anadyomene.

Dodgson put down his pencil.

"We must be apart for a while soon," he said gently, as if trying not to startle her.

"I know," said Jane brightly. "I must go back to Aunt Willis for a week, and you must go back to Oxford in a fortnight. You told me that. We may be apart for a few weeks."

She put her hands upon his shoulders, as if to keep her balance more surely on the rock surface. With a mixture of sickness and hope, he began to explain himself.

"Not for a few weeks," he said. "It will be for years, while you grow up, marry, and live a woman's proper life. Then one day, when all this is changed and even these cliffs exist no more, we shall be together always. Perfectly happy."

The hands upon his shoulders moved as she hugged him and her face turned, pressing a cheek against the black jacket.

"Supposing I should not fancy a woman's proper life?" she asked thoughtfully.

Because it was instinctive and there was no other pose he could easily adopt, his arms crossed behind her shoulders, cradling her.

"You will," he said gently. "One day you will. You must not mind it, for I shall not. There will be so much to look forward to for us both, so far away."

"You forget I am your Unknown Quantity."

He laughed, still holding her as she held him.

"Even an Unknown Quantity may fall in love."

Jane answered him with hardly a pause.

"And what if I should love you?"

It came like the confirmation f a disease that he had long suspected his body of harbouring. There was no answer he could make when Jane confirmed all his hope and dread in her simple question. At length he spoke on behalf of the world.

"That would never do."

It was a debate in which words were useless. They remained together, he perched sitting on the ledge of the rock, Jane standing before him. Even when he eased himself down to stand as well, the position of their arms about each other scarcely altered.

"Things change," he said vaguely, as if explaining himself to her at last. "You have no idea how they change!"

"Does love change always?"

"No," he said, "I shall always love you, wherever you are and whoever you are with. Only, remember, that is the love of an aged, aged man and not at all what you mean."

"I know what I mean," Jane answered softly.

"I suppose you do."

She broke from him and turned a pirouette upon the sand-strewn rock.

"Well, then," she said impatiently, "that settles it!"

For the rest of the afternoon she behaved not as one in love but as a girl who felt the gaiety of relief in having got rid of an oppressive burden. Heat shimmered from the stone surfaces as they waded in pools, examining the underwater world of thin green weed, the conical tents of shells, and the tiny fish that darted and vanished like scraps of tissue paper in the miniature grottoes of the rocks.

As the sun moved behind the downland, throwing the fore-shore into shadow, she dressed and walked barefoot beside him on the strip of sand still dry and soft before the encroaching tide.

Mrs. Dyer was easily placated by a story of times and distances, a lunch taken at Beachy Head, by which Dodgson meant the humbugs. He saw Jane and her Aunt Willis's maid safely to the railway station and put them onto the Lewes train. Then he walked back to Lushington Road in a wide circle through the Meads with their brick, gabled houses set in fine gardens of trees and shrubs behind the walls of Sussex flint.

That night he slept uneasily, finding that it seemed not to be true night at all. When he woke, as he did every hour, the sky to the north betrayed a flush of light as if the sun travelled only just below the summer horizon.

Major Tiptoe noticed the same phenomenon. Work, rather than insomnia, kept him from sleep. By the time that the pale green of early dawn touched the sky over Hastings he had made good use of a hired room above a chemist's shop in Terminus Road. The glass-plate negatives showing Jane naked among the rocks while Dodgson drew her were finished. But the major's true *pièce de résistance*, for which he had lain in wait so long, was the embrace of the sombrely dressed little clergyman and the naked girl.

He looked at himself in the discoloured square of glass that served as a mirror on the wall of the room. The chimney pots and spires rose sharply in black silhouette against the pale flush of daybreak. The major patted his bottle-brown locks into place and straightened his moustaches with the edge of a finger.

"Dicky Tiptoe!" he said admiringly to his reflection, thinking that for a man who had not seen his bed that night he looked remarkably fresh. "Dicky Tiptoe, you old devil!"

He was so bucked with the outcome of his visit to Eastbourne that he drew breath to whistle on his way down the stairs. Then he remembered that the occupants of the other hired rooms were probably still asleep. Major Tiptoe released the breath in a long sigh of satisfaction.

19

Oxford in the Long Vacation possessed for Dodgson a melancholy not altogether unpleasing. The busy streets among the larger colleges assumed a Sunday calm as the dons and their protégés deserted them for reading parties in the Scottish Highlands or the mountains of Switzerland. He could sit for an entire afternoon looking out across the wide lawns of Tom Quad and see no more than two or three figures pass.

There was an elegiac quality to the scene that prompted reflection rather than sadness in his mind. The elm trees and oaks of the meadow beyond the cathedral rose in all the green glory of high summer, yet the blossoming was done and the leaves carried within them their acids of decay. College business or visitors of his own would usually bring him back from the seaside for a week or two during July or August. Sometimes, as on this occasion, he was alone for much of the time. Hall dinner was a matter of three or four ancient dons clustered together, eating in silence at one end of the long timbered room. He preferred to dine alone in his room on mutton chops.

From time to time there would be some splendid display or celebration as the citizens of Oxford took over the streets and spaces appropriated during the rest of the year by the members of the colleges. In the wide thoroughfare of St. Giles, the booths and stalls would soon be going up for the late-summer fair.

On one or two days, Dodgson walked the riverbank alone. At other times he would set out for a whole day, tramping across the Cumnor hills or walking downstream as far as Culham or Radley. When there was no time to undertake walks of such length he was content to stroll in Christ Church Meadow, the University Parks, or the Botanic Garden opposite Magdalen.

A week to the day after his return from Eastbourne he chose to visit the Botanic Garden after lunch. Turning in through the stone archway, built as if for a Roman triumph, he followed the series of paths of the Jardin Anglais, flanked by the rich-smelling tobacco plants and old-fashioned roses. He entered the wrought-iron hothouse, a long and elegant conservatory where the gardeners in green baize aprons and white smocks were watering the plants. Tall and overlapping, the lush green stalks and white flowers of tropical foliage rose from the wet earth. The air within the sun-warmed glass was thick and steamy, oppressive to the lungs.

Dodgson walked along the brick-paved alleys of this contrived jungle until he came to the far end where small window panes, a foot square, opened to allow ventilation. The hothouse itself was deserted except for the last of the gardeners, who was emptying the remains of his can over the roots of the orchids. Perhaps he would not even have seen the other man who stood in the fresh air beyond the glass, had the voice not caught his attention.

"A word with you, if you please!" said Major Tiptoe peremptorily.

It was so unlike the joviality of the man's tone at their seaside meetings that Dodgson looked again to make quite sure he was not mistaken. Then he saw a second figure farther off, head bowed as she stood in bonnet and gown of deep cream. It was Prudence. Dodgson and the major faced one another through the open square of glass. They were separated by a greater distance in another sense, since Dodgson could only reach Major Tiptoe by walking back the length of the hothouse to the door and then round its exterior.

After the last letter he had written, he did not doubt that Tiptoe's presence promised a disagreeable encounter. The major had removed his hat as he spoke, apparently in a gesture of courtesy that Dodgson declined to return.

"I trust, Major Tiptoe, that you have not travelled to Oxford on purpose to see *me*." Hands folded on the knob of his stick, he returned the other man's stare. "I should regard that as both unnecessary and ill-judged after our last communication."

"Would you?" Tiptoe's moustache moved as if his lips might be forming a smile under cover of it. But there was no smile. "I daresay you would. Perhaps it will change your mind if I tell you that I have come on purpose to return certain property to you."

The major put out his hand and offered Dodgson an envelope through the open pane. Dodgson shook it open and tipped a thin pile of cards into his hand.

"Yours?" asked Major Tiptoe sardonically.

The first two cards were taken from the glass plates of Jane Ashmole that he had made on Christ Church roof. Each was inscribed with the caption "Jane, by an Oxonian" and its individual title.

"These are not mine," he said quietly.

"No," said Tiptoe reasonably, "but the glass plates might be another matter. Go on, please."

Dodgson turned the other cards and saw the sunlit beach. One of the prints showed him sketching Jane while she lay naked, propped on her elbow. Each of the other three showed her face as he held her in his arms. In one of them his own features were clearly identifiable. There followed another four of the house in Lushington Road. None of this last set would have meant a great deal on its own. Sally was no more naked than she was on the trapeze. Without some suggestion, the figure of the man in the background was far from distinct. Taken with the others they made his condemnation doubly sure.

In the moment that he saw them, ten prints in all, he believed that he must do whatever Tiptoe asked. On the base of each print had been pencilled the captions for publication. "Do you like me this way?" followed by "Or do you prefer this sort of thing, eh?" One of the set that showed their embrace was entitled

"Oh, sir! I did so want to be good!" and another, "But this wicked seaside air makes a girl so frisky!"

"They'll go well as a set," said Major Tiptoe conversationally, "to be called 'Jane, by an Oxonian.' "

But then Dicky Tiptoe was somewhat discomfited as Dodgson merely handed the photographic prints back to him through the open window pane. There was a hint of wretchedness in the little clergyman's long pale face but nothing approaching the fear that the major had rather hoped to see.

"Why do you bring these photographs to me? They are not mine except the first two, which were taken in the most innocent manner and with the permission of the girl's mother. There is nothing I can do for you."

"Oh, don't say that, sir!" said Major Tiptoe encouragingly. "Never say that, when there's so much you might do, for Miss Ashmole if not for yourself."

"What has Miss Ashmole to do with you?"

The major laughed. Behind him the summer flowers rose from the garden beds like bright-tuniced regiments of hussars and lancers.

"Why, bless you!" he said pleasantly. "I know as much about the young lady, about good Mrs. Ashmole and wise Mr. Thomas Godwin, as they know about themselves."

"What has it all to do with you?" There was such weariness in Dodgson's voice now that Tiptoe judged it best to come to the point of his visit. He edged a little closer to the open pane and put his face to it.

"It concerns me as your friend," he said gently. "Imagine, if you will, the effect of so charming a set of photographic gems issued in a racy magazine. How will it be when that publication is perused by the learned Dean of Christ Church, or the bishop's secretary, or Mrs. Ashmole and Mr. Godwin? Why, I daresay it wouldn't stop this side of the police court for you."

Dodgson's cheek twitched and for the first time his anger shone out at the major's fatuous *bonhomie*.

"If you believe that any one of them would read such purulent rubbish, you are most grievously mistaken. I bid you good afternoon, Major Tiptoe."

"A moment!" said Tiptoe quietly, and Dodgson turned back because he knew he must.

"You'll come round," the major resumed. "Not now perhaps, but when you've had a chance to think what all this must mean for Jane Ashmole. I came here, friendly-intentioned, as the man who might arrange for you to buy the glass plates of those pictures and never hear another word of the business. Still, if you won't buy them there's others will. And if they must see the light of day in a frisky journal, then there's but one trade for our Miss Ashmole to follow. Savvy?"

Had it not been for Jane, Dodgson would have sent the major packing and invited him to do his worst. Yet now that worst would be done to Jane. All his life, when blackmail was a subject for discussion, he had never understood why the victims did not face it out with their persecutors. Too late he realised how badly he had misjudged the skill of the professional extortioner.

"What if I should agree to your proposal? Mind you, I do not say that I shall!"

"That's the ticket!" said Major Tiptoe encouragingly. He was secretly delighted that he had landed the fish whom Howell had allowed to slip the hook. "All ten plates shall be yours for fifty sovereigns each. Five hundred yellow-boys. Tomorrow afternoon at three, in this very spot. Mark you, I shan't appear until I see you inside there. The glass between us and the distance to go round it make it the place for a tête-à-tête. An exchange through the window pane and we go our separate ways."

He waited for Dodgson's expression of dismay at the sum of money asked, but he waited in vain. Major Tiptoe felt annoyed with himself and wondered if he might have asked for more. Dodgson was not thinking about money.

"How would it be, Major Tiptoe," he asked quietly, "if all but my two portraits of Miss Ashmole were fakes? How would you stand with Dean Liddell, the bishop's secretary, and the police in that case?"

"Fakes?" The earth seemed to move under Tiptoe's feet. There was indignation in his voice, a hint of affronted honesty, as he repeated the word. "Fakes? You know damn well they can't be fakes, you canting little prig!"

"You forget, Major Tiptoe," said Dodgson quietly, "I did not take those eight photographs. I know no such thing. A man of your talents must consider how easily, with two glass plates and the means of copying, a skilful artist may do the business. One head substituted for another. A naked body for one fully clothed."

"You mean to perjure yourself?" Major Tiptoe's lip curled a little under the dark moustaches. "You would perjure yourself in court upon your Bible oath?"

"If I believed you when you say that the photographs are untampered with, Major, it would be perjury to maintain that they were fakes. But who would believe you? Certainly not I! Be sure that if you attempt anything of the sort you have threatened, I will not spare you."

"And Miss Ashmole?" murmured Tiptoe. "How will it stand with her when the photographs you admit taking become public property? How will it stand with you as well?"

Jane. Like a hostage in the hands of the enemy, her name was brought forward to bar every reply. "And what if I should love you?" In his mind he heard her voice again, the words spoken even while Major Tiptoe among the rocks was taking his mean, sardonic photographs. If money would save her, all the money in his possession, ought he not to use it?

"Well, then," said the major brightly, "here we stand. Each day you may find me at this spot, prompt on three o'clock. Mind you, I don't say that after tomorrow we can do the business for quite five hundred sovs. Inns and livery stables charge the very devil in season. A fellow mayn't stop in a town like this under fifty pounds a day. He really mayn't, sir. After tomorrow, then, the price must rise a little, by that much each afternoon. To-morrow you shall have 'em at cost—five hundred—though Dicky Tiptoe shall be a fool to himself in letting the goods go so cheap. The day after tomorrow, they must stand at five hundred and fifty. Think it over and see if I'm not right, sir. Now's your time to buy, while the market's low and the other bidders aren't yet in the ring."

The other bidders? As Dodgson opened his mouth to demand an explanation of this, Major Tiptoe turned about and marched smartly away. Dodgson walked quickly down the length of the hothouse, out through the doorway, and round to where the major had been standing. The gardens were still and empty. A dragonfly sailed on a current of air above the roses, in a blue sky over Magdalen Bridge and the river.

Shut from the sunlight of the afternoon as securely as in the deepest cell, Dodgson walked alone up Longwall Street and came at length to the pillared façade of the Clarendon Building on Broad Street, where he had a matter of business in the proctors' office.

Sixty miles away on the same afternoon, Charles Augustus Howell returned to his apartments in Southampton Row from a visit to Mr. Freeman, "Pawnbroker to the Discerning," in Farringdon Road. He was in a particularly buoyant mood as he swung his stick through the little Bloomsbury streets and beamed at the nursemaids and their laden prams in the public gardens of Russell Square.

Mr. Freeman had just made a most satisfactory offer for a Japanese lacquered cabinet that stood in Howell's study. In other circumstances, Howell might have felt a pang at parting with so handsome a piece of furniture, the immaculate black gloss highlighted by green and gold. On this occasion he was more sanguine, since the cabinet was not his. It belonged to James McNeill Whistler, who had sold it to Sydney Morse on departing for Venice. Whistler had left Howell to attend to the transaction. At present, Whistler believed that Morse had the cabinet. Morse was under the delusion that it was still in Whistler's possession. For six months or more it had stood in Howell's room until, as he said, it seemed fair to let it earn its keep. The matter had turned out most satisfactorily in every way.

Going up the steps of the house in the warm afternoon with the dust-laden sunlight falling on street vendors and parasols, handsome porticoes and laughing children, he could almost imagine himself in some city of northern Italy or Spain. Turning the key in the lock, he opened the door and went directly to the room.

Since Mr. Freeman would be there with cash and carriage that evening, it seemed the best thing to empty the Japanese cabinet straight away. Clearing a space on the top of his desk, he opened the main doors of the cabinet and took out several pieces of delicate china, setting them admiringly on the desk top. Outside in the warm afternoon the children called, and the ice-cream cart made its noisy way towards Holborn. Howell stroked the fine pale glaze of the china with its mandarin figures as if they could sense and approve his caress. The possession of material objects was the great satisfaction of his life, and he found it hard to understand those who could not share such a pleasure.

The papers in the drawers, consisting of unpaid bills and un-answered invitations, were unimportant to him in his present mood. Howell disliked correspondence and relished personal encounters. In consequence his letters were few. There was something so final and binding about words committed to paper that he shunned them in that form.

All that remained was one drawer in the back of the cabinet. Like most artefacts of its kind, the Japanese cabinet possessed this secret compartment, devised in deference to the European market. To reach it, one had to remove two of the other drawers and find a long tongue of metal running between them. By press-ing this a catch was released. What appeared to be part of the inner structure of the cabinet frame could then be drawn out as a wooden compartment some six by eight inches. Poor Whistler, he thought, had not even known of its existence. It was in this drawer that Howell had deposited certain papers and photo-graphic plates. They related to Dr. Vaughan of Harrow, to a royal prince, to Major Kitchener and another gentleman, and even to the Grand Old Man himself. Now, of course, the little collection boasted a pair of gems unwittingly provided by Story-Book Dodgson.

Even these items of trade would cause him a moment's regret when the time came to part with them. He felt as he supposed an artist must feel when selling his latest work. Like the artist he was driven by necessity. Unlike the artist he found no consolation in receiving the world's recognition.

He opened the secret drawer, wondering as he did so where its contents might be safely kept. The plain wooden space was empty. Howell frowned. His first thought was that he must have transferred the contents to another hiding place and then for-

155

gotten about it. Absurd though it might seem, he had practised this precaution from time to time with such success that a lapse of memory had once hidden his treasures even from himself. This time he had not doubt. This time he was quite sure that the papers and glass plates had been there two days before and that he had not looked at them since.

Walking across to the porcelain bell-pull set on the wall, he wrenched its lever, jerked the thin wires, and heard the distant jangling in the servants' quarters below. Mrs. Jones with her dark skin, slant eyes, and pert young body came bustling to attend him.

"Who the devil has been in here since Sunday?" said Howell unceremoniously.

Her sharp little nose and almond eyes watched him suspiciously as she thought about this. The young servant had been his companion in bed from time to time and, trying to take advantage of the situation by familiarity later on, had found herself treated at once as an insolent menial.

"Who has called on me since Sunday when I have been out?" Howell was shouting at her now.

"No one!" she wailed indignantly.

"You certain!" Howell raised his hand as if he might strike her. "Someone has been in this room! If there is no one but you, believe me, there will be a reckoning to be paid!"

She was frightened now and, in consequence, her confusion increased.

"Major Tiptoe!" she cried. "But you were here! He was the only one!"

In his mind, Howell re-enacted the events of Tiptoe's visit on Sunday evening. The cabinet had been locked throughout, but that would not have been a deterrent to a thief of even the major's modest abilities. Howell himself had been absent from the room on a couple of occasions. Perhaps none had been long enough for his companion to empty the secret drawer on one of them, yet taken together there was time enough. The hidden drawer was a secret. Had Tiptoe ever been there when he opened it?

Could young Mrs. Jones—who boasted no Mr. Jones—be believed? Where had Tiptoe gone? A remark about Paddington

Station came back to Howell's memory. Story-Book Dodgson and Oxford! Suppose the lynx-eyed Mrs. Jones was lying? There might be others who had entered that room in his absence.

"If you have been whoring while my back was turned," he said pleasantly to her, "if you have had your damned fancy-men in here, I shall break you! See if I don't!"

With that he dragged her protesting to the water-closet, as the most convenient prison. Fetching a short chain and padlock, he secured the girl's right wrist to a pipe so that she could stand, sit, and relieve herself. Finally he went to the kitchen and found a roll of bread and some cheese. He put these and a jug of water where she could reach them.

"Tomorrow morning I shall go out," he said, as her mouth worked in fear of him. "I shall be away for several hours. When I come back I daresay I shall know the truth."

He was gratified to hear that, when the door was closed upon her, her cry was scarcely more than the mewing of a cat. With his mouth set and the blood beating in his head with fury at what had happened, he strode back to his study and consulted Bradshaw for the first morning train to Oxford.

20

In the dark hallway of the old coaching inn, Howell began to shout. His anger was not appeased by the servants of the Mitre Inn, who did their best to receive his inquiries with apparent courtesy.

"I have come to Oxford to see Major Tiptoe!" His fist hit the top of the table again. "See him I will—and must!"

The truth was that Howell had never been robbed before and he took the experience badly.

"Indeed, sir!" The keeper of the inn, with his dark suiting and port-wine waistcoat, bowed his head a little as if in compliance. Then the head came up again. "But Major Tiptoe is not here at the present. He has gone out on a matter of business, I believe, and will be back for dinner at seven. If you would care to return then, I will have your card sent up to him."

Howell knew perfectly well that if he returned at seven it would be to find that Dicky Tiptoe had packed his belongings and fled. If that happened he might hide anywhere in the length and breadth of the land.

"I will wait for Major Tiptoe in his rooms."

The innkeeper's flat dark hair bowed again.

"I regret that is not permissible, sir. You are most welcome to wait for him in the parlour but . . ."

"Then show me his rooms!"

Now the innkeeper looked at him as if Howell should have known better than to ask this.

"If you were our guest, sir, you would not want your rooms shown or occupied in such a manner. I beg you will not insist upon it."

Unable, in his anger, to judge the best action, Howell glared at the man. His dark eyes were narrowed and a pulse of fury beat visibly in his sallow cheek. Then, without another word, he swung round and walked out of the Mitre's doorway into sunlit High Street. From within white-barred sash windows the other guests watched him as they sat at lunch. Then, as the altercation seemed to be at an end, they returned to their cold meat and pickles.

The innkeeper drew back into the darker regions between the dining-room and the steamy kitchens. Major Tiptoe stepped out from behind a corner, where he had been concealed and poised for flight. He pressed a sovereign into the innkeeper's hand.

"Poor devil!" he said sadly for the man's benefit. "Till last month he was a patient in the Surrey Asylum. Believes in a legacy that never existed and that I have taken it from him! If he were not my own cousin, I would give him in charge to a constable."

The major did not suppose that the innkeeper was convinced by his story. It mattered little so long as his main purpose was served. Thanking the man again he slipped up the back stairs to his rooms.

The major was not concerned about the papers and plates he had acquired from Howell's Japanese cabinet, for those were securely lodged in the innkeeper's safe. What mattered much more to him was the busy afternoon ahead. First there was a letter for the penny post, addressed to Sarah Ashmole. He glanced over it and his eye caught the essential phrases. ". . . the nature of your affection for Mr. Thomas Godwin. . . . the unfortunate circumstances of its discovery by a person of ill repute. . . . the public disgrace that must attend its revelation to society at large. . . . a sum of money substantial enough to purchase the silence of the scoundrel who threatens your peace. . . . to undertake such negotiations esteemed a privilege by your loyal and admiring friend, Richard Tiptoe."

It was not a masterpiece, Tiptoe thought, but under the circumstances, well worth an afternoon's work. He sealed it and sent it down. With commendable efficiency, the local post would deliver it to the house beyond Folly Bridge in a few hours. Time was all important to Major Tiptoe just then, and he was appreciative of such speed.

The proposed meeting with Dodgson was his only rendezvous for the afternoon. He would keep it if possible, though there might be no harm in letting his victim wait another day. If the little prig was hungry for the glass-plate negatives today, he would be ravenous by tomorrow. The major decided that he would see how events moved.

For the moment he had other fish to fry, and they must be fried this afternoon or not at all, he thought. In a small case he had packed away a hired box camera, a collapsible tripod, and the black hood of the photographer. Whistling a little under his breath, he decided that a man who could take such portraits of the prime minister of England would find his present quarry easy game.

With the camera case in one hand, he went cautiously down the stairs and stood in the hallway of the Mitre. The innkeeper watched him. Dicky Tiptoe took the silver watch from his fob, consulted the clock on the wall, and wound his own timepiece. He nodded to the innkeeper, slipped out through the rear door to the stable yard, and came out unobserved into the narrow, busy lane of Turl Street.

By back lanes and side-streets, he made his way to the boating station near Folly Bridge. Handing a sovereign to the boatman, Tiptoe laid the camera case carefully in the stern of the little skiff and took the sculls. It was just as well, he thought, to be launched upon the water when the time came. Pulling gently out into the stream he drew across to the towpath on the far side. Astern of him, as he looked back from his rowing bench, the dismasted college barges like a row of white-painted frigates lined the meadow bank.

He was little more than twenty feet from the far side of the broad river, preparing to turn the skiff, when he heard the voice at his back.

"Tiptoe! You damned thief!"

Could Howell have followed him? He doubted it. Tiptoe swung the skiff round and saw him standing there on the towpath, tall and furious in his cream linen suiting, bareheaded and hands on his hips.

"Go home, Charlie Howell!" called the major reasonably. "Leave the business to me! You shall have your share of the dibs once I get them!"

"The devil take that! Where in damnation are my papers?"

The wine that the major had consumed at lunchtime left him agreeably relaxed in the afternoon heat.

"A man that can't reap the harvest has no right to the scythe, Charlie Howell! A fellow that's green as a leek and soft as new cheese ain't the chap for work like this!"

Howell looked about him, seized a stone the size of a brick, and pitched it at the major in his skiff. It landed several feet to one side with a gulping splash. The major hastily pulled from the bank.

"Now, see here, Charlie Howell!" he shouted back. "You've had your try and come up with a handful of shine-rag and damn little else. Now it's my turn, and see if I don't give you cards, spades, and a beating when it comes to it!"

Despite the growing distance, Howell pitched several more substantial pieces of stone and brick, as if hoping to sink the little skiff by knocking a hole in it. One of the pieces landed in the boat, causing Dicky Tiptoe to yelp and massage his foot. There was shouting from the boat station on the other bank, and one of the boatmen came running across Folly Bridge to prevent further damage to his property.

"I'll have you thrashed for this, Tiptoe! See if I don't!" Howell waved away the boatman's protests as he shouted after his betrayer. But he had lost the present battle, and he knew it. Dicky Tiptoe was like a troublesome fly, easily swatted in the end but distinctly elusive at the moment in his little skiff. Even if he waited at the boating station, Howell thought, Tiptoe had only to abandon the skiff at some other point on either bank of the river in order to escape him easily. Even if he caught him, what precisely could he do?

Added to this was the awareness that he must return to London sooner or later. The lynx-eyed young maid, Mrs. Jones, had been frog-marched from water-closet to basement. She was secured in a cellar with bread, cheese, water, and a convenient bucket. Now that Tiptoe's own words appeared to confirm the girl's innocence of the theft, Howell felt an added obligation to return and release her.

Dicky Tiptoe watched Howell from a safe distance as the tall, cream-suited figure, the hat now on its head, walked away towards Folly Bridge and the town. The clocks of Oxford struck two, the sound ruffling the warm air until an idyllic stillness returned upon river and meadow. The dragonflies hovered and the bees sang. Major Tiptoe could have dozed, indeed appeared to do so, his hat almost over his eyes as he lay back in the skiff.

No one would have detected a flicker of interest as his heart leapt with excitement. Sarah Ashmole, Jane, and the Chantrey sisters were standing on the slipway of the boating station while two watermen pulled one of the little craft alongside and helped them in. The major could not be sure, of course, but he rather thought that this was the afternoon for which he had been waiting.

He allowed the other boat to pass him as he lay under the branches of the meadow bank. Sarah Ashmole sat in the stern holding the lines. Jane and Nerissa Chantrey, as the two elder girls, had taken the sculls.

The stream was busier now, as the several picnic parties set out, yet by comparison with Oxford in June, the vacation river was well-nigh deserted. However, Major Tiptoe judged it safe to slip downstream in discreet pursuit of his quarry. They stopped, as he thought they would, near Iffley pool, where the river formed a natural bathing place on the thickly wooded bank. He waited until they had landed and their attention was given to preparations for the afternoon's bathing. Then he drifted past, just round a corner of the bank that would conceal his boat from sight. For all that, he was close enough in the still afternoon to catch the sound of their voices.

The camera and its tripod remained in the case. Yet it was the work of a moment to set them up when the time came. Indeed, the equipment was sufficiently light and simple for him to carry the camera already mounted to the place from which the pictures would be taken. He waited a little longer, however, telling himself that the time was not yet.

Just before three, the Christ Church porter noticed the prim black-suited figure of Mr. Dodgson going out past the lodge and turning towards High Street, perhaps en route to Magdalen Bridge and the Botanic Garden. It was the only event that disturbed the porter-s mid-afternoon tranquillity.

Another hour of high summer passed into history. Charles Augustus Howell sat in the corner seat of the railway carriage and watched the grey towers of Oxford recede. He sucked voraciously at a freshly lit cigar and fretted over the business of the day.

A mile or so away, Prudence stood outside the gates of Trinity in a yellow dress and bonnet, twirling a matching parasol over her shoulder. Her eyes seemed to follow those of every man who passed. She appeared to be waiting for someone, though not for any one person in particular. Presently there arrived a little man in a black gown and suit, a high collar and a white bow-tie, the black felt tile of a mortarboard set firmly on his head.

"Miss Tiptoe?" he asked politely. "Miss Prudence Tiptoe?"

It was not her true name and so she was hesitant to respond to it. She thought how old the little man looked.

"What if I am?"

"Daughter of Major Richard Tiptoe." Now it was a statement rather than a question.

"What's it to you?" Her defiance came out as a resentful squeal.

"What it is to me, Miss Tiptoe, is that I must take you under arrest."

"You?" She could hardly stop herself laughing. "You call yourself the police, do you?"

"Alas, no, Miss Tiptoe. I am the senior proctor of this university. I therefore hold the power to arrest and detain in custody any person in this city, whether a member of the university or not. A serious complaint has been made against Major Tiptoe and yourself by a senior member of a college. I must ask you to come with me."

Prudence was preparing a sardonic reply to the frail little man. Then she noticed the two other figures who stood politely at a short distance behind him, as if unwilling to intrude upon the tête-à-tête. Each was dressed alike in dark suit and waistcoat with black hat. Their broad shoulders and burly chests, the impassive strength of jaw and forehead, confirmed her fears.

"Please," said the little man gently, "if you will come with me and my men, I promise you that your detention shall be no longer than is absolutely necessary. We shall endeavour to make you comfortable in your confinement."

The girl had long ago learnt how to deal with the police in such situations as this. Now she felt a fear of the unfamiliar world, a place where the ordinary laws and customs she had known ceased to apply.

"I wish I'd stayed home in London," she sobbed quietly, as the little man shepherded her away. "I wish I'd never come near this nasty, beastly place!"

"There, there," said the little proctor gently. "No need for a scene in the street, if you please!"

When they reached the tall, sunlit room in the Clarendon Building, the little man sat at a desk. Prudence was given a chair facing him. The two muscular "bulldogs" stood behind her with arms folded.

The proctor looked up at her kindly, his pince-nez twinkling a little in the light as he set them upon his nose.

"Now then," he said, in a tone that was almost paternal. "What we must know from you is where we can find Major Tiptoe."

"I don't know!" she squalled. "May I never set eyes on the nasty brute again!"

"Your own father?" said the proctor in quiet reproof.

"He's not my father! He has me when he fancies me and blacks me eye when he don't! That's who he is."

"Oh, dear!" The little man rose and walked to the window, looking down the sunlit vista of Broad Street in his black plumage, tapping the pince-nez on his thumbnail. "Oh, dear. Oh, dear."

While the courteous interrogation continued in the fine corniced room overlooking Broad Street and the formal gardens of Trinity, the under-porter opened the glass-panelled door of the lodge in the archway of Tom Quad. The senior porter of Christ Church was on duty just then, behind the broad wooden counter. His deputy stood before it with an air of importance allowable in a man with bad news to impart.

"Well?" said the senior porter.

"Mr. Dodgson's dead," whispered the deputy, hardly bothering to conceal a curious pleasure in announcing the tragedy. "Found drowned in the river a few minutes ago. He'd been at his photography again."

The under-porter gave his superior a straight look, as if they both knew what the photography implied in Mr. Dodgson's case.

"No he's not," said the senior porter dismissively. "Mr. Dodgson went up to his rooms ten minutes back. Called in for his afternoon post on the way."

The second porter, who had been anticipating an outburst of dismay or astonishment, or at least a philosophical reflection such as "It comes to us all in the end," sat down hard on a small wooden chair and shook his head in bewilderment.

Sergeant Lumley of the Oxford City Police attended the senior proctor's office soon afterwards. His port-wine face, a match for the waistcoat of the Mitre innkeeper, and the moisture of his dark whiskers were the only evidence of the light perspiration gathering under the dark serge of tunic and trousers. Helmet clutched awkwardly in his hand, he joined the little group around the proctor's desk.

"Mr. Inspector Merriman's compliments, sir! Thought you'd like to know a man's been pulled from the river down at Iffley. Looks like it's 'im you want."

"Well, I never," said the little proctor mildly, taking the bereavement easily.

"They sent the dogcart straight to Woodstock for Inspector Swain. He's there on a matter of missing jewels. Mr. Swain's a Scotland Yard man, sir!"

The sergeant's pride in the magnitude of the tragedy was visible. The proctor contrived to be courteously impressed.

"Is he? Is he indeed? How very remarkable!"

The senior porter of Christ Church had slipped away from his duty, leaving his deputy at the counter in the lodge. He followed the general direction of the crowd that was moving across Folly Bridge and along the towpath towards Iffley. The distance was not great, and he came soon enough to the place where the sightseers were being coaxed back with difficulty by several uniformed policemen.

It seemed that the catastrophe had occurred at the weir. A little boat still turned in slow circles in the pools of the currents below it, despite the efforts of the officers on the bank to draw it in with their boathooks. On the grass, by the overhanging trees, lay a body in suiting that had been darkened to plum colour by immersion.

"Mr. Dodgson, indeed!" said the senior porter, impatient at his deputy's foolishness. "In fancy clothes like them!"

Yet as he walked away along the bank, he saw how the mistake might have occurred. Deserted now, but for a single policeman in careful attendance, the wooden box of a Piozzi-Smith camera stood upon its tripod behind a clump of hawthorn like an abandoned totem.

Rumour murmured through the crowd of onlookers, drawing attention to each new arrival in case he should be the Scotland Yard man, Inspector Swain. Perhaps it was a tribute to his professionalism that when he arrived, the flamelight of torches already wavering upon the mournful scene by the river, no one gave him a second glance.

To say that Alfred Swain had a face like a horse was not altogether an insult. It was a long equine face that suggested good breeding and mildness. The willing intelligence of the species showed frequently in his steady gaze. Alfred Swain's father had eloped with the daughter of the manor house. The young woman had died in childbirth and the father, a country schoolmaster, followed her to the grave when Alfred Swain was ten years old. He left the boy nothing but a few small debts and a curiosity about books.

At twenty-nine years old, Swain liked to regard himself however modestly as a thinking man of the Victorian world. He was as yet too poor—and indeed too cautious—to be anything but a bachelor. In his leisure he was apt to console his solitude with *Idylls of the King* for pleasure and *Modern Science and Modern Thought* for improvement. Naturally he was regarded with suspicion by his superiors and with ribaldry by his subordinates.

Despite such petty hostilities, Swain had made his way in the Criminal Investigation Division. Eccentricities were not more tolerable there than among the uniformed men. However, among his other equine gifts, he had the aptitude for learning and remembering the tricks of the trade. In the tall skull, under the dome of straight fair hair, the strategies of the criminal and the tactics of the hunter had been learnt and filed for easy reference.

Among his other vices, Swain was apt to speak so softly on occasion that his companions did not hear him and were obliged to ask him to repeat what he had said. By the time they reached the place on the riverbank where the torchlight flared upon the sodden corpse, Inspector Merriman had given up all attempts at conversation.

Alfred Swain stood over the dead man, looking down at the face now rubicund with a post-mortem flush and the brown locks flattened by their sousing in the waters of Isis. He did not stoop, nor did he examine the corpse more closely.

"Dicky Tiptoe," he said gently, as if the major could hear the soft regret in his voice. "Ah, yes, we know him, gentlemen. We know him very well indeed."

— IV —

Inspector Swain

VI

Inspector Swain

2 I

SWAIN AND SERGEANT LUMLEY arrived at the Mitre Inn as a
riot began. A high-spirited coaching party had drawn in from
town and was in the process of putting the rest of the customers
to flight. Swain knew the type as soon as he saw the first young
man, flushed with wine, standing in the hallway, splendid in bottle-green riding coat, top-boots, and the blond whiskers of a
dragoon. The kind of young devil, Swain guessed, who shot
pigeons at Hurlingham, drove four-in-hand in the Park, had a
box for his women at every racecourse, and thought himself the
most dashed good-natured fellow in London.

Just now, the young blood was cracking his long coachwhip
down the length of the panelled hall, sending the maidservants
scurrying back to the kitchens with screams of agreeable apprehension.

"Give me a mop and a bucket of dirty water!" shouted a woman
from the scullery. "I'll soon trundle the nasty thing out of his
fist!"

The panting young hussar took no notice of Swain in his plain
clothes but the sight of Sergeant Lumley in constabulary tunic
and helmet had an immediate and quieting effect. Outside in the
High Street the way was still blocked by the coach, whose horses

171

were now beyond the control of their driver. They reared and champed, breasts flecked with foam, as he cracked the whip over their heads and tugged at the reins with hopeless cries of "Oh, you would, would you, you beasts!"

Swain regarded such young men with a contempt tempered by unease. He had no intention of involving himself with the commotion their arrival had caused. Seeking out the keeper of the Mitre, he produced his warrant-card, demanding to see Major Tiptoe's rooms and any possessions of the major's that might have been entrusted to the keeper's care. He was extremely gratified when the small deed-box was produced. If there was a clue to Major Tiptoe's death anywhere in the Mitre, a locked deed-box was by far the most promising place.

The innkeeper waited, his fingers touched together in an attitude of prayer, while Swain wrote out an official receipt for the deed-box and the key to the major's rooms. Followed by Sergeant Lumley, he went up the carpeted staircase to the floor above.

Two uniformed constables were already posted outside the door. He gave Merriman credit for that, never expecting that a provincial police inspector would have acted with such speed. He sent them away, left Lumley to guard the door in their place, and let himself into Tiptoe's rooms, carrying the deed-box under his arm.

Only the oil light from the street outside cast a tawny glow through open curtains as Swain crossed the room and put the deed-box on the desk. Then the gas mantles above the mahogany table in the sitting-room spluttered into harsh brilliance as he put a match to them. He drew the heavy velvet curtains across the windows to deaden the sound of iron-rimmed carriage wheels on the cobbles of High Street.

A search of the rooms revealed little enough. There was a wardrobe of cheap, flashy clothing of a "sporting" kind. He found a small travelling cabinet containing proprietary medicaments for the trivial embarrassments of middle-age. Also in the cabinet were a bottle of dye, the colour of Major Tiptoe's fine dark hair and whiskers, and a little box of rouge that brought the honest tan of the newly returned Indian officer to the sallow cheeks of the trickster. There were one or two well-thumbed novelettes, a small box of cigars, and a dimple-bottle of whisky. Rather more promising was a set of female clothing—the clothes of a child, he thought—in one of the drawers.

Swain had been vexed to hear that the girl known as "Miss Prudence Tiptoe" had been released by the kind old proctor on the news of her "father's" death. Yet the mistake was not irretrievable. She was better known to him, and a good many others, as "Posture Prudence" for the displays of her slender nudity presented in certain penny gaffs and cigar-divans. It would not be too hard to find her again when she was needed.

Among the rouge and hair-dye was a key that fitted the deed-box. Strictly speaking, he should have waited until some authorisation was given before opening it. However, enough time had been wasted already, and there would be ways of concealing so small an irregularity. Swain unlocked the tin box and raised the lid.

He was disappointed at first to see nothing more than a few photographic prints and plates in a green box, and a roll of papers tied with pink ribbon. Blackmail, of course; he had expected that, for it was Dicky Tiptoe's profession. Yet the first items seemed so trivial to him.

There was a copy of a letter to one Mrs. Sarah Ashmole, alleging improper conduct with her lodger, Thomas Godwin. Poor Tiptoe, he thought! How the mighty were fallen!

Among the prints were several of a naked girl, "Jane, by an Oxonian," that looked no more than the postcards sold by the sham-indecent trade near the Strand. Then there were pictures of the same girl, naked with a man in clerical dress. That was more like it, but still blackmail on a modest scale. Next he unfolded a scrap of paper. This time the letter was incomplete and had apparently been discarded in favour of the other sent to Mrs. Ashmole. No mention of Mr. Thomas Godwin. Instead, there was a proposal that for a sum of £200, photographs of young Jane Ashmole naked with the Reverend Charles Dodgson should be returned to the girl's mother, complete with glass-plate negatives.

Swain looked again at the pictures. In his mind he saw again the portrait published in the *Saturday Review*, some years before, in an article about *Alice's Adventures in Wonderland*.

That *was* more like it! His respect for Dicky Tiptoe's professional skill was largely restored. There was evidence of other schemes in preparation. Assignations between a certain Major Kitchener and a young gentleman. A mere beginning for a blackmailer but full of rich promise. Two private notes from young ladies—the original manuscripts—complained of the conduct of Mr. Asquith, a rising young Treasury counsel. He had revealed his manhood to their astonished hands while on the sofa at a respectable house party. Again, Swain admitted, Dicky Tiptoe had begun well. A sentimental, romantic letter of proposal from the master of Balliol, Benjamin Jowett, to Miss Florence Nightingale, with that lady's reply. Some people, Swain thought, would pay a high price to prevent such of their literary manuscripts from going to auction.

That had proved to be the case with young Mr. Swinburne's effusions. How the price had mounted when the rogue Howell began to give semi-public readings of the rich young man's fantasies of his own sexual humiliation. And how eagerly the price was paid!

Swain opened the last papers. Then he knew that his estimate of Dicky Tiptoe had been grievously in error. He saw before him now a "a real show," the dream of every extortioner. It was the absolute guarantee of immunity. To bring Tiptoe to court and reveal what lay in the deed-box would be to risk bringing down in tatters the fabric of respect for Church and State.

There was one letter, in unambiguous terms it seemed to Swain, from the young Prince Albert Victor, second in succession to the throne, to another young cadet on HMS *Britannia*. It had every appearance of authenticity. Yet such a letter alone might have been dismissed as youthful folly, even as a joke. Setting that letter aside, there was much worse to come.

Swain saw before him the documentation of a scandal, past and present, that had grown into the very structure of law and government. There were amorous notes, going back for more than twenty years, detailing the unnatural practices of Dr. Vaughan, headmaster of Harrow, with those boys whom he selected as his "bitches." Swain read the names with fascination. They included several who, if the case came to court, must have taken a part as counsel in the prosecution.

Nor was that the worst. Several parents of the boys had, it seemed, discovered the truth. Dr. Vaughan resigned to forestall a prosecution. There then followed several notes between Downing Street and Lambeth Palace, the archbishop and the prime minister revealing their knowledge of Dr. Vaughan's conduct. Yet the purpose of the notes was to determine whether, as a reward for his sense of duty in resigning, he should be given the Bishopric of Rochester or some lesser recognition.

The effect of such revelations would scarcely be reduced by certain photographs at the bottom of Dicky Tiptoe's treasure trove. They did not rival the revelation that the prime minister and the archbishop had combined to conceal and even reward Dr. Vaughan's corruption of the nation's future leaders. Yet there, as a general election approached, was William Ewart Gladstone smiling and talking to young women with painted faces whose trade was not hard to guess. The photographs had been taken surreptitiously with one of the new, easily concealed cameras. Most showed the Grand Old Man accosting the girls in city streets. In one picture, however, he was sitting beside a girl on a park bench, addressing her earnestly. His arm was injudiciously stretched along the top of the wooden seat behind her shoulders.

Anyone who knew the great man's reforming zeal would see that the photographs showed nothing sinister. Among those who did not know him, the effect might be explosive. The House of Commons tolerated his eccentricity and called him "Old Glad-Eye." Lord Taunton had asked privately why only the *pretty* prostitutes were taken back to the wholesome atmosphere of Downing Street? Would the electors of England be as tolerant? Swain doubted it.

Below him, the coaching party had begun to yodel and crow with drunken enthusiasm. Swain took two of Major Tiptoe's erotic novelettes and locked those in the deed-box, as if they were the truly private papers. The papers and photographs of "the real show" were another matter. He slipped them into an attaché case. Next morning, he decided, he must take them himself to Chief Inspector Montague Toplady, commander of the Criminal Investigation Department at Scotland Yard.

22

THE SECTION-HOUSE OFFICER, whose own premises were full, had found a billet in Oxford for Swain. He was to lodge with Mrs. Wilberforce in St. John Street, a row of unpretentious Georgian houses behind the grander spaces of St. Giles with their fashionable churches and full-leaved elms. The arrangement suited Alfred Swain, who had little taste for the intrusive comradeship of the section-house. Mrs. Wilberforce was younger than he had expected, however, scarcely more than thirty. She was a widow whose husband had been a sergeant in the Oxford City Police. Her soft white skin and dark red hair had a prettiness which called to Swain's mind the appeal of plump young chickens. It was in her eyes that he saw a certain predatory feline instinct.

Despite the arrangements made for him, his first duty was to return to London and wait as long as necessary for a decision about Major Tiptoe's "real show." Sergeant Lumley, under Inspector Merriman's supervision, would be left to ask the obvious questions. Swain set out to walk from St. John Street to the police office in St. Aldate's to record his departure.

As he walked, Swain thought of the dead man, Richard Baptist Tiptoe. Born Richard Baptist, as far as anyone could tell. There was little in his character to appeal to a man of Swain's type. Tiptoe did not fit the cliché of an amiable rogue. Under the bluff *bonhomie* of his bogus military pretensions, he was mean and devious. His erotic novelettes, turned out to order for the slum presses of Holywell Street, showed a sardonic mockery of women that was far more shocking to Alfred Swain than any gross pantomime of copulation. However sad the truth may be, Tiptoe had once remarked, a man must be all-important to himself.

Why, as he walked through the Oxford streets in the fresh leafy brightness of the August morning, did Swain feel a sense of loss, even of bereavement, at Tiptoe's passing? It was, he supposed, a mere pang of mortality. There were passages that his father had recited to young Freddie Swain in his childhood. Quick and retentive, the young memory had stored them away, understanding little of their mystery at the time. Now they made up such formal literary education as he possessed.

"Any man's death diminishes me, because I am involved in mankind." Swain repeated the words to himself. With that, his feelings for Major Tiptoe were carefully classified.

The city mortuary was conveniently situated as a brick extension of the police office. Swain showed his card to the keeper and was admitted to a brightly lit room where the bricks were still unplastered. Major Tiptoe had been carried naked from the main hall on a hurdle. Now he lay upon the copper surface of the autopsy table where a jet of water played upon him to allay the more disagreeable odours. From time to time a sickly whiff of spirit came in Swain's direction.

Dr. Hammond, the police surgeon, was familar to him from a previous case. Hammond nodded curtly, then returned his attention to the saw, the scalpel, the brace and bit with which he proposed to dismember Tiptoe's mortal remains. Swain swallowed hard. It was at times like this that he wished he had acquired the habit of a pipe or a cheroot to shroud himself from the aroma of death. On the other hand, he thought, an enthusiast of Hammond's kind would have been just the sort to resent the intrusion of tobacco smoke.

Swain had never been able to hold his stomach down without a struggle at the preliminary sound of canvas being rent, which the pathologists dignified by calling it an incision in dead flesh. It sounded as if Tiptoe was being torn limb from limb. Swain decided to ask his questions and go.

"Any signs from the preliminary examination, sir? Anything I might take back to tell them in Whitehall Place?"

Hammond's lips drew back in a grin of exertion as he parted Major Tiptoe's flat bedraggled hair with the saw blade, choosing a place to begin his carpentry.

"A blow to the head, Mr. Swain. A hole more than an inch square in the crown of the skull. Made by a paling taken from the fence that divides the riverbank from Lord Rodric's lands. Paling thrown in the river, but found under the bank by one of your men this morning. Matching splinter, size of a darning-needle, tweezered from the wound."

"Struck by an assailant before he went into the water?" Swain asked. He was beginning to feel distinctly unwell in the odours of death and preservative, so that the question sounded more stupid than he realised.

"Hardly likely, Mr. Swain, that he'd be swimming in the Isis with a hole the size of a gob-stopper in his skull. Two inches into the grey matter it goes. Come, Mr. Swain, see for yourself how you may insert your entire finger into it, almost to the knuckle."

Swain shook his head and swallowed hard. Dr. Hammond had won this round and they both knew it.

"Come, Mr. Swain! Wait till I saw him through along the line of his parting. We shall sit him up and you shall greet Major Tiptoe without his cranium! A miracle in nature, Mr. Swain, and nothing to blanch at!"

Swain headed for the door. As he closed it behind him, he heard the voice still murmuring. Yet it was no longer for his benefit. Alone on such occasions, Hammond was in the habit of conversing in subdued monologue with a corpse as he dismembered it.

Walking round the side of the building, Swain entered the

police office, presenting himself to the duty inspector in his sentry-like office near the entrance. Sergeant Lumley had been at work since the early morning. Despite Swain's forebodings, Lumley had assembled an impressive collection of evidence from various witnesses, as well as from Tiptoe's effects.

"The watch in his pocket, sir. Stopped with the blow at 3.35. That might come in handy. Worn in the front fob. Struck from behind, he'd have fallen right on it, sir. It's busted flat."

"And the persons whose names I gave you last night?" Swain asked.

"Mrs. Sarah Ashmole present, close by at Iffley pool with three young ladies. Her own daughter, Jane, and the two Chantrey sisters. There from three o'clock until gone five. Heard nothing. Anything known of her?"

"No," said Swain, "not by the police anyway."

"Mr. Thomas Godwin," Lumley glanced at his list again, "came there at about five to escort the ladies home. At least an hour and more after the blow stopped Tiptoe's watch. Several witnesses to place him in Christ Church until after four. Never out of the sight of the rest of the bathing party when he was at Iffley pool. Anything known of him, sir?"

Swain shook his head and frowned.

"Mr. Charles Howell," said Lumley. This time Swain's eyes brightened.

"Howell? From London? Friend of Tiptoe's?"

"Hardly a friend, sir. Shouting at Tiptoe and threatening him, near Folly Bridge about two. Very fierce. Attempted to strike him. Something about the major robbing him. Mr. Howell also seen catching 4.15 train to town, sir. Definitely able to be at the place of the murder when it happened."

"Good!" said Swain enthusiastically.

"Criminal record, sir?"

"No, Mr. Lumley."

"But known to the police, sir?"

"Oh, yes, Mr. Lumley, known to the police all right."

"How's that then, sir?"

"Official application from Mr. Howell for the exhumation of

the body of Mrs. Elizabeth Rossetti from Highgate Cemetery, to retrieve a volume of Mr. Rossetti's manuscript poems from the coffin. Details of the application passed to Scotland Yard from the Home Office for information. That's how he came on the files."

"Not criminal then, sir?"

"Also, Mr. Lumley, a private word from Admiral and Lady Swinburne. Howell was holding to ransom a score of silly indecent letters signed by their son—Mr. Swinburne, the poet. Written when he was a thoughtless boy. Describing himself beaten and abused by old lechers, as he wished to be. Most embarrassing to him in his fame. Either the Admiral and Lady Jane were to buy them for a small fortune, or Mr. Howell must put them to auction."

"Charges brought, Mr. Swain?"

"No, Mr. Lumley. No charges. The Admiral and Lady Jane paid the price. Mr. Howell's lawyers said he was entitled to sell literary manuscripts in his possession. By offering them to the family first, he showed the consideration of a true gentleman."

"Very neat," said Lumley, admiring Howell's professionalism

"Anyone else, Mr. Lumley?"

"The Reverend Mr. Dodgson of Christ Church, sir. Walked alone beside the river from three till nearly five. No witnesses, no other account he can give, sir. He spent all that time alone."

"Did he, indeed?" said Swain softly. In his mind he saw the photographs again. Jane, by an Oxonian. The surreptitious naked embrace. He thought of what Mr. Dodgson might do to a blackmailer, either to protect himself or the child.

"Looks like either Mr. Howell or Mr. Dodgson must be number one for this, sir," said Lumley cheerfully. "That narrows it down. So does the watch being smashed at half past three."

Swain nodded without committing himself further. He took his leave of Inspector Merriman, had his movement order signed by the station superintendent, and set off to catch the London train. As the sooty brick of warehouses and Gothic churches overshadowed the hansom cab, Swain felt a new satisfaction. It had surprised him that a petty blackmailer of Tiptoe's kind should have assembled such a "real show." That Howell, friend of the mighty, should do so was far more plausible. Not that it made his task easy. Charles Augustus Howell was a man of great intellectual agility, what Swain preferred to think of as slippery as a greased pig.

23

THERE WAS A PAUSE as Hannah the maid came in to light the lamps. Jane Ashmole stood before Godwin's chair, her head bowed and her hands folded at the lap of her lavender-blue dress, as if in a gesture of protective modesty. In the garden, beyond the French windows, the deepening dusk turned the pink flower petals to an appearance of mauve. The whisper of gaslight now obscured the rasp of grasshoppers in the warm undergrowth. In a moment more, the servant blew out her taper and withdrew from the drawing-room.

The girl raised her eyes enough to see, glancing upwards under her brows, the embroidery-screen, the tawny carpet, the dark and aquiline features of Thomas Godwin scrutinising her from his buttoned-leather chair.

"Again," he said quietly, "again! Properly this time. Otherwise I shall conclude that you must be sent away somewhere to be taught these things in the correct manner."

Hardly able to get the words out for the breathlessness that the ordeal brought upon her, Jane struggled with the recitation once more.

> "From an eternity of idleness
> I, God, awoke. In seven days' toil made earth
> From nothing. Rested and created man . . ."

It was repulsion rather than loss of memory that made her stumble at the words that followed.

"Continue, if you please!" Godwin tossed back his dark hair. "Or must I think you deliberately defiant in refusing to learn your lessons?"

"I planted him a paradise . . ."

"No! 'I placed him in a paradise'!"

"I placed him in a paradise . . ."

The carpet shivered through a haze of unshed tears as she prayed to be forgiven for what she must say.

"... and there
Planted the tree of evil, so that he
Might eat and perish, and my soul procure
Wherewith to sate its malice...."

"Stop!" he said, scorn in the sudden laughter. "I do not think that Shelley's verses deserve to be tortured any more upon such a tongue."

There was so much relief in knowing that, for the present at least, she need endure no further. His insults were nothing by comparison with that. It was not, of course, any pity on Thomas Godwin's part that made him end the recitation, the inquisition as it became. Jane guessed that he had seen the figure of her mother, ghostlike in her grey dress, coming through the twilight from the garden alleys.

For all the bitterness between them, Jane and her tormentor had a curious compact, almost a complicity. He might do as he chose, she might weep as she wished, yet Sarah Ashmole must not see the tears.

The girl went over to a chair and sat with her head bowed, unseeing, over a volume of Stevenson. She and Godwin had not been quite quick enough, however. Mrs. Ashmole stood in the opening of the French window, the white and flame of freshly cut madonna lilies drooping over her arm. She might have been a woodcut for Tennyson or Rossetti.

"The child is far too tired by now," she said gently. "Let her say the lesson in the morning."

Godwin laughed good-naturedly. He got up, went over to Sarah Ashmole, and took the lilies to a vase. Presently he chose a cigar from the cedarwood box and went out onto the terrace with her. Their voices grew more distant and a silence settled once more upon the room where the girl sat alone.

Without waiting for any instruction to do so, she went up to her own room. By the light of the fluttering candle flame, Jane Ashmole undressed and hung up her clothes for the next day. Pulling on her white nightgown she knelt by the bed and prayed, dreading that the performance in the drawing-room, the committal to memory of *Queen Mab*'s blasphemy, might build a wall around her, proof against all prayers. It was not a pedagogic whim that had made Thomas Godwin order her to learn the lines by heart. Their scornful sacrilege was woven into her mind, their sneering had become part of her soul's fabric. She knew there was a mark upon her unlike that of any other guilt, for it could never be wiped away.

Lying in bed, she thought of this again, hearing once more the voices on the terrace below her window. The conversation was more intimate than on the occasion of the dinner party, softer and with quiet laughter. At one point she knew that they had walked off into the garden alleys, towards the rich sweetness of perfume from honeysuckle and night-scented stocks.

The footsteps returned. Thomas Godwin stamped his heel upon the terrace and laughed again. There were movements in the rooms below and on the stairs.

It was entirely dark when Jane woke suddenly from sleep without knowing what had roused her or how long she had been dozing. The garden was silent now, not even the cry of the screech-owl sounding remote and mournful as it sometimes did. At first she thought the house was still. Then, through the wall dividing her own room from her mother's, she heard voices that were little more than whispering. It was not the volume of the sound that had woken her but, rather, that there should have been any sound at all.

Jane tried to blind her imagination to the events in the next room, upon which she was an unwilling eavesdropper. There was a sudden hollow gasp, a syllable of shock. Nothing beyond that was audible for several minutes. Then she heard her mother's cries, rising in soft intensity, measured as the rhythm of a heart or pulse. Jane Ashmole, like a child in a nightmare, turned away with her hands over her ears, as if this would protect her from her own destruction.

Before breakfast on the following morning, Thomas Godwin returned, striding over the water meadows from Christ Church with several letters and a copy of *The Times* in his hand. He sat for a moment reading in the same buttoned-leather chair. Then he looked up at the girl, who stood by the window wanting only not to be noticed by him.

"How very singular," he said to her humorously, "how very singular, after all those afternoons on which you have kept poor Mr. Dodgson such very close company, Jane!"

Her first thought was that he might be ill, or dead.

"Why?" she asked, alarmed.

Godwin smiled more gently.

"On that very afternoon of the dead man by the river, they tell me, Mr. Dodgson was alone there with no one to prove him innocent."

"But that's silly!" she said weakly.

He looked at her with ironic confidentiality.

"I wonder, Jane, do you suppose it is God's judgment on you both for your wickedness together? Hmmm? Or is it only a judgment on an evil little girl for reading the bad bold Mr. Shelley that you should not be with your friend when he needed you more than at any time in his life?"

As she continued to stare at him, Godwin dismissed her from his attention and opened the newspaper.

24

O<small>N THE FAR BANK</small> the reapers had begun the harvesting and hay-making in Godstow Meadow. While the labourers scythed the long grass and poppies, the workers from Wolvercote paper-mill constructed the ricks. There were men in waistcoats and breeches with broad-brimmed hats, women with white aprons and dark blouses, their heads kerchiefed and veiled at the back like nursing sisters.

Dodgson shaded his eyes against the bright reflection of sun on the silver and brown river tide, the water purling towards the overhung bank and the slow pool's turn where he had moored the skiff. He fetched the narrow case of glass plates from the boat and went back to Jane Ashmole.

She lay on the soft grass in a white gown of plain silk that he had brought for the occasion.

"Now," he said, "you shall be Ophelia with an armful of wild flowers, or you may be the Sleeping Beauty without them. The Sleeping Beauty, you may know, also went by the name of Miss Ann S. Thesia."

He put down the case of glass-plate negatives, arranged the white gown about her legs, and kissed her gently on the brow.

"The young lady," he explained, "fell into a deep sleep until the day on which she was noticed by a passing prince. He, being as they say in search of a sleeping partner, thought she would answer admirably. Taking her lily-white hand in his—as I do yours—he lifted it to his lips—in this way—and implanted upon it a kiss. This roused the young woman, who, in a most ladylike manner, hit him a resounding box on the ear for his impudence. After so striking a proof of attachment, they were married at once. The bride took several short naps during the ceremony and they lived happily ever after."

He kissed her again, released the hand, and went over to the camera on its stand. Jane lay on her back, her arms folded under her head as she looked up at the sky. It was not at all the pose Dodgson had envisaged.

"He sits in my father's chair," she said suddenly. "The leather chair. Why must he do that? Why does he? Why does Mama not tell him?"

Dodgson looked at her, the furrows produced in the white brow by her bewildered resentment, the tension of her hands, the impatient brushing aside of her fringe of dark hair. Releasing a long breath of resignation, he decided that this was one of those afternoons when photography was out of the question. With any other model, his disappointment would have turned to annoyance. In Jane's case, he felt only a shared foreboding at what was to come.

All his facetious cleverness was of no use now. He went across and sat beside her on the grass, taking her hand gently once more.

"One day, my dearest Unknown Quantity, you shall tell him all these things."

She shook her head.

"I shall never be brave with him. I am always afraid of him. However hard I try, I am afraid when he is in the room. I cannot say the words I mean and, sometimes, it seems as if I cannot make any sound at all!"

"Come now," he said gently, "that is quite absurd. How can Mr. Godwin hurt you?"

"He can!" There were tears in her eyes but she dared not explain herself. "He has ways of doing it! Ways to destroy me!"

"Then your mama will protect you."

She shook her head again.

"She treats him as my father. One day they will marry and then he will be my father, I suppose! But I know he can never be! He hates me so!"

Still he tried to reassure her.

"In a few years, my love, in a very few years from now you will be grown up. These things will not matter much then, for you will live a life of your own."

She turned her head, blinking away the tears as she looked towards the old women in their white aprons and headscarves, raking the hay together, tossing it with their forks.

"Before I grow up, he will make me as wicked as he is already."

"No," he said gently and kissed the crown of her head as she turned from him.

"Yes!" Her passion was close to anger with him now. "He has ways! He has such ways that you would never guess at. With me! With Mama at night, in the other room!"

Now she turned back and stared at him wide-eyed, as if dismayed by his failure to understand her in less explicit words.

Dodgson took a deep breath and tried to explain those things that were impossible to explain. To him the impossibility was more awesome, for he must describe a landscape of passion to which he possessed no more than a sketch map. He knew that such things happened, but he could scarcely envisage how they happened.

"There are men and women who play like children in a game," he said awkwardly. "A game is not the same thing as love. They are like one another's toys. If there is no more to it than that then, like children, they weary of the game and of the toys before long."

"Suppose it should be love?" she said at last.

"Do you believe your mama would ever love a man who did not cherish you?"

Yet as he spoke, Dodgson's assurance was mocked by his vision of Sarah Ashmole, the gentle, weak-willed mistress who would never match Godwin's power and resolve.

"Perhaps she loved him before she loved me," said Jane simply. "Perhaps that is why he hates me."

Dodgson stroked the lank fall of her hair insistently.

"He cannot hate you. Why should he? Even if he did, your mama will never forget that your home is there, with her."

Jane's firm pale face turned to him, her teeth set wonderingly on her lower lip.

"But you *know*," she said gently, "surely you know! I am at home with you. Whenever I am with you, wherever it is. Then I am at home. Never anywhere else."

They were on dangerous territory now, as Dodgson saw it. He was in no position to contend with Sarah Ashmole or even Thomas Godwin for possession of the girl's allegiance. There being no other reply he could make, Dodgson kissed her again and then stretched back on the grass, gazing up at the burnt blue of the August sky above Godstow and the river.

"If I'd been with you *then*!" she said softly, her shadow falling on him as she leant over and stroked his face. "If only I'd been with you then!"

He guessed what she meant. Without discussing the matter of Major Tiptoe's death and the investigations that had begun, he knew that she would have heard the rumours somehow. Godwin would know of them—Sarah Ashmole, too, he supposed.

"How could it matter?" he said gently.

"It matters a good deal!" Jane was indignant with the world on his behalf and he smiled at this.

"I don't suppose they will carry me off to prison for it," he said, laughing at her solemnity. "I should make a poor enough figure in the dock. As for the day Jack Ketch stood me upon his trap and fitted the rope to my neck, I should not have the least idea of the customary courtesies. Perhaps he would expect me to pay him for his services. And perhaps I should not even have the money."

The haunting folklore of judges and executioners, the two types indistinguishable in the girl's mind, filled her with awe.

"If only I'd been there and could tell them you had nothing to do with the murder!"

Now there was darkness over his face as she lowered her head even more and the brown hair hung to touch the grass.

"You would not be believed," he said, smiling at her again. "People who love one another are never believed. Why, they will tell lies for one another, they will even murder for one another."

"As I would for you—and you for me," said Jane fiercely, falling upon him in determined possession.

25

By THE TIME that Swain stood at ease before Chief Inspector Toplady's desk, it was evident that the chief inspector had spoken of Major Tiptoe to some very important people indeed.

"Here's a pretty pickle, mister!" He spoke habitually in the voice of one whose throat was roughened by shouting and argument.

"Sir," said Swain respectfully, and watched his superior turn to the papers again.

Toplady. What freak of genealogy had given this name, suggestive of feminine elegance, to the chief inspector? As it happened, Montague Toplady was the great-nephew of an even more famous bearer of those names—Augustus Montague Toplady, who had fought for Calvinism against free-will and had written a famous hymn, "Rock of Ages."

Chief Inspector Toplady had the appearance of a sturdy, bow-legged gnome. His head was absurdly large for his body. The grizzled hair was cut almost as short as a "Newgate fringe," so that it stood upright, stiff and wiry, with an impression of energy or fright. At every turn of his head the high collar scraped his cheeks. Swain waited in some apprehension, half expecting that a sudden downward glance might cause the cruelly starched collar point to pierce the chief inspector's eyeball.

"Here's a pickle, mister! Here's a pretty pickle!"

Toplady spoke without looking up from the papers.

"Yes, sir," said Swain again. He continued to stand at ease, like a soldier in the presence of his commander, one hand resting lightly in the other behind his back.

Beyond the window he could see the river, moving from Westminster down towards Blackfriars. Penny steamers with tall black funnels scurried among the rust-coloured sails of the collier barges. On the slime of the foreshore female mudlarks scavenged under the overhanging hulls of barges awaiting cargo. They waded thigh-deep in the ooze, picking stray coals from among the broken crockery and dead cats left by the receding tide.

Chief Inspector Toplady glared at the papers in his hand, as if he hated Tiptoe, the victims, and Swain himself. All of this, Swain thought, was extremely probable. A quarter of a century before, Toplady had been an artillery officer in the Crimea. When his position was almost overrun, he had fought hand to hand with greatcoated Russian infantry in the blind and bloody Battle of Inkerman. It had been a brief experience of the slaughterhouse of war. Yet alone among his officers he had seen such things and he was not apt to let the others forget it.

"Mary Anns!" he said suddenly, slapping the papers with the back of his hand and glaring directly at Swain from his dark little eyes.

"Sir?" said Swain courteously, the long equine face eager to understand.

"Mary Anns!" said Toplady violently. "Don't y'know what a Mary Ann is, mister? Don't you?"

"Yes, sir." Swain swallowed lightly. "I believe I do."

"Believe? You *believe* you do? How long have you been in the force, mister?"

"Nine years, sir."

"Nine *years*? And now I must tell you what a Mary Ann is? Have y'not seen them everywhere? The men that dress in so many frills and colours they might be taken for women? The soft voices? Have y'not heard them everywhere? The poetry books and the lilies? The white hands and the smooth cheeks? The country is ruled by Mary Anns, mister—has been these last twenty years and more."

Swain blushed a little and shifted uneasily. A glimmer of triumph shone in Toplady's dark eyes.

"School-miss poetry books, mister! White hands! Lady's hands!"

Swain, his own hands now clenched behind his back, coloured a little more.

"With respect, sir . . ."

"With respect, sir!" scowled Toplady. "Parlourmaid's language! I wonder y'don't curtsy, mister, and be done with it. Nine years! And y'must be told what a Mary Ann is. There are so many of them in Church and State a man could scarcely count 'em! If it were otherwise, such scoundrels as this Tiptoe would starve in silence."

"The papers may be forgeries, sir."

Toplady looked at him with despair for Swain's stupidity.

"If they were forgeries, mister, you would still be looking for our murderer in Oxford, and I should not be playing nursemaid to our betters. Since you came back, the Treasury Solicitor has asked a discreet question or two. The matter of the prime minister, the archbishop, and the Harrow master is beyond question. As to the rest, the worst of 'em are true. The small fry y'must see for yourself."

Swain drew out a list.

"If Tiptoe was killed that afternoon, sir, as it seems he must have been, only Howell and three others were close enough to do it. Mr. Jowett was in Tenby, all the rest at some more or less public function."

He had expected that Toplady might be pleased by his skill in narrowing down the number of possible murderers. Instead the gnome face with its bulbous nose continued to scowl back at him.

"You don't draw pay for telling me who *can't* have killed him, mister! Find me the man who did! For all you know, it may have nothing whatever to do with this pickle here!"

In this, at least, Swain was bound to concede that the chief inspector might be right.

"And y'may as well know . . ." Toplady's gravel voice sounded weary at last, pausing in mid-sentence.

"Sir?"

"Y'may as well know . . ." Toplady got to his feet, stocky and bow-legged as he faced the young inspector. "Y'may as well know that our masters have chosen you as their man. You are to tell them how Tiptoe died and what it has to do with this pretty pickle of extortion."

"I shall be honoured . . ."

"Yes, yes!" snapped Toplady. "They see in you a man like themselves with a soft voice and a liking for poetry books. They trust in your discretion. None of this—this blackmail in the papers—must ever be known. You understand?"

"Yes, sir," said Swain humbly. He could think only of the fact that in a few moments more he might be out of Toplady's presence and away from it for weeks to come.

"A discreet man!" said Toplady contemptuously. "A man fit to hold secrets! A man safe with the sort of secrets that ought only to belong among women!"

Unlike other men who were apt to think afterwards of the savage retorts they might have made to adversaries in argument, the chief inspector brought them effortlessly, like rabbits from a hat, during the course of conversation.

"May I . . ." Swain began again.

"Hold your tongue," said Toplady, with quiet contempt. "Not one word of all this." He shook the papers in his hand. "Not one word is to be told. When you have your man at last—or perhaps your woman—you will come to me. No arrest. No accusation. Not a word until I have been informed. You understand that?"

"Yes, sir."

Beyond the window, in the sunlight of the outer world, the female mudlarks were retreating up the foreshore with their haul of coals.

"A discreet man!" Toplady stood with his back to Swain, gazing out across the brown river. "Are you a discreet man, Swain?"

"I hope I may prove so, sir."

"Hope you may prove so!" Toplady followed this with a sniff of derision. "What kind of an answer is that for a *man*? Eh? What sort of an answer, mister?"

"The truth, sir."

Toplady stared at him with a certain curiosity for what seemed like a very long time to Swain.

"Go about your business," he said at length. Swain prepared to bring himself to attention, but the chief inspector had not yet finished.

"Great confidence has been placed in you, Swain, by those who decide upon such things. Be sure you justify that trust, sir. For, if you do not, mister, I will have you. You may depend upon it!"

Swain came to attention smartly and Toplady bared his teeth for an instant. It was an expression that anyone seeing him at a distance, and not knowing him, might have taken for a smile.

Alfred Swain gained his freedom at last, closing the door of Toplady's office as he left. He walked thoughtfully towards the communal office where the inspectors of the Criminal Investigation Department had their desks. A man on detail to other duties in another area was expected to clear his desk before leaving. It was a rule of Toplady's little kingdom, suggesting that the permanent departure of his subordinates might have given him a pure and lasting satisfaction.

Inspector Wilks, rotund and moustached, greeted Swain as he came in.

"You was lucky, you was!" he said.

"Oh?" said Swain mildly.

"Being in Oxford and all that when the Commissioner's annual parade and inspection was on."

"Oh," said Swain, "that!"

"Moth in the uniforms," said Wilks through a mouthful of cheese. "Holes the size of a half-crown down the arms. Bloody section-house. Can't darn them without it showing. We wasn't half roasted by bloody Toplady and the guv'nor, parading like that!"

He continued the disjointed account while Swain murmured sympathetically and looked at the note left for him. The Oxford

City Police had confirmed Swain's evidence to suggest that the late Major Tiptoe had died at 3.35 p.m. precisely on the day in question.

It was the first piece of encouraging news that Swain had so far received. Glancing up, he was confronted by the furrowed brow and ruminating jaws of Inspector Wilks, still pondering on the matter of the Commissioner's inspection. Wilks swallowed, clearing his mouth partially. He gave a half nod of his head.

"You was lucky, you was," he insisted. "No doubt about that."

26

THE BELL on the loop of steel gave out its dry cracked note as Swain pushed open the shop door. Ferdinando, who had been eating a bun as he stood behind the counter, stopped chewing. He looked at Swain with an expression of apprehension and malevolence.

"Come now, Ferdy," said the inspector gently, "that's no way for a cove to take his lunch. There's no call for a man to suffer the pains of indigestion on top of all his other troubles."

Ferdinando chewed a little more and then swallowed. He put the remainder of the bun down on the wooden counter.

"You've no right to be in here," he said gracelessly.

Swain was undismayed by the rebuke.

"A man may enter a shop, Ferdy. How can the world do business otherwise?"

He closed the door behind him. The cracked bell jangled again. A draught disturbed the dead flies and yellowed photographs of ballet girls in the dusty window. Ferdinando's head moved from side to side, trying to see beyond the inspector, to catch a glimpse of a raiding party—uniformed officers and porters of the National Vigilance Association—in the littered street outside.

Swain spread out his hands.

"I've come alone, Ferdy," he said in the same gentle voice, the long equine face pleading his sincerity. "I shan't call for company unless I have to."

Ferdinando was sufficiently reassured to take another bite from his bun.

"Is't about Tiptoe?"

"Yes, Ferdy, it's about Tiptoe."

"No use asking me, then. Hadn't seen him in donkey's years. He was always a bloody fool." Ferdinando concluded his statement with a suggestion of dismissive sympathy.

Swain came forward and placed his large, long-fingered hands on the counter.

"You won't mind me asking, though, will you Ferdy?"

"Nothing to say."

The shopkeeper seemed sulky rather than frightened in the face of the inspector's persistence. Swain appeared genuinely sorry.

"I think you have, Ferdy. Not for others, perhaps, but for me."

Before Ferdinando could stop him, his long arm had reached over the counter, the hand curving under it. Just below the counter was a box of prints that Ferdinando used to entice his gulls to the "special collection" of treasures he kept under lock and key. Swain straightened up with one of the cards in his hand.

"Jupiter and Anty-ope," said Ferdinando defiantly. "You could see much the same identical object hanging on the walls of the National Gallery, if you'd bother to walk half a mile!"

"The name is An-*tie*-o-pee," said Swain pedantically, "should you ever wish to refer to it in open court. Moreover, I would hardly think the figures or conduct of your photographers' models were a match for those of Correggio."

He handed the print back to Ferdinando, who continued to stare at him morosely.

"Who sent you here to bait me?"

"No one," Swain said reasonably. "I merely require certain information from you. After that, my interest in you ceases. When the good Major Tiptoe called upon you lately, what was his object?"

Swain knew from his own observation that Tiptoe had accompanied Howell to Holywell Street. All the same, he was gratified by a sudden affability in the sallow face as the shopkeeper snatched at the promise of Swain's interest in him ceasing.

"Almost nothing," he said eagerly. "Tiptoe was stony-broke. Had some photographs he thought I might use. I told him they were dead lead. He went on a bit and in the end I gave him a sovereign or two. He'd had words put to them but that didn't improve 'em much."

"Show me," said Swain quietly.

Ferdinando unlocked a drawer, rummaged in it, and produced the prints of Jane Ashmole, identical to the two in Tiptoe's box. As Swain examined them, he continued to express his willingness to help.

"If only you'd said, Mr. Swain! If only you'd said that was what you wanted, instead of coming in here with a face like winter and frightening a poor chap silly!"

"Who was with him?"

"No one!" Ferdinando gave a little laugh at the absurdity of it.

"I'll be having a word with a young lady of your acquaintance," said Swain pleasantly. "The one they call Posture Prudence. It might make the world go round a lot smoother if you were to tell me the reason of your introducing her to Mr. Howell and Tiptoe."

"I never had the pleasure of her acquaintance," said Ferdinando sincerely.

Swain sighed. He drew the shopkeeper's attention to a little pantomime being played in the street outside. From the direction of the Strand came a well-dressed man with a coat too warm for the season. However, by turning up its collar he was able to conceal his identity. As he drew level with the window of the little shop his steps grew slower. He paused and looked at the yellowing ballet girls and the novels of the harem. As if making a sudden decision, he turned sharply into the doorway and came face to face with Swain's uniformed constable from Maiden Lane. It was quite simple to step past. Yet the well-dressed man turned about and set off along the shabby street with a brisk stride, disappearing round the corner without slackening the pace.

Ferdinando looked at the inspector with consternation.

"Be fair, Mr. Swain! I can't do business with a uniformed jack on the bloody doorstep!"

Swain shrugged.

"You may need his protection, Ferdy. Some of the gulls who find that their sealed packets are nothing but Bible tracts might turn very nasty. I'll see there's a man in position from now on. Better safe than sorry."

"All right," said Ferdinando, as if it really did not matter to him at all. "Tiptoe knew Posture Prue. Don't ask me what they did together."

"And Mr. Howell of Southampton Row?"

The shopkeeper's face brightened again.

"Funny you should ask about it, Mr. Swain. He was in here the very afternoon poor old Tiptoe fell in the river. Came in about three o'clock."

"He was still in Oxford at four," said Swain coolly.

"Oh," said Ferdinando casually, "must have been some other afternoon." He took the rest of his bun and popped it into his mouth.

Swain gave another sigh and turned to the door.

"Anything else, Mr. Swain?" asked the shopkeeper quickly. "If there's anything I could do for Dicky Tiptoe . . ."

The offer remained unacknowledged. Swain opened the door and spoke to the uniformed constable in his mild, poetry-reading voice.

"Take this person into custody, Mr. Tulloch. See him lodged safely in Bow Street. My compliments to Inspector Brennan there, and perhaps he'd be good enough to take an inventory of the stock."

"Why?" howled Ferdinando angrily. "You got what you wanted! Why?"

Swain turned, his manner suggesting that an explanation was not required of him but that he gave it out of pure friendship.

"The Obscene Publications Act of 1857, Ferdy. It may surprise you to learn that you are in apparent breach of most of its provisions. Do your duty, Mr. Tulloch!"

He saw Ferdinando gather breath for expostulation at this betrayal and then turned on his heel. The outburst reached him as a volley of incoherent farmyard rage when he came to the end of the street and returned once more to the bustle and glare of the Strand.

27

HALF AN HOUR LATER Swain sat on the edge of the rumpled bed in the Essex Street room while Prue pulled the sheet close around her neck. She bit at her thumbnail while her hard little face scanned his own in hope and apprehension. Swain waited until the client had pulled the braces on to his shoulders, buttoned himself, and made a hasty departure carrying his jacket and shoes.

"Now, miss," he said cheerfully, "I propose to prosecute you as a common whore under the Town Police Clauses Act, also for obstructing a police officer in the exercise of his duty, also for conspiracy to defraud, also for conspiring to demand money with menaces. Why, since Mrs. Manning was hanged at Newgate there can hardly have been such a trial as yours shall prove."

For a moment he thought he had gone too far and that she was in a confusion of terror. Her hands went over her face and a disconsolate hooting of grief came from behind them. He snatched a hand away and saw that her hazel eyes were still dry. In the interests of realism, Prue managed a broken-hearted sniff or two.

"Tell me, then," he said coaxingly. "Tell me about that old rogue Dicky Tiptoe. Let us see if we may not strike a bargain."

The little mouth pouted at him reprovingly.

"I never killed him!"

"To be sure you did not!" He released her hand now. "To your great good fortune, the proctor had you in arrest all that time. Tell me, though, of the game that Major Tiptoe was playing."

"'How should I know?" Prue wailed as if in anger at his stupidity. "I was to go where he went and do as he said. I was to be paid for and get a present when all was done. Much hope of that! Look at me now!"

Swain looked at her.

"Where were you to go and what were you to do?"

"Go to the seaside," she said grudgingly.

"What for?"

"To catch a prig that was there. One that liked little girls. To make him like me and that."

"And what?" asked Swain, regarding her with calm curiosity.

"What men do that like little girls."

"And what was that?"

"I dunno, do I?" wailed Prue. "He never even liked me!"

Swain checked the comment he had in mind.

"And what about Oxford? What were you to do there?"

The sulky little face looked back at him for a moment.

"What'll I get if I tell you?"

He replied to her very gently.

"Think instead of what you'll get if you don't tell me."

The petulant little mouth faltered.

"I was to make a man like me."

"By pretending to be a little girl?"

"Not necessarily," said Prue, as if defending her maturity.

"Was it Mr. Dodgson?"

"No," she said. "He was the seaside prig."

"Was it Mr. Godwin?"

There was a long pause before she admitted it.

"It was just to make him like me," Prue said helplessly.

"Why?"

"To find out about him and a woman. What they did together."

"And what did they do together?"

Prue gave a squeal of resentment at the question.

"How should I know? I never even met him!"

Swain sat on the edge of her bed and thought about all this. He was weary of questions but there was one still to be asked.

"You're not still shielding Dicky Tiptoe, Prue? There's no use in that now."

She looked at him with such a contortion of her mouth and cheeks that he thought she might spit in his face.

"Protect that brute? He blacked me eye at the seaside! And that last night . . ." She pulled the sheet from one narrow shoulder to display the last oyster-grey traces of a bruise. "If someone put Tiptoe in the river, good riddance to bad rubbish!"

Swain nodded as if he was now satisfied that Prue had told him all he expected. He stood up, turned away, and then turned back again as she slid deeper under the sheets.

"When did you last see Mr. Howell—Mr. Charles Augustus Howell?"

"Don't know as I ever met him. Couldn't say, I'm sure."

But she hesitated a little too long and there was a catch of apprehension in her voice when she answered.

"Get up," he said gently. "Get out of bed and dress yourself."

"Why?"

"Because you are now going to be taken to Scotland Yard and questioned by Chief Inspector Toplady."

"Not likely," she said. "Not for bloody Toplady nor you!"

"Get up!" he said. "And show respect when you speak of Mr. Toplady!"

"I'm naked," she said defiantly. "You can't take me! Think of the rumpus! I'll see to it the whole street catches you at it!"

As if yielding in the face of this, Swain went to the door, where Constable Tulloch was once more in attendance.

"In here, if you please, Mr. Tulloch. Allow this young person three minutes to get out of bed and put her clothes on. If she refuses, light a fire under the bed. Use any means necessary to secure her compliance. On my authority, Mr. Tulloch!"

Prue looked from one face to the other. With a forlorn little cry of surrender, she slid out from the unwashed sheets and fumbled at the petticoat hanging on a wooden bedside chair.

Swain left her in the constable's charge. There was a certain aptness in ensuring that Posture Prudence and Chief Inspector Toplady should keep one another occupied for the foreseeable future. His own thoughts turned towards a more elusive subject: Charles Augustus Howell.

Howell was not an Oxford suspect, and yet he was a suspect all the same. He had been seen and heard arguing with Tiptoe by Folly Bridge at two o'clock or soon after. Swain's information was that Howell could not have caught another train to London until after four o'clock. It was possible, in theory, that he could have killed Tiptoe at 3.35 and reached the station in time to catch that London train.

Where was Howell? He might as easily be in Paris, Madrid, or Lisbon by this time. No crime had been proved against him and there was no ground for his extradition. Indeed, his Portuguese blood might make Lisbon an effective sanctuary against all the appeals of the British Foreign Office.

At the end of the Strand, Swain turned into Northumberland Avenue and so to Whitehall Place again. In their communal room, Inspector Wilks was pouring himself a large mug of sugared tea from an enameled pot. Swain had no idea whether this was the conclusion of his lunch or the beginning of some other repast.

"Gentleman to see you," said Wilks, studying the orange flow of tea anxiously. "Insisted on waiting. Most particular to see *you*. Told you was out. Insisted on waiting."

He raised the tin mug and his bull throat pulsed with the tidal surges of warm, sweet tea.

"Who?" asked Swain. Wilks lowered the mug and his forehead creased with an effort of memory. His eyes brightened.

"Howell," he said quickly, "Mr. Howell. He and his friend was told to make themselves comfortable in the interview room."

"His friend?"

"Another gentleman," said Wilks, his voice now coloured by a mild reproof at this interruption of his nourishment.

Swain walked towards the interview room. He reached the door, paused outside for a moment, and then turned the handle.

Howell, his dark eyes burning with a desire of acquaintance, his hand held out, rose to greet him. Swain recognised the other man at once. Sir George Lewis had been solicitor to many of the most famous names in the past twenty years. He was a pale, cautious man with a drily courteous manner. It was he who persuaded Howell to sit down and curb his effusiveness. Yet Howell was master of the situation to the extent of insisting upon his own explanation.

"I find myself, Mr. Swain, in a most invidious position. As soon as I saw that you had been appointed to inquire into the affair of the late Major Tiptoe, I knew that I must come to you in all frankness. You see, Mr. Swain, I knew Major Tiptoe."

"Indeed, sir?" Swain rested his elbow on the table beside his chair and endeavoured to sound surprised.

"We were acquainted," said Howell confidingly, "though not upon the best of terms. I had lent the poor fellow one or two small sums of money, never expecting to see them back."

"Indeed," said Swain again.

Howell was now well into his part, commanding the fluency and gesture of a great actor.

"Death, coming as it does to all, ought never to take a wise man by surprise. Yet, Mr. Swain, the news of Major Tiptoe's death came to me both as a surprise and an embarrassment. I was in Oxford that afternoon and had seen him not more than an hour before I left—not more than two hours anyhow."

"You left by the 4.15, sir," said Swain coldly.

"Why, Mr. Swain, and so I did. You see, then, what my misgivings are. That very afternoon I had an argument with Major Tiptoe—not a quarrel, you understand, but an argument. Lest you should put a worse interpretation upon it, let me tell you the reason."

Swain said nothing. He looked at the strong sallow figure of Howell and waited for the lie.

"I was robbed by Major Tiptoe only a few days before," said Howell simply.

"And you reported the robbery to the divisional police." Swain took a certain pleasure in this.

"No, Mr. Swain. To tell the truth, I did not. The robbery was not serious, merely a bloodstone ring taken from the top of my desk during Major Tiptoe's visit on the Sunday. A ring of little value but precious to me as having been in my family three generations. I suspected Major Tiptoe and, he having said something about Oxford and the Mitre Inn, I went there to confront him. The occasion of our meeting on the riverbank near Folly Bridge is something you are well acquainted with, I imagine."

"There were witnesses to it," said Swain drily.

"Was Major Tiptoe wearing my ring when they found him?"

Swain cast his mind back to the inventory of "personal adornments."

"There was some such ring, sir."

"Really?" Howell's eyes gleamed with enthusiasm. "And how its history will be embellished by having been worn by a man at the time of his murder! I shall be grateful for its return when convenient, Mr. Swain."

"As soon as may be, sir," said Swain expressionlessly.

"In the meantime, I thought it best to explain myself and to assure you that, however provoked by its loss, I am not the man to commit murder for the value of a ring! Twenty pounds would have induced Major Tiptoe to restore it to me with far less inconvenience than I have incurred now."

"None the less, sir, you were seen to display great anger with Major Tiptoe near Folly Bridge scarcely an hour before his death."

Howell laughed at this, like the good-natured victim of a practical joke.

"Believe me, Mr. Swain, I am no murderer! Even if I were, I hope I would not be such a fool as to kill a man an hour after having had a public row with him in front of a score of witnesses!"

"Anger has been known to override a man's judgment, sir," said Swain mildly.

"But never mine, Mr. Swain!"

Swain believed this. If Howell were a killer, he thought, he would be of the cold and meticulous kind. As casually as possible, scarcely daring to hope for an answer, he turned to another topic.

"After the disappearance of the ring, sir, did you find that any of your papers appeared to be missing or mislaid?"

The long equine face and the gentle intelligence waited patiently for a reply. Howell assumed the expression of a man in a state of honest and almost amused bewilderment at such a suggestion. Before he could answer the inspector's question, Sir George Lewis put down his gold pencil, with which he had been making notes, and interrupted.

"Mr. Swain, my client has come here to offer you an account of his conduct in a certain matter. He has done this in part to relieve himself of suspicion and in part as a public duty to prevent the expenditure of your time on an unnecessary investigation. It is my opinion that any further questions upon his personal affairs would be improper. Upon my advice, he will decline to answer them. Should you wish to question him further, it will be in my presence, and he will answer only those queries that in my opinion are proper. I believe that concludes all the business which you have with Mr. Howell, sir."

"Of course," said Swain gently. It was clear that Howell would say nothing more, on this occasion or any other. Whatever else he could discover about Howell must be unearthed by more subtle and devious means.

He opened the door and waited politely while his two visitors made their way down the panelled corridor of Whitehall Place, which had been a gentleman's residence long before it became a police office. Then, with a sudden resolve, he strode off in the other direction to the detention room where Constable Tulloch and a police matron kept watch over Posture Prudence.

"Show me how Dicky Tiptoe blacked your eye!" he snapped at the girl.

She looked up at him dumbly.

"Back o'his hand across it," she said feebly.

"Wearing a ring?"

"How else did this happen?" She pulled up her eyebrow a little and showed a tiny healed mark, on the underside above the eyelid, that she was likely to carry to the grave.

"Can you remember it?"

"If someone did that to you, you'd have cause to remember it, wouldn't you?" said Prue bitterly.

"A bloodstone ring?"

"Dunno."

"A *bloodstone* ring?" His hands were on her shoulders now as if he might shake the answer from her.

"Sort of ruby!" she squealed.

Swain relaxed.

"There's a good girl," he said, patting her cheek. "That's the sort of girl who might find she has no charges to answer."

He caught up with Sir George Lewis before the lawyer had reached his cab in the yard outside.

"Your client Mr. Howell, sir. I shall have to consider charges against him. I thought you'd best know, sir."

Policeman and attorney had encountered one another before in court without lasting malice. Sir George Lewis shrugged.

"There's nothing to connect Mr. Howell with Tiptoe's death. You know that, Swain, as well as I do. Not a charge that could be substantiated."

"I'm not talking about murder, sir." The long face looked at Lewis with mournful wisdom. "I'm talking of a charge of obstructing a police officer in the performance of his duties. I'm talking of being brought here to tell a pack of lies about being robbed of a ring. A ring that was in the other party's possession weeks before and probably belonged to that other party all along."

"Can you be so sure?" Lewis was lightly contemptuous in his scepticism.

Swain thought of Prudence.

"If someone blacked your eye with it, sir, you'd be sure. No better way."

"We shall see." Lewis pulled on his gloves and was turning away as Swain spoke again.

"And as for that other matter, sir . . ."

"Major Tiptoe?"

"As for that, sir. Mr. Howell may not have been connected until now. After his carrying-on here, he's well and truly connected. And that's the way he'll stay until all this is over."

"There's no charge that you could prove against him in that matter," said Lewis, beginning to take offence.

"I shan't charge him with anything yet," said Swain coldly. "What he's done I shall prove. Then, if there's proof, I shall charge him. And that charge will stick. Closer than sticky paper to a fly's front legs. You, being his solicitor, may tell him so."

With uncharacteristic lack of courtesy, Swain turned about and walked up the steps without any formal leave-taking. It was not merely that he felt a natural repugnance for Howell's type. Howell and Mr. Dodgson were now his two prime candidates.

28

CLOCKS. Swain knew that whenever he thought of Oxford in the future, he would remember the clocks. They chimed and sang from spires and towers every hour, every half-hour, and every quarter. Even in the inventory room of the police office he could hear them carrying time away in an obbligato of bells.

Two uniformed constables, perspiring lightly in their dark serge, stood at ease by the door, watching Swain and Lumley at work. The uniformed officers were always there to guard against pilfering by the detective branch and, in turn, to protect the branch against false accusations. These uniformed witnesses stood in watchful silence, apart from an occasional digestive groan, unobtrusive belch, or shifting of sinews.

Major Tiptoe's gems of blackmail had passed beyond Chief Inspector Toplady. They were in the care of men to whom even the Treasury Solicitor was a mere clerk. Swain was left to make the best of the major's remaining possessions. He surveyed them on the scrubbed pine table of the inventory room. There were the bloodstone ring, the broken watch, coins, pocket-book, handkerchief, and very little else. Inspector Merriman had taken charge of the two volumes of pantomime copulation, judging them most likely to be stolen. They remained under lock and key in his desk.

Sergeant Lumley pointed to the damaged, silver-coloured case of the watch.

"That was handy," he said confidentially, "stopping just like that. Gives the time to a minute."

Swain grunted sceptically.

"If it was right."

"Just it, sir," said Lumley with swelling confidence. "The keeper of the Mitre saw Major Tiptoe go out. The major stood there, in front of the Mitre clock that was right to the minute. Near enough half past one, the keeper says. The major wound his watch and put it right then. Just two hours before it was stopped for good by the weight of his fall. Far as anyone can tell he must have gone forward and the watch smacked on something hard. Being a stout man, his weight behind it would make a difference, too. As for the watch being wrong, sir, that's not likely. It'd hardly go far wrong in two hours after being wound."

Swain made a sceptical sound through pressed lips, but there was not the least reason to suppose Lumley wrong in the matter.

"And the camera? The Piozzi-Smith left standing on the bank?"

"Safer in the cupboard, sir. Left the glass plate in it. Seemed the best thing to do."

"The glass plate?" said Swain incredulously. "You left a glass-plate negative in the camera?"

"Yessir." Sergeant Lumley now seemed to realise that something—he did not yet know what—was badly amiss. "Best place for it, Inspector Merriman said."

At a distance, the easy-going feudalism of the Oxford police possessed a certain charm. For Swain, that charm had now faded to the point of invisibility.

"Mr. Lumley," he said gently, "there may be something on that glass plate."

"Couldn't say, sir."

"There may be a picture on it! It may have been exposed! Has no one tried to develop it?"

A look of smug reproof came over Lumley's face, as if Swain should have known better.

"Can't do that, sir! That'd be tampering with the evidence, as Mr. Merriman would say."

"Oh, would he?" said Swain menacingly. "Find me the police photographer."

Lumley looked uncertain.

"There *is* a police photographer, I suppose?" said Swain gently.

"Oh, yes." Lumley came to life again. "There's one of them all right, sir. Old Mr. Hills at Hills and Saunders in High Street. He comes at Superintendent Gravitt's invitation every autumn and takes the big photograph in the parade yard. Everyone in rows, rising on benches one behind the other. Anything else needs doing, Mr. Gravitt sends it to him."

"Get Mr. Hills," said Swain calmly.

"*Now*, sir?"

"Yes, sir! Now, sir! Arrest him for obstructing the public footpath with his camera, if you have to. Get him here! Is there a dark-room?"

"There's a cellar room that was used for the annual police photograph a couple of times, sir."

"Good. Then get Mr. Hills *and* his equipment."

Mr. Hills came with no trouble at all. He was an elderly, pedantic man, his dark suit stained here and there by sulphurous yellow. Inky patches on clothes and hands betrayed his use of the wet-plate process. Around him hung the unmistakable sour whiff of collodion.

The old man was installed in the makeshift dark-room and presented with the glass-plate negative in its holder.

"Mr. Hills," said Swain quietly, "there may be nothing on this plate. It may not have been exposed. If there should be an image upon it, that may be a matter of life and death. I beg of you to use all your skill and care to develop it successfully."

The old man showed no reaction whatever. Perhaps, Swain thought, he was deaf as well as doddering. Only when Swain reached the door of the cellar room and was about to leave it did he hear Mr. Hills call him.

"Mr. Swain! Do you know, in all my long life I do not believe I have ever come across anything that was a matter of life *or* death. Such choice is not given us, Mr. Swain. When the time comes, we die. Until then, we are alive. Be so good as to close the door tightly as you leave."

Back in the inventory room, there was a moment of uneasy silence. When Sergeant Lumley could stand it no longer, he said,

"No one ever told me about that glass plate, sir. Not about its being important enough to develop."

Swain nodded, still nursing his exasperation.

"No one said, sir."

He looked more kindly at the plump discomfited sergeant.

"Has no one ever asked *how* Major Tiptoe was killed?"

"Yessir. Knew that straight off, sir. Paling through the skull."

"Try it, Mr. Lumley," said Swain generously.

"Beg pardon, sir?"

Swain went to the cupboard, unwrapped the wooden paling from the waterproof cloth and handed it to Lumley.

"I'm about Major Tiptoe's height, Mr. Lumley. You're quite tall enough for Mr. Dodgson and Mr. Howell. Walk up behind me as I stand here and show me how it happened."

Lumley gave a fat embarrassed titter. He reached up with the paling in his hands. He held it some three inches above its sharpened end, the tip an inch or two above Swain's skull. The inspector turned while Lumley held the pose.

"That will never do, Mr. Lumley. You will never kill me by such means."

"Sir?"

"In the first place, even a man of your height has only a couple of inches to drive the paling down. Secondly, if you hold it so low down, you will never put enough force into it. You will bruise me, I daresay, but you will not kill me."

"Can't hold it any higher, sir, on account of the reach."

"Exactly," said Swain soothingly, "which is why Major Tiptoe was not standing upright when he was killed. And is it not odd that, in the open, he apparently never saw the man who stalked him?"

"Seems so," said Lumley, as if suspecting a trap.

"Read the medical report, Mr. Lumley. The hole in Major Tiptoe's skull was a treasure house of information. Bits and pieces, some from the river, others from the bank. Black cotton or thread, Mr. Lumley. Did you notice that in Dr. Hammond's inventory?"

"Hat, sir?"

"No, Mr. Lumley. Tiptoe never wore black. Not his style. No, the poor devil was stooping to take a photograph, the black camera cloth over his head, when he was killed. Blind to his peril. Easy for the man who killed him to dispose of a black cloth."

Leaving Lumley, he went down to the cellar room, through double doors. In the pale inferno-glow of the dark-room, old Mr. Hills knelt at a Bunsen burner, holding the darkened sheet of glass in one hand and brushing varnish onto it with the other. The liquid sizzled ominously as it touched the hot glass. Swain hoped to heaven that Mr. Hills knew his business.

"The flame!" said the inspector uneasily. "The heat on the glass!"

"Varnish!" Mr. Hills looked up proudly. "A man must hold the plate close enough to scorch his fingers. The image will be hard for ever."

He stopped brushing the varnish onto the developed plate but continued to hold the glass close to the jet for a moment more. Swain checked the most important question of all. He felt, quite irrationally, that to speak too soon would bring a judgment upon him, like a greedy child who forfeits a treat by persistence. The glass would be a sheet of uniform black.

At last Mr. Hills struggled up onto his frail old legs.

"There, sir! Now you may see all that you shall ever see of it!"

He came close to the inspector, and his breath whistled slightly through his teeth in the moment of confidentiality.

"Mark you, Mr. Swain, if this picture had come to me in the way of respectable business, I should have wiped the plate clean!"

"Indeed?" asked Swain nervously. But he took the plate and kept it firmly between his hands, as if fearing that old Mr. Hills's scrupies might yet get the better of him.

"A nasty sight!" said Mr. Hills philosophically. "Still, what may not suit the public eye is yet permissible in the dissecting room of human evil where you and I work, sir."

Glancing at Mr. Hills's own murky eye in the orange light, Swain detected a twinkle of enthusiasm that seemed ill-suited to the old man's words. He took the glass plate up the steps and held it to the full light of the window.

His heart jumped with excitement at seeing how strong and clear the image was, despite the period of neglect. For all his age and slowness, Mr. Hills was a professional in the smallest details. Not for him the excuse that the chemicals had "gone wrong," leaving the glass a square of deepest black.

It was a full-sized plate negative, eight by ten inches, and the details were extraordinarily good, so far as Swain could see at this stage. The view was that of a sunlit riverside scene. To one side glimmered the edge of a pool, overhung by branches of willow and ash. The other edge was a screen of bushes, with some rough grass in the foreground. Just in view, where the bushes ended, was a female figure. She was apparently naked and stood with her back to the camera. At first Swain thought she was alone. Then he saw that what appeared to be part of the foliage at a glance was in fact the head of another girl. A third girl, dressed in jersey and long bathing-drawers, faced the camera at a greater distance, though her head was slightly turned aside. Swain doubted that any of them had been aware of the lens or the man behind it.

"Mr. Hills!" he called down the cellar steps with the peremptory tone of master to servant. "I must have a print of this, sir! As quickly as it may be done!"

The old man's head appeared in the doorway below. He was wiping his hands on a towel and had evidently been packing away his equipment.

"Tomorrow, Mr. Swain?" he said hopefully.

"No," said Swain sharply. "Today, if you please. Now. This minute, Mr. Hills. I beg of you!"

The old man gave a whimpering sound of reluctant compliance. He took the glass plate and went down again to the dim Hades-glow of his dark-room. Half an hour later, Swain and Lumley stood side by side, the pair of prints which Hills had made spread on the table before them.

"Fancy a man being killed for that!" said Lumley quietly.

"Not for that alone," Swain answered.

Now that the picture had been printed, he found the result disappointing. Having seen Dicky Tiptoe's collection of prints, he had no doubt that the naked girl with her back to the camera was Jane Ashmole. In that case, according to their own evidence of the afternoon's events, the other two were the Chantrey sisters. Much of the scene was obscured by bushes, behind which, presumably, sat Sarah Ashmole. None of the witnesses had been able to give a precise time, but it seemed likely that the girls had undressed to bathe in the riverside pool at about half past three. That would be an hour after they had set out from the boating station.

"A man must want that picture badly to risk being killed for it," said Lumley respectfully.

Swain looked at it again. In his mind he saw Major Tiptoe crouching under his black cloth, the lens in focus upon the group of bathers. The lens uncapped and capped again. Yet even as this happened, at 3.35, there appeared behind the crouching major a figure of furious vengeance, paling raised, who drove the weapon through his skull. The blow and the fall were so faint that not one of the girls heard them. Then the dragging of the body back to the major's skiff, the pushing of both away from the bank towards the weir. The bathing party, unaware of anything amiss, left the scene some two hours later and returned to Folly Bridge.

Thomas Godwin cared little enough for such things, by all accounts, to strike a blow in the interests of bourgeois decency. In any case, there were a dozen utterly dependable witnesses to place him in Christ Church from two o'clock until four.

Sarah Ashmole, however outraged by this prying upon the girls, lacked the physical strength to deliver such a thrust as had killed Tiptoe. Nor was it likely she could have had a part in it without attracting the notice of the girls. All three had been questioned, gently enough. None of them showed the least trace of guilt or suspicion in her answers.

Charles Augustus Howell had cause and opportunity for killing Major Tiptoe. Yet, without a skiff, he must have followed him with difficulty. If Howell came upon his enemy at that moment, there must have been a large measure of chance in the encounter.

Charles Lutwidge Dodgson was another case entirely. By his own admission he was alone at the time, somewhere by the river. He had already been blackmailed by Tiptoe, Swain guessed, or was about to be. What he would not have done to protect himself perhaps he would do to shield his beloved Jane Ashmole. Like a peep-show in his mind, Swain saw the scene on the riverbank again. The Reverend Mr. Dodgson came silently upon the major at his tricks. Lewd and sardonic, the lens was trained upon the naked girl. In Mr. Dodgson, Swain could imagine the reason, the strength, and—above all—the fury.

Was the intention, perhaps, not to kill, merely to prevent the outrage? Did the blow miscarry? Or was Mr. Dodgson, like a suicide, in that state where the balance of his mind was disturbed? Whatever the truth, and whoever the assailant, could it ever be proved?

"Mind you," said Sergeant Lumley, with the plump satisfaction of achievement, "it's evidence, this is. It's evidence right enough!"

Swain looked at him sadly.

"There's evidence, Mr. Lumley, that makes a case. And there's evidence like this I'd rather be without just now."

Even as he spoke, Swain thought of the worst possibilities of all, explanations that would extend his list of suspects to infinity.

There were enough men and women who knew or guessed Mr. Dodgson's fascination with his child models. Was the blow delivered by a man, outraged at what he saw, who believed in all honesty that it was Mr. Dodgson's skull under the black cloth of the photographer's hood? Worst of all, was it an act of hot vengeance by a total stranger upon a photographic peeping Tom whose identity he neither knew nor cared about?

Swain dismissed such possibilities for the moment. He felt like a man crossing Niagara Falls on a tightrope. The great thing was to step resolutely forward in the direction he had intended, and not on any account to look down at the vertiginous drop below.

29

SUNLIGHT LAY across the polished mahogany and old oak of the deanery. A shaft of grey brightness lit the dust and pipe smoke in the air. Swain glanced appreciatively aside at the effect of such brilliance upon calf and gilt in the study shelves, the regimented ranks of Milman's *Histories* and Grote's *History of Greece*. He could almost feel himself part of the life of men whose duty it was to carry such knowledge in their heads.

Dean Liddell faced him from the depths of a leather chair on the far side of the fireplace. Above the faintly comic fringe of grey hair rose the bald dome of intellectual power. The long nose was turned to his companion with interrogatory precision. Swain felt as he imagined a freshman might, called for his first tutorial with the great man, the dean of Christ Church and a builder of the famous Greek lexicon. It was a feeling of admiration, tempered by a certain apprehension of being found out in his deficiencies.

"Forgive me, Mr. Swain," Liddell said, continuing their preliminary conversation. "I will help you in any way I can. For the life of me, though, I do not see what use I could be."

"I must speak in confidence, sir," said Swain awkwardly.

"Of course, you must, Mr. Swain," said the dean unhelpfully. "Of course, you must."

Even the volumes of Milman and Grote seemed to confront the inspector with dumb hostility in their gilt and plum-coloured leather.

"There are two men of your own college, sir, whose names are bound to be implicated in the present case."

Liddell spread out his hands.

"Do your duty, Mr. Swain. Above all things, do your duty. Go to them and put your questions. I do not suppose you need my permission to do so. If it is necessary, however, I give it freely."

"There are certain matters, sir, of which I cannot ask these gentlemen to speak."

Dean Liddell gave a short laugh, as if at the absurdity of the problem.

"Then, Mr. Swain, you can hardly expect the answers from me!"

This was exactly what Swain had expected, and his heart sank a little further. How much easier it had been to deal with a rogue like Howell. Hard as he tried, he could not envisage himself threatening Dean Liddell with a charge of obstructing a police officer in the execution of his duty.

"I need to know something, sir, of Mr. Dodgson and Mr. Godwin."

Liddell considered this for a moment.

"On matters and questions of fact, Mr. Swain, I will try to oblige you. But I will no more betray the confidences of those two men to you than I would betray yours to them. Isn't that fair?"

Swain inclined his head and then looked up at Liddell.

"I must ask something of Mr. Dodgson's relationship with Miss Ashmole, sir."

The dean returned his gaze with a detachment bordering on distaste.

"Then you must inquire of the gentleman himself, Mr. Swain. I can tell you only that I have entrusted Mr. Dodgson absolutely with my own son and three daughters. I would do so again at this minute. Mr. Dodgson is a solitary man in many ways, a man who cultivates privacy. Yet his feelings for children are pure and benevolent. There is nothing he would not do to protect a child from harm."

"That's rather what I meant, sir," said Swain gently.

"I beg your pardon?"

"I meant, sir, that Mr. Dodgson might be such a man as would go to any length to protect Miss Ashmole's innocence from ruin."

For the first time, Dean Liddell shifted uncomfortably in his chair.

"I do not think it right, Mr. Swain, that I should discuss such matters further with you. They have no possible bearing on the inquiry that I can see. Even if they had, I cannot answer for what Mr. Dodgson thinks of Miss Ashmole."

"Believe me, sir," said Swain, with the same remorseless courtesy, "I have no wish to harm either Mr. Dodgson or Mr. Godwin if they are innocent. Yet it is plain, sir, that a child is caught at the centre of this web. If I do not unravel it, it is she who must be destroyed."

He watched the dean's fingers tap the arm of his chair in a nervous outburst and guessed what would happen next.

"Very well, Mr. Swain. I believe that Mr. Dodgson loves the girl." Liddell paused. "As a man may love a child, with a love holier than any other granted to humankind. I believe he may love her as he has loved many children in the past. In certain respects I think him unwise but his piety, his virtue, and his benevolence are beyond all question."

"With respect, sir," said Swain, "that was not entirely what I meant."

"It is entirely what *I* mean, Mr. Swain. As for your meaning, whatever it may be, I do not think I greatly care."

There was nothing to be done in this direction, Swain decided.

"Then, sir, as to Mr. Godwin . . ."

"As to Mr. Godwin, Mr. Swain, I can help you very little."

"What sort of a scholar might he be, sir?"

The question caught the dean entirely off balance, coming as it did from such a different direction.

"A scholar, Mr. Swain?"

"Yes, sir."

"For the life of me, Mr. Swain, I do not see what this has to do with your inquiry."

"Might one call him a Hegelian, sir?"

For a moment, Dean Liddell assumed the look of a man who has run face first into a plate-glass wall. His intellectual processes seemed almost visible, like the muzzles of an artillery battery shifting to a new elevation.

"Yes, Mr. Swain. A romantic philosopher of idealist inclinations. A man of German sympathies."

"A sceptic, sir?"

The dean smiled again.

"Mr. Swain, we do not indulge in such hunting out of rationalism any longer. Provided a man abides by the articles of religion in form, the university insists on very little more."

"There are some who would call Mr. Godwin an infidel, sir. As much was said at the time of *Essays and Reviews*."

The dean looked distinctly uneasy. It was impossible that the young inspector with his lean, long face could know of such matters in depth. Yet it was disquieting that he knew of them at all.

"It appears, Mr. Swain, that I need tell you no more of Mr. Godwin's views. He has been called an infidel by the High Church party. So has Mr. Jowett. So have I, for that matter."

"And what may Mr. Godwin's relationship be with Mrs. Ashmole, sir?"

"Really!" said the dean. "That is an improper question if ever I heard one."

"Yet it must be asked, sir. I would rather learn the answer from you than embarrass Mrs. Ashmole herself. Embarrass her I will, if I have to."

Liddell gave way once more.

"Mr. Godwin lodged with her a short time ago. I believe he admires her greatly. I should not be surprised to hear of their engagement to marry. Mrs. Ashmole has been a widow some years. Mr. Godwin is not debarred by statute from marriage, as some fellows of colleges are still. If he courts Mrs. Ashmole, there is no irregularity in that whatever."

"Not if it be true courtship," said Swain doubtfully.

Dean Liddell's brows contracted in a discouraging frown.

"Neither you nor I, Mr. Swain, have any cause to regard Mr. Godwin's conduct by any other light. If you tell me that there have been—that there are, indeed—fellows of colleges who are fornicators or adulterers, I could not deny it. A man may live a quiet enough life here and yet have some woman of his acquaintance in the town. Unless he makes himself notorious in the matter, the liaison rarely becomes an issue to the university. I am no more prepared to regard Mr. Godwin as a libertine than I could accuse him as an infidel."

Swain folded his hands gently, as if with some relief.

"Then there is no more to be said about that, sir."

"Indeed there is not, Mr. Swain."

"Yet I must put one further question to you, sir. Who is the father of Jane Ashmole?"

At first it seemed that the dean might find offence in the question, but he chose to take it merely as an inquiry after fact.

"Mr. William Ashmole, who died eight years ago, after some seven years of marriage to Mrs. Ashmole. A most estimable Christian man, Mr. Swain, and a scholar of Hebrew. He died quite suddenly of a ruptured appendix and you may see his memorial in the cathedral nave."

"Were there any other children of the marriage, sir?"

"Two," said Liddell curtly, "both boys, and both taken from us in their infancy."

"And Mr. Godwin . . ." Swain began, but the dean cut him short.

"It may save some indiscretion on your part, Mr. Swain, if I tell you that from the time of the Ashmole marriage until the birth of their first child, Jane, a year later, Mr. Godwin was at the University of Göttingen. If you know as much as you pretend to know in such matters, you will be aware that he was engaged then upon his translation of Goethe's *Wilhelm Meister*."

"I see, sir." Swain raised his head and took in the tranquil view of mown grass and deep-shaded trees in the deanery garden.

"No, Mr. Swain, I do not believe that you see at all. One reason only permits me to answer such questions as these. If I do not reply to them, I fear you will put them to those who may be more hurt by them than I. The matter of Mr. Godwin cannot concern you in the least. At the time when you say your man was killed, Mr. Godwin was within these walls, the walls of the House, that is."

"The House, sir?"

"Christ Church," said Liddell bluntly. "We are in the habit of calling it the House. Mr. Godwin cannot be at the bottom of all this."

"No, sir," said Swain, agreeing quickly. "I know who's at the bottom of it all. It's not Mr. Godwin. Miss Ashmole, more likely."

Liddell stood up, indicating the end of the discussion.

"What utter nonsense! The child could not have struck that blow."

Swain got to his feet.

"Exactly, sir. But in cases like this, who's at the bottom of it all is generally more to the point than who dealt the blow."

Dean Liddell shrugged, as if the ways of detective investigation were beyond comprehension or caring about. Yet as they walked to the garden door of the deanery, he softened a little.

"Mr. Swain, if I may advise you, have a care of what you believe. In a place like this, rumour is fertile. There never was a man more like nature's bachelor than Mr. Dodgson. Yet, if you believe what you hear, he will seem quite a ladies' man. Why, when he came over to the deanery so often to see my own children in years gone by, nothing would satisfy the world but that he was courting my daughter's governess. As it happened, he rarely set eyes upon the good lady. They were almost strangers. You would not have thought so had you questioned his colleagues as you have questioned me today."

"I'm obliged, sir," said Swain courteously. "I must speak to Mr. Dodgson and Mr. Godwin, for all that."

"Then so you must, Mr. Swain."

Swain, about to take his leave, paused as if something had quite unexpectedly come to mind.

"Would it not be strange, sir, if Mr. Godwin *were* an infidel?"

"Strange, Mr. Swain?"

"In the light of his enthusiasms in philosophy, sir. The nature of the Hegelian absolute being essentially spiritual rather than material."

Suspicion bordering on unease once again clouded the dean's blue eyes.

"You are not a university man, I take it, Mr. Swain?"

Swain reassured him at once.

"Not the least, sir. Not in the slightest."

"Yet you know of Hegel?"

"By subscription to the *People's Penny Educator*, sir. Under the letter 'H,' when that part was issued, there was a half column for Hegel, with a paragraph by Mr. Jowett and another taken from one of Mr. Godwin's own lectures, sir. Most instructive, they were. Most instructive."

"Ah, yes." There was a visible relaxation and relief in Dean Liddell's features, as if the world had come right again. "Quite so. In the *People's Penny Educator*? Of course. Entirely admirable, Mr. Swain. My best wishes for a speedy resolution of these other difficulties."

With that, Liddell turned about and sought the shady refuge of the deanery, leaving Alfred Swain to make the best of his farewell.

That evening, Mrs. Wilberforce (Roxana, she assured Swain, was her true name, in tribute to her chestnut hair) sat on the other side of a humbler fireplace in St. John Street, and listened to him reading from *Idylls of the King*. Swain enjoyed reading aloud, feeling privately that he did it rather well. Sometimes when he was alone he did it to increase his enjoyment of such verse as this.

Opening the worn and much-read little volume, he had chosen "Merlin and Vivien," thinking it the most likely to appeal to one unfamiliar with the works of the Poet Laureate.

> "A storm was coming, but the winds were still,
> And in the wild woods of Broceliande . . ."

He looked covertly over the book's edge, saw the satisfaction on young Mrs. Wilberforce's soft features, and missed two lines.

"... At Merlin's feet the wily Vivien lay."

The young widow listened with sighs of appreciation and languid motions of her brown eyes, conveying all too surely that her admiration was directed as much to the reader as to the poem. Swain missed another line and then, flurried by error, found the track of the poem again at last.

> "And lissome Vivien, holding by his heel,
> Writhed toward him, slided up his knee and sat,
> Behind his ankle twined her hollow feet
> Together, curved an arm about his neck,
> Clung like a snake . . ."

Swain had already begun to feel a little warm in the face and to doubt the prudence of choosing such a passage. He glanced up, caught the tender smile in Roxana Wilberforce's brown eyes, saw the tight youthful plumpness of a partridge through her cotton merino gown. Going hastily back to the page he hurried onwards through the lines. The carpet stirred. A gentle warmth pressed his leg and the soft weight of hair was pillowed on his knee.

The little volume of Tennyson seemed damp between his hands. High above its usual place, his heart was beating hard and quick. With constricted throat, Alfred Swain plunged into the next stanza.

> "I saw the little elf-god eyeless once
> In Arthur's arras hall at Camelot . . ."

"I like a lovely poem," said pretty Mrs. Wilberforce, looking up softly from his knee, curling her legs under her on the green carpet. "You like a lovely poem, don't you, Mr. Swain? Anyone can tell you do."

30

M<small>R. DODGSON</small> did not sound to Swain like a man who knows he may be suspected of murder. The inspector presented himself to the porter's lodge and was led into the sunlit calm of Tom Quad. During such an afternoon, in the depths of the vacation, the stillness grew oppressive as the heat. A scout with a silver tray was approaching from the direction of the buttery, his face still no more than an indistinct pallor beyond the expanse of grass and gravel paths.

It was then that Swain heard the shout and the storm of juvenile female giggling from the open windows of the room, high up in the north-west corner of the courtyard.

"Twinkle, twinkle!" shouted the voice. There was a shriek of comic terror from one of the girls and the thump of falling furniture. Looking up, Swain was astonished to see a bat fly out of the open window in broad daylight and dart across the quadrangle. It headed towards the white-coated scout with his tray of college crockery and silverware, bound for the rooms of a senior student. Then the bat seemed to find its target, diving in a last thrust of energy directly into the contents of the tray.

Startled and incredulous, the scout dropped the tray and its contents with a clatter on the gravelled path. Dodgson appeared, straw-hatted, at the open window.

"Twinkle, twinkle little bat," he called, to an accompaniment of girls' laughter. "How I wonder what you're at! Up above the world you fly! Like a t-t-tea t-t-tray in the sky! I am most t-t-t-terribly sorry, Jenkins! The demise of the b-b-beast in this manner was quite unin-n-n-tentional!"

He was stammering with laughter, quite unable to continue the apology, the face under the straw brim showing the fatuous dismay of the stage comic.

"My dear J-J-Jenkins!" he cried at last. "It's not a real b-bat!"

With that he disappeared, hauled back from the window, it seemed, by unseen hands.

Swain and the porter, who had stood motionless in admiration during the display, continued on their way towards the arch of the staircase. Dodgson had not apparently taken notice of them. In any other circumstances, Swain thought, he might have been mistaken for a drunken reveller. Perhaps he was. Drunk on something more potent than alcohol: the admiration of those whose admiration he sought most of all.

They went up the stone staircase in the cloister darkness. Swain, in his ignorance of such matters, had assumed that Dodgson and his colleagues would each possess a sitting-room, a bedroom, and little more. What more could they need? He was astonished to find, when the porter opened the outer oak, that in Dodgson's apartments the doors stood open to four separate sitting-rooms or studies, and a pair of bedrooms. A game of some sort was being played that involved access to them all. Louisa Brereton, an infant screaming with excitement and carrying a silver cup, ran past him into one of the sitting-rooms and slid under the table, concealed there by its velvet cloth.

"Mr. Swain, sir," said the porter glumly as Dodgson appeared through the doorway of one of the sitting-rooms. Dodgson regained his breath from laughter with a deep inhalation and took the straw boater from his head.

"Ah, Mr. Swain!" he said, holding out his hand. "I fear you find us in something less than a responsible mood just now. Excuse me one moment."

He dived into the other room, caught Louisa Brereton's leg gently under the table and drew her slowly into view. Then he

229

gave her and two other little girls into the charge of the porter to be taken to the lodge and refreshed with lemonade.

"Now, Mr. Swain," he said, still a little breathless. "We shall be undisturbed. Please come in."

Swain entered a sitting-room that combined the calm of a study and the chaos of an ill-organised nursery. A distorting mirror, propped against the pillar of the mantelpiece, reduced the inspector to an obese dwarf with the head of a melon on the body of a pumpkin. Two rag dolls, limp and gaudy, sat in the fireside chairs. There were a scattered army of tin soldiers, a clockwork bear with its forepaws rigidly extended as it stood upright, and folded exercise paper whose conical shapes would do equally well as hats or boats. Dodgson removed the rag dolls and put them with his straw hat on the table.

"So, Mr. Swain." He waved his visitor to the other chair. "You are the London detective about whom everyone is talking."

"Yes, sir," said Swain, taking in the appearance of the pale face and dark curls. "I regret the necessity of troubling you."

"We were busy with weighty matters this afternoon, Mr. Swain, as you saw for yourself." Then he sat down and gave a solemn sigh. "It is very pleasant to me, Mr. Swain, to know that such children are so absolutely at their ease in my company."

Swain ignored this.

"I have come about the matter of Major Tiptoe, sir."

"Why, Mr. Swain, I never supposed you had come for any other reason. I am at a loss to see how I may help you. Was the man's name *really* Major Tiptoe?"

"Tiptoe was a slang name, sir. He was never a major, not even in India. A corporal or a sergeant, I believe. Perhaps a lieutenant."

"How very singular, Mr. Swain."

"On the afternoon of his death, you were walking alone on the riverbank, sir. You were alone there from about three o'clock until five, during which time it seems that Major Tiptoe was killed."

"Not quite, Mr. Swain. I left here at a quarter to three and walked down to the Botanic Garden. I strolled there for some time and then crossed the road to Magdalen. I went along Addison's Walk, strolled as far as Parsons' Pleasure, found my way to the University Parks, and so back here again."

"You met no one who might recognise you?"

"No, Mr. Swain. So you will now tell me that, as far as you are concerned, I might have gone the other way along the river, murdered Major Tiptoe, and come back here in the same manner."

"It is a possibility, sir."

"So it is, Mr. Swain. So it is, to be sure. However, I did not."

"Where were you at half past three, Mr. Dodgson?"

"Now *that* I can tell you precisely, Mr. Swain. I had an appointment at the Botanic Garden at three o'clock. By half past three that appointment had not been kept. I decided to wait no longer and set off across High Street to follow the Cherwell northward along Addison's Walk."

"And can you say no more, sir?"

"What else would you have me say, Mr. Swain?"

"Most unfortunate, sir, that no one came to keep that appointment with you. You might have had a witness then."

Dodgson straightened his white tie.

"I could hardly expect that, Mr. Swain. My appointment was with Major Tiptoe. He was attempting to blackmail me."

Swain felt once again like a man walking a tightrope that an unseen hand had begun to jerk vigorously at one end. In a few minutes, his interrogation of Dodgson had gone quite against all the rules of experience. The little clergyman with his twinkling smugness had offered both opportunity and motive for murdering Major Tiptoe. Swain had imagined himself revealing the knowledge of blackmail as a final blow to Dodgson's composure, then drawing the truth gently from the broken suspect. This bright, birdlike self-assurance was not at all what he had expected.

"Blackmail?" he inquired impassively.

"Yes, Mr. Swain. But surely you know about that? To be sure you must. If you will excuse me, I shall put the kettle on for tea."

"Which blackmail was that exactly, sir?"

"Are there so many, then, Mr. Swain? Major Tiptoe confronted me in the Botanic Garden on the previous day. He produced several photographic prints of Miss Ashmole—did you not find them in his effects?—and demanded a large sum of money for their return to me. Only two of them were mine. The others he had taken of the girl surreptitiously. He threatened to publish them in an indecent manner unless I brought the money— some hundreds of pounds—to the same place on the following day. I kept the appointment to repeat to Major Tiptoe what I had already said. I would not pay him a penny piece—not a brass farthing. If he should attempt to publish the photographs in the manner he proposed, I would see him visited with the full rigour of the law."

Swain watched Dodgson fill the kettle and put it on the hob.

"Did you not consider the harm to Miss Ashmole, the public disgrace, if the law took its course, sir?" he asked sceptically.

Dodgson looked up at him from the hearth, where he seemed to be encouraging the kettle.

"I did not judge Major Tiptoe resolute enough to put the matter to the test. However, if I had thought of murdering Major Tiptoe—which I did not—consider the far greater harm to Miss Ashmole that my trial would have brought about. No, Mr. Swain. I might have paid Major Tiptoe—if it had been agreeable to my principles. I might have told him to go to perdition, as I did. Those are the only two courses of action that reason or logic condone. Mr. Charles Augustus Howell, whom I take to be Major Tiptoe's confederate in these matters, had already visited me several weeks before. He represented himself as a friend, eager to purchase the glass-plate negatives—purloined from this room— on my behalf. He, too, was sent about his business."

The revelation of Howell's implication in the blackmail was not a surprise to Swain. He watched Dodgson scald the teapot and then add the crisp dry leaves over which the boiling water was poured.

"There are moments of anger, Mr. Dodgson, when reason and logic do not prevail. A man who loved Miss Ashmole deeply and purely might come upon a scoundrel photographing her naked and unawares upon a riverbank. In his rage, he might strike a blow of such force that the man was killed."

Dodgson turned and faced him, teapot in one hand and kettle in the other.

"A photograph, Mr. Swain? Of Miss Ashmole naked? But what possible purpose could there be? Major Tiptoe, however reprehensible the reasons, had several photographs of that nature already. What possible use could there be for another, taken under circumstances in which she was so palpably innocent?"

"No reason that I can find," said Swain gently. "Yet it might rouse the anger of a man who cared for her."

"So it would, Mr. Swain. Why, if I had caught the rascal at that trick, I daresay I should have kicked Major Tiptoe and his camera into the river. As for murdering him, I should not know precisely how to begin. A blunderbuss? A sharp knife? Who knows? But you are quite wrong, Mr. Swain. I cannot believe that Major Tiptoe went to so much trouble to take another, quite unnecessary picture of Miss Ashmole."

"Yet he hired a camera and a boat," Swain insisted. "He stalked the party and he took that picture."

"There were Mrs. Sarah Ashmole and the Chantrey girls," said Dodgson reasonably.

"Mrs. Ashmole does not appear in the picture." Swain clung to his hypothesis like a lost sailor to a rope. "Miss Nerissa Chantrey's head alone is visible, and that not entirely. Miss Belinda is at a considerable distance, dressed, and turning so that her face would hardly be recognised. Miss Ashmole, though with her back to the camera, is revealed naked from head to toe."

Dodgson poured the strong tea into two cups, handing one to Swain.

"Would you grant me a great indulgence, Mr. Swain?"

"If I can, sir."

"I know you are obliged to suspect me of having murdered Major Tiptoe—will you take sugar, by the way?—but I have some little experience in the matter of photographs. Would you be so kind as to show me this one?"

Alfred Swain was wearing a Norfolk jacket of which he was rather proud. Its belted waist carried a suggestion of the squirearchy. It also had unusually capacious pockets. From one of these he drew a folded card, containing the photograph, cut for convenience of carrying into two halves.

Dodgson took them and laid them on the table. He fetched a magnifying glass from the desk and examined them more closely. He saw a pleasant grassy scene by the riverbank, a glimpse of Nerissa's head above the foliage, Belinda at a distance in profile, Jane with her back to the camera in an opening of the bushes. It was a badly composed photograph, yet it caught the tranquil leafy moment with great suggestiveness.

"The party reached the place about quarter past three," said Swain helpfully, "and changed for bathing about fifteen or twenty minutes later. It all makes sense."

"Indeed, it does, Mr. Swain, if one could only find the sense in it. The man who took this was no photographer."

"Nor was Major Tiptoe, sir."

"The man who took this did so to no apparent purpose, Mr. Swain."

"Yet he must have had one." The inspector raised his teacup.

"The man who took this photograph was not Major Tiptoe," said Dodgson gently.

Swain gulped down a mouthful of hot tea and blinked away an involuntary tear. He looked again at the two halves of the sepia print. There was no reason that he could see for Dodgson's deduction.

"How can you tell?"

"Major Tiptoe was dead when this photograph was taken," said Dodgson in the same gentle voice. "I do not in the least blame you for overlooking the detail. I should not have noticed myself, had I not had cause to examine this so closely. See, here and here. Most of the scene is in the shade of the trees and the sunlight is diffused by the leaves above. Yet, towards the edges there are saplings in full sunlight. Did you ever see such a sapling cast so long a shadow at half past three in the afternoon on a summer day, Mr. Swain?"

Swain's eyes followed the neatly clipped fingernail as it traced the faint shadow of two trees by the margin of the water.

"Was this the only photograph taken by the camera on that afternoon, Mr. Swain?"

"So far as we can tell," said Swain slowly, his attention still on the shadow patterns. "The negative plates were ready-made by Hill-Norris. They were all still in the case with their seals unbroken. Whatever he went there for, he was killed before he could use any but this one."

"Major Tiptoe did not use this one, Mr. Swain, I promise you."

Swain took up a last line of defence.

"The bathing party changed at half past three," he said firmly.

"And at what time did they change back again?"

"Later," said Swain awkwardly, "about two hours, I should think."

"Exactly, Mr. Swain. Now, tell me, have you ever photographed or sketched a nude model?"

An image of Roxana Wilberforce in all her glorious abundance glowed briefly in Swain's mind.

"No," he said, "but you can tell from the picture that Miss Ashmole's hair isn't even wet!"

"A lady does not immerse her hair in river water, Mr. Swain. Perhaps she does not do more than dabble her toes. Now look again."

Swain saw nothing and said so.

"Exactly!" Dodgson's finger delineated the extent of Jane's pale figure. "Now, whatever its deficiencies as a work of composition, the photograph in this area is remarkably bright and clear. The very hairs of her head might be separately counted. Now, if you were a photographer, Mr. Swain, you would know that it is utterly out of the question to begin taking a picture of your model for a little while after she has disrobed. You may pose her and correct your focus. But you would not expose the plate."

"Would I not?" Swain grew more intrigued by the notion.

"No, Mr. Swain. Dresses and petticoats, let alone the hideous forms of corsetry and confinement in which modern young ladies imprison themselves, leave impressions upon the flesh. Those impressions remain for a while after the garments have been removed, deep and clear as any scar. You would not, I assure you, choose to make a photograph marred by such ugliness."

Swain considered the image of Jane Ashmole, unblemished from nape to heels.

"You see, Mr. Swain? That is the vision of beauty that has been lightly clad—or not clad at all. It is not the visage of beauty imprisoned and just released."

Swain sat down in his chair again.

"A picture taken two hours after Major Tiptoe was killed? A camera standing alone on the riverbank, where someone comes upon it, takes a picture of the bathing party, and leaves the plate in the camera? Where's the sense in that?"

"The sense is in it, Mr. Swain, if it happened."

"But why a picture of this?"

"Perhaps to draw your attention from something else, Mr. Swain. Do you yet know why Major Tiptoe went to the riverbank with his camera on that afternoon? You think you have the reason. I suspect that you must still seek it elsewhere."

Swain put down his teacup.

"Miss Nerissa Chantrey's hardly in the picture," he said. "Then, sir, Miss Belinda's too far off. As for Mrs. Ashmole, she's not there at all."

"Precisely!" Dodgson seemed to spring upon the idea with a new eagerness. "The truly remarkable features of a picture in a puzzle are often those things missing from it."

Before Swain could demand an explanation of this, Louisa Brereton ran up the stairs, shrieking with laughter, the college porter in vain pursuit.

31

" 'Ô SATAN, prends pitié de ma longue misère!' " Thomas
Godwin read in a fine resonant voice, sitting on the grass with
his back to the bole of the horse chestnut tree. Above him, among
the sunlit leaf clusters, the outer skin of the chestnuts formed
blobs of unripe yellow. Sarah Ashmole sat in the garden chair,
her needle working slowly at the hem of the white shawl that
draped her blue dress. Jane sat cross-legged on the mown grass,
her face bowed as she endured the recital. Godwin deepened
and relished the Frenchness of the pronunciation, so that some
of the vowels became a sardonic growl.

" 'Père adoptif de ceux qu'en sa noire colère,' " he continued.
" 'Du paradis terrestre a chassés Dieu le Père, Ô Satan, prends
pitié de ma longue misère!' "

He closed the copy of Baudelaire and looked up, throwing his
dark hair back and allowing the admiration to shine fiercely in
his eyes. Jane, who understood enough French to gather the
blasphemous purport of the poem, kept her face lowered, watching her fingers pick daisies.

"There you hear the poetry of the future," said Godwin, as if
the thought stirred brave emotions in him. "Not the school-miss
verses of our Laureate, or the scented pap of Mr. Rossetti and
his kind!"

Sarah Ashmole snapped off the thread and began to sew again. She did not interrupt Godwin, any more than if his remarks had formed part of the reading. He was the performer and she merely the audience. Godwin turned his attention to Jane. Had it not been for his words, his tone might have been taken for one of affectionate mockery.

"Tell me, child, when you go to Harrogate in October to be made a pupil-teacher, what will they hear from *you*?"

"I don't know, I'm sure." There was a constriction again in her throat that might have been the prelude to tears. It was not the blasphemy, not even the carping of Thomas Godwin whose eyes she could not bear to meet, that brought this about. The causes were in the prospect he offered. Separation. Distance. Loneliness. At other times, when she submitted in such words, he would turn from her as though she were a hopeless case. Today he pursued her.

"I fear," he said, "it will be Maud in her garden or the wretched Damozel of the pale Rossetti. Or will you tell them that God is in heaven and all's right with the world, as old Browning has it?"

Sarah Ashmole folded the shawl and stood up.

"What questions to ask the child!" she said impatiently. "How can she tell when she is to be a pupil herself of Mr. Shergold for two years more?"

"Ah," said Godwin, sardonically sympathetic. "Then it shall be the elegies of the drawing-room and the deanery, the moral humbug of the swindling shopkeeper and the petty clerk!"

Sarah Ashmole laid down the shawl by her blue sewing basket and walked towards the house to fetch another reel of cotton. Jane turned her face aside a little and stared at the pale mauve trumpets of the tobacco plants, withered and drooping like stained silk in the late summer. She dared not follow her mother without being accused of discourtesy in leaving their guest alone, and so being forced again to account for her feelings towards Thomas Godwin.

"I do not suppose that Mr. Dodgson would like Monsieur Baudelaire, Jane, would he?"

"No," she said, brushing her short fringe and still looking aside.

"I am sure he would not," Godwin persisted, in the same tone of mocking concern. "Mr. Dodgson would think him very wicked indeed, would he not?"

"Yes," she said hesitantly, guessing that he was manoeuvring to a position from which he might more easily strike at her.

"Yes!" Godwin echoed her derisively. "And do you suppose that Mr. Dodgson is right?"

"Yes." It was a small, uncertain syllable of defiance.

"Ah, then how such wickedness shall be punished hereafter! Imagine, Jane. Imagine the agony of touching a red hot coal with the tip of your finger. More than that, imagine the torment of it applied to the entire surface of your skin, and swallowed within you as well. Hmmm?"

She looked up suddenly and saw the contempt in his eyes.

"Now," said Godwin, folding his hands quietly. "Think what it must be like when such indescribable torment lasts not for a second, not for a minute, not for an hour, but for all eternity without a moment's respite. An intensity of torment a thousand times worse than the most terrible pain felt upon earth. If Mr. Dodgson is right, Jane, that is the punishment awaiting those who offend in this life."

The guilt repressed by love flickered in her mind again.

"We shall be forgiven," she said, almost pleading with him.

"Not for our crimes, Jane. Not for such impurity and lewdness. Not for such things, if Mr. Dodgson and his kind are to be believed. If he is right, you have good reason to be terrified at what lies in store for you both."

"No," she said miserably, "it's not true. How can it be?"

"Ah!" Godwin looked at her triumphantly. "I think you understand then why men and women prefer to give their allegiance to Satan. For if it is true, Jane, are you not lost already?"

So Jane bowed her head again, thinking nothing of Godwin's theological acrobatics. The tobacco plants appeared vaguely through a haze of tears that she knew she must not shed. If her mother returned now and found her crying, it would make matters worse than ever. Mrs. Ashmole would demand reasons, reasons that could not be explained. Dumb tearfulness, Godwin had called it to Sarah Ashmole in Jane's hearing, as if it might be a disease. Disease or not, every occurrence of this kind made the departure for Harrogate, the separation and bereavement, more absolute and more to be desired by Mrs. Ashmole herself.

Godwin had picked up the book from the grass and was looking at its pages, though without reading them in detail. Jane could only think that he was congratulating himself upon the terror that he had inspired in her. In this he was mistaken. It was October that she dreaded more than the pains of hell. What he had woken in her heart was not fear but the great vacuum of desolation.

Presently he put down the book and stood up, stretching himself with an appearance of animal enjoyment. He walked round behind Jane, his hands pressing on her shoulders so that her back was supported, tense and unwilling, against his legs. To Sarah Ashmole at a distance, the two figures offered a reassuring image of a man's pure affection for the child of the woman he loved.

Indeed, Godwin now began to behave in a gentler manner towards her.

"Should you like to go to Mr. Dodgson now, Jane?"

"No," she said quickly, as if fearing the consequences of her answer.

Godwin's hand stroked the crown of her dark hair and the sweep of it to one side of her face.

"Truly? Are you determined to desert him, then, after so many happy hours tête-à-tête?"

"You will not like it if I go to him. You are always angry if I do!"

The hand moved a little and stroked her cheek.

"You do me an injustice, Jane. You may see him as often as you please. What is it to me if you choose to spend your time among pale English clerics with their canting ways?"

"Then what must I do if I am to please *you*?"

"Go to Mr. Dodgson, Jane. Find some maidenly pretext for your visit. Entice him to undress you again and take a pretty picture. A picture that we may all admire. Be his little girl-angel!"

The innuendo was lost on her. While the conversation continued she was looking at the familiar garden and thinking that when the leaves fell she would see it no more. The life of the house would continue, her mother and Thomas Godwin leading

240

their strange dual existence. Neither they nor her home would be part of her own life for many months, perhaps for years. When she saw the house across Folly Bridge again, she and the world would be changed beyond recall.

"Why must I go in October?" she asked plaintively, hoping to soften him by the process of explanation.

"Mr. Dodgson will tell you why, Jane. Mr. Dodgson is well versed in matters of Christian duty. It is his trade to reconcile foolish girls to the ways of the world, the duty of a daughter to her mother!"

In order to placate him and as a means of avoiding his caresses, Jane got to her feet. In this she would obey him.

"You will tell Mama where I have gone?" she asked doubtfully.

Godwin looked at her, ignoring the question. She stepped away and stood in the green shade of the horse chestnut, brushing the pink pleats of her dress into place. Turning at last to the shrubbery, she looked down at the road, along which the Welsh drovers brought the wild ponies to the market at Gloucester Green.

It was rare for her to visit the rooms in Christ Church without warning. He might be out. More likely, he would be writing or entertaining some other guest. Still hesitating, she glanced back. Thomas Godwin watched her from the lawn.

"Go!" he said savagely. "There is nothing here for you!"

He went back to the tree, sitting with his book in his hand, not deigning to see whether the girl had obeyed his command.

Beyond the towers of St. Ebbes and Carfax, the afternoon sun in its decline lengthened the shadows of battlements and archways.

Dodgson perched on one knee before the chair, as if about to attend to the fireplace. It was Jane who was the object of his care.

"I knew a young lady once," he said confidentially, "and how she cried and she cried! Do you know, my dear? She cried a whole pool of tears, so that they quite surrounded her boots. And then do you know what happened? Why, it was the most extraordinary thing!"

He paused and looked up at Jane, a comic concern on his face as if he feared she might not be attending to the story. The handkerchief he had lent her was still pressed close to her eyes and he heard the sudden deep breaths of her checked sobs.

"Well," he said emphatically, "this young lady, she cried so that her boots stood in the pool of tears. Now, as you know, any object standing in water displaces a volume of liquid equal to its own bulk. So the soles of her boots displaced the water and the pool of tears rose a tenth of an inch. But that tenth of an inch of boots and legs displaced more tears, and so the flood rose higher still."

Despite herself, she caught her breath and listened.

"Why," cried Dodgson in alarm, "in no time at all, it was at her knees! And then, to be sure, she cried all the harder. What with the tears that were falling and the ones that were being displaced as the level rose as she sank farther in, it was at her waist before you could say 'Knife, fork, and spoon.'"

He heard the quick gasp that might have been laughter, and so made his own voice seem the more solemn.

"Then, alas, poor young lady, it was all over with her. The flood rushed upward and swallowed her entirely. Had it not been for a good-natured marine diver in the next room, who so happened to keep a spare diving-bell on the premises, they might never have brought her out alive. Since that day, she has never shed a single tear, and is known to all her friends as quite the jolliest young lady for a hundred miles around."

Jane put her arms down in an awkward attempt to hug him to her. Dodgson got up, raising her at the same time, and they stood before the fireplace with their arms about one another until Jane was calm again.

"*Why* must I go?" she said softly. "Why? I could be a pupil-teacher as easily here as there! What sense is there in sending me away?"

Dodgson led her to a chair by the teatable and sat her down.

"Because your mother loves you and wants what is the best thing for you, my darling," he said gently, "and because she thinks that Harrogate is the best thing."

"But how *can* it be when I am happy here?"

Dodgson poured the tea and put the image of Thomas Godwin resolutely from his mind.

"Perhaps you may be happy *now*. Perhaps your mother sees that you must be a little unhappy now in order to be a lot happier in years to come."

"I shall not be able to see you." The brown eyes in the firm, pale face looked up at him as if hoping for contradiction.

"Then *I* shall come to see *you*!" Despite the joviality of his tone, the obligation to be cheerful was making him feel more wretched at every attempt.

"It won't be the same!" Jane announced with something approaching sulkiness. "I believe they want me out of the way, that's all."

"You must obey your mother, Jane," he said, with a threat of severity. "That is your duty."

"Is it my duty to be thoroughly miserable every day of every week?"

"There are many girls of your age, my dear, who would think your misery heaven on earth if they could change places with you."

Jane ignored this.

"It is *his* doing!" she said helplessly. "Why should he hate me? I have never done him harm, nor wished to."

Dodgson could not answer her. The image of Godwin returned to him, the dark sardonic infidel. Godwin and Sarah Ashmole, a weak, compliant woman. He sensed that Jane was about to weep again.

"Will you help me, Jane?" he asked, sitting down in the next chair. "I have a great ambition to be a London detective. Who knows what may happen if I solve the famous mystery of the riverbank murder?"

Jane Ashmole shivered at the words.

"Ah," he said, "I shall not talk of dead bodies and clues. But will you tell me, as a secret, what happened on that afternoon while you were there?"

"Nothing," she said indifferently. "It was all horrid, of course, but it must have happened a long way off."

"Why?"

"Because," she said, searching for a likely reason, "I should have heard it if someone was being murdered close by. It must have made an awful noise."

"You went to the river with your mother and the two Chantrey girls?"

"Yes," she said, "of course."

"No one else?"

"There wouldn't have been room in the boat for many more."

"What time did you go there?"

"We went to the boating station at about half past two," she said thoughtfully, "and tied up by the bank soon after three. Then we sat and talked for a while. At about half past three I changed to go bathing. Then Nerissa and Belinda did the same."

Dodgson was certain that Jane could not have been told about the photographic plate left in Tiptoe's camera. Now he was more confident still that his own interpretation of it was correct.

"So," he said gently, "you had changed into bathing-drawers and vest while the others were in their frocks."

Jane looked at him, trying to help without knowing why.

"Yes, I suppose so."

The only time, then, when she could have been naked and Belinda Chantrey still in bathing costume was when they changed back again. He was sure of it now.

"When did you put your clothes on again?"

"I don't know," she said helplessly. "About two hours later, I think. After Mr. Godwin arrived. He came along the towpath."

"And when was that?"

"About five o'clock, I expect."

"And your mother and the other two girls were with you all the time?"

"Of course, they were. Mama would not have left us alone."

"I'm sure she would not. Did you hear and see nothing all this time?"

"About the man who was found drowned?"

"About him, Jane."

"No!" she said, shaking her head with emphatic earnestness.

"There was nothing. Nothing that we heard or saw. Not even the camera on the bank."

"Perhaps it was hidden by the trees."

"Perhaps it was," Jane said, lowering her face a little in bewilderment. "Whether it was or not, we never saw it."

Dodgson took her hand between his own.

"Now you may think that I am *your* Unknown Quantity, Jane, with so many questions. Will you mind if I ask you one more?"

"No," she said uncertainly, "I shan't mind."

"Tell me about the bathing."

"We were in the pool, and Mama sat on the rug. After a time we lay on the grass in our bathing things, in the sun, and got warm."

"Was that when Mr. Godwin came, while you were in the sun?"

"Yes," she said, recalling the sequence of events with an effort. "Yes, it was. Then Nerissa began to feel cold because the sun had gone behind the trees. So she changed into her proper clothes again. Then I did. And then Belinda. After that we all went home."

He leant forward and kissed her on the cheek. As he did so, he knew that Jane had quite innocently lied to him. Godwin had not been with them all the time, nor perhaps had Sarah Ashmole. Whatever her weakness for her lover might be, Mrs. Ashmole was unlikely to allow him to watch the three girls in their nakedness as they changed from one set of clothing to another. Even if she cared nothing on Jane's account, she must have known that the Chantrey girls were likely to confide such an incident to their governess or their mother.

There had been a time, then, when each of the bathing party— the three girls, Mrs. Ashmole, and Godwin—had been concealed from the rest.

In his mind, Dodgson saw again the photograph that Swain had shown him. He had, naturally, assumed that Sarah Ashmole was within its boundaries, though concealed as she sat on her rug behind the bushes. Now, in imagination, he extended the view of the camera's eye to include Sarah Ashmole and Godwin standing in the trees, in conversation together while the girls were concealed from them. Perhaps they even stood in one another's arms.

Thoughts of a similar kind occupied Alfred Swain as he set out the facts of the evidence like the incompatible shapes of a Christmas puzzle.

"What it comes to," he said severely to Sergeant Lumley, "is that every fresh scrap of news does nothing but make nonsense of all that came before. It's not the way that evidence ought to be!"

Lumley's plump jaws moved comfortingly and he exuded a faint odour of peppermint. He spoke confidentially.

"I can't say I've ever held with evidence, sir. Not to any great extent."

They stood side by side, looking down at the full-plate print upon the table.

"He's right," said Swain, rapping the sepia card with a pencil. "That can't be half past three. Even allowing for it being a fortnight earlier in the summer. The shadows on those trees won't be that length today until after five o'clock. I went down to the exact place yesterday and saw for myself."

"Best forget it, then," said Lumley, with the air of one who had been right from the first.

"No, Mr. Lumley. Best remember it and what it means. At half past three, if the facts are to be believed, Major Tiptoe was struck down from behind by a furious blow, a blow of great force, while attempting to take a photograph on the riverbank. His body fell, or was pushed, into the water. His boat was set adrift. Perhaps his murderer hoped that it would seem as if Major Tiptoe lost his balance and fell, head first, onto some projection, or that there had been a boating accident. The splinter from the paling scotched that."

Swain tapped the print again and continued.

"Perhaps it was Mr. Howell, and perhaps Mr. Dodgson. It may have been a complete stranger whose name was unknown to Major Tiptoe as it is to us."

"The blackmail again, sir," said Lumley, in an attempt to be helpful. "It all keeps coming back to it."

Swain ignored the assistance offered.

"Not Mrs. Ashmole or any of the girls. Such a blow would be beyond their power, even in desperation. And Mr. Godwin was safe and sound in Christ Church College at half past three."

"They don't call it a college, sir," said Lumley, in a gentle tone. "Just Christ Church or the House."

"I know all about the House," said Swain bitterly, "from Dean Liddell himself."

To some extent, he felt, that levelled the score with Sergeant Lumley.

"Now," he said, writing the figures on the margin of the print, "two hours go by, half past three until half past five or so. No one comes along. Mrs. Ashmole and party have no cause to go farther along the bank. If anyone did come along, he failed to notice what had happened—a camera standing on its tripod in the middle of the path and the body of a man floating in the water. Not to mention a boat adrift."

"It's a quiet part of the bank this time of year," said Lumley. "Not what you'd call frequented."

"And then," Swain went on, "a man or woman comes by about half past five. That person saw the camera standing there. That person pointed it at the girls dressing, uncapped the lens, and hooded it again. Someone who knew about photographs, Mr. Lumley, depend on that. Then, having taken the picture, the person leaves the glass-plate negative in the camera and walks on. Not Mr. Howell, who's half-way to London on the train. Not Mr. Dodgson, who's now seen back in . . . in . . . the House. Two hours after the murder, someone who couldn't have done it comes along, sees the body, and takes a photograph of girls undressed—which that person then deliberately leaves there to be found. Why?"

"That's evidence, sir!" Lumley took a red-spotted handkerchief from his pocket and patted his moustaches, thereby impeding any possibility of further explanation.

"Exactly!" Swain slapped the table with his palm. "That photograph was taken by someone who knew all about evidence."

"Sir?"

"If you committed murder, Mr. Lumley, what's the first thing you would do."

"Cut and run," said Lumley with a rich chortle.

"I'd find you and hang you, Mr. Lumley. Try again."

"Get rid of all the evidence, then cut and run!"

"You'd never even guess the things that might be evidence, Mr. Lumley. I'd still find you and hang you."

"You don't mean I'd add to the evidence?" said Lumley, his large red nose wrinkling with incredulity.

"It's what I'd do, Mr. Lumley. I'd scatter enough clues there to keep Scotland Yard chasing its own tail for the next twelve-month."

"And that's what you think?"

"Yes," said Swain shortly. "That photograph was left by some-one who knew all about evidence. Someone who knew what a bloody nuisance evidence can be!"

During this discussion, Jane Ashmole made her way in Dodg-son's company, across the water meadows to the house beyond Folly Bridge. At the gateway they separated.

That night, the girl lay in bed while the cloud castle of western sky hung bright enough with twilight to show the sudden flut-tering of moth and bat, like leaves in the wind. Sarah Ashmole and Thomas Godwin were talking in the drawing-room, the win-dows open and the tawny oil light falling in a thin panel across the terrace outside.

Most of the words were audible only as a murmur without meaning. Then, as the girl lay in bed, watching the last of the twilight on the ceiling, she heard her mother's voice, raised as if in protest.

"The child knows nothing, and would not understand if she did."

Godwin's gruffer voice replied, and then Sarah Ashmole spoke again.

"I tell you the child knows nothing of it. How could she?"

The words were no more than a repetition of the previous statement. Yet the tone of the voice was duller and more weary, suggesting to Jane that her mother was close to tears. In the lime tree beyond the lawn a screech-owl set up its shrill and mournful descant.

32

ALFRED SWAIN still lay in bed while Roxana Wilberforce in her petticoats combed her hair before the mirror. He watched the even strokes of her arm in the reflected mirror-light from the street window. Her fair skin upon her shoulders seemed paler still by contrast with the rich red and gold lights of the abundant tresses.

Any painter would have taken her for a model just now, he thought. There was such grace and feminine strength in the movement of the pretty arm, such slow self-admiration as she stared into the mirror glass before which she stood. Though she was several years older than Swain himself, her soft, appealing prettiness was Mrs. Wilberforce's unchallengeable asset. Each morning she examined it carefully, as if to assure herself that it had not depreciated since the previous day.

The loves of Swain's life had been few, and they had always come upon him unexpectedly. At one moment the happiness with a woman belonged to another, unattainable world. Then, in a few hours, the pattern of existence changed. The knowledge of years came to him in half a day. He lived a new life and emerged from it to find that the sun had scarcely moved half-way across the sky.

There was a knot in the dark chestnut hair. Roxana Wilberforce fretted at it with her tortoise-shell comb for a moment and then it came free. After that, the silver-backed brush swept in long, sensuous strokes, the hair whispering like silk under a hand. The sound of it soothed Swain as much as the young woman herself. How soft and enveloping the hair as she stooped over him!

He closed his eyes and listened to her sounds. Outside in the early morning, cart-wheels passed by in a clattering of iron rims. A familiar voice cried out: "Milk down below!"

The brushing stopped. He thought at first that Roxana Wilberforce was going downstairs in her petticoats. Before he could open his eyes, she was upon him. It was her energy rather than her soft weight that threatened to squeeze the breath from his lungs.

"It's very important today, Mr. Swain, is it?"

She spoke close to his ear, nibbling at it.

"Yes, Mrs. Wilberforce, it's very important."

"It wouldn't do tomorrow, if you was to have a bit of a rest today?"

"No, Mrs. Wilberforce. There are things that must be done today."

She got up with a sigh and went back to brushing her hair.

"I don't see the odds of being in private clothes," she said, "not if it's like that. You might just as well have to go in uniform and parade in the police-office yard. Like poor Mr. Wilberforce always did."

"Never a truer word, Mrs. Wilberforce." He swung his legs out of bed and kissed her on the cheek. "Never a truer word than that."

"Oh, Mr. Swain!" she sighed again, affectionately. "You don't know a lot, do you? About women and that?"

"I might know a lot more by the time I come back this evening, Mrs. W." With this cryptic dismissal he turned from her.

Two hours later, Sarah Ashmole received him, alone in her drawing-room. In strands of woollen plumage, the macaw upon the embroidery frame was still unfinished. Sunlight on chintz and lace dazzled the darker velvets of the cushioning. Swain imagined that the house might be a place of great tranquillity with its garden of green spaces and butterflies sunning their wings on broad leaves of nettles and flowers. Yet the uneasy spirit of Sarah Ashmole perturbed the air of rooms and garden alleys like a ghost.

She sat opposite him, dark hair bowed in a study of her hands folded in her lap. It seemed a pose of modesty, not concealment.

"I fear you will think me most unhelpful, Mr. Swain. Yet I should be a poor witness if I improved the truth by invention."

She looked up at him quickly, such soft kindness in her pale face. Then the dark hair bowed again in a study of her hands whose thumbs fretted one another as she spoke. Swain knew she was close to tears.

"I took the girls to the Iffley pool by boat, Mr. Swain. Only the four of us. We were slow in making the journey, I believe, and came there after three o'clock. We first thought of a nearer place on the bank but that was occupied already. So we went on."

She paused for so long that Swain had to prompt her.

"Then," said Mrs. Ashmole, "the three girls changed to wade and paddle in the water. I sat on the rug and read Mr. Stevenson's *Travels with a Donkey*, which the circulating library had sent. I had taken it as a book suitable for reading to the children when they finished bathing. Mr. Godwin knew the direction in which we had gone and upon which bank. When his business in college was over, he walked down there until he came upon us."

"And when was that, Mrs. Ashmole?"

"I could not tell you exactly, Mr. Swain. At about five o'clock. Soon after that, we made room in the boat for one more and Mr. Godwin rowed us back."

"How soon, Mrs. Ashmole?"

"A few minutes," she said. "Ten minutes at the most, perhaps."

"You saw nothing, heard nothing, out of the ordinary?"

"Nothing, Mr. Swain. This thing—this terrible thing which happened—was farther along the bank. We had no occasion to go in that direction, Mr. Swain."

"When you entered the boat to come home, you saw no camera standing on a tripod?"

"No, Mr. Swain."

"And you saw—you saw nothing in the water?"

She shook her head vigorously, without looking up or speaking.

"Then, Mrs. Ashmole, I have very little more to trouble you with."

It was a customary technique of Swain's to stimulate a sense of relief in his subjects before coming to the more important questions. Sarah Ashmole looked up, her mild face expressing unconcealed surprise that the ordeal of interrogation had been so trivial.

"Just to help me a little, ma'am," he said gently, "you and the three young ladies were together at that place all the time from your arrival at about three o'clock until you left with Mr. Godwin soon after five?"

"Yes," she said, "of course."

"And Mr. Godwin was with you from the time that he arrived until you all left together?"

"It was such a little while," said Sarah Ashmole.

"Thank you," said Swain courteously. "One last point. You can, I assume, vouch for the characters of the two young ladies who accompanied you and your daughter?"

She looked at him in astonishment.

"They are children, Mr. Swain! You cannot believe . . ."

He reassured her with a laugh.

"I do not believe them murderers, Mrs. Ashmole! Nothing of the kind! No more do I believe it of you or your daughter. I speak only as to their reliability as witnesses, if the need should arise."

"They are good and truthful children," she said, a spirit of indignation lighting her dark eyes on behalf of Nerissa and Belinda Chantrey.

"I'm sure they are, ma'am. And what of Mr. Godwin?"

Coming at the moment when she least expected such a question, it caused an involuntary quiver in the line of Sarah Ashmole's graceful mouth.

"Mr. Godwin?"

"Yes, ma'am. Your feelings in respect of Mr. Godwin."

"I cannot say, Mr. Swain. I do not . . . Such a question is beyond all reason."

He pitied her for the confusion in her beautiful eyes and guessed that in her astonishment she had almost said "I do not know."

"Forgive me, ma'am. I speak only of your feelings about Mr. Godwin as a witness. My question was most thoughtlessly phrased. I apologise."

She caught her breath audibly.

"As a witness?"

"Exactly, Mrs. Ashmole. Might he have seen or heard something that escaped you and the young ladies? I would not trouble any of you unnecessarily but it might be to my advantage to seek an interview with Mr. Godwin in addition."

The thankfulness at seeing a way out of her dismay was clear, and she followed it with gratitude.

"As to that, Mr. Swain, you may ask him for yourself. I do not think it possible that he can have heard or seen anything that escaped us. Why, he was hardly there for any time at all."

It was not in Sarah Ashmole's nature to be a liar, Swain thought. Perhaps in her own mind she was not even conscious of being one. And he pitied her for that, too.

It was an hour later when Sergeant Lumley, in the room at the police office, said,

"You're not a cruel man, Mr. Swain, I'll say that! You might 'a' been hard on her if you chose!"

"No, Mr. Lumley, it wouldn't do. Even you might have sworn to being together with a party all afternoon. Whereas, girls that are bathing mightn't notice if she sat on that rug every minute. Then, again, Mr. Lumley, there are such things as calls of nature. It's not common for several people to spend half a day in company without an interval. An interval long enough to strike a man down or take a photograph."

Swain's frustration was compounded on the following morning by a note from Bedell, the Oxford solicitor of Mrs. Ashmole. Mr. Bedell recorded his client's assistance in the inquiry and requested that she should be put to no further distress in the matter. Upon his advice, she would not answer further questions, except in his presence.

"Evidence of guilt," said Sergeant Lumley with a nod.

"No, Mr Lumley." Swain folded the paper again. "Not of guilt."

"What then?"

"Evidence perhaps that Mrs. Ashmole, too, saw what Major Tiptoe saw through the camera lens in the instant of his death. Fear, Mr. Lumley, not guilt. Fear for herself and her daughter, and for others, too. We'll get nothing more from her now."

33

THOMAS GODWIN was more elusive than Swain's other subjects. He was not to be found in his rooms at Christ Church nor had there been any sign of him when the inspector visited Sarah Ashmole. It was the assistant porter in the archway of Tom Quad who suggested to Swain that his man might be found at Roebuck's Gymnasium in Tanners Lane.

Swain walked slowly along the narrow streets of St. Ebbes, the eyes of slum children and women in their doorways watching him warily. They knew him for what he was, there was no doubt of that. In the passageway of Tanners Lane, the old damp buildings tall on either side, there was a courtyard with a small public house at its far end. Even at midday the gas was lit in the dark interior. From the open windows came the sound of pewter beating time to "Slap! Bang! Here we are again!" There were shouts of laughter and the stamping of heavy boots, a breaking of glass. The doors opened abruptly and two men reeled out, one of them stumbling to his knees in the gutter choked by refuse.

To one side of the public house, apparently part of the same building, were two windows with a door between. On the windows themselves, white appliqué lettering announced "Colonel Roebuck's Gymnasium. Billiards. Pool. Pyramid. Sparring."

It was not hard to imagine, Swain thought, how such a place might become the rendezvous of raffish undergraduates during term, young men of breeding and spirit, prepared to defy the vigilance of the proctors. He opened the door and went up the bare wooden stairs to the floor above the public house, which constituted Colonel Roebuck's Gymnasium.

The atmosphere was heavy with cigar smoke and steam from the baths that lay to one side. In one of the quieter rooms a pair of masked fencers engaged in conflict with a faint insect sound of two foils touching in a light preliminary test of each other. The main hall of the gymnasium was a long gaslit room crowded by draymen and bargees with a sprinkling of swells in sporting tweed. Numerous trophies, cups, and shields of uncertain authenticity were elegantly framed or cased along the walls. At the centre of the room an area had been roped off as the "ring." A roughly painted board promised sparring and boxing among tanners and costermongers "for beer and a lark," with gloves to be hired at twopence a match. The winner was to be the man who first gave his opponent a "noser" or worse.

Swain edged his way round the ring, under the coloured prints of past giants, Dutch Sam and Jem Belcher, Black Charlie and American Tom. So far as Swain could see, one of the present contenders had his right eye almost closed by a cut and extensive bruising on his left arm, while his opponent pelted away without ceremony. The timekeeper also did duty as umpire. Behind him, each man's bottle-holder stood in a corner of the ring clutching a dark flagon of beer anxiously.

"Mr. Godwin?" said Swain presently, picking him out easily as the one black-suited figure there. "Inspector Swain. May we have a private word?"

Godwin turned to him. For the first time Swain appreciated the acute intelligence in the tall brow and the sharp, dark eyes from which one was tempted to flinch. In the Middle Ages, he thought, they would have burnt the man as an alchemist or a sorcerer.

"Inspector Merriman has had a good many words with me already, Mr. Swain. I assume you refer to the matter of the man who was killed."

"I'd be obliged for a word myself all the same, sir."

They walked aside to a corner of the room, away from the hearing of the crowd.

"I should not have bothered you here, sir," said Swain gently, "had I been fortunate enough to find you at home. I did not know, of course, that you were a follower of the prize ring."

Godwin looked at him sardonically.

"If you consider this to be a prize ring, Mr. Swain, your experience is sadly limited. As to being a follower of the noble art, until I was wellnigh forty I sparred with gentlemen of my acquaintance once or twice a week. Contrary to appearance, this sport is the best in the world for improving one's knowledge of and respect for the man one fights."

"Indeed," said Swain, hardly concealing his lack of interest in the matter. "I will not then detain you from it unnecessarily, sir. Be good enough, if you will, to recount the events upon the riverbank that afternoon of Major Tiptoe's death."

Godwin sighed, as though his tolerance was under stress.

"I did not see the riverbank, as you call it, until five o'clock or thereabouts. I went by arrangement to collect Mrs. Ashmole and the girls. They were almost ready when I arrived. A little while after that, we entered the boat and came back. It is a harder exercise to row upstream, Mr. Swain, and a man is better suited to it."

"You saw nothing of Major Tiptoe, alive or dead, nor of his camera?"

"Nothing," said Godwin simply.

"You went no farther along the bank towards the weir?"

"I had no occasion to, Mr. Swain."

"And you have no other significant recollection of those moments?"

"My dear Swain," said Godwin tolerantly, "you surely do not want me to improve the truth by invention?"

"No, sir," said Swain humbly.

"Then I can tell you no more."

"When you were a boy, sir . . ."

"What the devil has that to do with it?" For the first time the anger of impatience glittered in the dark eyes.

"As a boy, sir, you were sent to Harrow School."

"So I was, Mr. Swain. Well?"

"Major Tiptoe was a boy there, sir."

Godwin gave a gentle snort of contempt for the inspector's stupidity.

"If you had cared to inform yourself in such matters, Mr. Swain, you would find that the dead man is reported as seven or eight years younger than I. Therefore, I would have left Harrow before his arrival. I neither knew him nor knew of him. It is possible that he may have heard something of me as one who had been there. I really could not say and do not care."

"Then you did not know, sir, that Major Tiptoe was blackmailing you?"

For the first time, Thomas Godwin lost his composure and looked at Swain without appearing to understand hm.

"No one was blackmailing me, Mr. Swain! Not Major Tiptoe or any other rogue."

"Not directly, sir," Swain conceded. "Mrs. Ashmole was being blackmailed, on account of your association with her."

"Rubbish!" Godwin regained his spirit at this. "Utter non-sense!"

"Among the dead man's effects, sir, was a copy of a letter he'd written to Mrs. Ashmole, all to do with her and you."

"Ah!" said Godwin softly. "The letter!"

"Yes, Mr. Godwin."

"When we returned that evening to Mrs. Ashmole's house, a letter had come by the afternoon post. It was a piece of trivial moral poison, unsigned. A young widow who takes a bachelor as her lodger is a helpless target for such vermin. There was no demand for money, however, merely the vapourings of a sanc-timonious prig who had not the courage to sign his name or to write except in block letters. You may ask Mrs. Ashmole."

"As a matter of delicacy, Mr. Godwin, I preferred to ask you first. What became of that letter?"

"The safest place," said Godwin darkly.

"Where?"

"Upon the fire, where such moral spite belongs."

"Did you never care who sent it?"

Godwin looked at Swain as if with pity for his stupidity.

"I *knew* who had sent it, Mr. Swain. That good and pious prig, the Reverend Dodgson!"

"And why should you think that, Mr. Godwin?"

Godwin beckoned him to a pair of wooden chairs a little farther off and the two of them sat down.

"Mr. Swain, you are an innocent in matters of the world for all your cleverness. That world has turned full circle in our time. A timid age of reason was fired sixty years ago by great men in our own land—Shelley, Byron—into a great revolution of the soul. Men such as I stand for the future, Mr. Swain, the freedom of the mind and even of man's love for woman. The god within the mind is reason, the only god there can be. Poor Mr. Dodgson may believe his Bible myths and his narrow bitter obligations of chastity. See how it shrivels him! A man among children and a child among men! A poor wretch whose only lust is to ride his own loins like a saddle. I pity him, Mr. Swain, pity him greatly. Do you understand me?"

"Very clearly, sir," said Swain equably.

"He is of the past, Mr. Swain, and I of the future. The world will one day see the jealous evil of the narrow marriage bonds that turn each man and woman from the greater love of mankind. I see such things now, Mr. Swain. I would kiss any pretty woman and be proud of it, Mr. Swain. I would sleep with a pretty woman and be so little ashamed that the entire world might look on. Do you still understand me, Mr. Swain?"

"Yes, sir, I understand you."

"Then you will see how it affects poor Dodgson, who sees his own timid world of moral humbug and religious cant washed out like footprints on the sand. How, like a scorpion that stings itself in fury, he must lash out vainly at those who represent the new order of enlightenment. Human dignity, Mr. Swain, proud and upright, not cringing before an ancient fetish! Reason, the god within the mind! The ultimate liberty of man and woman."

"And Major Tiptoe?" Swain inquired.

"Ah," said Godwin, "the blackmail! He might blackmail Mr. Dodgson, perhaps, a poor wretch who lives in shame. I live otherwise, Mr. Swain, and so shall Mrs. Ashmole and any other for whom I care. Blackmail me? Major Tiptoe might as well kick his own arse for all the profit it would bring him."

Thomas Godwin ceased, at that point, to be the Byron of his day and broke out into a lusty, bawdy laugh entirely appropriate to the smoky atmosphere of Roebuck's Gymnasium.

"Now, Mr. Swain, permit me to wish you good afternoon!"

34

SERGEANT LUMLEY received Swain's account of Thomas Godwin with well-fed scepticism.

"All he wants, Mr. Swain, is the world as a whorehouse and himself as lord and master of it. That's what it comes to! A man of his education talking no better than a heathen savage!"

The two men turned from the leafy expanse of St. Giles and walked down the Georgian avenue of Beaumont Street. Swain rang the bell of a house with a panelled front door.

"Wait here," he said, pointing at the pavement.

When not engaged as police surgeon, Dr. Hammond presided at this address over a lucrative practice, caring for the hearts and lungs of prosperous north Oxford. He greeted Swain with an air suggesting that the time bought by the coroner's fee had long expired.

The two men sat at a broad desk inset with green leather. Ground-glass lamps on tall bronze columns rose at either side. The noon sun filled the high, sash-windowed room from Grecian cornice to deep skirting.

"The time of his death," said Swain gently. "How close can you come to it, Dr. Hammond? For a certainty?"

Hammond regarded him across the desk, reluctant to reveal the secrets of medical magic.

"In Major Tiptoe's case the situation was a little unusual."

"Was it now?" said Swain, prompting him helpfully.

"Food, Mr. Swain. A man that takes lunch at noon will pass the food from his stomach to his tripes at about three."

"And Major Tiptoe?"

"Major Tiptoe had not done so. Major Tiptoe had eaten no lunch that day! It was, you may say, irregular. Extremely so!"

Dr. Hammond gave a little scowl as if in disapproval of the late major's rackety habits.

"What other evidence?" asked Swain bleakly.

"Well," Hammond waved his hands in a tolerant gesture at the possibilities, "in default of the entrails, the temperature of a cadaver, which cools at about two degrees an hour, is a normal guide to the time of death."

"In Major Tiptoe's case?"

"In Major Tiptoe's case," said Hammond confidentially, "the drop in the temperature of the cadaver would indicate death occurring between three and four o'clock."

"With certainty?"

"More or less."

"More or less will not do, Dr. Hammond. Should there be a murder trial and should you be cross-examined by defence counsel, it will not do to answer more or less."

Hammond thought about this for a moment.

"It is the water that creates the difficulty, Mr. Swain."

"The water?"

"Yes, indeed. The cadaver was found floating in the river whose temperature was some forty degrees below that of the body at the time of death. It must have had some effect on the rate of cooling—who can say how much? At seven o'clock the temperature was lower than that of a cadaver that would have met its death at three-thirty under normal circumstances. If the river cooled it more quickly than we assume, then the time of death *could* have been later."

"Later?" Swain sat up straight in his chair. "How much later?"

"Who can say, Mr. Swain? Only a little. My report was quite conclusive. There was nothing in the medical evidence inconsistent with the death of the victim at about half past three."

"But you don't know *when* he died!" Swain shouted.

"Do me justice, Mr. Swain! You tell me he could not have met his death before half past three, on the evidence of the watch. I tell you that he died between that time and half past five. The medical evidence, even in setting such wide limits, accommodates your belief that Major Tiptoe was struck down at 3.35."

"Unless the watch was wrong," said Swain morosely.

"If you allow such arbitrary possibilities, Mr. Swain, then no evidence is worth a button. What becomes of the body temperature if Major Tiptoe takes a steam-bath or, for that matter, an infusion of ice-water? The watch had been wound and set only an hour or so before. You had much better assume that it went correctly for that short period."

Back on the pavement of Beaumont Street, Swain gave the news to Sergeant Lumley.

"Then there's only the watch?" said Lumley with a sigh. "Only that and whoever killed him to say when it happened?"

"Not quite, Mr. Lumley." Swain turned and began to walk back along the street to St. Giles. "There's also the person who was there when he was killed. The person who saw him killed."

"Who's that, then?"

"Mrs. Ashmole," said Swain grimly. "That's what she saw! I'm sure of it."

"She never told you, Mr. Swain?"

"Yes, Mr. Lumley, though she didn't realise it at the time. Nor did I."

"What'd she say?" Lumley's eagerness caused him to pant a little as he walked faster to match Swain's stride.

"She said it wouldn't help me if she improved the truth by invention. Her very words. Then she said that she had no occasion to go farther along the bank than the pool where the girls bathed."

"And you saw it all in that?" The admiration shone in Lumley's eyes.

"No, Mr. Lumley, not at the time. I saw it when I put much the same questions to Mr. Thomas Godwin. He gave me a dozen answers, if he gave me one. Yet he, too, said he had no occasion to go farther along the bank—not cause or reason, but occasion.

I let that pass. Then he said it wouldn't help me if he improved the truth by invention."

"That's not much," said Lumley, the disappointment audible. Swain stopped in mid-stride.

"You hear a lot of people of your acquaintance talk about improving the truth by invention, do you, Mr. Lumley? One of them coached the other in what to say. Now, I can't imagine a silly frightened woman like Mrs. Ashmole putting the words into his mouth. I *can* imagine a bold, shameless man like Thomas Godwin telling Mrs. Ashmole what to say. A few days more and he'd forgotten the precise words he gave her. His mind threw them up again and he never even recognised 'em."

"Don't necessarily mean she saw murder, Mr. Swain."

"She was there from half past three until half past five," said Swain determinedly. "What else did she see that would put her in such fear and make a liar out of an honest woman?"

"And Godwin?"

"Five o'clock," said Swain reluctantly. "He couldn't have been there much before."

For most of the afternoon, Swain fretted in silence over the problem. He was well aware that his chance to question either Sarah Ashmole or Thomas Godwin had been spent. They had submitted to interrogation as far as their civic duty required. Next time there would be a solicitor present. And that, as Alfred Swain knew from experience, was as good as not asking questions at all.

Yet a half-formed memory plagued him, the echo of a voice he had first heard ten years ago. It had been a witty, self-assured, lunatic voice. The voice of the Reverend Mr. Dodgson. What precisely had it said? Something about being late, Swain thought. A rabbit with a watch. The riddles of time.

That evening he avoided the entreaties of young Mrs. Wilberforce and withdrew to his room carrying a carefully wrapped treasure. It was a copy of *Alice's Adventures in Wonderland*, bought that day as he made his way back to St. John Street. With a sense of utter contentment, Swain lay down on the bed and began to read to himself in a murmur.

Alice was beginning to get very tired of sitting by her sister on the bank and of having nothing to do. . . .

For more than two hours he read, the murmuring subsiding at last into a silent scanning of the pages. The long equine face relaxed in an expression of sheer good-natured enjoyment, the mouth curving in humorous appreciation of the book's endearing nonsense. He wondered why he had left it so long before re-reading the story.

Then, at "A Mad Tea-Party," the easy enjoyment vanished and his face tightened with suspicion.

"If you knew Time as well as I do," said the Hatter, "you wouldn't talk about wasting it. It's him."

This was what he remembered. The words seemed to come back to him almost before he read them.

"Now, if you only kept on good terms with Time, he'd do almost anything you liked with the clock!" Swain sat upright in his excitement. *"For instance, suppose it were nine o'clock in the morning, just time to begin lessons: you'd only have to whisper a hint to Time, and round goes the clock in a twinkling! Half past one, time for dinner!"*

Swain sprang from the bed and looked around him in eagerness. Now that he was so close to the answer he could not bear to wait a moment more. The tin-plated watch, regulation police issue, lay on the table. He wound it fully. Putting it on the floor, Swain took the boot from beside his bed and smashed the heel down on the timepiece with all his force. He looked at the remains: the splintered glass, shattered dial, and hands broken clean off. Now his face assumed a woebegone look. It was not at all what he had expected.

35

THE SHELVES BEHIND THE COUNTER of Mr. Treadgold's shop were filled with black Corinthian mantel clocks, each representing some temple of the ancient world. At his back, Swain heard the rumble and clatter of cart-wheels in Oxford High Street as the wagons made their way with poles and canvas to begin erecting the booths for St. Giles Fair.

"Your friend," said the little watchmaker confidentially. "His watch is of the American kind, the Elgin railroad watch. That is to say, it is of a standard of accuracy that permits its use by railroad officials in the United States. We import a good many, sir."

"Expensive?" asked Swain.

"No, sir. A good reliable watch for half a guinea and a year's guarantee."

"Show me."

The little man took out a tray of identical watches and laid the collection on the counter. Swain recognised them at once as the type Major Tiptoe had been carrying at the time of his death. He handed the watchmaker half a sovereign and six pennies. Taking the watch, he set the hands to their place and wound it fully.

266

"An excellent choice," said the little man politely. "A modern timekeeper that will give years of reliable service. I congratulate you upon your purchase, sir."

Swain said nothing. He stooped down, placed the watch, face upwards, on the shop-boards, and then brought his heel down upon it, his teeth clenched to give force to the blow. As with the police watch on the previous night, there was nothing but a flattened shell, the hands broken clean away. He straightened up and looked reproachfully at the little man who had sold him the piece. By this time dismay was turning into panic in the watchmaker's eyes, and he seemed about to bolt through the door that led to the back of the shop.

"Six more," said Swain firmly. "I'll take six more of them."

"But why, sir? Such a beautiful timekeeper as that!"

Seeing that he was likely to need the man's cooperation in the experiment, Swain produced his warrant card, the battered remains of Tiptoe's watch, and explained his apparent lunacy. Now there was a different excitement in the watchmaker's eye and he took to the task of dismemberment with as much relish as his customer.

An Elgin railroad watch lay open on the counter.

"First off, sir," said the little man, "you must understand what makes a watch like this go before you understand what makes it stop."

He pointed to the metal drum that dominated the rest of the workings when the back of the watch lay open.

"Now, sir, here we have the going-barrel, as they call it, round which the mainspring is drawn. When the watch is wound up, the mainspring is drawn tight upon it. Follow the tip of my pencil, if you will, and see how the metal thread of the mainspring is connected to the wheel, which is the mechanism for turning the hands. How simple it is! The going-barrel releases the mainspring gradually, like a capstan paying out rope. The ratchet governs the speed of release. When the full length is paid out, the watch will stop until it is wound up and the mainspring is tightly coiled again."

"And my friend's watch?" asked Swain sceptically.

"Why, sir, your poor friend's watch was never struck such a blow as you imagine. It is one thing for a watch to be hit while in a fob, protected by the cloth of the suiting. The impact will certainly rupture the mechanism but it will not crush the piece entirely, as would be the case when stamped upon by a man of your build. Falling upon a stone, for example, would cause the damage to your friend's watch. Did the poor gentleman fall?"

"Oh, yes," said Swain drily, "he fell all right."

The watchmater poked at the workings of Tiptoe's watch with the tip of his pencil.

"There you have it, sir. Now, see. The glass is gone but the hands are still attached. The dial marked but not broken. Why, sir, the watch may have been back to front in the fob, and the face of it protected from the worst. But see here! The fastening of the going-drum is broken away completely. The ratchet gone. Quite beyond repair, sir. Never worth it. Buy a new one."

"Show me how it would have been," said Swain quietly.

With visible reluctance, the watchmaker took another of the Elgin railroad pieces. He put the hands at 11.25 and wound it fully. Then, opening the back, he set to work to reproduce the damage done to Tiptoe's watch. In one jerk of a small pair of pliers he snapped free the going-drum and ratchet. There was a brief fizzing sound from the mechanism and then silence. He turned the watch over. The hands were set at quarter to two.

"I'll be damned!" said Swain admiringly. "So that was it. 'You'd only have to whisper a hint to Time, and round goes the clock in a twinkling!'"

"I beg your pardon?"

Swain ignored the question and asked his own.

"If such an accident were to happen, the hands might whirl round the dial to any point?"

"They might," said the little man doubtfully. "The Elgin being a modest watch—twenty-four hours only—they would most probably come to rest a little over that period from when it was last wound. When there is nothing to hold the mainspring, it will release its force upon the driving wheel, and the hands will be propelled until the spring loses its force. But that will only happen in such a case as this, where the hands and driving mechanism are intact but the mainspring free of restraint."

"If a watch of this type was fully wound at two o'clock, and if such an accident occurred to it, the hands might stop at about half past three?"

"Very likely."

"Regardless of what time the accident happened to it?"

"If the mainspring ran the rest of its course in a few seconds and carried the hands with it, the moment of the accident would make very little difference, sir. Mind you, in nine cases out of ten, the hands of the watch will point to the time of the blow for they are crushed and immobilised. Indeed, the mainspring might not be set free by the impact. Only a man who knew or suspected what had happened to the workings of your friend's watch would think of such a thing as this. I congratulate you, sir."

"Then there are cases . . . ?" Swain began.

"Indeed, sir," said the little man enthusiastically. "Did you never hear of the sinking of HMS *Ion*? All hands lost, no witnesses to the tragedy. The divers went down and saw the engine-room clock stopped at four. Naturally that was given as the time of the tragedy. Later the clock was brought up. The time of the tragedy was not four o'clock. The sea water had rusted away the fastenings of the mainspring. Long after the ship sank, the hands of the clock were sent spinning round the dial to the point where they were found. There again, you see, the mechanism of the hands was still in order."

Swain gathered up the other watches he had bought. Slipping them into his pocket he seized the little watchmaker by the hand with unfeigned gratitude.

"Thank you, Mr. Treadgold," he said sincerely. "Thank you very much indeed. What you have proved to me here will be welcome news to many, many people!"

The watchmaker looked at him doubtfully but Swain was already on his way to deliver the good news to some of those who, he supposed, might welcome it.

Swain walked slowly past the lanes and archways of High Street, deaf to the clatter of iron wheels on cobbles and the rumble of barrels rolling down the draymen's ramp into cellars of inns and colleges. He had yet to resolve the final problem of time.

It was likely that the hands of the watch came to rest at 3.35 as a matter of chance. The watch had been wound at two o'clock. It would normally run down in a little over twenty-four hours. In that case 3.35 was a reasonable time for it to stop.

But it was also possible that the murderer had set the hands to that time after Tiptoe's death in order to conceal the truth of when the blow was struck. Swain felt that, had he committed the murder, he would have used this deception.

Yet the murderer might not even know that the watch was there, let alone that its mainspring was broken by Tiptoe's fall. Even if the criminal had thought of the broken watch, he would know it must be likely that the hands or their spindle would be snapped by the impact. Swain revised his opinion. He would not, as a murderer, stand over the body investigating the state of the watch mechanism, liable to be seen at any moment by a stroller on the riverbank. No. He would dump Major Tiptoe in the stream and trust to Fortune to improve his alibi.

He walked thoughtfully among the tulip beds of the Botanic Garden, hearing the laughter of the picnic parties from the boats going under Magdalen Bridge. A watch and a camera were two very different articles, he decided. A watch might suggest time. A camera might hang a man.

Cheered by this thought, he turned smartly about and marched back to where Sergeant Lumley was waiting for him.

36

"SUCH FUN!" said Roxana Wilberforce, her voice luxuriating in the pleasure of it all. "I do think making photographs is such fun. Such clever fun!"

Swain stood self-consciously in the costume of King Arthur, a helmet like an inverted colander on his head, a pair of horns rising from it. The armour of chivalry was represented by a knitted tunic, resembling chain-mail at a distance and indistinguishable from grey dishcloths when seen up close. On the battlements sat three little girls. They watched with what their admirer Mr. Dodgson might regard as a quizzical smile and what Swain called a smirk. They were smirking at him, no doubt of it.

"Such fun!" murmured Roxana Wilberforce. She knelt on the leads of the sunlit roof hugging his right leg to herself, rooting him to the spot. Dodgson, straw-hatted and pedantic, was arranging the wooden box of the camera on its tripod for another picture.

In her robe of green samite, faithful to the poem, Roxana Wilberforce shook her chestnut hair free and drew the sleek silk more tightly over her plump hips for effect. Dodgson stood up from behind the camera, where he had been taking a view of the subject. He looked uneasy but presently stooped down again.

It was not Swain's idea in the first place. Yet their nightly readings from *Idylls of the King* had inspired young Mrs. Wilberforce with such obvious devotion to the poem that he could hardly refuse her. Wanting to return her kindness without compromising himself more than was necessary, Alfred Swain had offered to take her on a treat. The treat was to be of her choosing. He was not greatly surprised when she suggested they might go to a photographic studio and have a "keepsake" photograph made of themselves as two of the actors in the poem. There were studios, Swain had heard, where costumes and camera could be hired for these occasions.

Just then it had been his pleasure to call upon Mr. Dodgson again, to tell him of the matter of Tiptoe's watch, and to inform him that he was free of immediate suspicion. The probability now was that the major had been killed at about the time of the photograph found in his camera. On the same visit Swain had inquired of Dodgson if there were any photographic studios in Oxford of the sort Mrs. Wilberforce had described. With a certain show of awkwardness, though grateful for Swain's news about the watch, Dodgson had volunteered his services in the matter of *Idylls of the King*.

"Now," said Dodgson, "if you please, Aggie!"

One of the little girls sitting on the battlements stopped smirking, opened a book, and began to read.

> "Vivien, being greeted fair,
> Would fain have wrought upon his cloudy mood
> With reverent eyes much-loyal, shaken voice,
> And fluttered admiration . . ."

Swain felt only the tightening clutch of Roxana Wilberforce about his leg as the child's voice limped, scarcely comprehending, from syllable to syllable of the poem in the same flat style.

> "With dark sweet hints of some who prized him most . . ."

Dodgson's dark waves of hair popped from the black cloth behind the camera.

"Quite still, if you please!"

Swain held his breath and felt the perspiration upon his cheeks. He sensed that the trim blond beard and moustache, fixed with spirit gum to transform his face into that of a knight of chivalry, had begun to work loose. From the corner of his eye, he saw Dodgson stand upright and take the cap from the brass lens of the camera. Closing his mind to the present ordeal, the inspector listened to sounds in the distance, the rattle of wheels and harness along St. Aldate's, the more remote jangle of noise from St. Giles Fair, where a band was playing among the booths and stalls set up in the broad street that led north from the centre of the city. He tried to count the seconds of the exposure, as if this would shorten the time. He had got to forty when Dodgson said,

"Excellent!"

The brass cap went back on the camera lens. Roxana Wilberforce continued to hug Swain's leg for what seemed like an unnecessary length of time. Unseen by the others, her finger tickled him behind the knee as if in a mocking reminder of what had passed the other night.

Dodgson slid the exposed glass plate into a case and began to pack away the camera. Swain watched him lower the polished wooden box into its carrying grip and fold the legs of the tripod. The little girls were sent for lemonade, and Roxana Wilberforce went down from the photographic glasshouse to the rooms below to change into her other clothes.

Swain took the colander helmet from his head and sat on one of the battlements in his dishcloth chain-mail. He watched Dodgson for a moment longer as the busy little clergyman packed away his equipment and then said,

"Half past five."

Dodgson looked up at him in astonishment.

"Already? Surely it cannot be?"

"No," said Swain. "That day on the riverbank. Major Tiptoe. It happened at half past five. I'm sure of it. That's when the photograph left in the camera was taken, as near as I can judge. He was dead by then, just before. It's the picture he really meant to take that interests me."

Dodgson frowned, possibly with concentration, as he bent over the wooden carrying-box.

"So I imagine."

"Something so terrible that he had to be killed because he tried to take a picture—perhaps because he merely saw it. Can you imagine what that might be, Mr. Dodgson?"

"No," said Dodgson, standing up abruptly.

"Not just the sort of thing that might happen between men and women," Swain persisted. "Something worse than that, something truly evil."

"I really have no idea," said the little clergyman quietly.

"Now," said Swain, "Mr. Godwin and Mrs. Ashmole were there at about that time . . ."

A flush of annoyance coloured Dodgson's pale cheeks.

"Do not ask me to impute such things to those people, Mr. Swain! In fact, do not ask me to offer any advice that may send someone to the gallows—whoever it be—for Major Tiptoe."

"No one's going to the gallows for Major Tiptoe," said Swain wearily.

Dodgson straightened up from his task again, tripod in hand. For the first time he looked at the inspector with pure astonishment.

"Not going to the gallows? How can that be? Is such leniency in fashion now?"

Swain shook his head.

"Leniency's not in it. There can't be a public trial. There was enough in Tiptoe's little box to blow up Church and State like a Guy Fawkes plot. I can't say more than that. They want to know who killed him and why. When that's written at the end of my report, the matter is over."

"Will you take a Bible oath on that, Mr. Swain?"

"I give you my word," said Swain quietly, "as others have given me theirs. Believe me, there are times when men of power prize silence above justice."

"I find that hard to believe, Mr. Swain."

"Do you?" Swain stood up from the balcony. "What of Edward Oxford that shot at the Queen and nearly killed her on Constitution Hill? Detained as a poor lunatic. Never brought to trial."

274

"What of him?" asked Dodgson uneasily.

"Sane as you or I, sir. Acting for a certain duke that would have had the crown in his grasp if the bullets had struck home. The two pistols were that nobleman's own, and the written instructions were found in the assassin's rooms. Never a trial, Mr. Dodgson, never a public account. The villain safer than in any prison, the duke left to rot in Germany until he died. When so much is at stake, Mr. Dodgson, silence takes precedence over public justice."

Dodgson put down the tripod.

"You ask me to accuse Mrs. Ashmole? You must know that I, of all people, cannot do that."

"Not to accuse," said Swain. "Save her, Mr. Dodgson. Save her and her daughter. If I'm right, the greater evil is not past. It has yet to come. Come it will, sir, upon them both."

Dodgson thought about this for a moment.

"You take an oath as to the truth of what you say?"

"If you wish it."

The little clergyman looked out across the quadrangle of Tudor stone, the roofs of cathedral and deanery, towards the meadow trees with the first yellowing of decay upon their leaves.

"I make no promise, Mr. Swain. Please understand that. I make no promise to you, but I will see what may be done."

With that they went down to the other rooms. Roxana Wilberforce, now in her town clothes and feathered hat, looked appreciatively at Alfred Swain's muscular thighs in their dishcloth hangings.

37

On the following morning, Inspector Swain gave his attention to the Piozzi-Smith camera that Major Tiptoe had hired for his excursion to the riverbank, in pursuit of his victims. It was, in appearance, a smaller version of the model that Dodgson had used in his photography the afternoon before. The reddish wood of the camera was sleekly polished and the brass accoutrements of lens and focus screw seemed identical.

Swain set it on the tripod and examined it from every angle. He took a view through the lens and saw only the drab interior of the police-office room upside down. The duty constables just inside the door shifted impatiently and emitted their faint dyspeptic rumblings.

He regarded the polished wooden box with a mixture of irritation and awe. It appeared to yield no secrets. Yet, for however brief a moment, it had contained an image, an image of the crime Major Tiptoe witnessed and for which he had died. He must have died before he could take a photograph of it, Swain supposed, leaving the murderer to preserve upon the glass plate a scene of the bathing party, so that the investigation might be diverted in another direction.

Swain was about to put the camera away when his attention was held by a curious mark. It was not on the camera itself but

276

upon one of the legs of the tripod. The mark had been stamped there when the tripod was made. Had he not been so long preoccupied with the body of the camera, he would have noticed it as a curiosity. In his experience, it was a very common mark upon certain manufactured items, consisting merely of an inverted arrow stamped upon the wood. He called Sergeant Lumley.

"This tripod, Mr. Lumley. It's government issue! What the devil is a private shop doing with tripods made for the public service?"

Lumley frowned for a moment, then his bewilderment cleared away.

"That'll be the leg!" he said confidently.

"Which leg, Mr. Lumley?"

"The leg on the other tripod. Uneven. Risk of damage, as Mr. Merriman said, if the tripod should go over and the camera fall. Protect the exhibit of the crime, as Mr. Merriman said. So we put it on one that's used in the police office for taking the annual photograph of the city constabulary in the parade yard."

It was not good nature but excitement that prevented Swain from saying something about Inspector Merriman.

"Mr. Lumley! Where is the tripod upon which this camera was standing when it was found upon the riverbank?"

"That's easy," said Lumley with a look of pride. "In the cupboard."

He opened the tall cupboard and took out a long bundle of waterproof sheeting. Inside it lay the folded legs of the hired tripod.

"See?" He held the tripod feet up for Swain's approval. "There's a metal cup that sheaths each of 'em to protect the wood from fraying when the tripod's standing. Like a ferrule on a walking stick or umbrella. Only there's not one on this leg," he added unnecessarily.

"Nor is there," said Swain admiringly.

"If the camera'd been left on this, it might have gone over, Inspector Merriman said. So we put it on the other one. I hope that was all right, sir?"

"Oh, yes, Mr. Lumley!" Swain spoke without a hint of irony. "That was quite all right."

He examined the two silver-coloured steel ferrules that remained in place and then looked up at the sergeant again.

"Mr. Lumley, I want as many men who can be spared. The riverbank is to be searched for fifty yards around the place where the camera was standing when it was found. I can't imagine that anyone lugged Major Tiptoe farther than that. I want the other ferrule found and the place where it lay marked precisely. Tell them to take magnets as well as scythes."

"Magnets, Mr. Swain?"

"Yes, Mr. Lumley. These ferrules look remarkably like steel."

Lumley walked as far as the door and then turned back.

"Suppose it was missing before the camera was hired?"

"Shops that hire expensive cameras do not care to trust them to uneven tripods, Mr. Lumley. There is a danger of their falling over and taking the camera with them—as Mr. Merriman said."

Under other circumstances, Swain would have relished the tranquillity of the afternoon. It was a scene such as one of the Dutch masters might have painted, he decided, had they returned in the latter part of his own century. The bright, brown river ran gurgling and rushing towards the weir between banks overhung by ash and willow. Pools and ripples glittered in the Oxford sun. Through the trees he could hear the stamp of boots and the rhythmic swishing of scythes as the city constabulary worked over the area for a second time.

The entire search might prove to be no more than an embarrassment to him. He was well aware of that. Yet it was not likely that the tripod would have been hired in a deficient state, nor could the ferrule have been lost easily while the tripod and the rest of the equipment was still packed away during Major Tiptoe's boat journey. Far and away the most likely time for it to have come loose was when the tripod was set up and the camera screwed upon it. Then, as the tripod was lifted, the ferrule would simply come away and remain on the ground.

No doubt the major would have noticed this when he came to put the tripod down again. A murderer, working against time, might not have noticed the loss as he set the camera up again, nor had opportunity to do anything even if he had observed it.

All the same, as the hours passed on the pleasant sunlit bank, Swain's confidence diminished. At last the area had been covered three times and it appeared as certain as he could expect it that the ferrule was not upon the ground covered. To extend the scope of the search was unthinkable without devoting days of effort to the task. Apart from that, Swain thought, anyone dragging or carrying a body to the river to throw it in would go to the nearest part of the bank. Major Tiptoe must have been a heavy load. If it was to seem that he had been drowned at the weir, there was no sense in carrying him a considerable distance beyond it.

Inspector Merriman appeared with the pleasure of a sceptical onlooker at a performance of magic.

"And what's our next trick, then, Mr. Swain?"

Swain drew a dignified breath. Before he could answer there was a sound of swearing. Sergeant Lumley, who with the discretion of rank had stepped behind a bush to relieve himself, reappeared with his face a deep wine-red. Evidently excitement rather than some unexpected encounter had caused this blush.

"Growing on a tree!" he called, waving the discovery in his hand. But it was not fruit or berry that he held. Coming up to Swain he opened his meaty fist and disclosed the missing ferrule in the palm of his hand.

It had been lodged in the lower twigs of a bush on the edge of a small clearing. The clearing itself was no more than ten feet across and remarkably secluded. It was for that reason that Lumley had chosen it.

"Every inch," said Swain vindictively to Merriman, "every inch to be combed. Any object, no matter how small, to be bottled."

There was a sound of grumbling and cursing, like the hum of a hive disturbed. Twenty uniformed constables went down on hands and knees, like the figures of some ritual dance, round the edge of the clearing. They worked inward, bottle-noses to the ground and large serge-clad rumps raised in the strange performance.

The station-clerk produced a case with rows of small screw-top jars into which the fragments of stone and leaf among the blades of grass were to be dropped.

"It's quite plain, Mr. Merriman," said Swain tolerantly. "When the tripod was lifted, the ferrule must have been already loose. So loose that a scrape against the twigs of the bush brought it off. This clearing. This is where he was."

The search continued until the heads of the constables met at what was the approximate centre of the grassy space. Swain, alone in the clearing and imagining himself as Tiptoe, looked about him. The elder and bramble, hawthorn and wild plum, were so thick around him that there was very little view of any other part of the riverbank at all. Only at one end, where the opening lay, was there a clear view, such as a photographer might have considered. A man could step through the bushes at other points, but any view between them was blocked within a yard or two by further brushwood or bramble. It was ideal cover for an assailant.

At first Swain was uncertain of the area he was looking at. He stepped forward, following the line of a camera's perspective. The way led him, within thirty feet, to a place that was almost familiar. It adjoined the scene of the bathing party, screened from it only by the convenient protrusion of the trees.

"There's this, sir," said Lumley at his side, holding up one of the little glass jars.

Swain tipped the single scrap of stony substance into his hand. He considered the appearance of the hard pale crust and confirmed the lightness of its weight. He was no specialist in such matters, merely an unwilling spectator at the post-mortem frolics of Dr. Hammond and his kind. Yet it would not surprise him to learn that the hard white pellet in his hand was a dew-washed fragment of Dicky Tiptoe's skull.

That night he turned with more than customary gratitude to the magic world of chivalry in the *Idylls of the King*. The pretty Widow Wilberforce combed her chestnut hair alluringly through her white fingers, eyeing him as he read aloud.

> " 'The swallow and the swift are near akin,
> But thou art closer to this noble prince,
> Being his own dear sister'; and she said,
> 'Daughter of Gorlois and Ygerne am I':

'And therefore Arthur's sister?' asked the King.
She answered, 'These be secret things,' and signed
To those two sons to pass, and let them be."

Roxana Wilberforce pulled the green silk tighter about her and leant forward with lips parted a little.

"Lovely names, Mr. Swain," she said, the desire making her eyes wander as if she might swoon. "Aren't they such lovely poetry names?"

Alfred Swain looked at her as if he could not see her.

"Yes," he said absent-mindedly, "aren't they just?"

"Mr. Swain? Mr. Swain? You feeling all right, Mr. Swain?"

"Yes, thank you, Mrs. Wilberforce. Perfectly all right."

38

JANE ASHMOLE sat opposite him on the broad window-seat overlooking the grass and gravel paths of the great quadrangle. The morning sun through leaded lights caught the dark sheen of her hair. Dodgson put out his hand and laid it upon hers. He was startled to feel how cold she was, even in the warmth of sunlight.

"It's really very simple," he said eagerly. "I call it Doublets. You may play it with a friend or you may play it on your own. Now, see here . . ." He took the sheet of paper and withdrew his hand. "Choose two words. Come, let us try 'head' and 'tail.' Now, write 'head' at the top. You must change 'head' into 'tail' by altering one letter at a time. Each time you change a letter, the word you make must be a real word. Like this. Start with 'head.' Now change it to 'heal' and write that underneath. Now, change 'heal' to 'teal' and then to 'tell.' Now, next in the column, change 'tell' to 'tall' and there you have it. 'Tall' into 'tail' at one go! Whoever does it in the least number of changes wins the game!"

Jane gave a slight wordless smile and took the pencil from him. She showed no enthusiasm for the game or its cleverness. It was one of those occasions when she, at thirteen, appeared

282

the adult in experience, humouring Dodgson, the precocious child.

They began to play the game together so that he might be satisfied that she had grasped the rules. Jane engaged her attention in it with the air of one putting from her mind some more important but unpleasant task. Jane had the forced jollity of a mother indulging a child from whom she must soon part for ever.

"Now six letters," he said presently, squeezing the cold hand again. "My clever Unknown Quantity is getting too good for four. 'Walker' into 'sitter.' Try that."

They played the game, taking alternate tries at changing the letters, one at a time, until the column of words extended down the page: walker, talker, tasker, masker, master, mister.

"Come on!" said Jane, brushing her fringe impatiently with the edge of her hand. His own enthusiasm for the childish riddle had drawn her into the game sufficiently to beguile her melancholy.

Dodgson looked at the sheet of paper, as if he could not hear her voice.

"Come *on!*" she said, showing an adult's impatience with a dim-witted child. "Anyone can see the way now. What lies between 'mister' and sitter'?"

Dodgson looked up at her, as if rousing himself from a profound spiritual meditation. The words on the paper were only part of it. In his mind he began to recall phrases from conversations long ago. The 1860s, he thought, the small talk at a wedding feast. Thin cotton of regimental flags hanging in the tall pale arches of a cathedral nave. Sunlight on bridal silk. A scent of orange blossom.

He took Jane by the hand and led her to one of the large leather chairs. Gently, he stroked her head and kissed her forehead.

"Wait here," he said quietly, settling her in the chair. "Wait until I come back. Wait until suppertime if necessary. Whatever you need, ring for Mr. Draycott in the porter's lodge."

Her brown eyes scanned his face, believing in him but not understanding.

"I must go home, though!" she said doubtfully. "There are things to be done and people to be seen . . . before Harrogate."

"No," he said softly, "don't go home. Don't go anywhere until I come back to you. You shall not go to Harrogate unless you choose to."

The misgiving in her face was now tempered by a look of uncomprehending hope. Her hand tightened on his own.

"Not go to Harrogate?"

Despite his preoccupation with other matters, he smiled at her.

"Did you truly think I could bear to part with my own beloved Unknown Quantity?"

He kissed her again and left. From the window above Tom Quad, she watched the dark-suited little figure striding energetically towards the cathedral chapter-house, his unbuttoned frock-coat wafting out behind him.

Even Long Vacation meant nothing to the diocesan librarian, who remained at his duties regardless of time and season. In a few moments, Dodgson found the register and noted the details of the entry. They were in a separate leather-bound volume of abstracts, in which the details were preserved of ceremonies involving senior members of the college. There were not many of these and, after fifteen years, William Ashmole's was still one of the most recent. A few weddings and a handful of baptisms followed, as well as several funerals, including Ashmole's own.

Dodgson shut the register and thanked the librarian. He strode back across the gravel paths of Tom Quad. The lawns were smooth and soft as a bowling green, the stillness broken only by the water in the fountain of Mercury.

This time he went directly to the arch under Tom Tower and the street outside. Striding with the same determination, he crossed St. Aldate's, making for the castle mound and the unsalubrious area of Hythe Bridge Wharf and the Botley Road. A mile beyond this, he turned down a lane and crossed a stile into the fields that fringed the city on its industrial side.

Half an hour brought him to the old church of St. Margaret at Binsey, lost among the fields and trees of the meadowland that stretched towards Godstow. The old woman who was the parish pew-opener sat in the porch where slabs of stone made a rough bench on either side. She took his sixpence, curtsied, and went to fetch the sacristan. In the sacristan's company, he hurried down the aisle, with its musty parochial smell and cool light, to the vestry, which opened off the chancel.

The sacristan unlocked the vestry door and they entered together. Time and dust had made the diamond panes of the leaded windows almost opaque. A dim watery light fell upon the heavy leather volumes, ancient bindings crumbling to powder, some of which bore the arms of the Stuart kings. Here the ancient and obscure muniments of church lands and titles had mouldered undisturbed since the days of civil war and Oxford Parliaments.

"Have the goodness to show me the baptismal entry for Maria Lang's child in July 1846," said Dodgson abruptly.

The sacristan went along the tall gold-stamped volumes in the wooden case. He found a recent binding in dark green, lugged it out, and dropped it on the table in a cloud of fine-powdered leather. The thick parchment rattled as he turned the pages for Dodgson's benefit and came at length to the summer of 1846.

Dodgson glanced down the entries in the high, sloping copper-plate of the parish clerk. There were none between 15 April and 31 August.

At first he thought that it must be the volume for another year or that his own information was wrong. But the year was boldly marked and his own transcript from the cathedral register was clear. In any case, was it probable that there had not been a single child born—or baptised—in the parish of Binsey for a period of more than four months? Such things were possible, he thought, but not likely. He pressed the pages wider apart until the binding began to creak. Then he saw the jagged little tongues of paper that told their own story.

"Someone has torn a page from this register," he said crossly to the sacristan.

"Can't be!" The man looked closely at the open binding. "There's no cause for that!"

It was pointless to debate the matter now. It did not even matter greatly who had done it. Major Tiptoe, perhaps. Or Maria

Lang's child. To find that it was missing served as the best confirmation of his suspicions.

Handing the sacristan half a sovereign, he walked back down the aisle of St. Margaret's and out through the rustic porch. The old pew-opener in her faded brown holland dropped her curtsy with a crinkling of her weather-lined face and a toothless smile. Dodgson gave her a perfunctory nod. He stood by the glimmer of river margin, hearing a drone of flies and the sigh of osiers in the warm breeze. He looked across the broad expanse of the river bend towards the pastureland, yellowed by sun, and the harvesters piling a wagon with hay. That, after all, was where the whole thing had begun. Now, it seemed to him, he knew all that he would ever need to know.

In the damp interior of the church, Alfred Swain stepped out from the cover afforded him by the base of the pulpit. There had been a most unpleasant five minutes when he believed that Dodgson was going to lead him on a twenty-mile walk through the Oxford countryside to no purpose whatever. Swain's relief had been considerable when he saw the dark-clothed figure disappear into the porch of St. Margaret's with such a sense of purpose.

Having other sources of information at his disposal, Swain had not consulted the diocesan librarian. For many reasons he preferred not to do so. Yet this was a different matter. A parish register that stood comparatively unprotected in the vestry. What happened to such a record might prove very interesting indeed.

As the sacristan came out and turned to lock the vestry door again, Swain laid a hand upon his arm.

"A word with you," he said pleasantly, "a word with you before you close that door."

Dodgson, striding back under the sooty brick of the railway bridge, past the cattle market and the canal, felt like a man who has won a battle but cannot yet formulate the terms of the treaty that must be imposed in consequence. Proof? Proof, he thought, would never exist anywhere but in the hearts and minds of the culprits. Perhaps not even in their hearts and minds but in their consciences. Of all the soul's organs, the conscience was the most easily put to rest in such cases. A man was a fool whose conscience offered his neck to the hangman's noose.

There remained, of course, the diocesan archives. It might be years since the page had been torn from the Binsey register. On the other hand, Major Tiptoe might have done it a few weeks before his death. Whatever list of baptisms had been compiled in the diocesan records—if any—would be less easy to tamper with. At Binsey, the major would have picked open a locked vestry door in minute or two. A chapter-house, or a cathedral library, was a different matter.

With this in mind, Dodgson returned under the archway of Tom Quad and began to cross the deserted gravel path towards the cathedral buildings. Just then the door of the Common Room under the main hall opened and Thomas Godwin came out. He looked about him, saw Dodgson, and began walking towards him on the same path. With mathematical exactitude, it seemed, they would meet at the very centre of the great quadrangle, by the fountain of Mercury.

At this moment, Dodgson would have preferred to avoid the encounter. Now it was out of the question. Godwin, the dark hair shadowing his long sardonic features, blocked the gravel path.

"Where is Miss Ashmole?"

"In my room," said Dodgson quietly, "where she will remain as long as she chooses."

Godwin shook his dark hair back with a magnificent gesture of contempt and gasped with amusement at the outlandishness of the reply.

"My dear Dodgson! Infatuation is the stuff of which great poetry is made, but in this case merely farce. The child is only thirteen. For your sake and hers, this enticement must cease!"

Dodgson looked back at him, unmoved.

"There is another child who concerns me more, Mr. Godwin. The child of Maria Lang. Her baptismal entry has been torn from the church records."

Godwin's smile vanished and he shrugged like a sulky schoolboy.

"The devil it has! Maria Lang is nothing to me any more."

"Her child, Mr. Godwin," said Dodgson softly, "the child of a poor seduced governess, the child with no father to stand at the font. The child born as Sarah Lang, who became Sarah Ashmole upon her marriage fifteen years ago."

"Ah," said Godwin contemptuously, "because you have perpetrated a crime against Mrs. Ashmole's daughter, I daresay, you intend to excuse yourself by slander."

"Maria Lang was your governess, Mr. Godwin."

Godwin laughed with scorn at the absurdity.

"Until I was sent to Harrow at twelve! Do not credit me with seducing the lady at so tender an age, Mr. Dodgson! You do me too great honour. I never saw our poor Maria after that."

Dodgson stood, it seemed to him, in the labyrinth of dilemma. He might draw back in safety, handing the victory in this matter and the future of Jane Ashmole to his antagonist. Or he might attack now and risk his own destruction. There could be no retreat. He took a deep breath.

"I accuse you, Mr. Godwin, of Lord Byron's crime!"

Godwin did not look pale with fear or red with anger. He set his hands on his hips, threw his head back, and shouted his laughter to the sky.

"Lord Byron's crime!" he said at length, the contempt for his accuser unconcealed. "How can a man be angry with so prim a fool as you? What crime?"

There was no going back now. Dodgson took another deep breath.

"The crime that comes of Mrs. Sarah Ashmole being the daughter of your own father, Joseph Godwin, fathered upon his governess, Maria Lang. A child born at your father's house in Herods Park the very year you were sent to Harrow!"

"My poor fool!" Godwin shook his head. "You can prove nothing of my father and Miss Lang. You may try, to be sure—and be damned as a slanderer for your pains! I confess I never loved my father much. Yet he gave shelter to Maria Lang, gone with child. The child was his? Prove it if you can!"

"The world knew it, Mr. Godwin, at the time. Major Tiptoe knew it a few weeks ago."

Godwin's fingers tightened into fists.

"You will never prove she was my father's child, if she is not. Even if she were, you could prove nothing between us now that might not pass between a man and his half-sister. She is my half-sister, you think? Then what more proper than that I should have lodged in her house? She is my half-sister and a poor widow? What more laudable than that I should care for her and her child?"

"Twenty years ago, your father sent you to Germany for what you might have done to Sarah Lang!" said Dodgson firmly. "When your father died and you came back to Oxford, she was Sarah Ashmole with a daughter of her own. Did she not betray your love by that marriage, Mr. Godwin? Is not Jane Ashmole the fruit of that betrayal in your eyes? Is that not why you hate the child and would be rid of her? Is she not the only obstacle that stands between you and the triumph of a passion that is both insane and criminal?"

For the first time there was a tremor in Godwin's cheek and a movement of anger in his dark eyes.

"Damn your canting impudence, you sickly little prig!"

Dodgson looked steadily back at him.

"I do not fear you now, Mr. Godwin, for we stand here in this open space with the eyes of a dozen others upon us. You will not raise your fist against me here, I think. If I were alone with you on the riverbank, I believe you would strike me now. Would you strike with such force that I might never tell the world of it afterwards?"

With a visible effort, Godwin unclenched his fingers. Yet the pulse in his face did not slacken.

"The terrible act that Major Tiptoe would have photographed," Dodgson continued. "What was it? Between other men and women it might have been innocent enough. Tender kissing and caressing out of sight of the girls as they changed—even lying in one another's arms is not the worst crime in the world. Yet, if they be brother and sister it is another matter. If they are blackmailed already for their crime . . . if the blackmailer, thinking they have not observed him, would take a photograph, a scene that would damn them for ever . . ."

"To be sure, you have polluted the child's mind!" said Godwin savagely. "You have heated her imagination with filthy suggestions!"

"One might imagine," Dodgson went on coolly as if it were a matter of mathematical demonstration, "how the woman would continue to act as if her lover were still close to her. How the lover would move softly aside and stalk the spy. How, without the woman ever suspecting he intended such force, the poor scoundrel at his camera might be done for without a cry."

Godwin stood rigidly before him with eyes narrowed and lips tight.

"What do you want of me?"

"One might imagine," said Dodgson, ignoring him, "that even the man who struck the blow scarcely intended the consequence. How urgent, then, the matter of dragging the body to the river above the weir, setting the boat adrift. And, as a last refinement, the carrying of the camera to that place on the bank and taking a photograph that must direct all attention from the true purpose of Major Tiptoe's spying."

"What the devil do you want of me?" Godwin had ceased to argue now and had fallen back on the gruff phrases of concealment.

"To advise you," said Dodgson gently, "for your own sake. Go back to Germany. Go where you choose. Leave the child alone. Leave the woman alone. There is no hope for you here."

"Be damned to you!" The first trace of a scornful laugh was returning to Godwin's voice, and his spirits seemed to rise now that he saw how much of Dodgson's case against him must be conjecture. "You think to terrify me by such bogy tales? I have no part of a slave religion that forbids a man to be what a man desires. The crime of Lord Byron! The language of a prig. If, as his lordship put it, I choose to tumble the pillows of a sister's bed, I shall do so. And be damned to you all!"

"Then," said Dodgson sadly, "you must answer to Inspector Swain. He knows as much as I. Indeed, he was at Binsey church this morning, though he thought I did not see him. Mrs. Ashmole and her daughter must bear his questions too. How long will they elude him?"

"The questions of a man who knows nothing but what his imagination can conjure up!"

"The questions of a man, Mr. Godwin, who will send you to the gallows. It is not religion but the hangman's pinions and the noose that shall forbid you to be what you desire."

Godwin looked at him evasively. Dodgson felt like a man who was shaking the dice for the last time.

"You are no photographer, Mr. Godwin. That will hang you if all else fails."

The look of uncertainty deepened as Dodgson continued.

"You do not even know why photographers use their hood of black cloth."

Now the uncertainty contracted into a scowl.

"What has that to do with it?"

"One purpose of the hood, Mr. Godwin, is to prevent light entering the camera through the aperture where the photographer takes his view. On so small a camera, it is easy to remove the lens cover while your head is under the cloth. But if the cloth is not in the correct position, the light will reflect an image of the photographer as he takes his view, superimposed upon his subject."

It was as if the dice had rolled and shown a pair of sixes, Dodgson thought.

"The plate that Inspector Swain possesses, Mr. Godwin. It has upon it the image of Major Tiptoe's murderer. The likeness is a faint one but its accuracy is beyond question. By the process of photographic tracing it can be extricated from the rest of the picture on which it lies and can be strengthened. By tonight, my poor friend, that process will be complete, the image plain beyond denial."

Godwin's jaw tightened and he gave Dodgson a last burning look of moral contempt. Then he strode towards the porter's lodge and the archway of Tom Tower that led to the world beyond.

For a moment more, Dodgson stood with his eyes closed, praying unobtrusively by the fountain. He sought, among other things, forgiveness for the monstrous photographic lie of which he had just been guilty.

39

"THE MAN THAT HOPES to make a fool of me shall drink a bitter broth for it, mister!" said Chief Inspector Toplady, pleased at the promise of a fight.

Swain stood at ease, his gaze fixed ahead of him, beyond the window. He watched the mudlark girls stooping and scrabbling once more under the overhanging hulls of the beached collier barges.

"Sir," he said, in respectful acknowledgment.

"Sir!" said Toplady with scorn. He was standing behind his desk, the grey spiked hair rising upon end like the comb of a fighting cock. His bandy legs seemed braced for exertion, as if he might come round the desk at any moment and box Alfred Swain man to man.

"Incest?" The chief inspector spoke with dismay that any man would stoop to take account of so trivial a matter. "A fellow that bedded his sister? And only his half-sister at that?"

"Thomas Godwin, sir. Son of the late Joseph Godwin of Herods Park near Oxford."

"When I was a boy," said Toplady, becoming uncharacteristically mellow with nostalgia, "there was not a labourer's family in the village where something of the sort was not a common occurrence. Was that *all*?"

"Sir," said Swain obligingly.

Toplady roused himself to customary belligerence.

"And y'have the proof of this, mister? Y'have the proof, I may take it, of the half-brother bedding the half-sister? Hey?"

"Not entirely, sir."

"Not entirely, sir?" Toplady's hair and eyebrows moved as if in the continued preliminaries of combat. "What sort of answer is that?"

"The proof of such crime is difficult in the nature of things, sir." Swain set his eyes on the mudlarks and stood his ground. "Mr. Godwin lodged under her roof and was taken by all the world for Mrs. Ashmole's lover."

"Say he was her lover, did he, mister?"

"No, sir. But he looked it and acted it."

Toplady's mouth moved for a moment in a ruminative manner.

"Looked it!" he said at last. "What use is that?"

"There is a child, sir, a daughter of thirteen but her evidence could scarcely be corroborated. I daresay Mrs. Ashmole might be brought to confess if she were questioned hard enough."

"Half-sister?" asked Toplady with some doubt.

"Daughter of Mr. Godwin's father and the governess Maria Lang, sir. A good deal of scandal in the neighbourhood of Herods Park at the time—enough to touch Thomas Godwin as a boy at Harrow. A year or two later, when it was Major Tiptoe's turn to be a Harrow lad, the story was still in the mouths of schoolboys. That was how he came by it, sir."

Toplady sat down again.

"And treasured it all these years until he might use it for his purposes?"

"But for their unnatural association, sir, there would have been no purpose."

"Don't preach, mister!" said Toplady, getting up again. "You have your man. Tiptoe photographed 'em in the act—or would have done. Godwin, glimpsing him, slips round and drives the paling through his skull, then takes a picture of his own. Is that what you say?"

"It brings the strands together, sir. Mr. Godwin and Mrs. Ashmole as lovers in the normal way could be nothing to a blackmailer. He might tell the world, if he chose. As brother and sister, the least embrace of an amorous kind was another matter. At every other moment, their love was secret in this respect. They enjoyed the shelter of Mrs. Ashmole's house. On the riverbank they thought themselves alone, out of sight of the young ladies who were changing from their bathing things. It was for that moment that Major Tiptoe had waited. In a few minutes he would have had proof of their criminal conversation. The proof of their consanguinity as half-brother and sister he had possessed since his own boyhood."

Toplady went across the room to the window and glared out at the Thames. Then he turned back again.

"You have a story, mister. You have no *proof!*"

"The proof will be in their actions now, sir."

Toplady snorted with contempt.

"And what the devil does that signify to us? There can be no case from such a jumble of guesses. Do you imagine I should take *that* to the Treasury Solicitor and demand a proceeding against Thomas Godwin? If I did, do you not think the grand jury would throw it back in our faces at the first hearing? You have no proof, mister!"

"No, sir," said Swain humbly. "I thought that might be welcome news to some, knowing what must come to light if the matter of Major Tiptoe and his extortion were brought to court."

Swain knew at once, by the expression on Toplady's face, that he had made a grievous error of judgment in mentioning the blackmail. Toplady looked at him as if Swain had taken leave of his senses.

"Thought that, mister? Thought *that*? Why, the best brains in the country have examined those papers you called blackmail. And, mister, do you know what?"

A grin of ghastly horror split Toplady's wrinkled gnome face as he looked at Swain.

"No, sir."

"All made up, mister! Fabrications! Poor forgeries by the scoundrel Tiptoe. Dammit, how you have been imposed upon! A man that can be imposed upon as you have been is no man for me, sir!"

Swain had expected something of the kind. Yet, when it came, the cynical assurance of the denial shocked him more than he had expected.

"The photographs were no forgery sir, with respect. Mr. Dodgson was good enough to confirm that in his own case."

Toplady's mouth quivered, as if he had just bitten on sour fruit.

"Mr. Dodgson? Who the devil cares for Mr. Dodgson? It is of the others that I speak. Prime ministers and archbishops, royal sons and masters of our colleges. Forgeries, mister! The imaginings of a scoundrel."

And still Alfred Swain stood his ground.

"May I request, sir, a further examination of the watermarks on the paper by Mr. Walter de Grey Birch of the British Museum?"

Chief Inspector Toplady favoured him with another wicked grin. To Swain's surprise he said,

"You may request it, mister, as soon as you please."

"And a specimen of the handwriting, sir?"

"All of it, mister! Every dot and comma."

Something was wrong and Swain knew it.

"I shall be greatly obliged, sir."

Toplady replied with a short barking laugh.

"By God, you shall be obliged, mister, for the whole nasty mess of it was burnt a week ago. Now request to your heart's content, for all the good you shall get by it!"

So that was that, Swain thought. The gallivantings of a prime minister, the unnatural loves of the heir to the throne, the headmaster of Harrow, the complicity of the archbishop, had crumbled to ash, as though they had never existed. Unlike the promise of the *Magnificat*, someone had exalted the mighty and put down the humble and meek. Mr. Dodgson, Sarah Ashmole and her daughter, even Major Tiptoe and Thomas Godwin in their way, had been the sacrificial victims. For the rest, their troubles were no more than a handful of ashes in the Treasury Solicitor's grate.

"May I request to know my orders respecting Mr. Thomas Godwin, sir?"

"You have no proof, mister," said Toplady, wearying of the subject. "Let the fellow go to the colonies for a year or two. Let him keep his head low. Tongues will wag, to be sure, but they will not wag forever in respect of him. There will be new scandals soon enough to divert the gossip of Oxford and London."

"Then no one's to be charged, sir, and nothing's to be done?"

Toplady's high starched collar scraped his cheek as he turned from the window.

"A policeman mustn't always be expecting to arrest people and indict 'em, mister! There's a good deal more to constabulary vigilance than that!"

"Then, sir, a murderer must go free?"

Toplady sat at his desk again and took up the pen once more.

"He's nothing unless you can prove him so, mister. And, as y'say, y'can't! As for the other matter—to be sure a man ought not to bed his own sister! No, sir, he ought not. And yet a man that beds his sister is still a *man*. Give me that, mister, rather than a soft-voiced lily-poem Mary Ann! And now, Mr. Swain, good day to you!"

Swain came smartly to attention and took his leave. In the communal office with its tall counting-house desks, Inspector Wilks had just taken the first bite from a shiny currant bun. He greeted Swain through a mouthful of yeasty sweetness.

"You was lucky, you was, Mr. Swain, being in Oxford when the Volunteer Review was on in the park. All back in uniform for that. Eight hours at attention and never a drop nor a bite! Enough sun to raise blisters on an elephant's hide."

"I've been seen off, Mr. Wilks!" said Swain quietly. "We've all bloody well been seen off! By them upstairs!"

But Wilks was not so easily to be deflected from the tenor of his thought. He gave a slow, sideways nod of his head as an aid to swallowing what was in his mouth, and returned to the topic of the Volunteer Review.

"You was lucky, you was," he said emphatically.

Swain gave up the attempt at conversation and endeavoured to ignore Inspector Wilks's monologue as he lapsed into thought. There was, of course, Charles Augustus Howell. What more might be got from him? He sighed, concluding that there was little point to the mental exercise. There was to be no case and that was that. Howell might be anywhere by this time.

As it happened, Howell had never left his familiar territory. He was just then strolling along the pavement outside the solid fashionable houses of Church Street, Chelsea. No less than two of these belonged to Mary Jeffries, a handsome widow. The law had never troubled Mrs. Jeffries, nor did Howell propose to do so now. Yet within her houses, provided he was prepared to pay the price, a man could have whatever a man was likely to want. Because her customers were in general well-known men in their way, there was a room from which they could see the girls and make their choice without being seen themselves. There were rooms beyond that, some of them strangely equipped.

Under his waistcoat Howell felt the reassuring metal disc of the Stirn novelty camera, the lens protruding through his waistcoat button-hole. He glanced at his watch, as if waiting for the arrival of a cab. No one paid the least attention to him. He turned as there was a murmur of activity outside the handsome panelled door of the house he had been watching. A fat, bearded man came out, his hat brim tilted a little over his face. Yet the pop-eyes and the fatuous expression were clear enough. The little button lens of the Stirn camera winked at him and winked again. The fat man drew on his gloves as a chief inspector opened the door of the plain carriage for him. They drove away and presently turned into a mews entrance. It was there that they changed vehicles. Charles Howell had seen the grander carriage waiting in the mews. The three white plumes and the bold *Ich Dien* were set squarely on its door panels.

The photographs in the Stirn camera were not the stuff of blackmail. In choosing his victims, Charles Augustus Howell had more modest aims. Yet once again he had begun to build up "a real show" as he and Dicky Tiptoe used to call it. No Treasury Solicitor, no Attorney-General, would ever dare to parade before a court the revelations that a prosecution of Charlie Howell must include. There was only one way for men of power to deal with him. Despite Dicky Tiptoe's misfortune, he did not think they would dare to follow that path. For the moment he needed only a wealthy prig with one or two secret yearnings. Story-Book Dodgson had seemed the man for him. But Story-Book Dodgson had proved to be nothing of the kind.

Charlie Howell hailed a cab. In its darker interior, he eased the camera from its place and returned it to a carrying box.

40

AUGUST RAIN CLOUDS, soft as smoke and dark as twilight, deepened the green majesty of the meadow trees. Dodgson went up the staircase at the north-east corner of Tom Quad where John Fell's statue in its niche stood above the archway leading into the eighteenth-century grandeur of Peckwater.

In the course of the night he had considered Godwin's situation over and over. Because he understood so little of the other man's feelings, so little of his beliefs, it was impossible to imagine how life might be tolerable to him now. Every hour, it seemed, Dodgson had heard the clocks strike. The first dawn-light above the far battlements had found him still awake and fretful. By breakfast time he was convinced. Devoid of the consolations of religion, forbidden the only human love tolerable to him, Godwin would escape the hands of the hangman only to die by his own. As the scout removed the shattered eggshell and the cold tea, Dodgson believed that Godwin had hanged himself.

At nine o'clock Dodgson went up the staircase and found the oak closed across the entrance to Godwin's rooms. In any other circumstances Dodgson would have respected the sign. By the tradition of centuries, any man finding another's oak closed would turn and leave without knocking or questioning. This was different.

He tried the handle of the oak and found that it not been bolted. Inside, the doors of the rooms stood open and the curtains were pulled back to admit the daylight. He moved cautiously, almost fearfully, expecting at any moment to see the dangling feet, the shrivelled body with its hideous mask of self-destruction, hanging from beam or hook. There was no sign.

The rooms themselves were in that curious state where the owner's possessions—books, tablewear, pictures—were still in their places, arranged with unnatural neatness. Though a few of Godwin's belongings remained there, he thought, Godwin would never see these rooms again.

Turning about, he went quickly down the stairs and across the quadrangle to the porter's lodge.

"Mr. Godwin?" he said breathlessly.

"Yes, sir?" said the senior Porter guardedly.

"Where is he?"

"Mr. Godwin, sir? Gone to Switzerland, I understand. Left last night. Dr. Chantrey's taken a reading-party to Switzerland and Italy, sir. I expect Mr. Godwin's gone to join them. More than likely."

A darkness, worse than Godwin's possible self-destruction, fell upon Dodgson's hopes.

"Did he go alone?"

"He was alone when I saw him, sir. After that I couldn't say. His boxes went from here first thing this morning, to follow him."

Dodgson turned away and began to walk back. That Godwin's guilt was confessed by flight seemed unimportant. Christ Church had seen the last of him. The man who committed Lord Byron's crime with his half-sister would scorn the world as his idol had done. In the footsteps of the great romantic rebel, Godwin might spend his next years crossing Lake Leman, coming down into the sunlit plains of northern Italy, wandering with his train of gipsy girls and countesses from Venice and Ravenna to Florence and Pisa. What if he had not gone alone? Would Sarah Ashmole's humility in love stifle all moral protest in her heart? Would she and her daughter take the place of gipsy and countess among the followers of the Byron *de nos jours*?

That mattered more than Godwin, more than murder itself. For Dodgson could imagine too vividly the slow death of Jane Ashmole's hope, like a winged soul caged by the bars of Godwin's scornful intellect and bitter lust.

He would take the hat from his room, he decided, and go at once to the house beyond Folly Bridge. Whatever had happened, it might not yet be too late to retrieve the hopes of yesterday. Even Switzerland was not large enough for an Englishman with his mistress and her child to hide for long. The same lakeside hotels were common to English tourists, the same routes and the same guides. He went up the stone stairs and pushed open the door.

She got up from the armchair, where she had been waiting for him.

"There you are!" she said brightly. "You see? I am not to go to Harrogate after all!"

Dodgson stood upon the threshold, the pale anxiety of his face changing into wild surprise and then amusement. He ran a hand through his dark curls and gave a convulsive chortle. They smiled at one another, at the absurdity of the situation, where so much fearfulness had been superseded by victory after all. He came forward and let out the breath he had been holding in an explosive laugh. How absurd, he thought, that in a few hours more he would have been on his way to Lausanne if Sarah Ashmole and Jane had not been at home. The ridiculousness of it made him laugh again. Jane stepped forward and he held her to him in a close embrace, thinking of nothing more exalted than the feeling of her warmth and shape in his arms, which proved her presence there.

Later on he sat in the armchair and Jane on the floor, her back against his legs and her head resting close to his knee as he stroked her dark smooth hair. She began to talk, unprompted, of the future.

"I shall be a pupil-teacher here in Oxford. Why not? Mama sees now that it is quite the best thing. If I were away from her, all the way in Harrogate, what would become of her?"

"What, indeed?" said Dodgson encouragingly.

"Suppose she should be ill or fret alone. Would it not be better that I should be here to help her?"

"In every way, my own beloved Unknown Quantity." Despite the tenderness in his voice he spoke as if his mind were upon other things.

"I shall stay in Oxford," she said, patting his hand emphatically with her own. "I shall have a school of my own one day. A college of learned women in which I shall preside."

The last words puzzled him momentarily until he recognised them as a quotation from Johnson's *Rasselas*, one of the novels they had read together during the previous winter.

"You shall be a bluestocking," he said, kissing the crown of her hair lightly.

"And you shall come and see me whenever you choose," said Jane. "You shall give lectures in logic to my young ladies."

Dodgson took the girl's hand again and smiled, in part at Jane and in part at the absurd ease with which the world had come right in the space of a few hours.

"I shall be a very aged person indeed by then," he said, making a joke of her ambition for him, "advanced in decrepitude and silliness."

"And then you must die," she said brightly, "and then in a little while so must I. After that we shall be together, happier even than we are now."

There was no piety in her tone and no regret. She recited the sequence of events as if they were the rules of a game to which she had been admitted.

"My Dodo has promised me!" She patted the hand again.

"Not I," he said gently, "not I alone. I merely repeat a promise made for us all long, long ago."

They sat together like this in silence until the turret clocks began to chime again from Magdalen and Merton, across the grey quadrangles and rain-shadowed meadows.

Jane brushed the brown fringe with the edge of her hand. In a sudden movement she settled the pink folds of the dress about her hips. She was not lost in thought now, he saw. Her eyes were staring intently out of the window, her jaw firm and the line of her mouth set resolutely. She twisted her back against his shins and turned her strong pale face and brown eyes towards him.

"Suppose I should be very wicked," she said with quiet curiosity. "What would happen then?"

He stroked her cheek lightly.

"You will not be *very* wicked, my love. Even to be very naughty is only to be a little wicked."

Dodgson wondered how much the child had heard of her mother and Thomas Godwin. The blind struggle of passion? The soft cry in the dark stillness of the house at night? It was not for herself that Jane was asking, but for her mother. Sarah Ashmole, he thought, the weak affectionate woman. Perhaps when she was sixteen, and Godwin in his handsome twenties was the clever son of the house, she had given herself to him with no idea of the relationship between them. Love came first and the discovery later. By then, the reality of love could not be denied.

"Very wicked," said Jane quietly. "Will there not be torment forever, fire and torture, as Mr. Godwin says?"

"Mr. Godwin?" There had been a time when the irony of such an unbeliever appropriating such visions of hell to his armoury would have made Dodgson smile. But Jane continued to look up at him, not in fear for herself but inquiring with dread on Sarah Ashmole's behalf.

"Do you not believe it?"

"No," he said, bowing his head to kiss her cheek. "And Mr. Godwin certainly does not."

"Not if a person did a very wicked thing?"

Dodgson paused and wondered how best to explain the theology of apocalypse and judgment by his own light.

"When we come to be judged," he said quietly, "it will be by a love greater than you can imagine."

It was evident that the abstract figure meant little to her. Lowering his voice still further and holding her close, he put the matter in his own way.

"Think of the person who loves you most in all the world, Jane. Someone who loves you more than you could ever love yourself. Imagine that person dearest to you as your judge. That is how it will be. Yet then, even the judgment of that dearest person will be held too severe by one who loves you still more."

"And will it always be so?" she asked.

Dodgson knew she was thinking of her mother again, of Sarah Ashmole and the sardonic passion of Thomas Godwin.

"A judgment shall be passed on those you love, my dearest, gentler and more understanding than your own. There is nothing to fear from a love greater than any the earth can hold."

"Truly?" The urge to believe him was clear in her eyes.

"My dearest Unknown Quantity," he said, "would *you* doom any creature—the merest animal—to be tortured for all eternity?"

"No," she said, with a shudder at such cruelty.

"Then how can you believe that one who loves us more than earth could tell, who numbers the hairs of our heads, would sanction such a thing?"

"Then Mr. Godwin . . ."

A faint light of anger shone in Dodgson's eyes.

"Thomas Godwin is a blasphemer!" he said sharply. "Any man is a blasphemer who speaks of the holiest love in terms of the vilest torments, which neither you nor I would allow a cat, a dog, or even an insect to endure!"

She believed him now, he saw. They put their arms about one another again and sat in silence until the clocks chimed the quarter.

"Now," he said, putting her gently from him. "I shall ring for the porter. There will be mutton chops and ginger-beer for mid-day dinner."

Their happiness became absolute and impregnable. Because the fulfilment of love was to be postponed beyond death, it remained as a secure joy of certainty and expectation. Before long, Jane might pass into the chrysalid state of maturity and marriage. At some point, his own death would separate them. Yet when she followed him to what seemed, in imagination, an eternal Oxford June of river and meadow, the chrysalid state and the brief parting would be irrelevant. The same thoughts came to the girl's mind in the lines of a poem learnt long ago.

" 'How brief that pause shall be,' " she said, holding him gently by the hand, " 'against the onrush of eternity.' "

This time the words in his own mind were distinctly secular, prompted by the thought of Jane emerging from the chrysalis of womanhood into the eternal loveliness of her present state.

" 'Beautiful as a butterfly,' " he said vigorously, " 'and as fair as a queen!"

He raised her to her feet, kissed her again, and rang the bell for the porter.

Sixty miles away, Alfred Swain was considering the love of man and woman by a less absolute standard. Roxana Wilberforce, being in receipt of a police widow's pension, had made her annual appearance before the trustees of the fund at the Home Office in Whitehall. Satisfied that their annuitant was still alive and not in receipt of other support, the trustees had retired to a board lunch at the Metropole Hotel. The cost to the exchequer was roughly equivalent to Roxana Wilberforce's pension for the next two months.

Swain escorted her back to Paddington Station for the Oxford train. He helped her into the carriage and they stood looking awkwardly at one another in the moments before parting. Under the wide glass and iron canopy of the station roof, the gush of steam and the drifts of black smoke from the engine stacks engendered an interior fog. Swain could taste and feel the grit of soot in his teeth. Words of farewell were punctuated by the clatter of wagons and the snort of engines.

"You won't lose the keepsake, will you, Mr. Swain?"

He smiled and shook his head. Then, as if to reassure her further, he drew his copy of the photograph from the brown folder. In sepia tones his image stared out at him, absurdly bearded and capped by the horned colander-helmet. It was Mrs. Wilberforce who had, undoubtedly, stolen the scene, hugging his leg as she lay with the silk tight about her soft hips. In italic script below the picture, the words of the poem had been inset.

> *Vivien, being greeted fair,*
> *Would fain have wrought upon his cloudy mood.*

Roxana Wilberforce's chestnut waves, now hidden under the felt hat with the pearl-topped pins, were abundantly revealed by the camera.

Self-consciously, Swain returned the photographic print to its folder and slipped it into his pocket.

"I must go back," she said hopefully. "I must go back to Oxford. You do see that, don't you, Mr. Swain?"

"Yes." Perhaps the agreement was a shade too rapid. "Yes, of course, Mrs. Wilberforce."

How could anyone guess, he thought, at the way in which he had watched the morning light on her bare shoulders as she combed her hair, the oil light in the evening glimmering on the silk drawn tight across her hips? Roxana Wilberforce lowered the dark net of her veil and her face was hidden from him—perhaps for ever.

"Goodbye, Mr. Swain," she said softly.

The railway guard consulted his watch, while the under-guard walked up and down the length of the dark, soot-crusted carriages ringing a handbell. Alfred Swain remembered, as if he had not known it before, that his next tour of duty did not begin for two days. Absence from London for that period required the permission of Chief Inspector Toplady or his superiors. But Mr. Toplady was not there to be asked. Alfred Swain opened the door of the railway carriage and stepped into it. Roxana Wilberforce raised her net veil, and the dark eyes in her plump, pretty face regarded him with affectionate mockery.

"Why, Mr. Swain!" she said quietly. "You'll be carried away in a minute more!"

Alfred Swain closed his eyes and kissed her. The young Widow Wilberforce gave a sigh of contentment.

"Why, Mr. Swain!" she said, softly reproving as the carriages jolted forward and the smoked glass of the station canopy gave way to bright west London sky. But Swain had made his decision. He might be carried away all right, he thought. All the way to Oxford and the house in St. John Street, the luxuriant chestnut hair combed on bare shoulders before the morning mirror. A head resting on his knee after supper, and tight silk on plump hips in the evening lamplight. Only two days? A lot might happen in two days. The world might end this very night.

Despite that, he decided not to go directly to St. John Street. First of all he made his way to the vaulted archway under Tom

Tower and gave his name to the senior porter. He was escorted by the usual path to the north-west corner of the quadrangle and the familiar stone staircase.

The oak was not closed across the entrance to Mr. Dodgson's rooms. Yet as the porter paused and prepared to knock, Swain heard the sound of the girl's voice coming from within and Dodgson's soft, laughing answers. Swain tapped the porter on the arm as the man raised his knuckle to the white-painted panel of the sitting-room door.

He shook his head vigorously at the porter to prevent the knocking. Then they went back down the staircase to the main gateway, where Roxana Wilberforce stood in the sunlight of St. Aldate's.

Postscript

Charles Augustus Howell died in 1890. According to the bibliophile Thomas Wise, he was found lying in the gutter outside a Chelsea public house. His throat had been cut and a half-sovereign had been wedged between his teeth—a traditional vengeance upon a slanderer.

The Reverend Charles Dodgson died peacefully at his family home in Guildford on 14 January 1898. To the end of his life he remained reluctant to acknowledge to the world that he was "Lewis Carroll." Letters addressed to him in that name were still apt to be returned unanswered to their senders.

After the crisis of 1879–80, this most gifted of Victorian photographers abandoned his camera for ever. On his death, however, he still had a collection of photographs of his "little nudities." By the provisions of his will, they were returned to the sitters, all of whom were by then middle-aged ladies.

Of the other characters in the novel, Inspector Swain and his colleagues, the Ashmoles and the Chantreys, even Thomas Godwin and Major Tiptoe are conjectures at the secret actors in the drama. Yet Dodgson had good reason to be haunted by such phantoms, if only in his riverbank dreams. He was a man much preoccupied by dreams, and it is also to be hoped that in a wonderland of his own there was a Jane Ashmole in whom all the perfections of his other "child-friends" were united.

The scandals associated with Dr. Vaughan, the prime minister, the archbishop, Mr. Gladstone, Mr. Asquith, and the rest of the "real show" were documented at the time but not revealed. The London Library now holds some of the papers but with restricted access and a ban on quotation.

The life of the Reverend Mr. Dodgson was not one of furtive guilt but of triumphant innocence—which ought not to be equated with ignorance. Perhaps he owed something to the time and place of his existence. His private Oxford idyll coincided with the last age of sexual innocence that England was to know.

>>> If you've enjoyed this book and would like to discover more great vintage crime and thriller titles, as well as the most exciting crime and thriller authors writing today, visit: >>>

The Murder Room
Where Criminal Minds Meet

themurderroom.com